The Oshadangw

By

D.P.O'Connor.

'

(Author's Note: This is a book about Apartheid South Africa. Authenticity demands that unpleasant racial terms are used throughout. The term 'kaffir' is highly offensive and banned in many parts of Southern Africa. It has similar connotations to the word 'nigger').

Between 1975 and 1990 the South African Defence Force fought a secret war on the Angolan border against the forces of Black Liberation.

Black and White soldiers fought on both sides.

None of them won.

Those who lived got a second chance.

*

This book owes a lot to Peter Giannone who got out of South Africa only a couple of steps ahead of the Bureau of State Security.

'This is the Intelligence Section,' said Captain Mostert, waving her arm airily at a room full of desks and typewriters. 'The brains of the operation. Top Secret. This is where we fight the MPLA, FAPLA, the ANC, MK, PAC, SWAPO, PLAN, the Cubans, the DDR and the Soviets.'

'Jeez,' said Sergeant Smith. 'There's a whole alphabet of enemies.'

'No 'U',' replied Mostert, with a smile. Mind you, once Rhodesia becomes Zimbabwe, it'll be a fair A-Z.'

01

Death of a Racist.

8th May 1980

Police Post 156.

South West Africa/Namibia

Sergeant Joshua Smith of the South African Police climbed up the thirteen steps of the ladder to the top of the rusting iron water tank and raised his binoculars northwards to the horizon. There was nothing there but salt sand; flat, white, grey, flat, white, grey and flat white again. Sometimes it was seeded, smeared with sparse khaki dried out grass like hair on the shoulder of a desiccated corpse; most times not; just flat, white, grey and white again. He lowered the glasses and slowly swinging through ninety degrees of unchanging vista, he looked eastwards along the straight scrape that qualified as a road in this part of South West Africa. He could tell it was a road only because the grass that had straggled across it had been shaved off by the blade of the road grader that had gone through four days ago. The raised lips along either side of the verge went like perspective lines straight to a vanishing point somewhere in the invisible distance on the sharp horizon. He raised the glasses. The view was the same. He lowered them again and looked west. No difference. He looked south. Another identical scrape ran to an equally empty horizon. It was Sunday and his team would not be relieved until Wednesday, when someone else would come out here and swing the binos around the horizon five times a day and see nothing.

He looked at his watch. Four-thirty pm and the burn under his eyes told him it was thirty degrees. His lips were cracked and his red arms, given no shade from the fine hair that had bleached from black to light brown, had peeled once this week. He didn't mind it really. Coming from Graaf-Reinet in the Karoo, he was used to the desert heat but this featureless white landscape had something different about it, something isolating, empty and oppressive and he felt the heavy hand of its presence on his forehead much more than he felt the burn of the sun.

He looked up into the blue, the perfect blue, the picture postcard, tourist poster blue of the perfect sky. It was always blue, always perfect, intense in a way that was similar to the blue of the Karoo sky, yet here in the Namib it was somehow one degree more perfect, one degree deeper where the sky was higher, one degree darker where it was lower; a blue without silver or soft sheen or low mist to lighten it. It was always blue; from Wednesday to Wednesday, it was always blue. Not even the sun could bleach its colour; from an hour after dawn to an hour before sunset, the blue sky was dominant and the sun passed over it like a scorch mark from a magnifying glass on a piece of graph paper.

'Tell me again why I'm here?' he said out loud, asking no one in particular. And when no answer came, he added: 'Fuck. It could be worse.'

As if in answer there was a hiss of static from the radio mounted in the ugly cross-eyed dog-faced armoured dump truck *Casspir* that served them as both transport and fortress, parked hard up by the wall of the square, white plaster police post.

'Get that, hey?' he called. 'See if they have sorted the monkey gland situation, hey?'

Konstabel Scholtz appeared from out of the building. He was wearing nothing but veldtschoen and a pair of khaki shorts and had not bothered to shave again, which gave him the appearance of someone much older than his twenty years should have admitted to. Without bothering to acknowledge the horizon, as though to do so would admit it existed, Scholtz trundled towards the truck, holding on to a bustling dream of his native Johannesburg. Distracted and whistling, he ambled around the Casspir, swung up into the back and made his way forward to the radio set. For a moment there was nothing but silence, the real profound silence of the bare salt desert, the silence that sucks up all sound and turns it into heat, flat light and emptiness, then Smith heard Scholtz trying to raise HQ through the staccato exchanges of other conversations.

'Hello, hello,' he announced, urgently and half-heartedly at the same time. 'This is Whisky Golf. Acknowledge, Over.'

Sergeant Smith pursed his lips and wondered how he was going to get through another endless, empty day in this endless, empty desert. He knew Scholtz was no conversationalist and knew that there was nothing much to talk about anyway, out here, where nothing happened, ever. They couldn't get music on the radio and the batteries on the cassette player had given out half way through *Redemption Song*, because Scholtz had broken the charger. There wasn't a generator to power even a fan, so the only debate that seemed worth having, about whether it was better to sleep the days away in the building, or outside in the shade of the building, or inside the Casspir, was the only one that they had not exhausted. It was almost a highlight, thought Smith, to see Scholtz take the shovel and the toilet roll and go out fifty meters to the same bleak spot every day, the same spot in a couple of thousand square kilometres of bleak emptiness, at the same time, every day, to take a *kak*.

The radio hissed and spat again and Smith heard Scholtz talking over it, as he always did, garbling both his message and everyone else's. For some reason, he had never got the hang of radio discipline; half the time he would talk with the handset on *receive*; always, he had the volume cranked up to maximum.

'Hello, hello,' he repeated. 'Is that you, Piet? Piet, for *fok's* sake we need monkey gland out here urgently. We stuck with these kak *Russians* and you can't eat them without monkey gland.'

The radio spat a stream of static like firework sparks and Smith heard an angry but indistinct voice radiating frustration telling him to get off the net.

'I think they've got some contact,' apologised Scholtz, his blonde head appearing from the rear of the vehicle. 'Casualties, maybe. The *terrs* must be active today, hey?'

'Try later,' said Smith, wearily. 'What else is there to eat?'

'Potato salad.'

'That'll have to do then.'

Scholtz climbed out of the Casspir and banged the door shut behind him. Inside the radio fizzed once more. 'When do you think Sisingi will be back?' he asked, hopefully.

'This evening, probably. When the Engineers come through to sweep the road. He'll probably thumb a lift with them.'

'You want tea?'

Smith nodded, let the binoculars dangle round his neck and climbed off the water tower. He dropped off the mid-way rung of the ladder, felt the crunch of the sand and rock salt beneath his feet and the give in his knees bend like wishbones. Straightening up, he screwed his eyes into a gritty slit and looked around his vast kingdom once more; one junction, one building, one water tank, one armoured vehicle, Scholtz's latrine and one long, stark encircling line of nothingness. It was all there, just as it had been since last Wednesday, with only the daily increase in kak and daily decrease in decent things to eat varying. It was only the fact that Smith had the date on his Timex watch that they knew the days were passing at a regular speed, separated by heat and light, heat and dark, and two very brief periods of purple coolness at sunrise and sunset. Not a rhythm but rather the absence of one; long hours, longer minutes, endless seconds which slowed to a stasis in which the stifling heat brought a suffocating torpidity. Police Post 156: his own private prison, penitentiary and penance.

'There's no creamer left.'

'Sisingi took it,' said Smith. 'He barters it.'

'Do you think he'll bring gem squash and beer?'

'I asked him for Redheart Rum if he can get it.'

'Redheart?' Scholtz turned his nose up. 'Better if he got Klippie and some cokes.'

'We'll see. Is it White Roses or Rooibos you have there?'

'Both,' replied Scholtz after a moment's investigation inside the post.

'I'll have Rooibos then.' Smith ran a hand across his itching face and decided that he would shave after all. It was Saturday and would make a change. He drew some lukewarm water off from the Casspir's water tank, propped his small round mirror, barely the size of a ladies' compact, up on top of the wheel and rubbed soap into his beard. Looking around him, he wished again that he had never joined the police and cursed the fact that as long as the war went on, it was unlikely he would ever get out. He ran the razor through the dark beard that clutched the lower half of his spade shaped face, cutting a swathe through the soap just like the road grader had through the desert, and examined the slight scar that ran along the top of his cheek under his left eye. It was a childhood mishap with a home-made cane bow and arrow, no more; an innocent mark. He kept his brown hair short normally, and parted on the right, but he had been so drunk so regularly on this tour that he had missed the barber each time he had tried to get it cut and now, in this heat, he felt it uncomfortably long, though it barely lapped his shirt collar, and he had to keep flicking it off his forehead. Sucking in his lips, he scraped away the stubble under his nose, broken (of course) in a rugby brawl and then glided the blade around the acne spot on the left of his chin, trying not to pop it.

'Your tea.'

He mumbled his thanks as Scholtz balanced an enamel mug on the tyre.

'I hope he does bring Redheart. I'm not bothered though. Not if we don't have ice. You need ice for Klippie and coke.'

Smith nodded in agreement.

'You got a spot. You going to squeeze it?'

Scholtz was five years younger and had a coffee blonde complexion that had never seen a blemish, ever.

'Fuck off, will you?'

He turned back to the mirror and caught his own searching eye for a moment, the briefest, fleeting moment of flecked hazel, then looked away and finished shaving without looking again.

'And see if the contact is over, so we can get some monkey gland up here. Or ketchup, peach chutney or anything. I'm sick to death of Russians without some sauce. I'm going back on the tank.'

'Can I take a kak first?' answered Scholtz irritably.

Smith ignored him and went back to the ladder, touching the metal gingerly before deciding that although hot, it was not hot enough to burn, and began his ascent. The binoculars knocked against his breast bone as the clean, new sweat of his armpits quickly renewed the soup plates on his shirt. His crotch was gritty and the thick cotton of his shorts was black where the sweat had gathered along the creases but he was glad of the movement because it put some ventilation in there. Once on top of the tank, he put the binoculars to his eyes and for the fifth time that day carried out his drill.

'Now I know how the Muslims in Durban feel,' he said to himself.

'What?' said Scholtz.

'Go take a kak. Then put some more tea on.'

'Can you see Sisingi from up there?'

'I'll tell you if I do. I promise.'

'OK. I'll go for a kak now.' Scholtz took the shovel and toilet paper from the back of the Casspir and began to walk in his habitual direction, marked now by a faint path. 'You won't look will you?'

'The day I need to get my jollies by watching you kak is the day I will start supporting England rugby.'

Scholtz smiled and walked on, the clumping of his boots made damp by the silence.

Smith put up the binos and began to sweep the empty horizon for signs of life, or change, or hope, or Sisingi, or monkey gland or Redheart Rum. There was nothing. He looked north; foreground nothing; distance nothing. South; foreground nothing, distance nothing. West; foreground nothing, distance nothing. South West; distance nothing, foreground Scholtz taking a kak at the end of the faint white trail that the dragging shovel had drawn in the salt, like a thin line of spittle between the lips of a madman.

'I know you're watching,' called Scholtz.

'What else is there to do?' Smith called back.

'It looks like the sweetcorn went right through me again.'

'You are shitting corn cobs now?'

'Ja. Corn cobs. You know the Kaffirs in Joburg use them to wipe their arses with after they have been for a kak? That is a very fucked up thing. It must hurt like hell.'

Smith sighed. 'Did you bring that copy of *War and Peace* with you this time, so that you might continue with your education?'

'Hey?' replied Scholtz, pulling up his shorts.

'Never mind. Check the radio before you make the tea, hey?' he called.

Scholtz clumped back, opened the rear doors of the Casspir like ears, threw in the shovel with a clang and the softer whump of toilet paper and then climbed in after them. Smith could see him moving around as he worked his way forward, past the narrow glass side panelled windows, towards the front where the radio set was fitted and then disappear as he squatted down. A long moment later, and he was climbing out of the commander's top hatch to the accompaniment of static and tinny radio voices.

'Ja, it's working now,' said Scholtz. 'I thought it was fucked. Maybe the heat got to it, hey?'

'Did you put the handset back properly when you used it just now?'

'Ja, of course.'

'OK. See if you can get some monkey gland then.'

Scholtz bobbed down into the cab and began trying to raise the base. 'Hello, hello. Whisky Golf here. You there Piet? Piet..?'

Smith put the glasses back to his eyes and ran foreground north, west, south and east again, then distance north, west and south twice more before he spotted it. Out on the road to the east, just before the night, there was a small smudge of white dust pluming up and trailing off. He watched for another minute or so, until he was sure it was a vehicle and then called out to Scholtz once more.

'Ja, Sergeant?' Scholtz replied, standing in the commander's hatch and holding the radio handset.

'Get the AK. There's movement on the road.'

'Is it the Engineers? Maybe it's Sisingi?'

'Get the AK.'

'Where did you put it? You had it last.'

'Where it should be. By your *fokken* feet.'

'Shall I still try to get the monkey gland?'

'Bring me the AK first.'

Smith put the binos back to his face and leaned slightly forward as if this might give him a better view of the distinct dust cloud on the road, now coming towards him faster than the advancing night. The plume was too big for a bakkie or a jeep, he guessed; it was something heavier. With luck it would be the Engineer's Buffels, or a stray Casspir with Sisingi aboard, but it could also be a truck commandeered by SWAPO and he didn't believe in taking chances.

'Here, Sergeant,' said Scholtz, appearing at the bottom of the ladder.

'Is the safety on?'

'Ja. No, wait. Ja, now it is.' Scholtz climbed up onto the water tank and looked eastwards down the road. 'I think it's the Engineers. Maybe, we'll get a braii out of them. What do you think?'

Smith concentrated. The westering sun was sending out clear, horizontal gold rays now and within a minute or so they touched the windscreen of the oncoming vehicle and sent back a single blazing reflection. He put the binos down.

'It's a Buffels,' said Joshu assessing the state of the ugly one eyed cross between a frog, a dump-truck and a moon landing unit. 'The Engineers. They'll want to laager up with us here. So, yes, we'll get a braii.'

'*Lekker.*'

'Give me the AK, then dig a couple of tins of potato salad out of the cool hole.'

'Shall I try for monkey gland again?'

'Let's see if these guys have brought Sisingi first.'

It took an hour for the squint, one-eyed armoured truck that Smith had identified as a Buffels troop carrier to come close enough to be recognised fully as the familiar truck it was. Throwing up the salt sand as though it were spray off a beach, it was being driven hard and as it came closer into view, Smith identified Lieutenant Els perched atop the driver's cab like a rodeo rider. He had recently acquired an afro, a Zapata moustache and a pair of aviator sun glasses, which effect he rounded off with a cigarette dangling from the side of his mouth, an AK-47 held nonchalantly on the hip of his nutcracker shorts and a new rampant rhino tattoo across his bare chest. Below him on the front bumper, a dead body in olive drab fatigues had been strapped like a hunting trophy and it flopped and bounced oddly, as though the limbs had become dislocated with the movement of the vehicle. On either side of the v-shaped troop compartment, a pair of elephant tusks had been fixed with rather more care and as Smith lowered the binoculars, he heard the sound of rock music coming from a speaker wired onto the side, accompanied by raucous drunken voices. As soon as it came within hailing distance, Els started bawling at him, his voice brash enough to be clearly heard over the noise of the engine.

'Smith, you *fokken poes*! What happened to your radio? We've picked up a couple of your Kaffirs on the road. There's been a big contact. 41 Mech have had an officer killed by the sounds of it. Name of Dietz: I think I know him. Big fella – handy in the scrum, but more of a Back than a Forward, if you get me.'

The growling vehicle came to a halt in a skid of gravel, soap powder sand and screaming guitars.

'It's been playing up,' replied Smith, looking pointedly at Scholtz, who was back standing on top of the Casspir. 'Where's the contact?'

'Up by the Cut Line - Chetequera. You're wanted up there tomorrow. Well, today, actually, but they won't expect you there now. You mind if we share your location tonight? We've got *Castle* and *boerwors*.'

Smith looked across at Scholtz, who was pretending not to know about the radio, and then nodded his assent to Els. Els cut the engine and five soldiers in bush hats and khaki tumbled out of the vehicle, stretching, scratching and looking around as though they had just arrived at a beachside camp site. They were followed by a tall black man, clutching a haversack.

'This your kaffir?' called out Lieutenant Els, sliding off the cab and landing like a cat on the sand.

'Sisingi is Ovambo, not a kaffir.'

Sisingi was a sharp faced man with a strong brow and a pointed jaw who stood just short of six feet and looked everyone straight in the eye. He was in his late twenties and accepted life as it came, though he was also a thinking man who could often be seen looking at the empty horizon and wondering what lay beyond it.

Els stumped into the Police Post, rooted around for a few moments and then reappeared.

'You got monkey gland?' he asked.

'No,' said Smith, climbing down from the water tank. 'I was hoping you might have some.'

'*Fokken* Russians without monkey gland. How do those *piels* in Pretoria expect us to clear mines all day without *fokken* monkey gland?'

Smith walked to the Buffels and inspected the corpse on the bumper.

'You know his head has come off?'

'What?' said Els, suddenly concerned.

'His head has come off.'

'Fok!' said Els. 'It must have been when we drove through that hut. How will we identify him now? Can we leave him here?'

'No, you *fokken* can't.'

'But you're police and will know what to do with a body.'

'Ja, and you're Engineers who should not be shooting at SWAPO in a police area. You must leave that to us, but now you have gone and shot someone, you must deal with the consequences yourself. We are here until Wednesday and that body will be stinking by tomorrow – I'm guessing you killed him today?'

'Can't you get your kaffir to bury him?'

'I told you. He isn't a kaffir – he's Ovambo.'

'What about your boy on the Casspir?'

'No way. I don't want any bodies buried around my post. Just the smell will attract lions and I do not need the million flies that that corpse is already impregnated with fucking up my life.'

'I'll give you first crack at the braii.'

'No. The answer is no.'

'OK,' said Els, stubbing out his cigarette on the ground and looking at the corpse as though it was no more than a damaged radiator grill. 'Well, he won't smell much tonight, so we can just leave him where he is and I'll dump him in Windhoek in the morning.'

Els walked off to the back of the vehicle where his section were busy with wood, charcoal, a large grill and a cool box full of good meat.

'You OK, Sisingi?' said Smith quietly. 'They didn't fuck with you or anything?'

Sisingi shrugged. 'It was good to get a lift. I brought Redheart and Cane.'

'No monkey gland?'

'They had none. I have *Mrs Balls* instead.'

'Good enough.'

Els' engineers soon had a fire going and while they waited for it to burn down to embers, they cracked beers, smiled in the firelight and pulled up boxes of ammunition to sit on. The night was full and starry and though it was still warm enough to justify shorts, hands were not shy in stretching out to feel the heat of the flames. The Buffels with the body had been moved at Smith's request, grumbling around the back of the Police Post like a disgruntled Quasimodo indignant at the extra work; *it was only a body*, it seemed to say, but Smith was insistent; he did not want to look at the mutilated trunk while he was eating. Later, when the embers were red and the ash white and the meat was sizzling, Scholtz scrounged some new batteries for the cassette player and the rustic Bavarian sounds of *boeremusike* were added to the sounds of rugby club banter which made Smith think of all the backyard braiis at home. For a moment he could see the pool, the tennis skirts and the swimsuits and when Els cracked another *Castle*, he almost thought he heard the clink of ice in glasses.

'What did they want me for?' he asked, coming back to the present.

'Hey?' said Els. 'Oh, ja. They didn't say. They just put the call out. Probably some fuck up. Anyway, I'm to give you a lift in.'

'Maybe they want you to investigate a murder,' chimed in one of the Engineers beerily. 'I hear they may have killed some kaffirs up there.'

There was a hoot of raucous laughter as a couple more tins were cracked.

'Sisingi and Scholtz must stay here and man the post,' said Smith. 'Can you leave one of your guys to keep them company?'

Els shoved a cigarette under his moustache, lit up and exhaled heavily.

'Ja. You're right. This water is valuable.' He looked at Scholtz and pursed his lips. 'And you can't leave the kaffir in charge. I'll leave Wilson. He's OK. He talks kak about kaffirs sometimes but he's a good guy.'

'Sisingi isn't a kaffir.'

'Ja, I know. He's Ovambo. You told me.'

'What's the difference between a *kaffir* and a *wog*?' asked Scholtz, breaking in on the conversation. 'I mean, I know that in America they're called *niggers*, but why are some blacks – like Sisingi - not *kaffirs*?'

Sisingi ignored the mention of his name and slowly drew on the neck of the Redheart before handing it on to Smith. Smith took a swig and then poured a shot into his tin of beer.

'*Kaffirs* are blacks in Africa and *wogs* are blacks in India,' explained Wilson, one of the Engineers. He was a burly man with a moustache like Els's, but it underlined a red nose permanently peeling and raw. '*Fok!* Didn't you go to school?'

There was more laughter but Scholtz persisted.

'No, but Sisingi is black, but he's not a *kaffir*. And there's Samoa; and the Fijians; and there are blacks who play cricket for England. Does this mean you stop being a kaffir if you leave Africa?'

'You think if a kaffir gets on a plane, he stops being a kaffir, hey? Man, you are *opgefokt.*'

'I once saw an albino kaffir,' another voice revved. '*Fok!* If that isn't bad luck, hey?'

'It's just that when I was in Ireland last year, there was a black who was Irish...'

'Like Phil Lynott in *Thin Lizzy,* you mean? He's only half-caste...' said Wilson.

'What were you doing in Ireland?' asked Els, turning over steaks. 'I thought South Africans were not allowed to go to Ireland.'

'My Dad has an Irish passport now,' answered Scholtz, slurping beer. 'He says since the kaffirs are taking over in Rhodesia, South Africa will be next and he wants his money out of the country.'

This came as a surprise to Smith. 'You are joining the chicken run?'

'*Ag* man! The Rhodies are all English *poes,*' said Wilson, wiping his mouth. 'The kaffirs will never beat the Afrikaaner. Not while there's one of us standing.'

'Fuck politics,' said Els. 'Who needs a steak? And Wilson – just how did you come by such a traditional *Afrikaaner* name, hey?'

There was another burst of laughter and then the conversation paused as the men concentrated on their meat, tearing it off the T-bones, eating with fingers and wiping their mouths with the backs of their hands. Sisingi took a length of the coiled boerwors, wolfed it and asked for more. Els gave him a T-bone and half a kilo of rump. Wilson handed round more beer and steaks as the firelight lit their faces with a hot infernal glow and the fat spat and sizzled on the hot coals, like flesh in purgatory.

'How did you come by the *terr*?' asked Smith.

Els grunted and put a bone down on his plate. 'Like I say, there's been a big contact here and up on the Cut Line.' He wiped his moustache with the first and second fingers of both hands. 'Typhoon unit trying to get down to the farming areas to kill a few whites. This one was on his way back. He was probably planting a mine or something because he didn't have a gun. We ran him down with the Buffels. He could run though. I'll give him that. Took Wilson three goes before he nailed him.'

*

9th May 1980

Joshua had seen dead bodies and death before, but not enough headless ones to get properly used to them, and he found it difficult to ignore the body on the front of Els's Buffels as they drove eastwards towards Headquarters in Windhoek. For most of the way, he stood up, keeping his head and shoulders above the parapet of the open topped vehicle, braving the whipping sand and the broiling sun and smoking cigarettes with Els, who didn't mind, and wondered why HQ wanted him in Windhoek. He tried not to think about it, ignoring the feeling of unease in his stomach and trying not to wonder why he did not feel glad about leaving Police Post 156.

'Cheer up,' said Els, noticing the frown.

'You don't seem bothered about the death of your pal, Dietz,' said Smith.

'Fuck all I can do about it, so I don't think about it,' answered Els. 'But as long as there's beer and rugby, the world is going to be fine man.'

Smith disagreed but kept his disquiet to himself. Els' rough counsel could not change the fact that the world was not fine, had not be fine for a long time and was unlikely to come anywhere near being fine in the near future. Nor did three more hours of thinking on it make it better and as they drove past the shacks and donkey carts on the road into the city to dump him at the guardroom at Police HQ, Joshua was still feeling uneasy, a feeling that increased aand intensified as he went up the steps, past the wired in windows, along the buff corridors, under the ceiling fans and past side offices full of clerks battering away at typewriters. It was noisy after the silence of the desert and Joshua felt curiously disorientated by the sounds of voices chatting easily, the rattle of a tea trolley going backwards and forwards on a squeaky wheel overladen with a large silver urn, a bowl of sugar under a fly cover, a white jug of milk and a plate full of rusks. Two African women in blue housecoats were sweeping the floors half-heartedly, their eyes down as they reached in to the waste paper baskets to empty them and the smell of sweat, heat, cigarettes and disinfectant made his head swim. He was familiar with the building but even though he came here every week to make his report, the sense of apprehension, of claustrophobia even, always came to him here, always in the same way. There was something menacing about the way the paper travelled around the offices bound up in manila folders from desk to desk, from filing cabinet to green, battered filing cabinet, with every detail of every person engaged in the war and every incident that took place in it neatly recorded on the printed forms, in triplicate. The paper machine fluttering and clattering on, never forgetting, never forgiving, always ready to serve up the information that might hang a man as soon as promote him, always ready with a version of the truth that never encapsulated it. There was something relentless about it all, something towering, like a wave building higher and ever higher, waiting to come crashing down on anyone it chose to. There was no resisting either, he knew; reports were reports; they existed independently of experience and somehow outside of it. A dead man in a shallow grave in the bush was experience; the terse report of his death, typed up in officialese, was not, but it would become truth enough for the machine. He lit up another cigarette, sat down on a bench for a moment, and tried to put it all down to the contrast between the isolation of Police Post 156 and the bustle of a busy office, but he knew that he was fooling himself and that the sense of unease he carried with him was due to much deeper causes.

A woman's head appeared from behind a frosted glass door, evaluated him from behind preying mantiss spectacles and then sniffed.

'Sergeant Smith?' It was more of a statement than a question.

Joshua nodded. Captain Botha's secretary knew him. She had known him for nearly four years. She had known him ever since he had been posted here. He had tried to chat her up once. He had even fixed a puncture for her once but she never varied her routine when he came to make his weekly report. He admired her. He liked her. She was dependable and predictable, a female version of his Police Post, and these were things to be treasured in a war. It was reassuring, even if it was dull.

'Captain Botha will see you now,' she said.

He stood up and she waved him into Captain Botha's office.

'Fancy a date later, Trish?' he said, as he always did.

'No,' she replied, as she always replied.

He went through the ritual because it was familiar and went someway to relieving the growing feeling of apprehension that he always had when reporting to Captain Botha. Today, he needed the ritual even more because this was not a normal meeting. He felt that he was going back into a bar he had once been banned from.

'Sergeant Smith!' Captain Botha's voice was rich with suppressed mirth. 'It looks like you have found a home where a welcome awaits you! Someone other than me wants you! Is this not a miracle?'

The pallid Captain looked down at the paper before him and then straight back at Smith. He was a fleshy man in his late thirties, his domed head camouflaged by the merest veneer of military stubble, pale faced and sweaty like bacon fat, and habitually happy, like a butcher. He had Smith's manilla file in front of him and was glinting with amusement at it. Snorting a little, he picked up a blue pencil, licked it and consulted the ragged, dog-eared documentation with exaggerated precision, as though he was about to despatch a consignment of special sausages to a valued customer. Joshua's stomach give a flip of anxiety.

'Sergeant *Smith*? Sergeant *Joshua* Smith?' he asked, with mock amazement, pausing after each question, like a stage magician expecting a contrary answer from a stooge in the audience.

'Sergeant Joshua Smith, *aged 25*, of *Graaf-Reinet*? Sergeant...'

'Yes, it's me, for fuck's sake, Captain.'

'Sergeant Joshua Smith, aged 25 of Graaf-Reinet, presently awaiting charges in...where was it?'

'Wilderness, George and Knysna.'

'Correct! For being drunk and attempting to go *three* rounds with the *eight* members of the local constabulary? Something about a girl – or the lack of one?' said Botha, gleefully ignoring Smith's repeated nodding of the head. 'Is this *you*?'

'Where is it? I'll take anywhere except Krugerburg or the Cape,' said Joshua, hoping that this was just a piece of routine nonsense.

'You have a high notion of police logic,' replied Captain Botha, smirking. Captain Botha liked to collect stories of the oddities, absurdities and singularities of service life in a counter-insurgency war. He looked up.

Joshua had the sinking feeling that came with the certainty that Captains only spoke like this when they had some wonderfully cheering news to divulge.

'I'm being charged then?' he asked, wearily.

'You are going to join the *big* boys, this time, Smithy my China,' Botha replied. 'What a lucky little copper you are! No position in the rear echelon latrine detachment awaits you quite yet because it seems that your breadth and depth of experience, education and heroic stature has combined to furnish you with the *unique* qualifications required by none other than 41 Mech! Their CO has asked for *you! Especially!* You have no doubt been chosen on the recommendation of your first Inspector, the great Inspector Du Toit of Graaf-Reinet, who so considered you to be a man of *great discretion and integrity* that he wrote it on your file in big letters and underlined it, Smithy - here! Congratulations! No wonder you were promoted so young!' He tapped the file significantly with a fat finger. 'You are going to join the army for a little while and help them win the war against all those Cubans and Communists and horrible, uppity SWAPO kaffirs! And be sure and give my regards to the Forces Armada Popular Liberation of Angola or whatever the fuck FAPLA are called these days, won't you?'

'What the fuck do they want with me, Sir?' said Joshua, as his heart went down to his boots.

'Search me, Smithy. All very hush-hush by the looks of things. Perhaps they think you will make a good secret agent, like James Bond, and send you over the border to fuck things up for the Communists and win all the kaffirs' hearts and minds for us? Or more likely, it will be a prisoner escort job; some officer or other caught with his hand in the mess accounts or the knickers of a General's wife and sent off to do jankers in Oudtshorn jail. It will obviously be something trivial, if irritating; something to do with kaffirs even.'

Joshua was disconcerted. He did not like the sound of this posting. He did not like being picked out *especially*. He did not want to go to the army. He did not want to go to a unit like 41 Mech, who he knew had a reputation for looking for trouble and finding it. He could think of no good reason why they should want him. These were enough reasons in his own reckoning to make him feel suspicious, uncomfortable and downright scared, but the fact that Els knew about Dietz, their dead officer, while Captain Botha did not seemed to be an absolutely unholy coincidence.

'Fucking great. That is just *lekker*,' he protested, hoping that a bad attitude and a convincing protest might just get him disqualified. 'I joined the SAPS so I wouldn't have to join the fucking army. Can't someone else go? What's going to happen to my Section?'

'Lieutenant Keegan is already on his way to take over your Section. No, there's no escaping your fate, Smithy, my China. This comes from up on high, Smithy. It has the stamp of High Authority, Smithy. It is probably a filing error, of course, but what can we humble mortals do in the face of officialdom, hey? You have been called, Smithy. You are the Chosen, the Elect.' Botha tapped his pencil on the file. 'Is it true you *like* kaffirs, Smith?' he asked, as though this was a new and uncertain concept.

'I got no problem with them.'

'You wouldn't let your sister marry one though, would you, hey?'

'Have you met my sister?' replied Smith.

Botha digested this for a moment and then, with a meaty smile returned to his circus impresario routine.

'Thanks for visiting with us,' he said, pointing. 'Enjoy Oshadangwa. The door is behind you. Do come again.'

*

10th May 1980

'You're a policeman, Sergeant Schmidt? That right?'

'Graaf-Reinet's finest, Sir – and the name's *Smith*, Sir. Sergeant, South African Police Service.'

Major van der Merwe was a good six feet and forty something in age, with a pale complexion under a bush tan, more like a bank manager than a farmer. He also had the silence of the fisherman; brown eyes, red nose, brown moustache with grey coming through; bat-shaped jug ears, brown hair receding above the temples, going grey like his moustache; a conscience; a mole on his right cheek; a man too sensitive for the job he had been given.

'It's Sergeant Joshua Smith, *attached A Company, 41 Mech* here,' replied van der Merwe through a tight smile, before dropping his eyes to inspect the backs of his hands for a moment. They were laid palm down, soft fingers spread wide, with clean, obsessively scrubbed fingernails, set off by a gold wedding band. He seemed to be counting them, then exercising them, moving each finger in turn, feeling the soft wood of the desk and wishing instead that the keys of a piano were under them. He looked sideways at the Company Sergeant Major and chewed his lip. 'Unfortunately,' he added, more to himself than to the room.

'Smith?" said the Company Sergeant Major, grimly. 'What's an English *poes* doing in a good Afrikaaner town like Graaf-Reinet?'

'Locking up Afrikaaner *poes* – when I'm not fucking it,' answered Joshua belligerently. He was trying to look hard, un-military, a barrack room lawyer who would best be posted back to the SAPS as soon as possible. He was also trying to ignore the fat bluebottle buzzing around the bare bulb that hung down from a twisted wire tacked to the roof truss that ran under the thatch.   Straight ahead of him on the otherwise bare wall of the spartan office was a tired, mildewed portrait of ex-President Vorster in a frame that the woodworm had got at.

The CSM raised a heavy eyebrow before replying.

'Your shoe lace is undone, Sergeant Smith. I suggest you tie it up like the good copper you no doubt are. After that we may well get around to instructing you in the use of an implement called a *smoothing iron.*'

'You heard about Lieutenant Dietz?' asked the Major rhetorically.

'Yes Sir,' replied Sergeant Smith, mechanically. 'The driver told me something on the way in from the airstrip.'

'We all mighty sorry about this,' continued the Major. 'He was a good officer. His folks will be heartbroken.'

'Of course, Sir. Quite right too, Sir,' Smith replied in a voice that was almost parody. 'But what you need is a military policeman, Sir. This is a military matter, isn't it?'

Major van der Merwe ignored him, tilted his head sideways and coming to a reluctant decision, or rather, an unwilling acquiescence in accepting the unpleasant fact of Smith's appearance as the solution to his problem, nodded to the CSM. CSM Landsberg, bull necked, broken-nosed, barrel-chested, ironed, pressed, creased, starched and ironed again, pragmatically military to his core, understood the request instinctively and clunked heavily across the wooden floor of the Company office to the door. He tore it open and ordered the startled clerk revealed in the outer office to double along to the armoury and ask for a long stand and a short weight. The clerk also understood what this meant instinctively and cleared off hurriedly in the direction of the canteen. Looking to see that there was no-one else present and ignoring the black man pushing a mop and pail around the office, the CSM closed the door, firmly but carefully, as though snapping shut the breech block of a field gun, then picked up a thick, folded newspaper from a locker and held it behind his back.

'Have you ever worked on a murder case?' asked the Major, dropping his voice and his lids simultaneously.

Sergeant Smith started. Murder was something that he was acquainted with yet barely qualified to handle.

'Just kaffirs,' Smith replied, cautiously, suspiciously. "Black on black stuff – nothing serious. No one gives a shit in Graaf-Reinet if a couple of kaffirs decide to settle their differences with a panga, Sir. Who's been *donnered*? I mean, who's been murdered, *Sir*.'

Major van der Merwe picked up his service hat and indicated that Smith and the CSM should follow him. They walked out into the flat, bright sunshine of a blazing hot desert day, ignored the chatter of the monkeys plaguing the canteen and the tinkering of spanners by the workshop area and trotted briskly over to the infirmary, a low whitewashed building, thatched and shaded by bluegums. It was cool by comparison inside, but the distinctive smell of rotting meat made it feel warmer, close, suffocating. As the CSM dismissed the duty medic and led the way into a deserted ward, Sergeant Smith's eyes quickly adjusted to the relative gloom and he took in the magnolia painted brick, the single curtained window, the fly screens and the mosquito net hanging down from a meat hook in the ceiling. Beneath the yellowed muslin a black body bag lay on a rusted, paint-peeling iron trolley. It was taut, full, like an inflatable pillow. It was dripping heavily too, smelling foul and attracting a swarm of flies and roaches.

CSM Landsberg tucked his stick under his arm, swept away the netting and deftly unzipped the bag all in one movement, then stepped quickly back to avoid the stench that billowed out from the decomposing body. Major van der Merwe pursed his lips in regret as he recognised the handsome, blonde bearded face of Lieutenant Dietz, now grey and green-tinged. The bluebottles were already greedily at their work, preparing the way for the maggots.

'Tell me what you think," said van der Merwe, quietly.

Joshua hesitated, then stepped forward as the CSM tied the mosquito net into something resembling a shroud and wafted away at the flies. Assuming a professional detachment that he had not used since leaving Graaf-Reinet, he sniffed and decided that it could do no harm to take a look, however reluctant he was to be involved in an army case. The murdered bodies of strangers didn't bother him much, and a first glance reassured him that he'd seen corpses in a worse state than this; this was nothing to match the ones when the animals had had first go. Once, previously, he had bagged up the leftovers of a corpse that had fallen out of a tree, bit by bit, just as the leopard had devoured it.

'How long has he been dead?'

'Does it matter?' replied the CSM, and then. 'Two days.'

Ignoring the gathering flies as they dropped out of the thatch, Smith ran his eyes up and down the head and shoulders of the corpse, then looked up for permission to open the bag all the way. When CSM Landsberg gave it, he ran the zip down, laid bare the torso and put his fingers gingerly around two small, dark-ringed, symmetrical bullet holes, on the front of the naked body. He let out a little whistle.

'No blood,' he said, carefully. 'These shots didn't kill him. Dead bodies don't pump out blood. Somebody did this afterwards. From close up.'

Van der Merwe pursed his lips again and told him to continue. CSM Landsberg touched his nose and looked on impassively. Both men, it seemed to Smith, already knew the answers to the questions they were asking. He waited for them to say something, but when it was clear they intended to remain tight-lipped, he moved his fingers towards a crusted scab of black blood just below Dietz's heart.

'Can I?' he asked. The Major assented. Smith pulled a bit of rag from his camo uniform pocket and picked the scab off. A plug of thick, granular, dried blood, like a piece of black pudding came away and Smith whistled once more. 'This is what killed him.' He put a finger into the gash. 'A deep stab; delivered from someone standing behind him, who reached around and directed the blow upwards towards the heart, I'd say. The killer was probably right-handed, and used his left to restrain the victim.'

'*This* is what killed him," replied CSM Landsberg, unwrapping a bayonet from the folded newspaper, passing it from hand to hand and then handing it to him, blade first.

Smith looked up. 'That's one of ours. How'd the kaffirs get hold of that?'

'They didn't,' said van der Merwe, sadly. 'I've got seven good soldiers who swore no SWAPO got anywhere near him....And three good soldiers who came back from the Chetequera Op without bayonets. And I need them back on Ops, quick.'

Smith looked from the Major to the CSM and back.

'Did they do it?'

There was no answer. He straightened up.

'Who found the body?'

'Some of the lads in his platoon,' said van der Merwe. 'They didn't see anything suspicious.'

Smith took a deep breath, like a used car salesman about to punt a rotten deal.

'You know, you could just tell his parents that he was killed in action,' he offered. 'It wouldn't be the first time that the truth has been watered down to spare the grieving family – or keep it out of the newspapers. That way your problem is solved and I can get back to my unit.'

'And leave us with a murderer running round scot free in the Company?' answered the CSM. 'How would *you* feel about sharing a trench with him?'

'He's *connected*,' said van der Merwe, looking straight at him. 'Dietz's people are big in government, big in the National Party. They will need answers. That's why we need someone with experience of a murder investigation. A civilian investigator. The military police have other fish to fry.'

'Then you need a proper detective, Sir,' said Joshua, stepping back. 'I don't want anything to do with anyone big in government. You need someone with experience.'

'And I have been given you,' replied van der Merwe. 'You may not like it. I may not like it, but this is where we are and this is what we are faced with.'

Joshua took in van der Merwe's evident reluctance and shook his head again.

'You don't have a choice, as I understand the situation,' said the Major.

'Meaning?' answered Joshua warily.

'I have been given to understand that the charges relating to several unfortunate incidents on your recent leave are still pending,' said van der Merwe, looking at the floor. 'I understand that they are serious enough to warrant a prison sentence.'

'No they are not,' protested Joshua. 'OK, maybe a couple of days in the *tronk* but nothing more. This is bullshit. You have been misinformed, Sir.'

The Major looked up and then across at the CSM.

'Just do the investigation, come up with something convinving and you can clear off,' said Landsberg. 'Like the Major says, Dietz's people are connected. Unless you want to really piss them off, I'd do what they asked.'

Joshua considered for a moment.

'How did you know about the charges?' he asked.

Major van der Merwe gave the merest shake of his head and looked down again.

'And you say he is *connected*,' said Joshua. 'As in *connected*?'

The Major looked up and straight into Joshua's eyes. He didn't say a word, but Joshua knew exactly what he meant.

'Shit,' he said, his heart sinking as he realised that there was no way that he could avoid taking the case. 'How long have I got?'

'Two days,' replied van der Merwe. 'Then we are back on Ops. You'd better start with the suspects.'

'And you don't breathe a word about this to anyone but the Major or me,' added CSM Landsberg. 'Understand?'

Joshua didn't understand. He didn't understand why he was standing in a room with the body of a murdered officer; he didn't understand why or how he had been chosen to deal with this case; he didn't understand how the army knew about his charge sheet; he didn't understand why the Major seemed so uncomfortable; he didn't understand why he felt like he was being blackmailed, but he did understand what *connected* meant. And as a member of the South African Police Service he understood everything about how the law worked in Apartheid South Africa and he understood even more about how the law worked up here on the border, where there wasn't any.

*

02

Roses amid the Thorns.

Outside the infirmary, Major van der Merwe left them with only the briefest of farewells. Joshua watched him as he walked across the dusty ground, his shoulders slightly stooped, his steps lacking the bounce normal in military men, ignoring the helicopter that suddenly appeared above the base. The little dust devils that he kicked up were half-hearted, his gait slightly rolling as though disorientated or a little drunk and half way across the open space he hesitated and changed direction, took a few paces and then looking about him, changed direction again. It was not indecision that gave him his zig-zag course though. Rather, the impression he gave was one of deep sorrow, a sorrow that went deeper than the loss of one of his officers, a sorrow that he did not wish to express because it was indeed so deep. It looked like a sorrow that he could not escape, would never go away or be assuaged, a sorrow that was recognisable to anyone who lived the lives that they lived now and Joshua recognised it as in some way his own too. He turned the corner and stepped on to a veranda, his footsteps becoming hollow and disappearing into the sound of the haze.

'You've got a charge sheet then?' said Landsberg. 'Serious?'

Joshua shook his head. 'Like I said, its nothing.'

'Why did the Major bring it up then?' said the CSM.

'You'd better ask him.'

'Sounds like politics,' said Landsberg, tapping his nose with his stick. 'I don't like politics. Neither does the Major.'

Turning on his heel, CSM Landsberg led Joshua away through the vehicle park, packed full of armour – Ratel infantry fighting vehicles, Eland armoured cars, Buffel troop carriers - and all manner of weaponry, then down towards the Armoury where the infantry of 41 Mech were stripping, cleaning and assembling their rifles, checking kit and sharpening their bayonets. The heat was intense; only the sounds of metallic tinkering could penetrate the tinnitus of the cicadas, and no bass sounds intervened to give depth to the day. The only variance in the timbre came from far out beyond the perimeter wire, where an armoured car was being put growling through its paces, but even this sound struggled against the muffled weight of the beating sun. The soldiers were quiet, eschewing conversation as too much wasted effort, concentrating intently on scraping, scrubbing away gunshot residue with sharp iron tools and pan scrubs dipped in orange bowls of soapy water. From time to time, one or two lit up cigarettes, handed them on to grunted thanks and then stretched their necks up to watch the blue smoke gathering for a moment under the shade of the awnings rigged up between the acacia trees. It hung there, like a gun shot, before the slow movement of torpid air bore it away. Everywhere, the smell of oil, canvas and rubber was present, a comforting military fug that lacked only beeswax and starch to make it complete. There were more than a hundred men here in A Company, Smith reckoned, each armed with a rifle and bayonet capable of doing what had been done to Lieutenant Dietz.

With a sinking feeling in his stomach, Joshua realised that he had been thrown into a haystack made of needles and he rated the likely chances of finding the rusty one at just short of zero. Stumping along after the CSM, his feet rattling along in the loosely fastened boots that he had hoped would make him look un-military, he wondered what the consequences for the inevitable failure would be; if the army was anything like the police, arses would have been covered, blame assigned and scapegoats sought from the moment Dietz was pronounced dead. And as potential scapegoat material, an English copper Sergeant in an Afrikaaner outfit with a blameless reputation like 41 Mech - well, it seemed pretty obvious who the scapegoat would be. It was probably why he had been brought up here.

At the end of vehicle park, Smith saw the familiar shape of a long, low whitewashed shed with a green painted corrugated iron roof and bars over the windows. Alcatraz it was not, but Joshua saw as he approached that it bore all the hallmarks of a military jail; too much whitewash, not enough care, too much military bullshit, not enough permanence, and always the smell of carbolic and bad latrines and the rattle of enamel mugs against the cage.

'They're in here,' said the CSM, as the guard came to attention and saluted.

'Better let Sherlock Homes at them, then,' said Joshua, sourly.

CSM Landsberg stopped short and eyed him up and down.

'Take this seriously, *laatie*,' he warned. 'A good officer – a good man – is dead and one of these...' he paused, as though dismissing a squad full of words. '....these *citizen* soldiers, is a traitor to his country, his regiment and his mates.'

'Oh I take it very seriously, CSM, Sir,' answered Smith, with only a hint of exasperation. 'No evidence, no witnesses, no fingerprints on the murder weapon except yours and however many others have handled it, a wide selection of means for murder in every fucking hand on the base and more opportunity to kill someone than a fucking Redcoat at Rorke's Drift, on top of which I'm in pole position to be shafted when I draw a fucking blank into the bargain. Yes, CSM. I am taking this very fucking seriously.'

CSM Landsberg eyed him up once more, then smiled, almost genially.

'I take your point, *roinek*,' he said. 'And you're right; something does smell about this investigation business. But some *poes* killed Dietz and I want to see him pay – slowly, over a long period, and with sound effects.'

*

Joshua went past the guard and into the cell block and saw straight away that he had yet another problem. As per the regulation design, the cells were just bare cages extending all the way down one side of a narrow corridor, each equipped with a bunk and a bucket and little else and although the prisoners were not in adjoining cages, communication between them was free and open to the elements. He looked at the CSM with despair, who recognised his appeal.

'The jail was only designed to keep *houtkops* and *jollers* in 'till they were sober,' he explained, almost apologetically. 'Do your best. These boys are too stupid to cook up a curry between them, never mind an alibi.'

'Who you calling stupid?' cried a voice from a cot in the nearest cage. 'I nearly passed the *Matric*, I did. Oh, sorry, CSM.'

Sergeant Smith turned to look as a huge, barefooted young man climbed out of the bunk and came to the bars. He was over six three and had a head elogated by the forceps which had never gone back to shape. His ears shot out like radar from the sides of his dark, quizzical brows, and the cap of black, wiry hair gave him a mule-like countenance that a bent nose, weak chin and full lips did nothing to correct.

'Who's the plough-horse?' asked Joshua. 'And does the vet know he's missing?'

'Meet Private Kassie Strydom,' replied CSM Landsberg, drily. 'Some of the kaffirs say he's part human, but not many people agree. Still, he's useful for holding up Ratels when we need to change a wheel, aren't you Strydom? Now stand to attention like the good Boer you are and answer the Sergeant's questions.'

Kassie Strydom stiffened up and dropped his brows, as though he were struggling to follow the conversation.

'Where did you lose your bayonet?' began Joshua, sighing and tugging out a small notebook and pencil from his shirt pocket.

'Are you writing this down?' queried Private Strydom.

'And you only just failed Matric,' answered Joshua, flipping to an empty page. They were all empty. He licked the end of the pencil and found it to be too blunt to use. 'You must have been unlucky. Now tell me where you lost your fucking cutlery.'

Strydom looked as though he didn't understand the question and then shot a glance at the CSM, hoping he would tell him the answer. His lips ruminated and his tongue flicked out nervously.

'Am I in trouble?' he blurted.

'You're in the fucking *tronk*, and I'm a detective so "yes"; you are in trouble,' replied Joshua.

'Tell him what you remember, Private Strydom,' coaxed the CSM. 'And I'll give you a banana. There's a good lad.'

Kassie Strydom looked puzzled and hunted at the same time. He started scratching his balls and closed one eye in concentration.

'I left it in a kaffir,' he began to babble, hopping from foot to foot. 'The same day that Lieutenant Dietz got *donnered*. This kaffir jumped up at me out of a dugout and I went to shoot him but...but...but, I forgot to count my rounds and my magazine was empty, so I stuck him like a pig. Except the *bladdy poes* wouldn't get off the end of my bayonet and when I put my foot on his chest to boot him off, the *houtkop* fell sideways and twisted the *bladdy* thing like one of that yid *poes* Yuri Geller's forks. So I unclipped the Vector, reloaded and double tapped him in the *fokken* head.'

'You didn't retrieve the bayonet, then?' enquired Joshua.

'What for? It was bent.' A glimmer of understanding passed momentarily across Strydom's face and a light went on. 'I got to pay for a replacement, have I? *Kak!*'

'Did anyone see you lose your bayonet? continued Joshua.

'*Ja!*' exclaimed Kassie, excitedly, jerking a thumb towards his fellow inmates. 'The *rooinek* and the kaffir here were in my squad.'

'He's telling the truth, hey,' called the man in the cage half way down. 'He's a dozy fucking Dutchman and thinks Dietz is – *was* - a fellow member of the Master Race. I'm telling you, it would never enter that bone head of his to kill a white officer, even if he was fucking his mother, sister and grandmother at the same time. Don't look so shocked, Sergeant,' the young man added, as an afterthought. 'They're probably all the same person anyway. He's from the Orange Free State.'

Joshua took a couple of paces down the line and stopped in front of the Englishman. He was in his early twenties, blonde, with brown eyes and a wide grin and looked like a winger rather than front row. His hair was longer than it should have been and Joshua guessed that this was a boy who would rather spend more time in the surf than in the army.

'Private Merriman, David,' intoned the CSM. 'He is what is known in America as a hippy and if he wasn't such a *rooinek poes*, he would make a half decent soldier. Rumour has it that he is actively engaged in undermining the future security of the nation by fucking kaffir cherry and producing as many piccanini coloureds as he can, so we will be swamped. The other side has it that as he is a dab hand with a 20mm, he is balancing his overall contribution to the black peril.'

'Where you from, Merriman?' asked Joshua, tucking away the useless notebook.

'Cape Town, Hofficer! Guilty as charged! But I wasn't never there and didn't see fuck.'

Joshua dismissed the sarcasm. 'My mother lives in Cape Town,' he replied.

'Groovy! Why don't you come round for a braai just now?' said Merriman with an enthusiastic grin. 'I'll invite some blacks and you can detain them without trial or shoot a few for turning up without a pass. What do you say? It'll be cool.'

Joshua slid the pencil behind his ear and turned to CSM Landsberg.

'Do I have to kick the shit out of him personally or do you have some kaffirs to do that for me?'

'As you wish Sergeant,' replied Landsberg. 'Or we could have him in full kit running behind a Ratel for a couple of hours - in the nice sunshine.'

'Now, Merriman,' continued Joshua, turning back to his suspect. 'Why has the CSM got your bayonet?'

'Because I dropped it during the battle,' replied Merriman with the same grin. 'And someone picked it up and gave it to him after they had spitted Dietz with it. That's *if* it's my bayonet, of course. They all look alike to me; like kaffirs.'

'Did anyone see you drop it?'

'No idea – ask them.'

Joshua looked blankly at the CSM and, giving a little flip of his eyebrows moved on to the last cage. Merriman began to hum the national anthem, just audibly enough to be irritating: *Uit die blou van onse hemel....*

'Corporal Sanchez, 23 Leopard Battalion, attached,' said Landsberg. 'He was in Dietz's platoon as translator.'

Corporal Sanchez was an upright, square faced mature man, with chocolate skin, dimpled cheeks and large, square glasses sitting on a squat nose. He stood easily, not rigidly, to attention as the CSM introduced him and Joshua spotted immediately that here was a professional soldier, simultaneously relaxed, tough, observant and permanently switched on.

'What's a black man doing fighting for Apartheid then?' asked Joshua, provocatively.

'I am not fighting *for* Apartheid,' replied Sanchez evenly. 'I am fighting *against* Communism. If you wish to debate the dialectics of this apparent dichotomy, I am happy to oblige at some later date. At present, I suggest we concentrate on the issues germane to our present predicament, viz. the whereabouts of my bayonet.'

Joshua smiled in acknowledgement of the riposte. 'Where did you go to school?'

'I *taught* politics and philosophy at the University of Lisbon,' he replied, in a scholarly velvet tone. 'That was before I joined the FLNA and *before* the FLNA became 23 Battalion.'

'FLNA?' asked Smith.

'Angolan rebels,' answered the CSM.

'That appellation would not stand up to a rigorous analysis, Sergeant-Major, Sir,' interjected Sanchez. 'But it is accurate enough for our purposes, I suppose. The bayonet?'

Joshua shrugged. 'Where is it, then?'

'It was stolen from me.'

'You sure?'

'I have been fighting the Communists since 1974,' intoned Sanchez. 'Believe me, Sergeant, I do not lose my weapons.'

'When did you notice it was missing?'

'It was after I had retrieved my webbing from the sanitary block where I had hung it up to enable me to answer a call of nature,' Sanchez asserted. 'I reported this to the CSM immediately.'

'True,' confirmed Landsberg. 'He's only in here for being honest. Any other kaffir would have just stolen someone else's bayonet.'

'Sergeant-Major,' declared Sanchez. 'May I respectfully remind you that I am a Catholic and a Bakongo Angolan. I am decidedly *not* a kaffir, unless you mean *kufr* in the Islamic sense; in which case we are all here kaffirs, black and white.'

'But you are an uppity *poes*,' answered Lansberg, unimpressed. 'And I can't wait to get your clever black arse off my base and back to 23.'

'I think I've got everything I need for the time being,' concluded Joshua, looking up to the ceiling where a large spider was scuttling across a dark web.

*

Once outside, CSM Landsberg returned the sentry's salute and asked 'Any ideas?'

'There isn't enough evidence there to convict a kaffir, never mind one of these here war heroes,' Joshua replied, blinking in the light and rubbing a hand across his scalp. 'What happened to Sanchez's bayonet?'

Landsberg pursed his lips and rocked back on his heels. 'It hasn't turned up. Could be anywhere. Is it important? I thought you coppers had a nose for the guilty, whether there was evidence or not?'

'It could be all of them or none of them,' said Joshua. 'The only thing I can suggest is to let them all out just now and see if they kill someone else.'

'Be serious.'

Joshua didn't reply for a moment and then turning his hands up said: 'Have you still got *that* bayonet with you? Yes? Then let's see if it matches a weapon.'

The CSM led the way to the Armoury where, amid the hot smell of oil and the cold smell of steel, he pulled out the register for Deitz's platoon. Taking down from the racks the three rifles corresponding to the serial numbers of their three suspects, Joshua looked carefully at the bayonet mounts. On the top of the bayonet was a groove into which fitted a lug on the underside of the rifle barrel to hold it firm. Both metal components were parkerized to reduce corrosion, but the grey coating wore away with use and Joshua looked to see if there was a match between the wear patterns on the bayonet and rifles in question. Sanchez's rifle was of recent issue and the lug was hardly worn. The groove on the guilty bayonet was almost clean of coating so, Joshua reasoned, it probably didn't belong to this one. The lug on Strydom's rifle made a reasonable match, but Smith also noted that the barrel itself was bent a little out of true, as it would do if the weight of a man had been held on it; Strydom was probably telling the truth too. That left Merriman's. Looking closely, Smith saw that the scratch marks and scrape shapes corresponded, more or less, to the murder weapon.

'What do you reckon?' asked Landsberg, expectantly.

'I reckon they should all stay in jail until I can find a motive,' answered Smith, decisively. 'Any chance of a shufti in the personnel files?'

*

Back in the Company office, the CSM pulled out three mildewed manila folders, tossed them on the battered desk and settled a canvas chair by it.

'Help yourself,' he said, indicating the buff sheets spilling across the desk like a canasta hand. 'Dietz, Merriman and Strydom.'

'Only three?' observed Joshua.

'Sanchez's file is at 23 Battalion,' replied Landsberg. 'No doubt with copies in triplicate filed with SWAPO and FAPLA.'

'You think he's a traitor?'

'He's a kaffir,' answered Landsberg, sweeping a cockroach off the table. 'He's hardly likely to be in favour of racial segregation, is he?'

Joshua wrinkled his nose and wiped away the sweat gathering on his eyebrows.

'I suppose it might be too much to ask a black man to die for someone else's country,' he chuckled, picking up Dietz's file and glancing through it. 'The time to worry though is when he decides to die for his own.'

'Don't be a smart arse, Sergeant,' Landsberg reprimanded. 'You a politician or just soft on kaffirs?'

'Sanchez isn't our man,' he said, and then spluttered. 'Fuck me! He is one of *the* Dietz's. He is *connected* in spades! They claim they were here before Van Riebeck; employed Kruger to look after their cattle and Smuts to clean their boots. The family owns half of Jo'burg, about a million farms, gold mines, diamonds and most of the National Party.'

'That's them,' answered the CSM. 'Now you know why we have had a *poes* copper like you foisted on us. The Brass are *kaking* themselves about what will happen when the family get the body and find out someone in this regiment – someone in *this* company – murdered him. They're hoping that they'll look better if they bring in someone from outside. You're supposed to give 41 Mech something to get our bollocks off the meat-hook. A nice quick confession and conviction would do it, I dare say. Especially if you were to find that the murderer was off his head at the time and should never have been posted up here to us. That means we could blame it all on some *poes* in recruitment.'

'Jesus,' Joshua coughed. 'The Dietz's have pissed off half the farmers of Graaf-Reinet; they nicked the water rights on most of the Sunday's River and reduced a lot of families – *white* families – to scratching around Port Elizabeth for jobs the kaffirs wouldn't do.'

'So?'

'That mule Strydom's a farmer isn't he? May be they did it to his family too? Pass the file.'

Landsberg slid Strydom's file over. Joshua laid Dietz's folder down carefully and flicked through the new one.

'What kind of farm does he come from?'

Landsberg thought for a moment. 'Chickens, I think,' he said after a moment. 'They call him *hooender naaier*, often enough.'

'*Chicken fucker*,' answered Joshua, thoughtfully. 'The Orange Free State is beef country. They classify chicken as a vegetable there. Good Boers wouldn't be seen dead farming chickens up there. Can we find out?'

'We can ask him,' confirmed Landsberg, handing the third file over. 'What do you make of Merriman.'

Smith wiped the sweat away again and felt the flannel collar chafe at his neck as he read, his finger tracing down the page.

'My mother knows his, I think,' he said tentatively. 'That's if his mother is the same Sheila Merriman who was active in the Black Sash with my mother a few years ago. They went to the same church.'

'Your mother's in the Black Sash?' said Landsberg in disbelief. '*Fok* me sideways, the Communists have already taken over!'

'She's an Anglican,' answered Josua, drily. 'She worked for General Smuts – that's the Afrikaaner bloke who fought the British in the Boer war, before he went off to join Churchill's war cabinet. I hear he was against racial segregation too.'

'You *are* a *fokken* politician, aren't you?' proclaimed Landsberg.

'My dad hated kaffirs though,' offered Smith. 'Split up with mum because of it – that's why I was brought up in Krugerburg before I moved to Graaf-Reinet. Things aren't always so black and white are they?'

'And you are a *fokken* smart arse,' replied Landsberg.

'With a copper's nose. Can we call my mother on the radio, hey? There can't be many Merrimans in Cape Town.'

'You can try,' said Landsberg. 'But the rear link is pretty ropey. Here to Windhoek, to Uppington and then down to the Cape – 1500 klicks as the crow flies. Does she have a phone?'

'Ja, she got one put in last year.'

'Ok, use the one in the Clerk's office,' said Landsberg. 'Report to me when you have finished.'

Joshua's relationship with his mother was, like most men's, somewhat strained. She was English and churchy and had been involved with the Black Sash anti-apartheid movement since the 1950s, which Joshua had found to be something of a two-edged sword. On the one hand, he admired her stance and having grown up in Cape Town close to the mixed race District 6, he had never really understood the logic that led to the unpicking of such a racially complex city. He had played with plenty of black friends as a child; race was not something that he had ever thought about at the time and it was only later, at school, that he had been introduced to the concept of white supremacy. Even then, he had not really listened to the lessons; he had never really been interested, being more absorbed by cricket and rugby. On the other hand, he resented the fact that her outspokenness had led to increasing tension with his father, who had entirely the opposite views on apartheid; he approved of it; he thought it natural.

How his parents had ever got together was beyond him. He could only put it down to the the attraction of opposites but that was a very weak reason because it seemed to him that they had always been repelled by each other. Ever since he could remember, they had argued. He said her head was all full of flowers and trees and seagulls in the sky and that she should just accept facts as facts and get on with enjoying the good life that South Africa offered instead of wasting her time over politics and religion. She would shout back that the facts that he accepted as facts were not facts at all and that we were all God's children and how could he live with himself when there was such injustice and unfairness all around? There were variations on this theme, but none of them much out of the way of the original and though the exact circumstances at the beginning of the row might vary, they always ended up at this same point, which was when Joshua would put his head under the pillow and try to go to sleep. The resultant tension, building ever higher, never shorted out by love or lightning had resulted in cloudbursts of tears until separation and divorce was the only way they could prevent murder being done. His father had insisted that he have custody of Joshua and, given that his mother had been in and out of courts and committees and meetings and petitions all related to her political activities, he had been able to insist on the move to Krugerburg. This was not something that Joshua wanted to happen and in the end he resented his father for taking him away from Cape Town to that grim one horse dorp in the Eastern Transvaal and his mother for allowing it to happen. Although he visited her regularly during his teenage years, there was always a semi-detached feel to the relationship. It irritated him that she always seemed to want to know more than he was willing to tell about school, friends, girls, his father and he knew he irritated her by not telling her. The resultant friction generated too many sparks for them to feel entirely at ease in each others' company and Joshua always felt a wave of relief come over him when he finally got on the bus to go back to his father's house.

Not that he looked forward to going back to Krugerburg for his relationship with his father grew increasingly tense through his teenage years. He was always so keen that Joshua become a man's man that Joshua began to kick against it just because he hated having it shovelled down his throat. Sure, he played rugby and shot game and braiied, but when it came to running down the kaffirs, he found the coarseness of the language uncomfortable.

Later on he would ponder on the injustice of being an only child and *not* spoiled or doted upon by an adoring mother. Later on still, he came to terms with the fact that she did actually believe in all that religious stuff and that her politics sprang directly from it; she thought that the welfare of all mankind came before the needs of just one little boy and that she just didn't have enough love to go around everyone. He knew he still resented this, but it was also the case that he admired her for it because he knew in his heart that she was right and his father was wrong. Her disapproval of the police was one reason why he had joined up, paying her back for not thinking enough about him. His father had applauded, of course, but neither had Joshua joined up to please him; the desire of the only child of a divorce to belong somewhere was strong in him and although the SAPS was not exactly an ideal family, it had at least given him shelter from his natural one. On the day he caught the bus for Police College, he had had the same sort of feeling he had when leaving his mother's place and looked back and swore that Krugerburg would never feature in his life again. The truth was that at the time, he hoped that his father would also never feature in his life again but this was something his mother would not allow. He maintained an arms length relationship with both them; he sent money to his father and promises to his mother. Neither were satisfied by this, but then, neither was he. It was also the reason why he had been overjoyed when his first posting turned out to be Graaf-Reinet; it was pretty much equidistant between Krugerburg and Cape Town so he could sell it to his parents as being half-way between them. For him, the important thing was that it was equally distant from them both.

It took a while to get a connection along the long radio and telephone link, but just before the canteen announced dinner, he finally got through.

'Joshua? Is that you,' crackled the voice. 'Where are you? I have been calling you these last two days and you have not answered your telephone at all. Why is that Joshua? I should like to know.'

'Hi, ja, Mom. This is kind of urgent, Mom.'

'Speak up, Joshua. This is a very bad line.'

'OK, Mom...'

'Joshua?'

'Ja, Mom?'

'Where are you if you are not at home?'

'I'm on police business, Mom,' said Joshua. 'I'm working on a case.'

'What sort of case, Joshua? You are not doing anything that would not make me proud of you, are you?'

'No, Mom. I'm not,' he replied.

'You know that I do not really approve of some of the things that the police do?'

'Ja, Mom. I know this, but this is not anything to be concerned about, hey?'

'Say 'yes'Joshua. Remember you are English, please. Remember it was the English who fought against slavery, Joshua'

'I'm half-Afrikaans, Mom, remember?'

There was a pause and the crackle of words being swallowed.

'Joshua?'

'Yes, Mom.'

'You would not deceive me now, would you?'

'Mom...'

'Because I know that you are not in Graaf-Reinet. Mrs Durand's husband was just over there last week and he called in but you were not in and I have been telephoning often too.'

'Mom, I'm on a case and have been called away,' he said, pinching the bridge of his nose. 'I have just a simple quick question for you, hey?'

'What sort of a case, Joshua? Because you know...'

'Yes, Mom. I know but it is not a *political* case or anything, OK?'

'When will you be home again, Joshua?'

'What? Where?'

'I mean home, *here*, in Cape Town.'

'Oh, er...I don't know yet. I must just finish this case and then maybe I can motor down.'

'You have bought a car, now? Is that what you have spent all your money on so you don't have money to come visit?'

'No. Look Mom. I need a little piece of information...'

'*Information*, Joshua? What sort of information?'

'Do you know if Mrs Merriman has a son in the army?'

'*Sheila* Merriman, do you mean?'

'That's right, Mom.'

'Why do you want to know?'

'It's just a little detail.'

'Is she in trouble?'

'Mrs Merriman? No. I just want to know if her son is in the army.'

'Do you mean *David*?'

'That's him.'

'Is he in trouble?'

'Mom; just tell me; please, if he has gone to the army?'

'Well, I don't suppose it is a secret.' There was a pause and a long distance crackle of clicks. 'Joshua?'

'Mom?'

'Is this line tapped?'

'What?'

'Am I being bugged by State Security?'

Joshua pinched the bridge of his nose harder.

'No, Mom. It's just a bad line.'

There was another pause.

'Has he deserted?'

'I don't think so Mom, but thanks for telling me he has joined the army.'

'I said no such thing!' said Mrs Smith indignantly. 'You should not think it so easy to interrogate me, Joshua!'

'No, Mom. I just made a guess, hey?'

There was a forgiving pause.

'So when will I see you again?' she said.

'I must just finish this case, hey?'

'Joshua?'

'Yes, Mom?'

'Don't do anything you might be ashamed of doing.'

'I won't Mom. I promise.'

Joshua put the phone down and blew out a long sigh. *Don't do anything you might be ashamed of doing.* If only she knew, he thought. He had done many things since joining the police that she would not approve of. One the other hand, they would all be approved of by his father, which wasn't an entirely comforting thought.

As he walked over to the mess, he thought of Sheila Merriman. She and his mother had been inseparable for a while before and just after they were married. A pair of fashionable Cape Town blondes, they swapped clothes, make-up, gossip, played tennis and swam together, living in each other's pockets as his father put it, not without a twinge of jealousy, all the time that Joshua was growing up. He didn't know David though because he lived in a different part of Cape Town and had then been sent off to the expensive boarding school in Petermaritzburg that Sheila's English husband insisted on. Schools like that were never within the reach of the Smith family finances. That was the thing about Sheila Merriman though; she was always a little richer, a little more glamorous, a little racier than his mother. He had a very early memory of catching a glimpse of envy on his mother's face when Sheila had been showing off a pair of new high heels, cherry red shoes whose lacquered finish announced that were beyond the reach of the housekeeping allowance doled out to her by Mr.Smith every Friday. They were so bright that they seemed to flash in his childish eyes and in that moment he understood that there was competition between his mother and Sheila where before he had only ever seen companionship. This seemed strange to him at the time because he didn't understand yet how complex friendships could be but he quickly concluded that they might not be as deep as they first appeared to be and that he would need to be wary.

As an only child, he would need to be even more wary, because he had not the imagined luxury of brothers and sisters to fall back on if his friends turned out to be false.

After those shoes, Mrs Merriman seemed to be a less frequent visitor to the house, which seemed to confirm the correctness of his conclusions but then, thinking back, so was his mother for that matter. They were too busy making a nuisance of themselves over the disturbances in District 6 or getting religion to look after their husbands and children, so his father said. Even when the shoes had gone back into a box or into the bin though, Joshua could never quite rid himself of the lingering memory of those heels, the shapely calf muscles accentuated by them, and the glimpse of velvet leg that the split in the back of her skirt revealed. The thought of them had made him blush throughout his teenage years whenever he thought of them in church.

Pushing through the doors into the Sergeants mess, Joshua turned over the curious possibility that David Merriman, family friend, was the murderer of Lieutenant Dietz. The murder weapon could have been his means, he was connected through his mother to the Black Sash anti-apartheid movement which might provide a motive, and the circumstances of battle provided the opportunity. It was a weak case, he admitted, but it was at least the beginnings of one and it went through his head again that if he could get out of this situation, he would; his mother would never forgive him if he sent her best friend's son to jail; the recriminations would go on forever.

Catching his eye, CSM Landsberg detached himself from three other NCOs, called him over and then drew him aside.

'David Merriman is the son of Sheila Merriman and she is Black Sash,' said Joshua.

'You're sure?' asked CSM Landsberg.

'My mother is.'

'Is she sure?'

'There's only five million of us whites in the whole fucking country,' answered Joshua. 'And most of them are Afrikaaner half-castes. So between her and me, yeah, I'm sure.'

'Right,' said CSM Landsberg, letting out a sigh and drawing himself up. 'That's good enough for me. Merriman is following in mummy's footsteps. Job done. Good effort. Case closed. At 0800 tomorrow we charge Merriman with murder, at 805 you get back on the chopper to Windhoek, and at 810 I kick him into the middle of next week before consigning him to the deepest dog hole in the Republic, God rot him. Then everyone's happy.'

'You know it's possible he didn't do it?' Joshua yawned.

'It doesn't matter,' replied Landsberg. 'Merriman's a bad hat that we can do without. You don't need to be concerned with him anymore.'

'Fine by me,' said Joshua, shrugging his shoulders. 'I take it I've got a billet somewhere. Sergeants' Mess, is it?'

'No fucking chance whatsoever,' said Landsberg with a broad grin. 'CO's orders; 41 Mech only. You are officially a leper. Fuck off to the Company clerk and see what he can find for you. Answers to the name of Bornmann.'

But it wasn't fine by him really. He had said it out of tiredness and petulance and regretted saying it as soon as it had come out. Going out into the warm evening in search of Bornmann, the weakness of the case shouted at him. The Dietz's were important people and wouldn't be so easily fobbed off. They would want to know the facts. Merriman could not be easily disposed of; it was getting more and more difficult to disappear troublesome blacks these days and the thought of getting a white man connected into an activist network convicted on facts as sparse as these was hopeless. He could see it now; he would be there, up in the witness box holding the baby and squirming while the case was torn apart by some smart liberal lawyer trying to make a name for himself as a rebel. Meanwhile, his mother would be sitting in the gallery disapproving, his superiors would be asking what he thought he was doing posing as a detective, the newspapers would plaster his face all over the billboards and every terr in South Africa would have him as their new pin up boy. There was no way he could send Merriman for trial; even if it was as complete a fit up as could be managed by the army, it wouldn't work. Such a botched investigation would come back to haunt him sooner or later and he had enough ghosts in his past to cope with already. No, he preferred his obscurity back down at Police Post 156 to anything that might make him famous for whatever reasons at all.

*

03

A Hard Rain's Gonna Fall

0800 hrs 11th May 1980.

Oshadangwa was not much more than a scuff of an airstrip and a bare square of wired in compound up beyond the Etosha pan, seventy kilometres south of the Angolan border and right in the centre of Ovamboland, heart of the rebellion. It was an arid, flat place where the grass was sparse, the buffalo thorn thick and the baobabs ancient. In the wet season it quickly greened up and blossomed, allowing the local villagers to raise their long horn cattle and millet crops and allowing SWAPO to move more safely, hidden from patrol aircraft by the dense canopy. About a thousand soldiers lived here, divided up into three mechanised companies and an HQ, billeted in long low ant plagued huts with thatched roofs and concrete bases, plonked down around a central vehicle park. There was cookhouse, an infirmary, the usual storehouse and armouries and a jail, all built on the same pattern, all whitewashed and ant plagued to the same degree, all full of mosquitoes, and two mess halls. The first was a room tacked onto the cookhouse which contained an ant-eaten dart board, an ant eaten pool table and a bar with an ice-maker that only worked intermittently; this served up beer and klippie for anyone below the rank of sergeant. The other was a separate building which though hardly less Spartan, did have a better bar, a wider selection of spirits and some softer chairs; the officers and sergeants' mess. In addition, just off to one side of the base, on the far side of the airstrip was the compound for the black ancillary workers, who had their own equally bare facilities, and were equally plagued by ants and mosquitoes.

Just to the north, separating the base from the SWAPO infiltration strongholds on the other side of the border was a kilometre wide swathe of cleared bush known as the Cut Line which the South African Defence Force had furnished with a wire fence and freely sown mines. It didn't stop the guerrillas, who used the cover of the bush to move during the wet season, but it made tracking them easier. This was a task that the army generally left to the SAPS counter-terrorist police, the *Koevoet*, while they waited for the dry season so that their vehicles could move more easily and take out the enemy on the other side of the border. 41 Mech had plenty of experience of doing this and now that the wet season was well and truly over, they were mounting raid after raid after raid in an attempt to punch SWAPO into a state of beaten contusion. It was a time of intensive warfare and the pressure was on to get results before the the rains came again and turned the dry river bends into muddy torrents and every scrap of dried out bush into a lush, green ready camouflaged base for the SWAPO Typhoon units. Everyone knew the stakes were high and there was a buzz about the base that spoke of tension, excitement but above all, impatience to get the job done well, heavily and properly. It was almost tangible and when Joshua reported for for duty at the appointed time next morning, he was waved in quickly to van der Merwe's office and motioned to stand easy while everyone else was trying to do two things at once.

'Just how much ice is left?' said Major van der Merwe into the telephone. There was an answering squawk. 'Well, I don't care. I need it. The men can drink warm beer for a couple of days, hey?'

The flies in the Company office were still circling around the light bulb but they seemed to be fizzing quicker than yesterday, driven to a frenzy by the just perceptible smell of rotten meat; or rather, the perceptible smell of rotting Lieutenant Dietz. CSM Landsberg was trying to maintain his patience as the essence of military self-control but he was tapping his stick in his hand as though it was a truncheon eager to break heads. Major van der Merwe was sweating and irritated and Joshua sensed that he and Landsberg had had words that were less than harmonious. Van der Merwe was too sensitive for the job, he thought once more, hoping that this might make his own position a little easier when he told them both that convicting Merriman at this stage was a non-starter.

Major van der Merwe put the phone down and raised his eyebrows in frustration. CSM Landsberg pursed his lips. Breathing out through tight nostrils and tight lips, the Major controlled himself and turned reluctantly to the manila folders in front of him.

'So Private Merriman is to be charged,' he surmised, sitting oddly still, as though his buttocks were clenched against the flux, but tapping Merriman's file with his middle finger. 'Is this your finding?' His voice was provisional as though hoping that Joshua's reply would provide sufficient leeway for him to pass the issue on to someone, anyone, else.

'Sir,' said Joshua, taking a deep breath and shaking his head. 'There isn't enough evidence here to convict anyone. And if Merriman's mother gets involved, there will be lawyers. She's Black Sash.'

'It's a communist organisation, full of churchy white Englishwomen,' interjected Landsberg. 'They got some queer notions about not letting the blacks develop separately.'

'I know who they are,' said the Major irritably, pursing his lips and letting his eyes travel up to the circling flies. 'And they will make trouble, I know it. So the evidence has got to be watertight.' He opened the file and read through it. Joshua saw that the CSM had already added his report to the slim collection of sheets it contained and he saw also that the Major was concentrating, still looking for something that might let him escape the case. It did not take him long. 'What do you normally do in circumstances where the evidence is thin, Sergeant Smith?' he said, looking up and directly into Joshua's eyes.

'We normally fabricate it,' he answered. 'But Merriman's white.'

Major van der Merwe touched his lips, touched his moustache as though there was a tick there, and then reached for Kassie Strydom's file.

'You sure it wasn't Merriman?' He paused again but Joshua did not budge. 'What about Strydom? I mean, there is no chance that he has a family conflict with Dietz?'

'It's possible,' Joshua conceded and then spotting an opening that might allow his own escape, continued. 'I would have to re-interview the suspect, and then go down to Bloemfontein to investigate properly. I would certainly need at least a week in Pretoria, to follow up any potential leads, Sir. Lawyers, hey? You've got to be so careful when they get involved. You don't want to cross them.'

'Out of the question,' stammered the Major, laying the folder aside. 'What about Sanchez?'

'I've got nothing on him,' stated Joshua, regretfully. 'He could be a SWAPO spy, I suppose, but you'd have to ask 23 Battalion about that.'

Van der Merwe went back to Merriman's file, flipped it open and laid it out in front of him again.

'They should be kept under arrest and handed over to the proper authorities for thorough investigation,' blurted Joshua, in a tone of blustering officialdom.

'*We* are the proper authorities - in this case,' said van der Merwe quietly, in a voice that was hesitant yet brooked no contradiction either. 'And *you* are the thorough investigator. Your job is to give me something I can tell Dietz's family. I do not need the Black Sash sticking its nose in.'

Joshua was conscious of his police camo uniform standing out amid all the khaki in the room, the outer office and the base outside and wriggled in discomfort at the continued chafing of his collar, which seemed to have somehow acquired a lot of starch since yesterday.

'Look Major,' he said, wriggling. 'I don't think Kassie Strydom is a likely suspect, so you can let him go. Keep Merriman in on suspicion and keep the kaffir locked up too, just in case. Then, after Merriman has sweated a bit, I'll interview him again and see if I can't get him to confess. What do you think, Sir?'

Van der Merwe pulled at his nose and then sat still again, buttocks clenched, as he considered.

'Sergeant-Major?' he asked.

'Can't you just…you know?' said CSM Landsberg, looking directly at Joshua.

Joshua had seen this look on the face of authority before; it was the nod and wink that Inspector Du Toit employed back in Graaf-Reinet and usually meant the constables taking some poor black kid out beyond Spandau Kop and handing him a beating. Joshua was used to it and usually had no problem with it; very often it was a quick way to solve any sort of problem back in tight-knit Graaf-Reinet, where the coppers knew each other, knew what each other had done and knew that peaching was against the code. This was the army though and Oshadangwa was a long way from familiar territory; and Merriman was white. There was no way he was going to solve *their* problem by making his own bigger.

'We're not doing anything that is not strictly legal,' said van der Merwe, grasping the meaning too. 'Understand? CSM?'

Landsberg nodded. 'Just a thought, Sir. In which case we should go with Sergeant Smith's suggestion. I'll see if I can square it with 23's Regimental Sergeant Major. And Sergeant Smith, here,' he added, almost as an afterthought. 'He can take Merriman's place in the Ratel and do the interrogation when he gets back.'

'Ratel? Where am I going?' said Joshua as his stomach flipped.

'Anti-terrorist operations are not going to stop because we've got a messy situation in barracks,' explained van der Merwe. 'We still have a war to fight and as you're intent on keeping two of my soldiers in jail, you will have to make up the numbers.'

'But I'm not army,' he protested. 'I don't know how you guys operate.'

'You did basic training didn't you?' interjected Landsberg. 'You can go in Strydom's squad. Give you chance to interrogate him informally, won't it?'

'I don't have a weapon.'

Major van der Merwe looked slightly disgusted and turned to the Sergeant-Major for support.

'We've got plenty of weapons, Sir,' said Landsberg.

*

41 Mech pulled out and headed north in arrowhead formation, looking like a great battle fleet convoy throwing waves of dust and sand out in its wake. The Ratels were the main armament, means of motion and *raison d'etre* for 41 Mechanised Regiment. They were their battleships, landing craft and lifeboats and they were tended with all the care that spanners, oil and socket sets could lavish on them. Two and a half metres high and seven and a half long, the 6x6 cross between a tank and a truck did indeed look like a boat because its lower half was v-shaped to direct the blast of a mine away from the body of the vehicle. There were crew hatches on top, to the side and the rear, a two man turret packing either a 20mm cannon or 90mm gun, plus mounts for two more machine guns and gun ports for seven soldiers and the driver. It was a formidable piece of firepower that could run off-road across desert, bush or veldt at 30kph, shooting all the time, and then drop seven hornet angry riflemen right on top of an enemy position. Van der Merwe's Alpha Company had twelve in all, organised into three platoons of three, plus a mortar platoon, and his own command post. Brought in to deal with the old Russian tanks that FAPLA deployed from time to time, there was also an Armoured Car squadron made up of the more heavily armoured 4x4 Elands, packing a 90mm gun in an elephantine turret and affectionately known as Noddy cars. Taking the rifles, guns and cannons together, and throw in artillery and aircraft supports, 41 Mech was capable of rapid movement, formidable aggression and lethal force, carefully and expertly directed by men who were used to killing. SWAPO knew it, FAPLA knew it, the Cubans knew it. The only people who did not know it were the South African public, for whom the war was a closely guarded secret.

As the formation spread out to avoid having to drive in each other's choking dusty wake, Joshua perched on top of the vehicle to take in the spectacle, looked back and forward, right and left at the echelons of Ratels, the Elands out in front and, high up in the May sky, a couple of Impala strike jets. Reluctant as he was to put on a soldier's uniform, he still had sufficient testosterone to feel the instinctive exhilaration of approaching battle and he mused on how effective movement was in dispelling the anxiety that had been nagging at him since Landsberg had told him to report to 3 Section; he had fought before, but much preferred to do it with his own mob rather than this unfamiliar horde. Looking around to identify Major van der Merwe's command group, somewhere off to the right, and then 2nd Lieutenant Steyl's Ratel, fifty metres in front, he wondered if anyone else was feeling the same heady mixture of excitement and apprehension and guessed they were. This he thought was comforting. They all seemed to be enjoying the ride and taking pleasure in the day - nothing more; just like Els. But then the thought of Police Post 156 crowded in on him again; familiarity was safety, he reminded himself. Routine was survival. He checked his newly issued weapon once more.

The Ratels trundled unstoppably on across the ruts and pockmarks of a band of red desert sand, then onto the yellow grasslands and green scrub, alternately sliding along the salt roads as though the white grit surface was made of ice, or kicking up clouds of dust that hung in the hot air like bushfires. They would get to the border at last light and laager just short of it while the 23 Battalion recce teams went forward to make first contact with the target, a SWAPO base at Dombondola 15 kilometers further on. The plan was to stir the enemy into committing as many men as they could to the battle and then, at first light, 41 Mech would sweep into them as the air force hit them from above with a co-ordinated strike of gunships and bombers. Smith's 3 Section Ratel was to take station as the extreme left vehicle of the regiment when they attacked and his job, along with Corporal Hofmeyer and Kassie Strydom, was to blast anything that came at them from the west, south or north of their position.

'Light me up a *skyf* before it gets dark,' called Hofmeyer on the 20mm to Kassie Strydom, as the sun began to wester. He was a man built from the same stuff as Els, right down to the Zapata moustache and afro. They could have been brothers. 'Last ones until tomorrow, *jollers*.'

Seizing the opportunity for conversation, Joshua pulled out his cigarettes and handed one over for Strydom to light. Kassie took it in his huge fingers, ducked down into the squad compartment, sparked up and handed it up in turn to Hofmeyer.

'I hear you're a chicken farmer back home,' he asked in a conversational tone.

'He's a chicken fucker, if that's what you mean,' bawled Hofmeyer against the wind before Kassie could reply. 'Ain't you Strydom?'

'We got beef,' returned Kassie defensively, putting another of Joshua's cigarettes into his mule's mouth. 'Chickens is just on the side like. And mealies.'

'You own your own farm or you renting?' probed Joshua.

'Own it,' grunted Kassie. 'Got a mortgage and everything. You a farmer?'

'He's a *fokken konstabel*,' Hofmeyer called again, his voice full of contempt. 'He's here to arrest SWAPO and charge them with being *kaalgat kaffirs*.'

'Hofmeyer, will you shut the fuck up, for fuck's sake?' Joshua shouted back, pointedly displaying the three stripes sewn on his camo shirt.

Hofmeyer farted. Joshua and Strydom ducked down to smoke out of the wind.

'He's always chaffing me,' complained Kassie. 'He thinks I'm thick. One day I'll *donner* the *poes fokken gat*.'

'Did Lieutenant Dietz chaff you?'

Kassie looked serious for a moment, then drew on his cigarette and began to think. Joshua thought he could almost hear the grinding of metal on a chain pump.

'Not Lieutenant Dietz,' he said firmly, after he had finished his cigarette. 'He was a *regt dopper*, a real gentleman. He bought us *Castles* every time we killed a kaffir. He had a farm too.'

'Who do you think killed him?'

'Probably a kaffir,' shrugged Kassie, without thinking, and then went back up top to see the last of the light.

'Laager up ahead,' called Hofmeyer, an hour later. '*Skyfs* out, dicks in, magazines checked, cock weapons. Smith and Strydom dismount and clear.'

'What?' answered Joshua. 'I'm a *Sergeant*. You don't get to give me orders.'

'Get out and check there's no kaffirs hiding on our *fokken* pitch! Jesus Christ!' shouted Hofmeyer in disbelief. 'Pretend it's a township riot, *Konstabel Poes*! Now – out!'

The Ratel lurched to a standstill as the detective and his erstwhile prisoner jumped down into the bush. As they hit the ground, Joshua looked across to see men from the other Ratels doing the same. One of them was Private Merriman, who caught his eye and grinned that wide-mouthed grin of his.

'Give me the radio, Hofmeyer,' said Joshua.

'Radio silence,' replied Hofmeyer, shaking an admonitory finger. 'Clear the position, as ordered.'

'Fuck that,' replied Joshua. 'I'm off to HQ.'

'*Poes*,' shouted Hofmeyer.

The bush was closing in with the purple sunset and Joshua felt unsettled by the shifting shadows. His head told him he was safe out here, surrounded by all the armour of A Company 41 Mech, but it was still not Police Post 156 where he could see every horizon from the top of his water tank. This was unfamiliar. It was new. It was close and every step into the wiry bush made him feel more exposed, even though he could see the outlines of the buff Ratels whenever he chose to focus. He looked down. The ground was not white salt sand. It had not been cleared for mines. He stopped.

'I dare say you're looking for the Major.' Landsberg's voice snapped him out of his paralysis.

'What the fuck is going on here?'

'You've seen him, then?' he said, coming close by him. The uniform had changed. Landsberg was in military browns, but there was no change in the whipcord.

'Has someone lost their mind or is this the way things are normally done around here?' said Joshua.

'Listen,' CSM Landsberg explained, tersely, pinching his elbow between a powerful thumb and forefinger. 'We need the men and the CO *told* van der Merwe to take him with us. No, I don't know what's going on either, but we're here, *he's* here and that's that.' He looked

Joshua directly in the eye. 'Look on the bright side. Tomorrow's going to be a big one and who knows,' he winked. 'Merriman just might not make it, hey?'

*

12th May 1980

'Man down! Man down! Oh! Oh! Oh! No! What will his poor parents say?'

'Fuck!' said Hofmeyer. 'This is not supposed to happen.'

Major van der Merwe was well known for his view that there was no reason whatsoever to risk his men in a close assault when he could stand off and reduce SWAPO bases to rubble from a distance. On this day, the attack had gone according to his plan and no-one in A Company had been hurt from the moment the air force screeched out of the sky with guns blazing and bombs so big it was possible to see the blast waves when they went off, to the moment when the Elands had gone skidding right around the flank of the position, nailing anything that looked like moving. The Ratels had blasted cannon and machine gun fire into buildings, bunkers and trenches in the approved fashion and the hopelessly under-trained enemy had flapped and run as expected. There had been some fire returned but nothing that was not high, wide or hopeless and the biggest nuisance had been caused when some White Phosphorus grenades had been carelessly tossed and a grass fire started. And then 2nd Lieutenant Steyl had been hit.

Joshua started the battle in a tremulous state, fearing the consequences of what the bigger, unfamiliar weapons of the enemy could do to him. He was also stunned by the decision to release David Merriman from jail and put a gun back in his hands and resolved to keep a weather eye open for him. He did not want to risk even the possibility that he might be the next notch on his rifle butt. As soon as the Ratels started forward and Hofmeyer fired the first rounds though, he calmed down a little and during the next hour or so, he found courage enough and confidence enough to become an interested observer of this remarkable spectacle. Watching Hofmeyer spray tracer and cannon fire into the enemy base was actually quite exhilarating and before long he was laughing giddily with excitement. Kassie Strydom was asleep in the bottom of the vehicle with three other troopers, while two more lounged at the rear, smoking, as relaxed as if they were behind the school bicycle sheds. It was at that point that the radio squawked and 2nd Lieutenant Steyl ordered Hofmeyer to send half his section forward to put out the bush fire as it was interfering with the artillery Forward Observer.

'And we don't want that do we, Strydom?' shouted Hofmeyer. 'Take the *konstabel* and the *skyf* brigade with you.'

Joshua jumped off the Ratel and went forward on foot, his sense of security and excitement instantly evaporating as he left the comforting protection of the steel vehicle. The straw grass was chest high and seemed to be smouldering all around as the wind fanned the crackling flames, and for a moment he was at a loss as to what to do. Casting around for something to use as a beater, he clutched his rifle, then put it on his shoulder as Strydom had done, and then almost tripped over it as it slid off. He cursed, put his foot in an ant-bear hole and fell over heavily, barking his shins on a tree stump. By the time he had recovered, Strydom was already tearing a branch off a bluegum and beginning to labour away at the smouldering bush, his tongue lolling out of one side of his mouth, his brow knotted in concentration. The two smokers were following suit, still with cigarettes clamped in their jaws, so Joshua did the same, tugging at a branch, losing his grip and tearing a finger nail. Only after a further struggle did he manage to separate the limb from the tree but before he had struck his first blow at a patch of burning grass, he heard the cry from forward and ducked down, put the rifle in his shoulder and peered nervously around.

There was a roaring of an engine and 2nd Lieutenant Steyl's Ratel came hurtling backwards through the grass and white smoke, like an elephant bursting out of an ambush. Joshua threw himself to one side, narrowly avoiding being run over, and saw a blood spattered soldier holding a field dressing to the head of a body slumped out of one of the top forward hatches.

'Medic! Medic!' cried the soldier, his voice straining to contain the panic and horror of what he was holding on to. 'Oh Jesus, Jesus! Medic! Lieutenant Steyl's down!' he shouted and then, his voice breaking. 'Head shot. Oh Jesus, he's fucked.'

Joshua's dive carried him over an anthill and into the arms of a tangled thorn bush which held him like a fly in a web. He tried to move, felt his skin tear where the thorns had hooked him and lost his rifle as it slid out of his stinging hands. Then realising with a rising panic that he was trapped and helpless, perfectly vulnerable to any guerrilla who happened to be scattering in this direction, he began to struggle more vigorously, more urgently but with even less effect. He made to call for help, but then as the Ratel roared away, he decided that perhaps he should not call attention to himself in this way and that the sensible thing was to keep calm. He made a conscious effort to control his breathing, take in his surroundings, get his heart rate down and come up with a plan of action that would as a first priority concentrate on him getting an arm free so that he could pick up his rifle. At least then he would be able to mount some defence against the guerrillas that he was now even more convinced were lurking nearby. Swallowing hard, he began what he realised would be a long, slow, painful and ignominious task, made more painful by the first bite from the fire ants that were now milling around his ankles. 'It could be worse,' he told himself, listening to the sounds of battle and forcing himself to be optimistic. 'At least there aren't any snakes.

He got one hand free and by tugging hard he managed to pull the rest of his arm loose from the snags and claws of the bush, tearing his clothes in the process but at least now being able to move half of his body. He reached out for the rifle lying muzzle down a foot out of reach and gave a lurch which he hoped would give him the momentum he needed to cover the distance and relieve at least part of his anxiety.

There was a grunt and a heavy rustle behind him, like the snort of a disturbed buffalo, and Joshua's heart came up into his mouth. He had been told that animals often got caught up in battles and went to ground in deep bush rather than stampeding away and there were few things in Africa more dangerous than a buffalo. He had come across them on the roads north of Graaf-Reinet and he knew them to be unpredictable, nervous, tetchy, bad tempered, grudge bearing beasts, apt to throw their 700kg into a charge at the slightest provocation. If that was what was in the bush, Smith did not want to be in there with it and he began to struggle harder against the thorns, accepting the claw deep scratches and the possibility of attracting a guerrilla as a price worth paying to be away from the buffalo. Under other circumstances, he might have just lain still, hoping that the buffalo would ignore him, but as more and more ants began to bite their stinging acid into him, he knew he had to escape. The more he struggled, the more the bush tore at him though, its branches whipping at him like spiked elastic and Smith began to fear that he would never escape. He made one more great lunge forward, felt a scratch just under his right eye and then a powerful hand grabbed the back of his webbing and whirled him round like a rag doll, tearing his clothes on the iron hard thorns, twisting him almost free.

He found himself staring straight into Kassie Strydom's mule face. Between his teeth was clamped a bayonet, as though in a vice, its blade a dull, cold gleam and above it the wide nostrils and dark, coal eyes of a face devoid of intelligence, remorse or understanding; the face of the slaughterman doing his duty in a yard full of cattle; the fox among the chickens. As the blood drained out of his own face, Joshua closed his eyes and cursed himself for suggesting that the big, stupid, evil, murdering Afrikaaner bastard should be let out of jail and hated the bloody silly way he was about to die.

'*Het roinek!* We got to *trek!*' shouted Strydom, pulling the bayonet out of his mouth and shaking him. 'We taking fire. Don't be a *poes*. Not 'till after.'

With a few deft, powerful slashes, Kassie Strydom cut away the remaining thorns that still pinned him, hauled him out of the bush and half running, half lifting him, propelled Joshua back towards his own Ratel as a volley of bullets shot pieces off the thorn bush he had just left. Joshua's feet barely touched the ground for forty yards and he saw nothing until Hofmeyer's head and shoulders appeared above a sand bank, loosing off the 20mm again and jerking a thumb towards the rear of the Ratel. As Strydom opened the rear door and pushed him in, a bullet *zeeped* between them and then a second and third hit the metal just as he was pulling it closed. A second either way and Strydom's face would have been spread all over the bush.

'The kaffirs have got round the flank! Eyes left; arc 6 and 12 o'clock,' Hofmeyer bawled as he ratcheted the turret round. 'Steyl's vehicle took fire from the left rear!'

The gun ports inside the vehicle were wrenched open and all eyes, from the turret to the crew compartment, searched the bush for signs of movement or fire. Back inside, Joshua was breathing hard, shaking with fear and relief now, his hands stiff and burning with pain, clutching his rifle and he determined never again to leave the vehicle, ever.

'Binos? Where are the *bladdy* binos?' called Hofmeyer.

Strydom, apparently unpurturbed, handed a pair up.

'There is nothing out there,' he called, after a full minute scanning the grassland and acacia bush. 'Let's go take a closer look. Gerrit! Put me on that *fokken* mound at nine o'clock.'

Gerrit the driver revved up and the Ratel bounded forward on its six run-flat wheels.

'You lot! Get ready to debuss!'

Joshua received this order with a dry mouth but checked himself over with shaking hands and prepared to obey.

'Check your pouches,' said Strydom. 'So you don't spill magazines when you jump out.'

Joshua saw the rest of the squad doing just this and decided that safety now lay not with familiarity but with doing what he was told and sticking close to Strydom, whose life was so clearly charmed. He followed suit, pulling off his bush hat, as they did, stuffed it temporarily into a pocket, and cocked his weapon, gritted his teeth and forced his blood up. As the Ratel bounced towards its objective, he decided that whatever joke god was dreaming up for him, however big the tidal wave, avalanche or rock fall heading towards him, he was not going to go under in the next half hour. He tried to think of all the times he had piled out of the back of the police van and laid into uppity kaffirs and forced himself to remember that it was speed and aggression that won the day in a scrap and that this would be no different, even though the stakes were higher, much, much higher. Just like any township raid or riot, he would follow his squad, stick hard by them, wield his weapons without mercy or discrimination and survive.

'Clearing the smoke now,' shouted Hofmeyer, and a moment later. 'Out! All Round Defence!'

Joshua, the *skyfs* and Strydom piled out of the rear doors and went left while the rest leaped out of the roof and went right. He scurried quickly into a small depression, crossed it in Strydom's wake and took up a position a few metres away, facing west, from where he was able to see clear across the veldt. Now that he had decided to survive, the rifle felt good in his hands and as he put it into his shoulder, he felt comforted by the solid wood of the stock and the weight of the warm metal. 'Have confidence in your weapon,' the instructors had always urged. 'When you see arms and legs flying off the bastards, you'll know what we mean.' Looking left and right he saw the *skyfs* burrowing into the soft sand like honeybadgers, digging the shell scrapes that gave an extra margin of cover, in a game where the marginal gains were everything. Hofmeyer atop the Ratel tore around further to the left like a terrier after a rat, and then the sound of the bush took over, as though a wave of normality had swept the war away, reducing it to a series of distant islands in an otherwise quiet ocean.

In this position, he might have been alone almost, and despite the *crump, crump-crump* of artillery shells landing on the Dombondola base, the peace of the wide open spaces of Africa descended on him. He was panting, true; but it was like being out on a game shoot now, looking for kudu or springbok to put on the braai or make into biltong. In fact, there *was* a springbok sixty meters to his front, nibbling at the last shoots on a thorn bush and Smith quickly spotted about a dozen more.

'There's no-one out here,' he called to Strydom in a low voice.

'You sure?'

'That springbok is,' he replied. 'They spook real quick.'

Strydom nodded and looked straight into his eyes. 'You done good back there, *rooinek*,' he murmured. 'You didn't panic like a *poes*.'

Smith smiled in acknowledgement of the compliment. He felt like he had passed a test and was proud of the fact. Suddenly, being a copper didn't seem half so attractive as being a full member of Hofmeyer's crew, with Strydom and the *Skyfs* for companions.

It was another ten minutes before Hofmeyer returned empty handed from his reconnaissance. He radioed in the report as 3 Section clambered back on board and then tapped his ear piece, as though he hadn't heard the full message that came in answer.

'Say again, over,' he barked into the mouthpiece. 'Roger that. Moving now.'

'Steyl's dead,' he announced. 'And *Konstabel Poes* here is wanted at Company HQ.'

*

Joshua jogged through a stretch of burning grass to where Major van der Merwe and CSM Landsberg were waiting for him. They were standing over a stretcher on which lay the corpse of 2nd Lieutenant Steyl, the head swaddled in bloody field dressings and already attracting flies in the 35C heat. Sitting a little way off was Corporal Parsons, his uniform covered in Steyl's blood, drying black and crusting, his emotions draining him into shock.

'Sir?' asked Joshua.

'Has there been any SWAPO activity to your flank and rear?' asked van der Merwe carefully.

'Nothing much,' answered Smith. 'A couple of rounds incoming, nothing more. No one in the platoon has fired their personal weapon all day. It's all been 20mm to the front.'

CSM Landsberg indicated the body. 'We need you to look at this,' he said. 'Parsons reckons Steyl was hit from behind.'

The body lay on its back, legs slightly bent, with a bootlace dangling. The shirt was ruffled where it had come away from the trousers and a couple of buttons were missing from where the webbing had been wrenched off but from then on it was all nightmare. Steyl's head was wrapped in field dressings, five or six, Joshua counted, but they hadn't stopped the wound up. He knelt down and pulled back the dressings one by one.

'You sure you're up to this?' asked Landsberg as Parsons began to sob.

Joshua looked back at him: 'Seen worse, probably.'

He hadn't. The whole of Steyl's face had exploded outwards and there was nothing now but a bloody hole a fist deep and a few teeth hanging onto a flap of cheek.

'Jesus Christ,' he gagged, swallowing back the rising vomit. 'Parsons is right. That's an exit wound.'

'It's a 7.62 bullet,' confirmed Landsberg. 'Nothing else has that kind of stopping power. Looks like we have a repeat of the Dietz situation.'

'Well, quick, then,' Smith urged. 'Tell everyone in Steyl's platoon that their ammunition is faulty and get them to unload. No-one has fired so we can count the rounds in the magazines. Whoever is short is the murderer. And where the fuck is Merriman?'

'Collect magazines. CSM?' said van der Merwe.

'Right away, Sir.'

'And have some of the guys check around Merriman's position for spent cartridge cases, just in case,' added Joshua, anxiously. 'Maybe take the mine detector if they need it.'

'Impala strike in one minute, Sir,' cried a voice from the command post, as the CSM went for the radio. '23 say they've located an ammo dump. It's going to be a big one.'

'Merriman?' asked Joshua.

Van der Merwe shook his head, tight-lipped with frustration. 'He should never have been allowed out,' he hissed.

Landsberg took one of the handsets and barked out an order to All Stations to check small arms fire and a puzzled silence fell over the Company, broken only by the swirling sound of approaching jets.

'Section commanders collect fitted magazines,' ordered Landsberg.

As if in open defiance, the sound of a rifle reported from the direction of Steyl's platoon. Four more shots followed, from at least two different rifles, then more.

'Merriman,' said Joshua, as the firing from that direction became general, and Hofmeyer radioed in a contact. 'He knows we're on to him.'

The rumbling sound of the jets continued to build as the Impalas raced towards them across the veldt at treetop level.

'If they find the spent cartridges away from the position, we should still be able to nail him,' the Major fretted. 'His Section commander will be able to tell us if he was alone when Steyl was hit.'

The whole of the Company ducked as one as the jets raced over, tearing open the sky like claws on silk, and as Smith straightened up he saw two black dots detach themselves from the underside of the lead Impala and drop in a perfect arc towards the ground.

'Fuck me, he's given them a double helping,' said Landsberg, returning from the HQ radio. 'This will be a big bang if he hits the target.'

The bombs hit the target and it seemed to Sergeant Joshua Smith that the Gods had come down to announce the end of the world. The blue sky seemed to be electrocuted as a series of crackling magnesium flashes went through it like the flutter of a Valkyrie's ring, followed instantaneously by the ghostly sword strike of the grey glass, visible, shock waves. The wall of roaring sound that followed made everyone fall to the ground with their hands over their heads, while the Ratels rocked and tossed like boats in a storm and the bandages on Steyl's head fluttered like ragged banners in the wind. Out in front, a column of thick black smoke towered up like some filthy tornado flecked with dark storm crows, spitting out cooked off RPG trails that span and wriggled like lightning worms.

'Get under cover!' bawled van der Merwe, as the men of 41 Mech stared in awe at the roiling cloud slowly climbing and toppling towards them. 'Get under cover!' he cried, dragging Joshua towards the nearest Ratel as the sound of hatches banging shut beat a tattoo.

'What?' gabbled Joshua as van der Merwe pushed him into the crew compartment of the command vehicle ahead of CSM Landsberg and slammed the door shut on them. 'What?'

A moment later the sound of metallic rain began to pitter on the armoured skin, as through the clouds had turned to brass and the rain to steel. Then the wet sound of something heavy, fleshy, bouncing off the roof sent the same deep reverberation through the Ratel that Smith had felt when he had hit a zebra that time on the road past the dam at Graaf-Reinet. And then, it seemed that the heavens opened in a storm the like of which he had never experienced, as iron, steel, wood and flesh cascaded out of the sky and clanged, banged and thumped on the Ratel's armour, as though the armed dead were trying to break in.

'It's the contents of the ammo dump thrown up high; human and material,' explained van der Merwe and then turning to the radio operator, said. 'Nobody moves, except on my order. There'll be unexploded ordinance all over this position now.'

As if on cue, there was an explosion nearby and then a second further off, followed by more metallic rain and the sound of rifle bullets cooking off in the burning grass. Van der Merwe looked at his watch and allowed a full five minutes to go by after the last explosion before he pulled the radio handset over and gave the order for hatches to be opened.

CSM Landsberg pushed open the rear door on the Command vehicle and grimaced. Apart from the burnt and blasted remains of a SWAPO storesman who had been lifted high into the air by and then slammed down, bouncing off the Ratel, there were hundreds, thousands, hundreds of thousands of rounds of 7.62 ammunition littered across the ground like twigs after a storm.

'So much for finding spent cartridges,' he said, stepping out onto the crackling veldt.

*

They had inched their way out of the remains of the exploded ammunition dump satisfied that the SWAPO base was nothing more than a smouldering crater and they could get back to their own quickly and without further danger. Usually there would have been celebratory beers once they were out of the combat area, but the news of the death of 2nd Lieutenant Steyl ran quickly through the platoons and blotted out any sense of triumph. Instead, as they left the columns of thick, oily, black smoke rising from burning tyres, vehicles and buildings behind them, heads went up to frown at the sky itself, darkening, leaning over as if to topple over on them, crushing them in vengeance for the violation brought by the exploding ammo dump. Back in Hofmeyer's Ratel, Joshua commented stupidly that perhaps rain was on the way, the platitude betraying the relief he was feeling at surviving the operation, but Hofmeyer demurred and Strydom shook his head anxiously.

'Fuck the weather. Two officers in one single week,' Strydom spat, his eyes glittering darkly beneath his heavy brows. 'It's a *fokken* tokoloshe, I tell you. Some kaffir witch doctor has put an evil spirit curse on us.'

'Ja, there's no logic here,' agreed Hofmeyer. 'This goes way beyond bad luck. There is some malign intervention here. You can't put this down to reason.' He scratched his backside and sniffed. 'You remember that piccanini that came out of that hut after we put two 90mm shells into it?' he offered, sure of the incontrovertiality of his evidence. 'I tell you, there was enough HE went into that shack to brew up a tank and that little kaffir came walking out, chewing on a mealie as though nothing had happened. He had a charm, I'm telling you.'

'Ja!' agreed Strydom, enthusiastically. 'And there was that one kaffir bullet that killed two twins at once, even though they were standing ten metres apart. There isn't a kaffir alive that could have made that shot normally. I'm telling you, it was *muti,* real black magic.'

'Then there was that Recce Captain who got lost coming in from over the border,' continued Hofmeyer, as though he were a lawyer presenting final arguments before a judge. 'I tell you there could not be any greater proof that you live and die according to what God and the Devil have already decided for you.'

'What happened?' asked Joshua, who was not much given to a belief in demons or evil spirits.

'What happened?' repeated Hofmeyer, as though he had said it once already and Joshua had not been listening. 'I'll tell you what happened: the poor *poes* asked the artillery to fire a smoke shell at a given map reference so that he could locate it on his map, take a bearing and get home.'

'Seems like a reasonable plan,' said Joshua.

'A *reasonable* plan?' answered Hofmeyer in disbelief. 'There was no *reason* involved at all except that God must have been pissed off with him that day. You know what happened?'

'No,' said Joshua. 'Enlighten me.'

'The gunners fired a smoke round as requested and it fucking landed right on the *poes* and killed him! Ninety thousand *fokken* square *fokken* kilometres of bush to choose from and it chose to land right, smack on his head. If that isn't God laughing at you, I don't know what is.'

Joshua was forced to agree that this was indeed extraordinarily shitty luck but he still couldn't be convinced that a jinx, a tokoloshe, a *sangoma's* curse or bad *muti* had descended on 41 Mech. Unless of course, and keeping this particular thought to himself, the tokoloshe was called David Merriman and the curse had descended on him personally.

'Was Steyl rich?' he asked.

'Owned half of De Beers,' called Hofmeyer, shaking his head. 'His old man's an Admiral too.'

Joshua closed his eyes and put his head back. Steyl was *connected* too and he would now be faced with two sensitive murders to solve. It was not a comforting thought.

*

The feeling that something bad was being deliberately visited on 41 Mech was not dissipated by the brief rain storm that Joshua had correctly forecast. Hofmeyer would not dismiss the unseasonal rain as mere coincidence; Strydom said that it just confirmed how crafty these kaffir *sangomas* were with their *muti*. Indeed, the conviction that something supernatural was at work gained immeasurably in credence later in the day when they reached the Company lines at Oshadangwa and the unmistakeable miasma of a decomposing body greeted their weary return. There was no concealing the dismay that followed on from the curious wrinkled noses of the troops as they debussed onto the square, slowly, stiffly as though they had laboured all day in the fields. As soon as the engines were switched off, and the exhaust fumes dissipated, the thick, rich smell of rotting meat and effluent seemed to descend like a blanket, and every man drew his own mental picture of the meat feast that so excited the plague of flies, thickest where the smell was worst, by the infirmary. The words followed, buzzing like bees among flowers; *muti; tokoloshe; sangoma, vengeance.*

'Ice machine has packed up,' said the waiting stores clerk, apologising, wringing his hands, and giving silent thanks to God that he was white. Joshua noted that none of the black ancillary staff were to be seen and guessed that if they were anything like the blacks in Graaf-Reinet, they would have learned to make themselves scarce at moments like this. 'Some fucking kaffir has broken it and I can't get the parts without a requisition chit from you, Major, Sir.'

'Get the chit,' said van der Merwe tersely.

'Let's get the fucking kaffir who did this and teach him a *bladdy* lesson!' called out a voice. Joshua reckoned it was one of the *skyfs* but he couldn't be sure.

'*Fokken houtkops*,' cried another in answer. 'Let's *donner* a few!'

There was the unmistakeable sound of a rifle being cocked. 'Let's do all the *fokkers!* Once and for all!'

Major van der Merwe drew himself up to a height that Smith had not seen in him before, then barked out in a parade ground voice that made the stones stand to attention.

'There will be no lynchings in this Company! No-one told you to stop working! Weapons to the Armoury! Stores to the QM! Platoon and Section commanders – get your men working! This is a war! Men get killed! You need look for no reason beyond an enemy bullet!'

'Chin straps and boot straps, gentlemen!' added CSM Landsberg, in his rolling baritone. 'Jump to it, now!'

The effect was galvanatic. Alpha Company, 41 Mech, was not used to hearing Major van der Merwe raise his voice and each soldier, having no desire to attract the attention of power in anger, leaped to his duties. The buzzing words did not disappear though, but wove their way into the ensuing swarm of activity and stuck there, buzzing furiously, flitting from pack to pack, alighting on weapons, ammunition belts, tools, spare tyres and the thousand and one pieces of kit that made up an mechanised infantry company, all feeding on the smell of Lieutenant Dietz.

Major van der Merwe watched for the effect of his own words, decided to settle for the activity and then turned to CSM Landsberg. 'Arrest Private Merriman.'

Landsberg did not move, but simply raised his voice a little above the norm to call Merriman over.

'Get in the *tronk*, you *fokken* murderer,' he growled as he presented himself.

'What me?' said Merriman, in an innocent affected whine. 'I didn't do nothing! Honest!'

*

Right from the start of the interrogation Joshua was doubtful of success because the opinion was forming in his mind that anyone who would commit a double murder such as this would have to be insane or extraordinarily confident of getting off scot free. Merriman was not gibbering, drooling or talking to imaginary friends, so that meant he wasn't a mental case. That in turn meant that, by a process of elimination, he was sure he would get off and that meant he either knew the evidence against him was worthless or he must have some smart lawyers. Either that or he was innocent.

'Come on, Merriman,' he began, hopefully. 'We all know you did it. Confess – you'll feel better once you've got it off your chest and God will forgive you when you go to your last judgement.'

'Any chance of a better deal?' grinned Merriman, through the split lip that CSM Landsberg had given him by slamming him into the cell door.

Joshua looked at Landsberg, counted the scratches on his hands, and then back at Merriman.

'Look,' he said, adopting a conciliatory tone. 'If you confess, I'm sure the CSM and Major van der Merwe will allow you to serve out your time here, with 41 Mech, so your parents will never know the disgrace you have brought down on them and you can repay your debt to society.'

Landsberg tried not to look startled at this extraordinary offer. Merriman sniggered.

'Is that it? That your best offer? Jeez – you should get another job, Sergeant. You rubbish at this.'

'Prefer a full Court Martial, would we?' interjected Landsberg, menacingly. 'It means a hanging for you *laatie*.'

'Yeah, sure,' replied Merriman, looking Sergeant Smith up and down with contempt. 'I think I'll take my chances in a court room, CSM. Especially if this Keystone Cop is presenting the case for the prosecution. Man! You will need a lot of ice to keep the bodies of the judges and court officials fresh after they have died laughing.'

*

'No confession, then?' van der Merwe asked hopefully.

'We can't beat one out of him or we'll have the Black Sash all over us,' grunted Landsberg regretfully. 'He says he's innocent and is starting to sound like a barrack room lawyer.'

'We need to find something that'll allow us to charge him,' insisted the Major. 'Steyl's family are out of the same stable as Dietz's. Construction, banking, shipping, sanctions busting, *everything*. They virtually own Cape Town. He was telling me the other day that they were the leading contractors on rebuilding Zonnenbloem.'

'Zonnenbloem?' interjected Joshua, choking. He was pulling at a hip flask of KWV brandy that van der Merwe had handed him and this news just piled on the woe. 'You mean District 6 in Cape Town?'

Van der Merwe shrugged and indicated that the flask go next to Landsberg. 'They cleared it under the Group Areas Act, to make it a decent place for decent people to live. You know it?'

'I know it,' affirmed Smith. 'I used to get curry at Dout's on Hanover Street before sneaking in to the Star Bioscope – I never, ever paid a penny to get into that place. Merriman will know it too, if he's anything to do with the Black Sash. They always protesting there.'

'You think there may be a connection between Merriman and Steyl over Zonnenbloem?' asked van der Merwe taking the flask from the CSM and putting it to his lips.

'If Dietz's family are involved with District 6 too, then you have motive,' confirmed Smith. 'The means were in his hands at the time of both killings and he certainly had opportunity.'

'Merriman was on his own, towards the right rear of the Platoon, when Steyl was shot,' Landsberg pointed out. 'But so were three others.'

'Doesn't matter,' declared van der Merwe, taking a second pull at the flask. 'It seems clear enough that Merriman's guilty. It's enough to charge him anyway.'

'It won't convict him,' warned Joshua.

'We'll see about that,' replied Landsberg.

Van der Merwe put the flask down on his desk and turned to the window. Joshua watched as he put his hands on his hips and allowed his head to go down and his shoulders to sag for a moment.

'First Dietz. Now Steyl,' he said quietly. 'Two fine young men. Is it worth it, I wonder?'

*

Joshua thought about showering but he was too tired to bother and settled for a dump instead. The mention of District 6 had given him a start and he turned his head to one side as he entered the ablutions block so as not to catch his reflection in the mirrors. He avoided mirrors these days and would only look into them when they were placed opposite each other, reflecting back a curving infinity of parallel worlds. Then he would wish that it was possible to jump into a different one, any of them, until he found one that contained a world that suited him better, or even, run through them smashing them behind him as he went, so that his past could not catch up with him. Somewhere in those reflections, he hoped, would be a better world than this one; one that didn't involve Krugerburg; one that was a little more like District 6; one that was clean.

District 6; the hot smell of damp concrete and warm water overwhelmed him and the memories sweated out of the walls to take him back to the streets he used to roam bare-footed as a kid. District 6 had been a treasure trove for him back then, always full of adventure, exciting smells and colours with endless opportunities for mischief. It used to lie at the foot of Table Mountain in the south of the city, up by the star fort, and was home to a mixed up melting pot of washed up flotsam, mismatched, marginalised, bohemian jetsam and any number of renegades, revolutionaries and roues. There were Lithuanian Jews peddling quiet books amid the screaming of newborns from out of the Peninsular Maternity Home; the muezzin sailing out from amid the palms of Vernon Terrace. *Stoep* gossip common to every race of every corner of the earth blew life into sparks of scandal while washing stretched and fluttered across the streets like the sails of tea clippers bowling down the Mozambique channel. Kids of every hue pushed into Parker's store to buy penny sweets and get in the way of the adults adding a little Cape Smoke on tick to the daily shop. There were whorehouses and opium dens concealed in the back streets, alongside the jazz and maskandi clubs catering for whites out for a bit of rough, which drove the church goers tutting to their bibles and white ankle socks. When Smith had lived there back in the late fifties and sixties, all the talk down Constitution Street was about the coming plan to build a new technical college, which would mean more clearances, more protests, more batons and tear gas and less business for the market stalls along the busy street that he used to steal peaches from. Thinking back, Joshua Smith had a distinctive picture of old Mrs Hendricks wondering just for how much longer Hanover Street would hear the minstrels singing '*Hyet kom die Alabama*' on a New Years Eve and how the people would get to work on time in Woodstock next door, if they were moved all the way out to the Cape Flats.

Dropping his trousers and taking a seat, he recalled with a grimace that it wasn't all romantic though. The area was already run down and due for redevelopment when he had left it and his dad hadn't been far wrong when he said it was the haunt of black gangsters who would rape a white woman rigid for a ticky and *dagga* cigarette. There was also talk then of building all over Woodstock beach and making a new district for big business to move into; progress was on its way back then, he remembered, and it was driving a bulldozer and packing a riot gun.

Casting around for the toilet paper, he realised that there wasn't any and began to root through his pockets for any odd piece of paper. From his present position, he realised that District 6 was probably why he couldn't care less about segregation and the Group Areas Act; it was just too much trouble to separate mixed up people into simple categories; just where would a Cape Malay with a Lithuanian Jewish father fit in? The National Party took a different view though and more than a decade ago the cops had finally gone in, shifted whoever was still there out for good and handed the better housing over to whites, who the National Party thought they stood for. He couldn't resist a snort. It was the white kids from the Cape who were bunking off National Service and sending the university up in riots against Apartheid. The National Party blamed the *bladdy soutpiels*, of course, as they did for everything; the English who had one foot in the Cape, one foot in London, and dangled their big, fat, communist, kaffir loving dicks in the Atlantic in between. Joshua sometimes wondered whether the Afrikaaners hated the English more than they hated the blacks.

Someone came into the shower block whistling and Joshua stiffened at the tune. It was V*er in die ou Kalahari,* a tune more redolent of lederhosen and Bavarian beer gardens than Namibian desert, and yet the familiar notes took him out of Cape Town and dumped him back in the complete opposite of Krugerburg, the East Rand shithole that his father had taken him to after the divorce. It was one of those towns that the National Party had poured money into so that the more sceptical parts of the white population would eventually be convinced of the rightness of Apartheid; a place where Greek refugees from poverty and German occupation lived cheek by jowl with their erstwhile enemies, the ex-POW Italians. Along the main street, dusty, arcaded with rusting iron work, there were Portuguese shopkeepers, a few Nazis keeping a low profile by claiming to be Polish or Ukrainian, Jews whose medical qualifications had been reduced to ashes in Soviet Russia and so were practicing as dentists, doctors and vets in the sort of place where bits of paper were not absolutely essential, all mixed in with the flotsam and jetsam of white trash unable to make it in sharp elbowed Jo'burg or not svelte or sophisticated enough for Cape Town. Back then, in the late 60s, there was something of a building boom and black men in blue denim overalls were laying the bricks for new flats, a better school with a decent rugby pitch and a new Church, right by the agricultural show ground where new tractors were on display. On the corner by Tognarelli's coffee bar, he remembered, the Boers liked to gather to gossip while their wives were inside eating the chocolate cakes and tortes that Mrs Tognarelli made herself. The talk was always business, which was always good, or children who were growing up strong, lithe limbed and white under the good clear skies and warm sun of the African sky, purified of the corruption of Europe.

'It's like being on an island here in Krugerburg,' his father had told him, soon after they had moved from Cape Town. 'The kaffirs are the immigrants here and they know their place. It's normal. It's natural. We eat beef and potatoes. They eat beef and mealies. There's none of those *bladdy* communists or liberals or those women at Church that your mother had her head turned by here. People here accept *reality.* Sure, it's a responsibility to rule the black man, but there also are benefits for everyone. Apartheid is good for both races. It's obvious the black man is not capable of governing himself, otherwise he would not have lost his country to us, hey? It even says so in the Bible. Look at them! I tell you, they know they are inferior. But it's OK, ja? They know who's in charge and they are happy with it. They can murder each other, fuck each other, get dead drunk and smoke *dagga* to their heart's content in their own Location, out of the view of us decent white people.'

Right opposite the church was the Rand Hotel, where his father liked to drink before, after and sometimes during his visits to the Bioscope. Sometimes he missed out the Bioscope altogether, but he had money in his pocket then and liked to do as he pleased.

'We have *space* here,' he explained as Joshua went off to his new school. 'Space to breathe, space to get on with life, space to do what you want and not be preached at all the time. I tell you, Josh, you will not grow up as a churchy, pasty milksop out here. You can really make something of yourself. I mean really make something of yourself in a manly occupation like the Police or maybe an Engineer. Ja, get your Matric, sure, but you don't want to turn into one of those *poes* types who only sit in offices and only come on site to tell you when you have done something wrong.'

At the end of the street was the Caltex and next to it a cafe which Joshua and the other school kids frequented because it had a pinball machine. Back then, he didn't think much about the advice his father gave him or the views he expressed. They were common enough, like stones, or hills or trees; they existed and that was it. They were as familiar as the silver balls whizzing around the machine and in Krugerburg the black people came and went with less noise and much less excitement. He was fifteen; his brain was still in its box and so he went to church when ordered to by the Christian Brothers, listened reverently to their sermons, did his trigonometry and hung out in the Bioscope or around the pinball machine, waiting for the day when something interesting would happen or, failing that, the day when he could drink beer legally or, even better, go somewhere else, somewhere where he wouldn't have to listen to his father anymore.

He found some paper, cleaned himself up and decided he would take a shower after all. Common sense told him that the last thing he wanted was for the ant bites and the scratches from the thorn tree to get infected. The nail he had torn while trying to free a branch was already looking angry and red and for the first time he noticed that his ankles had swollen up and his calves were covered in a rash of white bites. He could also smell the copper tang of Steyl's blood on his hands and he wanted to sluice away the sweat and dirt and blood and grime of not just today, but of the sound of the past too. Finding a free cubicle, he stripped off his torn clothing as though he was slewing off a skin and dropped it carelessly on the floor before opening the tap for the tepid water to cascade down on him. For a moment he stood there allowing the water to pour down his face, gather under his chin and then splash onto his chest. The feel of the water was refreshing and when he soaped his hair and felt the grit and sweat shifting like pebbles down a dirt road in a rainstorm, he felt better, clearer in his mind and a little more hopeful of coming through this posting in one piece.

He was sure that Strydom was clean; he was too stupid not to be, as CSM Landsberg had rightly pointed out and now that he had spent a day in his squad, he wanted to find for his innocence. Similarly, the fact that Corporal Sanchez was in jail when Steyl was killed ruled him out as the perpetrator. As he dried himself off and dressed in his dirty clothes, he concluded that it *had* to be Merriman, yet there was actually nothing to put him bang to rights in the frame. It could conceivably be almost anyone else; and there was still Sanchez's missing bayonet, the fact of which hung around in his mind as strongly as the odour of Lieutenant Dietz's bodily corruption hung around the infirmary. To which, he thought, would soon be added that of 2nd Lieutenant Steyl's, if they didn't fix the ice machine soon.

As he went back to the billet, his bare feet wet inside hs boots and his dirty socks in his pocket, he crossed the square once more. Even though he was preoccupied with the murder, he could not avoid hearing all the rumours of more action which were spreading through the tinker of hammers and spanners working on the Ratels, passing from mouth to mouth like shared smokes, but he had not time for them. Instead his mind snapped up and locked onto the sound of the accordion creaking out from a radio inside the one of the workshops. It was not V*er in die ou Kalahari*, but it was one just like it and he realised with a start that it was not his soiled and torn clothing that made him feel dirty all over again.

*

13th May 1980

Company Clerk Bornmann was already at his desk in the outer office when Sergeant Smith presented himself at the Company Office fifteen minutes late at 0815hrs. Bornmann didn't bother to get up. He was a small, dark gnome of a man, who sniffed and snaffled so much that he might have passed for something nocturnal had it not been for the fact of his olive skin. His arms were blue with tattoos, as blue as his heavily brylcreamed hair and he had the air of someone who liked listening at doors for secrets, yet not one who could tell the difference between something important and something trivial. He was selfish too, as Joshua

2

realised from the outset. As the man in charge of all the things that the CSM and Major were too busy to do, he had appointed himself to a position of authority on a par with them. It was he who had provided Joshua with his accommodation – a cot in a surprisingly well-appointed two room bungalow which he had managed to keep off the typed lists of available accomodation used by the rest of 41 Mech by labelling it as the Bedding and Secure Store. Joshua qualified to share this, Bornmann's private residence, because it was unlikely he would be staying long and Bornmann was careful not to impose extra bodies on already stretched accommodation in case anyone should look too closely into the accuracy of his accommodation lists. It was more than his cushy job was worth.

'Ice machine should be repaired today,' he said, lazily. 'That's one less worry for the Major. Mind you, I don't think he's too happy that Dietz's old man is on the way up tomorrow - just thought I'd let you know. Oh and you snore like a fat nigger washerwoman.'

'Thanks mate,' replied Smith brushing off his uniform and gingerly touching the sun burn on the back of his neck.

'23 want to borrow a platoon and half a dozen Elands,' answered the clerk, ignoring him. 'That means we can touch them up for some of their beef in return. You know they're keeping a herd over there?'

Joshua ignored the clerk's knowing wink.

'Is there anywhere I can get some tea now?'

'You want some tea now?' said Bornmann, as though the request was so incredible only a favour extracted in return would allow it to happen. He sucked on his teeth and then said; 'I can get the boy here to bring you some if you like. It'll cost you a *skyf* though.'

Joshua hadn't realised that a black man in blue overalls was kneeling by the filing cabinet, reaching to clean behind it with a red cloth.

'You didn't see him did you?' said Bornmann through a thin smile. Joshua tossed a packet of cigarettes down on the desk. 'The ability of large black people to become invisible is something that never ceases to amaze me. You always notice the kids and the young women but the bigger and fatter they get, the less you seem to see them,' he said, taking two cigarettes from the pack. He put one in his mouth and the other behind his ear. 'Sometimes, back home, I've seen people walk the whole length of the street, nip into CNA for a paper, go round for a cold one in the pub opposite the church, and then go all the way back home without ever noticing a single one of them unless they've got a panga or good titties. They're a bit like bushes; you only notice them when they're newly planted or got some nice flowers on them, or when they've been chopped back a bit.'

'Just make some tea, hey?' said Joshua, lighting up the clerk's cigarette. 'Which platoon is going out with 23 then?'

'Dunno,' replied Bornmann, blowing out smoke. 'What with two officers dead, I think the Major will try to pass this over to B Company. Especially with *Colonel* Dietz on his way here.'

Joshua raised an eyebrow.

'And Steyl's dad's an admiral.'

'I know,' said Joshua. 'Rear or Vice?'

Bornmann looked back blankly.

'Never mind,' said Joshua. 'Just tell the boy to hurry with the tea, hey?'

*

Major van der Merwe and CSM Landsberg had nothing to add to what the clerk had told him, but they took much longer to tell it. Van der Merwe was looking more sensitive than ever as to the grief over his two dead officers was added the anxieties attendant on the arrival of Colonel Dietz and Admiral Steyl, while the pervading presence of the decaying bodies focused his attention on how to prepare for the interview.

'It's no use! They're bound to want to see the bodies!' he snapped. 'We can't ask 23 to hold them until he's gone!'

'Maybe we could mask the smell a bit, Sir,' Joshua suggested, and wished he hadn't. 'Burn some shit next to the infirmary or something?'

'Maybe we could get the cooks to make an extra pungent curry, eh?' shot back van der Merwe, banging his hand down. 'That should do it, hey?'

'I've got a few gallons of disinfectant going in there now, Sir,' said Landsberg, leafing through a thick, red book. 'And the kaffirs are putting fresh whitewash on the walls, which should go some way towards a solution.'

'Jesus Christ,' said van der Merwe. 'And still nothing from Merriman? Is there any possibility he might come to his senses and confess to what he has done?'

Joshua shook his head. 'His senses are fine and he's refusing to answer any questions until he has a lawyer present.'

'Can he do that?'

'Apparently he can, Sir,' said Landsberg, holding up the copy of the *Manual of Military Law* he had found. 'He wants a full Court Martial.'

Joshua looked at the book. It was new and he had never seen one before.

'Which means we can't hush the deaths up either,' Landsberg continued.

This was not what Joshua had hoped to hear. He had lain awake last night listening to Bornmann snore and lighted on the idea that perhaps someone in 41 Mech would dream up something to explain away the deaths of the two officers. Failing that, he wondered if the Colonel of the regiment could be persuaded to lay the sympathy and citations on with a trowel and then send the grieving parents away satisfied, if not exactly happy. It was a thin hope and hardly survived the breaking day. As far as he could see, the Colonel wanted as little to do with this business as possible, otherwise he would have been over this whole affair like a rash. It seemed obvious that van der Merwe had been delegated the shit end of the stick and given the big hint that he should delegate that shitty stick further on down to the specially selected Police Sergeant.

'There'll be lawyers galore,' he said. 'Bloody fantastic.'

'And Black Sash women and vicars and newspapers and what have you all over the place,' said van der Merwe, drumming his fingers on the desk.

Bornman put his head round the door.

'Admiral Steyl on the radio, Sir,' he said, in his best Company Clerk voice.

'Jesus Christ,' said van der Merwe again. 'Can it get worse?'

14th May 1980

Joshua was in the jailhouse when the grumble of Elands announced the return of the 41 Mech detachments that had gone out to support 23 Battalion's attack on Dombondola. He had been chatting with Corporal Sanchez, initially in the hope that Merriman might have talked in his sleep or boasted to a fellow inmate about his deeds. Unlikely as this might seem to laymen and lawyers alike, Joshua had long got over his surprise at how often the criminal class gave in to the desire to brag about their misdeeds, and how easily their fellow lags would grass on them. After a while, though, he realised he was talking with Sanchez because he liked him. He liked the tone of his voice; he liked his scholarly air; he liked that he was so obviously a soldier; and he liked him because there seemed to be none of the barrier of suspicion that Apartheid had placed between men. Sanchez was black but Joshua did not see him primarily in these terms. He did not think of his friends as being blonde, or big nosed or short or tall and saw no reason why he should define Sanchez by his physical features.

'I see you are reading the Old Testament,' he said, keeping his voice low so that Merriman, three cages away, would not hear. 'I heard that lots of black people have benefitted from Christian, civilising influences. I mean, not like you, obviously, who is already civilised but, you know, in Black Africa generally.'

Sanchez finished reading the passage and closed the bible gently, reverently.

'I thought it was written by Jews,' he replied.

'Well it was, I suppose,' admitted Joshua. 'Which bit are you reading?'

'I was reading the Book of Exodus,' answered Sanchez patiently.

'Is that the one with Noah?'

'Moses,' corrected Sanchez. 'It is the story of the Jews leaving behind their slavery in Egypt and marching through the desert to the Promised Land. I believe it was President Kruger's favourite story; they say he followed its lessons when he left the British Cape Colony on the Great Trek to find the Boers' own Promised Land.'

'Ja,' agreed Joshua. 'I learned about that in school. Kruger wanted to keep his slaves and live a free and independent life away from British oppression.'

'And so he conquered the tribes of the Highveldt and established the Afrikaaner Republics of the Transvaal and Orange Free State,' continued Sanchez. 'Just as the Jews stole the land from the Canaanites.'

'Moses did that?' asked Smith. 'I never knew.'

'When can I go back to my Battalion?' Sanchez's voice was level, tired, but still contained something of the schoolroom in it.

Joshua dropped his voice to murmur.

'Has Merriman said anything to you about...'

'No, I haven't, you *soutpiel poes,*' shouted Merriman, indignantly. 'Do you think I am as stupid as you? *Civilising influences?* God, give me fucking strength!'

'Right, that's it, Merriman,' Smith declared, reaching for the fire bucket and a pickaxe handle. 'It's time for your confession, which I am going to extract a little at a time, by placing this bucket over your head and questioning you with *this*.'

Merriman squared up as he saw what was coming.

'You think you hard enough, hey? Come and take your pasting then, Sherlock Holmes.'

'Wait,' said Sanchez. 'Detective, you should not do such a thing. You should respect the law.'

'Why?' answered Smith, indignantly. 'That murdering bastard over there is the one with the lawyers on his side.'

'You should respect the law because when you lose this war, it will be all that protects you from the revenge of the black man,' replied Sanchez earnestly. 'And you *are* going to lose it. You are too few to resist the whole of Africa.'

'*What?*' said Smith. 'You think I need a lesson in legal matters? So that this bastard can get away with murder?'

'You need more than that,' shouted Merriman. 'You need a lot of friends because if you take one step into my cell, I will beat so much shit out of you, you will need that bucket to carry it away in.'

Sanchez pursed his lips and shook his head. 'Do you not see? Unless the black and whites unite in South Africa under the law, it will be the communists who will triumph.'

Joshua faltered at these words, but then quickly gathered himself together. Philosophy could wait until after he had stomped Merriman's smart mouth shut, he thought, as he pumped himself up. He patted his pockets and realised that he did not have the key for Merriman's cage. It was with the guard corporal.

'We can discuss the future of the continent later,' he called back to Sanchez, then walked past Merriman's cage, glaring right at him.

'*Poes!*' shouted Merriman, and spat at him. Joshua blew up ready to tear the cage apart with his bare hands but at that moment Bornmann appeared, breathless from running.

'Major van der Merwe wants you right away,' he announced, excitedly. 'Another officer's been *donnered*.'

Joshua looked back at Merriman and noted the stunned combination of puzzlement and surprise that had appeared on his face.

04

Naming Calls

'It's Lieutenant Keay,' said CSM Landsberg, quietly maintaining his composure. Major van der Merwe was looking out of the window, his hands behind his back, fingers agitatedly playing with his belt. '23 say they were taking fire, but not that effective. Keay copped it.'

'Any similarities with Dietz and Steyl?' asked Joshua.

'Strydom went with the Elands,' replied Landsberg. 'He says he wanted to get revenge for Steyl. I've got him isolated in the Sergeant's Mess.'

Major van der Merwe turned around and spoke from inside his black silhouette. His voice was irritated and bitter.

'It seems that you were wrong about Merriman, then, Sergeant Smith.'

'Actually, Sir,' replied Joshua, defensively. 'It was me who said all three of them should stay in jail and be investigated properly. It wasn't me who let Merriman and Strydom out.'

'Be very careful in what you say next, Sergeant,' warned Landsberg.

Joshua buttoned his lip. Van der Merwe held his position for a moment and then surrendered to his desk.

'What do we do now?' he asked despairingly. He picked up the manilla folders before him, flicked through them and then finally, banged the last one down on the desk. 'Three officers dead. Do you know when the last time the South African army lost three officers on one operation? Tobruck, 1941, that's when. And we can be reasonably certain that they were not shot by their own side.'

'It depends what you call *sides*,' said Joshua under his breath.

'Go and talk to Strydom,' said Landsberg turning towards Joshua. 'The others stay in the *tronk* until after Colonel Dietz and Admiral Steyl get here.'

*

'No ice,' said Kassie Strydom, burping. 'Never mind, hey? It still tastes *lekker*.'

Joshua watched the aircraft approach from the Officers and Sergeants Mess where he sat drinking a third brandy amid the smell of beeswax and silver polish. They were alone and Kassie was slurping noisily from his tankard and grinning at the good fortune that let him drink the officers' brandy and coke without having to pay for it. Joshua was happy for him; he couldn't help liking this big, stupid man, even though he disagreed with just about everything he said or stood for. There was something pleasing about such stupidity and Joshua envied the ignorance that kept Kassie Strydom in such a state of profound, comfortable peace. Nothing seemed to trouble him; it just *was*. He did not dwell on the past and drew few lessons from it. He did not appear to be much given to reflection or soul searching and thus was spared the pangs of an uneasy conscience or the regrets of deeds done hastily, in error or in downright malice. The future held no terrors for him either; what would be would be and Kassie would just take it on the chin or head-butt it out of the way. He did not understand much and so didn't bother trying to; he just ate mealies and beef, drank beer and brandy, grinned when he saw something funny, screwed when it was on offer, did what he was told, went were he was sent, lifted what he was told to lift and carried what he was told to carry. He thought no more about shooting an enemy than he did about shooting a springbok. It was just something that had to be done; he didn't even justify it with a *kill or be killed* or a *my country right or wrong* argument. He didn't really think it needed one and he wasn't sure how to go about finding one anyway. It was too complicated for him and he preferred to leave thinking and all that to officers or farm managers or predikants; it was their job to do things like that. It was why they had passed Matric and he hadn't. He just stuck to doing things.

Joshua looked up as the plane hung up, high in the blue sky, like an ill-omened albatross about to glide down and peck him out of the desert dunes like a sprat out of a wave. The death of Lieutenant Keay had just blown all prospect of nailing Merriman, whether innocent or guilty, for the murders. Now he had no suspect, no case and no prospect of sliding out from under the coming blow. *Connected:* he was fucked, he realised; he knew he was fucked; he was fucking fucked; the fucking fuckers had finally fucking fucked him. They were going to fuck him because he couldn't catch the fucking murderer. It was meant to happen, he realised; it was predestined, preordained; why else would they have chosen him? Why else wouldn't they have got a more qualified copper, a proper detective, to investigate the murder of Lieutenant Dietz? The brandy told him the answer was obvious; there had been a fuck up somewhere and it needed covering up. So they had found a nobody like him, who was English, who they could get to do a cursory investigation, fill in the forms and then exonerate them. And if there were any further questions, they could pin the blame on him for a shoddy investigation. The only thing that the fuckers hadn't banked on was that the murderer – or *murderers* - wouldn't stop at just one rich, influential, pure blood, National Party officer. And that really was no consolation; it just provided more fucking things for the fucking fuckers to fucking blame him for.

'What do you think, Kassie?' he slurred.

'We are jinxed. There must be a kaffir *sangoma* on the base.' He put a thick finger up his nose and rummaged for a piece of snot. 'You should look for *muti*; feathers and chicken feet and shit like that. Then you need a *Predikant* to exorcise it, like in that movie where that little American girl twists her head round.'

'Ever thought of joining the police?'

Kassie looked at the piece of snot on his grimy fingernail and then opened his thick lips to eat it.

'I only nearly didn't pass Matric,' he answered, dismissing the prospect. 'But I know a few coppers; *donnered* a few kaffirs for them, you know? The uppity *poes* ones.'

The aircraft was beginning its descent now, and Joshua was able to make out the wings and angry bird brow as it flew towards the drooping orange wind sock. It circled the airfield once, as if making sure it was in the right place and then lined up and grew bigger, fatter, more menacing, like a grub about to give birth to a cockroach. As the aircraft touched down, throwing up clouds of white dust as the wheels skidded and the turboprops went into reverse, Joshua threw up his hands, topped up their tankards with the last of the brandy and wondered how this fucking, fuck up was all going to end. That it would not end well was a certainty.

'Colonel Dietz is very rich and important and influential,' said Kassie. 'I seen him before. At a big meeting with the police before we *donnered* a load of kaffirs outside Bloemfontein.'

'He is going to be very pissed off today,' continued Joshua. 'Because I have been unable to find out who killed his son.'

'It will be a kaffir,' said Kassie, reassuringly. 'It always is.'

'Like Corporal Sanchez? Do you think I could blame it on him?'

'You could, but if he's in 23 then he's not really a proper kaffir, even though he is a *houtkop*,' offered Kassie. 'You got to find another one. Any will do.'

'But it might not be the right one,' replied Joshua. 'And there will still be a murderer stabbing and shooting officers.'

'Ja, I never thought of that,' conceded Kassie, picking his nose again. 'But it might buy you some time if you can say to Colonel Dietz and Admiral Steyl "Hey look! I got a kaffir here who has confessed. Now you can go home, have a burial and fuck *poes* and eat braais after church." That's what the cops do in Bloemfontein.'

'You sure you never passed Matric?' said Joshua, getting up. 'Fuck me.'

Patting Kassie on the back, he started for the door. He would be wanted soon and he thought he ought to wash and put a clean shirt on for the brass. He also thought that he should at least try to look sober, even if he didn't want to wash all the deadening comfort of the brandy out of him.

'You won't try to escape will you?' he said, thumbing the door.

'Escape?' replied Kassie, lurching up too but heading in the direction of the loaded, deserted bar. 'What for?'

'Good,' said Joshua, pushing out into the bright light of the morning and instantly regretting the brandy. He stiffened up and then, as though leaning into a gale, headed for Bornmann's bungalow and his own billet. It wasn't far, but it seemed far enough and he had to screw his eyes up to allow them to adjust. The route took him past the infirmary where the smell of decomposing bodies and disinfectant reminded him, if he needed it, of the impossibility of his predicament. Reaching the bungalow, he pushed in through the screen door and went straight to the bathroom where he found the light bulb to be missing and so had to screw his eyes up again to adjust to the gloom. He swayed a little as he tried to focus, then going forward, he stumbled across to a small wooden locker, knocked over the toilet brush and then banged his hip against the towel rail.

'Bollocks,' he cursed, as the metal ripped open one of his more tender camel-thorn scratches. He opened his flies and as his eyes adjusted to the light relieved himself, and then, when he had finished, put out a hand to steady himself on the cistern. Flushing and breathing as fully as he could to blow out some of the brandy fumes he looked for his toothbrush but then remembered it was with the rest of his kit in his own room. For some reason he had had the notion that Bornmann might use it and not willing to risk this revolting prospect, had returned it to his washroll that morning. Blundering out and across the narrow corridor, he pushed into his room, grasped the handle of his locker and turned to look into the recess there.

'Oh fuck,' he said out loud.

There was a handwritten note on the shelf stating clearly, bluntly, a message of such profound simplicity that it had to be genuine:

It would be better for you if you did not catch the hero who has struck these blows for liberty against the white oppressor. We know who you are and we know how you came by your early promotion. If you wish to stay alive, you will not catch this Spear of the Nation.

It was pinned to the shelf with Sanchez's bayonet.

Spear of the Nation, the armed wing of the African National Congress, operating here alongside SWAPO.

How could they know? How could they know who he was?

He slumped down on the bed and put his head in his hands.

Then, it occurred to him that he had told his mother that he was investigating David Merriman. She would have gossipped it to Sheila Merriman who would have put two and two together and concluded that Joshua and David were in the same place. Heaven knew who she would have gossiped that nugget on to, or who had overheard when she was doing so. Was that the link?

It's always a kaffir. Strydom's words echoed in his head. At every point on the chain of progress from the moment someone in 41 Mech had requested a detective right up to this very minute, someone else might have been listening in, flicking through the paperwork, looking at his face. There were black ancillary workers polishing around Captain Botha's desk in his office in Windhoek, handling the files, serving the tea, cleaning the toilets. Out at the airbase, they were pushing brooms around the control room, shuffling the movement orders, handling the baggage, serving the drinks in the mess rooms. The whole edifice of Apartheid depended on them, the cooks, cleaners, gardeners; all employed in occupations deemed too lowly even for white men like Kassie Strydom. They had found their way into every office, every home, every business, every base, seeping in, making themselves indispensable, subverting the system with every flick of a duster or wrench of a torque. All biding their time, all ignored, all talking to each other when the white man wasn't listening, passing the word from one to the next, each knowing who to talk to, each knowing to a greater or lesser extent what might be useful to the ANC, each one daring to do their little bit. They were the ants gnawing away at the tough teak and yellow wood foundations of Apartheid. Even up here, in secret Oshadangwa, they were present.

He picked up the cigarette and lit it, taking the smoke deep into his lungs and holding it there until his eyes began to spark and he almost passed out. Releasing it in a great blow, he snatched up the note and Sanchez's bayonet, reached quickly for his kitbag and concealed both objects inside, burrowed down in his spare shirts. He needed time to think about his next move, for this case had just become horribly personal. He was not just a copper being set up to take the blame by 41 Mech now. He was a target for the ANC too *and they knew who he was*. He drew in a breath quickly and then reached deeper into the kit bag to pull out a bottle of Redheart that he had put there for emergencies.

The sharp, sweet bite of the rum beckoned him into the bottle but no sooner had he taken the first slug than the greasy head of Bornmann appeared at the window.

'You're on,' he said, jerking a thumb in the direction of the office.

'I'll be along in a moment,' replied Joshua, keeping the quaver out of his voice and replacing the cap on the bottle. 'Talk about cannons to the fucking left and cannons to the fucking right,' he added, under his breath.

'I'll tell them,' he said, looking at the bottle. 'You are a wise man, I see.'

'What?'

'Got your kit packed for an early departure.'

'Fuck off, Bornmann.'

'And you're half cut.'

'Bornmann, fuck off, will you?'

'You have got about ten minutes before you are properly and royally fucked,' said Bornmann, laughing like a squeaky toy. 'Van der Merwe and his crew will be cooking up a fairy tale about your cock ups that Hans Fucking Christian Anderson would be proud of. And you do know the Colonel himself is in residence?'

'Go and make some fucking coffee, Bornmann,' said Joshua.

'That your last request?' scoffed the clerk, tossing in a tube of toothpaste like a handgrenade. 'Clean your teeth, man. Your breath smells like a kaffir on pay day. No point handing them another excuse to fuck you, hey?'

Joshua caught the tube and unscrewed the cap.

'Whose side are you on Bornmann?' he said, squeezing the toothpaste straight into his mouth.

'I'll tell them you're on your way, shall I?' said Bornmann, with a grin. 'Good. See you in a minute. And seeing as how you asked: *mine*.'

Joshua swilled the toothpaste around his mouth, felt the tingle as he pushed it around his teeth with his tongue and then swallowed. Bornmann gave a mock salute and turned to go.

'Bornmann, wait,' he called out. 'If one of the black staff had a death in the family, how would the family get a message to them?'

Bornmann turned and gave another grin. 'They would get the Labour Agent, the guy who recruited them, to give the Regiment a call and Regimental HQ would pass the message on.'

'Does it happen often?' asked Joshua.

'What, a death in the family?'

'Don't be so fucking obtuse, Bornmann.'

'*Obtuse*, is it?' replied the clerk, giving him the finger.

'Bornmann,' said Joshua, warning and pleading at the same time.

'All the time,' said Bornmann, repeating the gesture. 'They always on the *bladdy* phone'

Joshua watched him walk away towards the Company office and mused on this confirmation of his fears. For all the steel, cordite, aggression, muck and bullets, 41 Mech was no more secure than a reed hut in a tempest. The Ratels, the Buffels, the Casspirs, the Elands, the Impalas, the artillery, the tanks – all of it was an illusion because they could no more defend the Apartheid State against the softly spoken word of freedom whispering down a telephone line than they could turn lead into gold. They could batter away at every base the enemy could build and kill every man up there in Angola and beyond but it would do no good. The fortress had already been breached by…by *him.*

Joshua's view of Bornmann's retreating back had suddenly been cut off by the broad back of a man in blue denim overalls carrying a broom.

'Hey,' said Joshua, leaning out of the window.

The man turned and straightened up nervously. Joshua was close enough to him to see the stubble that lay on his cheeks and chin in tight little bunches, like the bush on Spandau Kop. He was in his thirties, he guessed, with a strong faced deeply etched, well built, muscular body but thickening and with long hams, but stooped a little, as though he had back trouble.

'Hey, man, what's your name?' he said conversationally.

'Just call me Mopboy, *Baas*,' answered the man. He dropped his eyes, rolled his shoulders and began to turn away. 'I come when you call, *Baas*, no problem, *Baas*.'

'Just stop what you are doing for a moment and stand still so I can look at you, will you?'

The cleaner did as he was told, came to a wooden attention, as though his mop handle was a rifle and exposed a cheap Timex watch on his right wrist, as though it was his pride and joy. He was clearly uncomfortable and put on exactly the same querulous face as Kassie Strydom had when he thought he was being given a trick question.

'You OK, *Baas*?' he ventured. 'You want I get you a *dokhotela*, maybe?'

'Just stand still while I look at you,' ordered Joshua. He could smell the earthy scent of hot denim and sweat coming from the man's overalls, a scent that reminded him of his father, but there was also the unmistakeable tang of Palmolive soap underneath it.

'*Baas*?'

'Where are you from?'

'*Baas*?'

'Which town? Jo'burg? Cape Town? Durban?'

'*Baas*?'

Joshua wondered if this was dumb insolence or just stupidity.

'Are you Ovambo?'

'*Baas?*'

'Never mind,' said Joshua, with a sigh. 'On your way.'

'*Yebon Baas*,' said the cleaner, shuffling away.

Tying up his kitbag and stowing it under his cot, Joshua tried to gather himself up for the coming interview. He felt his hair and wished that he had had it cut and then slipped on a clean shirt from the hanger in his locker. He gave his boots a cursory brush too, but in a half-hearted way, as if he knew that it would do no good. He stood up, sucked in his stomach and tried to blow some more of the brandy fumes away but he knew that too was useless; he was not drunk or glassy eyed but the dullness he felt was at least a comfort. Going out of the bungalow, he counted eight more men in blue denims on the way over to the Company office and one just coming off the stoep when Bornmann handed him a cup of coffee like a last supper. Kassie Strydom was there too, smoking, swaying and looking like he was waiting for a late night bus home from the pub.

'They want to speak to you, Kassie?' he asked.

'Just in case,' interjected Bornmann, leaning back on the rail. 'But the CSM has already told them he's plastered.'

Joshua looked at Strydom's eyes, heavy and closing.

'Getting pissed up before going into the witness box,' said Joshua. 'He's wiser than he looks.'

'That would not be difficult, my friend,' sniggered the clerk. 'Would it, Strydom?'

'Jah, you think I can't hear you because I am drunk,' said Strydom, slowly sinking down to sit on the wooden steps. 'But I can hear every word and I tell you I am not stupid at all. Ja, may be it will be me who cracks this case, hey? Then you will eat your words, hey?'

'You crack the case?' guffawed Bornmann, reaching down to rap his knuckles on Kassie's head. 'The case will crack you, more like. Man you are fucked up!'

'Leave him alone,' said Joshua, finishing the coffee. 'You shouldn't chaff him just because he's not so bright, hey?'

Bornmann laughed again. 'Your suspects are in and out of that jailhouse like a *piel* in a whorehouse,' he cried. 'At least now you are to be told who is guilty, you will be able to find him easily.'

'What?' said Strydom straightening up and flicking his cigarette butt away. 'They know who the *poes* who killed Lieutenant Dietz is??'

'They thought it was *you* for a while,' said Bornmann into Strydom's amazed face. 'Jeez, if I had a ticky for every dumb fucker in this man's army, I'd have enough money to be up de Beer's daughter's *poes* like a rat up a drainpipe.'

'I'm just going back to the billet to take a shit on your pillow, Bornmann,' said Joshua. 'Just after I've wiped the dandruff of it.'

'Me?' gasped Strydom in disbelief. 'I never did it!'

'They don't know who did it,' said Joshua. 'Relax, Kassie. He's just chaffing you.'

'They think they do,' said Bornmann.

'Ja, right,' answered Joshua drily, holding his hand up to his forehead, shading his eyes from the sun, his companions and his predicament. In front of him was the door to the Company Office through which he would be called any moment now. Fearing that what happened on the other side of that door would probably shape his life for the foreseeable future went some way to replace the fear that the note and Sanchez's bayonet had put there, but it did not assuage it. 'How can they know who the killer is?' he continued. 'There is just no way they can know.'

Bornmann lit up another cigarette. 'They can do want they want. They're rich and powerful people.' He puffed for a moment. '*Connected*, I bet. And they wouldn't come up all the way up here for nothing.'

'Have you heard anything definite?' The sudden sound of boots moving through the wooden building put a flutter in Joshua's stomach.

Bornmann looked over his shoulder, took a quick last drag of the cigarette and then nipped the end off, saving the rest for later.

'Only that it's someone already in the *tronk*,' he said, brushing ash off his trousers. 'Kassie, stand up quick and look military, you *poes*.'

Kassie Strydom lurched up and came to something approaching a military posture as CSM Landsberg appeared through the open door. Behind him the outer office was in darkness and he stood there in chiaroscuro for a moment, looking down at Joshua, then right towards Bornmann and then finally resting his gaze on Strydom.

'How much has he had?' he said.

'Don't know, CSM,' said Bornmann in a brick wall tone.

Landsberg looked at the clerk for a moment and then back at Strydom. 'When this is all over, Bornmann,' he said. 'You are going back to a Ratel Section.'

'Yes, CSM,' said Bornmann in the same brick wall tone.

Joshua admired the tone and determined to use it. A solid and relentless acceptance of what was meted out to him might suit better than squirming like a worm on hook or trying to pass the blame on to van der Merwe or, heaven help, the CSM. It seemed more likely to be successful, more resilient, than dumb insolence, pleading ignorance or trying to grovel out an apology. They might mistake him for a soldier, an ordinary foot soldier and conclude that he was just out of his depth. With a bit of luck, he hoped, they might put the blame onto the person who chose him in the first place. Then he remembered that the person who had chosen him was the Colonel of 41 Mech and so despaired of the thought.

'Sergeant Smith,' said Landsberg, turning back to Joshua. There was no indication on his face that the hearing might find him innocent or guilty, just a stolid, stalwart, professional blankness as impenetrable as Bornmann's brick wall. 'In you go then.'

Joshua came up on to the stoep. 'How is it?' he asked.

Landsberg shrugged. 'It is what it is,' he said, standing aside to let Joshua pass. 'Something from on high.'

Joshua took a deep breath and then straightened up, stood smartly to attention for a moment and then marched straight on, putting on as bold a front as a hanged man could.

'Good man,' said Landsberg, as Joshua went past. 'Take 'em head on.'

Inside Major van der Merwe's office, he saw that there had been some efforts to spruce up the general appearance. The bare boards had been newly scrubbed, a shade attached to the lightbulb and strong disinfectant had now replaced the malodorous presence of Lieutenant Dietz. Van der Merwe was standing in one corner, head stooped, hands behind his back fiddling with his belt, as though he had been sent there in mild disgrace, while his desk had acquired two more chairs, what looked like a gavel, and three new occupants. The centre chair was occupied by Colonel Malan, Officer Commanding 41 Mech, who in manner and appearance could almost have been dismissed as a larger version of van der Merwe; tall, military bearing, greying at the temples, thinning on top except, Joshua realised with dismay, that this man *was* comfortable in his post, and was *not* too sensitive for the job. There was something in the snub nose, straight mouth and thin lips that spoke of hard determination and there was conviction written along the set of his jaw line. Joshua had heard that the Colonel was respected, but not loved; the soldiers all knew without a doubt that he would spend their lives if he had to, whereas their collective judgement was that van der Merwe might accept a temporary setback if it meant the avoidance of bloodshed and that was something that they appreciated. Looking at him now through the motes of dust drifting through the bars of light between them he recognised the air of the courtroom and the tense smell of the trial. He marched up to within five paces of the table, came to attention, fixed his eyes on a rag of cobweb on the back wall and saluted.

'Sergeant Smith, Joshua, South African Police Service, reporting, Sir!' He barked and stamped his boot down sharper than he done since he passed out of Police College. The sounds echoed around the room for a moment before the damp wood and the humidity swallowed them, leaving a heavy emptiness hanging in the air.

'Sergeant Smith,' said the Colonel, after a pause that lasted an age. Joshua knew he was being inspected and could almost feel the cold eyes frisk him.

'Stand at ease, Sergeant Smith.'

Joshua stamped into the more relaxed position, yet still held himself parade ground rigid.

'Stand easy,' said CSM Landsberg behind him and Joshua relaxed a little more, but not so much as to give even the slightest impression that he was actually relaxed. This was ritual and not to be mistaken for anything else.

'These gentlemen – I'm sure you know who they are already -' The Colonel's voice was high pitched, sharp, precise and reminded him of a Singer sewing machine. It ran on a little, then paused, then ran on again, with its precise, stabbing needles. ' – they know who *you* are – are here to inquire as to what has become of their sons – and into the progress of *your* investigation into their murders. What can you tell them? Be brief and to the point please – but answer fully and *responsibly.*'

Joshua took a deep breath, came to attention, regretted the brandy and put on his courtroom voice.

'Three victims; one stabbed, two shot – in that order, Sir,' he began. 'Suspects: the first – Private Kassie Strydom, Afrikaaner, low intelligence, unlikely –'

'Would that not be Kassie Strydom, from the chicken farmers near Bloemfontein?' interrupted the man to the left of the table. From his uniform, Joshua identified Colonel Dietz, but it was obvious that Dietz was not a real, fighting Colonel. He was too old, bald, fleshy, with thick glasses, bushy eyebrows and the demeanour of a rudely awaken owl to be a soldier. He lacked the humour that crept around the corners of military men's eyes and his mouth was as stern as a toad's. 'A big Boer that looks like a mule?'

'That would be him, Sir,' answered Joshua. 'I take it you know him?'

Colonel Dietz nodded and set his grim mouth. 'He is not your murderer.'

'Suspect number two; David Merriman, English, connected through his mother to the Black Sash, had the means and opportunity to commit the first two murders but has a cast iron alibi for the third,' barked Joshua.

'Which is?' asked Colonel Dietz.

'He was with me, Sir, at the time.'

'That would be the latest murder,' surmised Admiral Steyl in a soft voice of cream, touching the white cap that lay at anchor before him on the desk. He was seated, or rather lounging on the Colonel's right, his chair pushed back a little and his foot stretched right out. 'Can you tell me the circumstances?'

Joshua looked at the Admiral. He was younger than Dietz; indeed, Smith thought him very young to be an Admiral - *Captain*, maybe – about forty, only a little snow on the roof, with hair still brown and full. He wore square sunglasses which made it difficult to see his eyes, but Joshua could still feel the coldness that emanated from them. Taken together, Malan, Dietz and Steyl made up an intimidating triumvirate of judges – and hanging judges at that.

'He was on Ops with 23. They took fire. He was hit. The report says he was hit from behind with a 7.62, just like ... just like your son, Sir.'

'Lieutenant Keay is officially part of 41 Mech but he was on loan to 23 Leopard to gain some experience,' explained Colonel Malan. 'We work pretty closely together.'

'So this murder might not be related to the first two?' asked the Admiral.

Colonel Dietz looked across at Steyl and gave him a curt shake of the head. 'We must assume that it is,' he said.

Steyl thought for a moment and then, pushed his dark spectacles back up his nose.

'Were any of the other suspects present?' he said, directing the question to Joshua.

'Strydom was out on the same Op, Sir.'

Steyl looked at Dietz with a question. Dietz brushed it away again with a glance.

'Your third suspect?' said Dietz, taking the lead once more. 'An Angolan Bakongo?'

'Yes, Sir,' confirmed Joshua. 'He has an alibi for murders two and three. Number two – he was in jail; number three – he was in jail with me.'

'He was in jail with you?'

'Sir, I was interviewing him,' said Joshua. 'David Merriman was in the next cage.'

'In the next cage?' said Dietz. 'You mean that the prisoners were able to communicate with each other?'

'It's how the jailhouse is laid out, Sir,' replied Joshua.

Dietz looked down at the manila folder before him and let out a sigh.

'Do you have any idea about how to conduct an investigation?' said Dietz, rapping a finger on the file.

'Sir, it's not my fault...' Joshua's voice trailed off.

There was a thick silence broken only by the distant ringing of a hammer on the vehicle workshop anvil and Joshua realised that, just as Bornmann had warned, he was about to be handed the shit end of the stick. He, more than anyone, knew how stupid he sounded.

For a long moment Dietz raised his eyes and looked across at Steyl, communicating something as if by telepathy. What seemed an age later, Steyl gave an answering nod of agreement and Dietz took a deep breath, the decision taken, the verdict confirmed and the sentence about to be handed down.

'Do you mind, Colonel Malan, if we might speak with the detective alone?'

'As you wish,' said Colonel Malan, scraping his chair back and standing up. He shook hands with Colonel Dietz and then with Admiral Steyl and then saluted them each in turn. Dietz and Steyl also stood and returned the salutes, but there was something faulty about the way in which they were delivered. Watching the three of them, Joshua had the distinct impression that they knew each other more on a social level than a professional one and that the military formalities were more of a show than genuine. 'Major van der Merwe? CSM Landsberg? Shall we take a stroll down to the mess?'

Van der Merwe nodded and headed for the door with his head down, refusing to look at Dietz or Steyl and avoiding Joshua's eye. Landsberg left only the shadow of a pause before following, but Joshua felt that there was at least a twitch of an eyebrow aimed in his direction. Colonel Malan shepherded them out without a backward glance, as though this was suddenly none of his concern and certainly nothing that he wanted to know officially about. He let the door swing shut behind him and Joshua heard him start up with some small talk before they had cleared the outer office.

'Do you know why we are here?' asked Dietz as the voices died away, replaced by the buzzing of two flies around the lampshade. The exit of Colonel Malan and the others had allowed a billow of hot air into the already stifling room and Joshua felt a bead of sweat appear in the hollow of the nape of his neck. In answer to the question, he started to speak but Dietz held a finger up. 'I will tell you. We are here for justice for our sons and also to defend our republic from enemies both within and without. Do you understand this?'

Joshua nodded, silent, apprehensive, aquiescent. The bead of sweat grew. It was cold.

'Does it not seem obvious to you that Merriman is the murderer?' continued Dietz. 'And that he has an accomplice, a fellow conspirator, in the ranks of this regiment? Perhaps another Black Sash traitor?'

Joshua nodded again. He could feel the weight of Dietz's presence building like pressure in a tyre just as the bead of sweat on his neck seemed to be growing ever larger.

'And how highly do you rate your chances of catching this second criminal and gaining the conviction of Merriman?' he croaked.

Joshua slowly shook his head. 'The evidence just won't stand up in court.'

'Is your Afrikaans fluent, detective? No? But I am sure you aware of the serendipity between the English and the Afrikaans language represented by the Afrikaaner word for a lawyer?'

'*Prokeurer*,' answered Joshua.

'Quite,' confirmed Dietz. 'A Pimp. So if we wish to achieve justice, we must look to achieve it in *unconventional* ways and not particularly through lawyers. As I am sure you are aware, the police in this country have a fine and inventive experience. In this case, the laws of war also have to be taken into consideration, because Merriman is quite clearly a traitor.'

'CSM Landsberg says he's killed lots of kaffirs with a 20mm,' said Joshua. The bead of sweat was joined by others now and he could feel it begin to trickle towards his collar.

'He is playing a long game,' replied Dietz evenly.

'Not all *kaffirboeties* are stupid,' announced Steyl. 'This is a mistake you should not make. And Merriman has been educated by the English. This means he will have hung around clever kaffirs and kaffir-lovers who will have filled his head with Marxism and subversion. Did you know his father left for England last year? Had a nice little jolly, then came back and has been hopping around at demonstrations ever since.'

Joshua did not.

'Why else would an English journalist leave a well paying job in the most beautiful country in the world to go to a strike ridden country about to collapse under the weight of its own liberal arrogance?' posited Steyl. Joshua noted the quiet, flat venom in his voice. 'And then *come back*.'

'Because he's a communist and a traitor?' The bead of sweat detached itself from his neck and ran down inside his collar making him itch.

'Correct,' said Dietz. 'So don't you worry about Black Sash pimps and lawyers. Take Merriman for a little ride, hey? You'll be doing us and the country a favour.'

'But he's *white*,' protested Joshua. 'There will be consequences.'

'There will also be consequences if justice is not done,' answered Dietz. He waited for a long, pregnant moment. 'Do you know who we *are*?'

'High ranking officers, Sir,' said Joshua. He was conscious now that sweat was breaking out all over his body now and that soup plates were forming at his armpits. He wondered if they would be able to smell the brandy and rum now exiting his system. 'And obviously you are well connected and respected members of society, Sir.'

Dietz gave him a withering look in return.

It clicked.

Suddenly, it all made sense.

That was why van der Merwe was kaking himself; *that* was why he had been called in to investigate; *that* was why the bodies had not yet been disposed of through the proper channels. It all made sense; simple sense, stupid! Dietz and Steyl were more than just *connected*. They were *Broederbond*. The sweat broke out all over his body and for a moment, Joshua felt faint.

The *Broederbond*, the Brotherhood, was not so much a secret society as an open provocation to anyone who was not a pure bred Afrikaaner. Everyone knew about them; everyone knew that they controlled the National Party – the 'Purified' National Party – and removed or sidelined anyone from office who wasn't a member. Everyone knew that they were a load of ex-Nazis who had wanted South Africa to come in on the German side during the Second World War; half their leaders had been interned for the duration. After that, they had got properly organised and in 1948, burrowed their way into control of the government like a worm into an apple. If you wanted a government contract for your business, you had to be in the *Broederbond*; promotion in the military or civil service? – *Broederbond*; if you wanted blacks dispossessed of a bit of land you wanted for a new farm or golf course – *Broederbond*; if you wanted a slice of District 6 – *Broederbond*. These were people who really did think they were God's Chosen People and South Africa willed to them by His hand; they really did think that black people were born to serve the Afrikaaner master race; and if there was one thing they hated more than a black man, it was the English. They hated the English so much that they wouldn't even let the white supremacists of Rhodesia join their Reich.

'Ja, now you get it,' said Steyl, watching the understanding run across Joshua's face and into his slackening stance. 'So do it, ja?'

'And don't you worry about lawyers and the like,' said Dietz, as he too watched his message sink in. 'They won't get a whiff of anything suspicious. *The beloved and heroic Merriman was killed by a SWAPO mine and as there wasn't enough left to fit in a beer can, he has been interred with full military honours in the cemetery at Swakopmund, where his name will live forever.* What do you think, *Sergeant*?'

Joshua kept his face set, even though it was now wet from the seeping sweat.

'Don't worry. Everything will be taken care of,' said Steyl. 'You just disappear Merriman, hey? Then everything will be *lekker*.'

'But...his accomplice?' said Joshua, swaying. He began to clench and unclench his toes inside his boots to keep the circulation going. It was a parade ground trick to prevent a man fainting at a review and earning himself a week of extra duties.

'We'll settle for Merriman first off,' replied Dietz. 'His accomplice will be sorted in due course.'

'Sir...this is not good. This is not *lekker* at all,' he protested. 'I'm just a Sergeant, Sir. This is above my rank, Sir. Maybe you could, you know, er, talk to my superiors or something?'

Dietz and Steyl looked at their hands. They had not moved from the desk during the conversation, but now Dietz got up and came closer, running a bloodless tongue along thin lips. Joshua, who likewise had not moved from his strict posture and now noticed how stiff his limbs had become, fixed his eyes on the light bulb, where the flies were slowly circling like miniature vultures. He pumped at his toes even more now, but the sweat kept coming and the feeling of faintness came and went in waves now.

'It would be good for your career,' said Dietz, shuffling around to the side, circling him. 'You are young for a Sergeant – and we know why you gained that promotion and approve. You could be young for a Lieutenant too. Or Captain, even.'

Joshua remained motionless, but he could feel his head swimming, just as his mouth went as dry as the Karoo.

'Or you could be back at a little post somewhere in South West Africa, where the mines are plenty, the *terrs* audacious, and help a very long way away.'

He paused and Joshua could feel him looking at the back of his neck.

'Take the rest of the day to think about it.'

Joshua felt the tension go out of his shoulders a little.

'Then kill Merriman,' said Dietz. 'Dismissed.'

Joshua tried to conceal the leap of nausea in his stomach under a sigh of relief but it escaped anyway. He saluted Admiral Steyl, and losing no time at all turned about, saluted Colonel Dietz and ran out through the Company office and into the warm breeze running across the stoep. Strydom and Bornmann were sitting there on canvas chairs smoking cigarettes and gossiping like old ladies but immediately plastered looks of alarm on their faces when they saw his face.

'Jeez, what happened to you in there?' said Bornmann. 'You sweating like a fat boy at a dance.'

'You look like you've been *donnered*,' said Strydom, shaking out a stone from his boot.

Before Joshua could say anything in return, the sound of Colonel Dietz and Admiral Steyl moving into the outer office turned Bornmann into a scurrying creature looking for a place to stub his cigarette out. Kassie Strydom was still trying to get his foot back into his boot when they came out together, touching their hats in acknowledgement of the salutes and pretending not to notice the blue smoke wafting up from Bornmann's hastily concealed cigarette.

'Hello Strydom,' said Colonel Dietz, catching sight of him. 'I heard you were...'

Smith didn't hear the end of the sentence because at that moment the Company office erupted in a maelstrom explosion of fire and splinters, something flat, hard and heavy hit him square on, and he was lifted up off his feet and dropped, smoking and naked, twenty yards away across the parade ground. Next to him was Bornmann's leg, which he identified from the non-regulation sock it was wearing, but there was no sign of the rest of him.

*

18th May 1980

Joshua came back to consciousness only slowly and tentatively. He was aware first of a dull pain in the fingers of his left hand and then the realisation came that any movement in any of his limbs would probably be even more painful. His next impression was that there was a pillow pressed to his face and as an eyelid flickered, it dawned on him that there was a thick bandage, a field dressing, attached to the right side of his head. He was vaguely conscious of something wooden being scratched down the sole of first his left foot, then his right, and low voices imparted the information that he was bloody lucky and his brain was still working OK. This seemed to be obvious to him and he smiled at how stupid these people were, not to be able to see that he was OK and his brain was still working. Swimming up to consciousness, he became gradually aware that he could feel his legs, both his arms, his groin and his torso, but that his mouth and nose seemed to be oddly configured and this made him twitch and think that a leap out of bed was a good idea. It was as if his body had taken on a life of its own and was demanding to be up and moving, to make sure everything was in working order, and as he tried to sit up a spasm of agonising pain swept across his chest, stomach, arms and legs. He felt like he had been slammed into the steel doors of the cells in the Graaf-Reinet police station and for a moment he wondered what he was doing back there.

'Easy now,' said the medic, laying him back on the cool sheets. 'You must just rest now.'

'I feel like I walked into a door,' he mumbled, groggily. 'What happened? There was an explosion....'

'The door walked into you,' answered the medic. 'Count yourself lucky because it shielded you from the worst of the blast. Now go back to sleep.'

'What is that smell?' The sweet smell of rotting meat was seeping through the disinfectant laid to mask it. The ice machine was broken again, he realised, and Lieutenants Dietz, Steyl and now Keay were making their ghostly presence felt from the room next door. Then he felt the sting of the needle and didn't care as he fell backwards and downwards into the well of muffled oblivion.

He came to again sometime later and upon looking around, was surprised to see a heavily bandaged black man on a cot at the other end of the ward. Then he drifted back into the pillow, trying not to move, trying to answer the demands of his body to lay still now, and let it carry out repairs.

The third time he came to, he knew he was not going to die because he could feel the flies on his arm so distinctly that he could count the steps of their individual legs. This was irritating, not reassuring, and as he moved to brush them off, he felt the tug of a drip fastened like a vampire into his left arm. He put his right hand gingerly to his face to feel the bandage and ran his tongue tentatively around his mouth counting the teeth. They were all there and although the skin on his face was hot and tight, stretched taut like springbok leather on a drying frame, he knew instinctively that he was on the mend, that his body had survived the trauma it had undergone.

Letting his eyes travel over to the black man, he noted that he had come off a lot worse; an arm bandaged up and pinioned to a frame to keep it high, his chest swaddled in dressings through which the blood was seeping and a head swollen on one side, as though it had been pumped up like a balloon.

'What happened to Strydom?' he asked as the medic appeared and began to take his pulse.

'Who? Oh the mule,' answered the medic, disinterestedly. 'Minor cuts and bruises. He'd already sewed up one gash himself by the time the Doc treated him. Said he did it all the time on the farm.'

'Bornmann?'

The medic shook his head.

'What about the brass?'

'Casevaced straight away,' said the medic. 'They'll survive.'

Joshua looked over at the black man again and noticed the regulation boots under his bed.

'Is that Sanchez?' he said, in disbelief.

'Oh him. *Ja*,' answered the medic glancing over. 'There will be hell to pay for what Strydom and his gang did to him. I hear 23 are furious.'

'What happened? How long have I been out?'

'You came to for a bit yesterday, but you have been in this bed for three days now,' answered the medic, looking at his watch and counting. 'Sanchez was admitted two days ago, after the CSM found him in a pool of his own teeth, shit and blood in the jail. Strydom and his mates *donnered* him up good. He got it into his thick skull that Sanchez had killed Lieutenant Dietz.'

'He is such a thick bastard,' wheezed Joshua as sharp pain across his ribs drove the breath out of him. 'Where did he get an idea like that from?'

'He says he nearly passed Matric,' answered the medic, raising his eyebrows. 'Now I'm going to give you another sedative. Do you want me to kiss you good night?'

'*Poes*,' Joshua gasped as the needle went in and the lights went out.

*

His eyes snapped open as his whole body surged with adrenalin and his senses screamed into life.

There was something in the room.

Something that his instinct told him represented a mortal danger. For a moment he feared that a leopard had got in to the infirmary, attracted by the powerful smell of rotting meat from the room next door, and his instinct told him to remain perfectly still as his eyes and ears and nose tried to seek out the nature of the beast. The darkness was so close he could touch it and his startled eyes could only make out the barest change in the depth of the penumbra that enclosed him. Lying still now, perfectly still, he heard a slight grumble, like a cough, but deeper, but couldn't tell whether it had come from a human throat or an animal one.

He listened harder. Sanchez was snoring gently and for a moment relief came to him; but in the centre of the room there was a dim square of silver moonlight, and a soft sound told him that the hunter was edging away from it, avoiding it. Beyond, he could just make out the shape of the doorframe. There was no door on it, never had been, but through it a single yellow glim of lamplight from a single jaundiced bulb in a billet on the other side of the Company lines could be seen, like a cat's eye. Joshua fixed on it, hoping to catch an outline of the danger in the room if it passed it and sure enough, there was a shuffle and the light went out for two heart stopping seconds.

It was the briefest time to make up his mind in, but he decided on that spur that whatever it was, human or animal, the hunter would not expect to be attacked by an invalid, sedated, sleeping and supposedly unaware. In this lay his only chance, for if it was a leopard, he was dead unless he could startle it into flight; if it was human, then unless he managed to get upright, he would be gutted like a fish or slit like a hog.

As his eyes adjusted to the heavy, velvet, choking darkness, he saw the shadow move towards the end of his bed. It was crouching, going carefully, and though he could not make out a definite shape, he saw it produce a gleam of cold light that could be a tooth, a claw or a knife, but which stood out as the harbinger of his doom.

It was human, not an animal.

He tensed himself, coiling up his muscles one by one ready to spring. He knew that he would have to give one great charge, perhaps his last, that could take no account of ripped muscles, spasms of pain from cracked ribs or torn stitches. It would have to be explosive enough to take the drip still biting into his arm with it; it would have to be powerful enough to sweep away the bed clothes in one movement, and sustained for long enough for him to scream for help at the top of his lungs while he held his assailant off and prayed that the tooth did not bite too deeply or too often.

The shadow came around to his right side, moving slowly and formed itself into a man. The gleam spread along the blade of a bayonet, flickering like moonlight on dark water and Joshua saw it retreat and rise, pulled back by a powerful arm ready to make a deliberate thrust. This was the moment. That blade would cut through his ribs if it went home and then it would jam there until it was wrenched and twisted free. It would drive all the air out of his body, as surely as a punch from a heavyweight boxer driven squarely into his solar plexus would and he would be paralysed with pain, outrage and terror, too shocked to resist the next agonising stab. And after that, as he tried to draw breath to scream, it would be too late because he would be drowning in his own blood, or trying to stuff his ruptured intestines back into his belly, or watching his blood spurt out, six feet high in a spraying fountain as the knife opened his arteries.

How long would he have to survive before help came? Minutes. It would be five long minutes at least, but the strike would come before that; it would come inside the next five seconds and as he closed his eyes to gather his courage he counted them up in his mind as though they were the ticking movement on a cheap Timex. When the second hand reached and settled at ten-to-two, just like in the adverts, he would make his move.

Closing his eyes, he drew in his breath slowly, steadily, as if he were a sleeper about to enter another dream and then made as though he was just changing position the better to enjoy it. From under one eyelash though, he kept his eye on the knife, saw it pick its spot, hesitate as he moved and then... he tore up the bedclothes with his right hand, dashing them into the face of his attacker and simultaneously wrapping them around his arm as a shield and buckler. Ignoring the terrible shout of pain that came from his own cracking ribs, he leaped up, forward and to the right, dragging the drip with him and feeling the needle tear out of him. His face was already bloody from popped stitches as he opened his mouth wide to scream for help and his fingers snapped again as he smashed his fist into the face of the shadow.

The shadow went over backwards and Smith gained a split second to throw the coarse blanket over its head. For a moment he thought that this could be Merriman, but then he felt the hair and realised that it was African; he could feel its wire through the sheet and tumbling out of the bed, he threw his body on the knife arm, determined to deaden it with his weight while he kicked at the blankets that had tangled around his feet. The surprise move gave him the advantage, but he could feel that the African was tearing free already. He was powerful, stronger than him, Joshua realised with horror. A big, strong, heavy man with muscles like buffaloes bollocks, and without a Sjambok and a truck full of constables, he knew he had no chance.

He screamed out again at the top of his lungs, 'Help! Help! I need help! Alarm! Alarm!' but before he could ascertain whether anyone had heard, the black man had freed his left arm and smashed a fist like ebony into Joshua's injured cheek. He saw stars and felt the pain running like electricity across and through the synapses of his brain. It was like having the dentist ram a probe through a broken tooth and all the way out of the top of his head, but he knew he must just hold on. He jabbed an elbow into the man's face, which was all he could do because now his own shoulder had become hopelessly tangled in the sheet. The African's head snapped back for a second, but then with a heave Joshua was cast aside, as though he weighed nothing, and the bayonet was jabbed right at his head. He moved just in time to avoid it going through the front of his skull, but not enough to prevent it gouging through his swollen cheek, opening it up like a boil and spattering hot pus over them both. The knife was retracted for the next blow and Joshua flung himself forward again, spitting blood and desperation and crying out in sheer panic, frantically scrambling through the pain to find the arm that held that dagger and stop it coming in again.

He missed, and his assailant pulled back, rising to one knee, tearing at the mess of blankets, the drip and now an overset locker, and drew back for a killing blow into the back of Joshua's head. He knew he was finished when he was rolled over onto his back, took another punch which made the enamel on his teeth spark like metal, felt another rib crack, and realised he had lost both the sight in his right eye and the use of his left hand, which was now a swelling, angry, blood bag flopping uselessly on the end of his arm. He put up his right arm to reach for the hunter's face, hoping to find an eye or a throat to drive his nails into, but his head began to swim and a choking, acid vomit started to well up in his throat. He saw the knife go back, into the air, and he knew that this was it. He was going to die and join Dietz, Steyl and Keay in Afrikaaner Valhalla.

And at that moment, there was a thump of something heavy, a boot, glancing off his attacker's head. There was a metallic scraping and then the iron bedstead was overturned, driving the hunter back against the wall. He heard a grunt, no more, then a rattling exhale, saw a movement and then pandemonium as the room was suddenly full of lights and 41 Mech.

'Well done,' congratulated CSM Landsberg, naked but for a pair of flip-flops and some yellowing Y-fronts, as Joshua began to pass out. 'You should get a medal for this.'

'Me?'

'No, not *you*. Him.'

Joshua flopped free, sobbing with wordless relief at his deliverance and saw the body of his attacker pinned to the wall by a length of surgical steel blasted through his temples. It was the cleaner who he had spoken to earlier, the one who called himself Mopboy, and Corporal Sanchez was standing over him, trailing bandages and blood and then he was collapsing on him like a crumbling titan and Joshua went under with the shock and pain.

*

19th May 1980

The next day, the clean sunlight woke Joshua to the relief that he was still alive. Someone had tried to kill him, first with a bomb and then again with a knife and he was still here, which he considered something to celebrate for the time being at least. There was still the problem that he had been ordered to kill Merriman by the Broederbond and ordered not to kill him by the ANC, which was a dilemma with real horns on it. He wondered if his injuries would be enough to get him sent to the rear, invalided out so to speak, but he knew they weren't serious enough. The fact remained that he had been chosen for this task and once he had been let into the dirty secret that the Broerdond wanted Merriman dead, they were unlikely to let him backslide from it. The same went for the ANC; the bomb, he decided, was probably not meant for him personally, but for the Broederbond. The knife had followed when they found out what had been discussed from whoever was cleaning the office or listening at the doors when the order had been given. Survival was, therefore, only a temporary state.

The simultaneous realisation that Corporal Sanchez had saved him cheered him up and though still far, far down in his drowsy state, he felt that the workings of bizarre chance might still offer him an escape. Peeping out from an almost closed eye, he saw Sanchez's broken body lying close to him in the next cot, drips into both his arms, bandages everywhere, a chart on the bed frame and, dozing on a chair by him, lulled to sleep by Sanchez's own deep, laboured, sedative induced breathing, another black soldier in an unfamiliar uniform. 23 had decided to look after their own, it seemed. Joshua let out a long breath. Perhaps one day he might come back up to the surface and breathe clean air once more.

Sanchez, his saviour. Joshua understood what had happened. Sanchez was in the hospital because Kassie Strydom, a big, thick, Afrikaaner, white supremacist had been told by the Company clerk that the murderer of his beloved Broederbond officers was in the jailhouse. With the blood roaring in his big ears and through his under-developed IQ, he had gone to the jail with his lynch mob and seeing two suspects, the English Merriman and the Bakongo Sanchez, had come to the only conclusion that his upbringing and stunted education permitted. It had to be the black man, because it stood to reason, hey? He was a kaffir and it was always the kaffir's fault.

The 23 soldier jerked awake, and spoke softly to him in what Smith took for Portuguese. Sanchez made no response, but settled again, and the soldier slid his eyes across to Smith.

'You the detective?' he asked.

Smith flickered an eyelid.

'You must be *homem bom*, for him to take this for you.'

Smith felt a heaviness begin to rise in his chest, a humbling, disgusted sadness, the like of which he had not experienced since that day at the Caltex, when Titch Janssens had *donnered* the old man all those years ago.

*

It was a Sunday and he was coming back from church when he saw Titch Janssens, a big, blonde country boy bred for the farms and Krugerburg's very own answer to Kassie Strydom. He was driving up Commissioner Street in his new wheels, a china blue Ford Consul, which was nine parts rust, four parts cannibalised Opel Rekord and three parts held together with baling wire.

'Hey what you think, *poes*?' Titch shouted, above the backfiring and the tin can rattle of the exhaust. Titch hadn't bothered with school much recently and Joshua now realised why. He looked a couple of years older than his real age, had a regular girlfriend and, because it was a small town and his dad knew the cops, reckoned he was ready to drive whatever the authorities thought. 'Fuck your schoolwork, man! This is living!'

Just ahead, an old black man was hobbling across the road. Madiba Buyisiswe was a familiar figure in the town; always drunk, always begging, always unwashed, always getting in the way. He was everything that white people hated about black people and the 'Madiba' of his name was given in mockery rather than respect. It was popularly believed that he refused to get a job because he was a chief of some tribe or other and it was beneath his dignity to expect anything less than the living the world owed him. The world had paid him what he was worth, went the corollary. Joshua had been told another story though. One of the teachers at school told him that Buyisiswe was stooped from years of digging coal and gold in cramped spaces underground, was deaf from the noise of the mining drill and was always coughing - always coughing - from the river of dust that had silted up his lungs. He had turned to the solace of alcoholism only after he had returned home one holiday to find his two sons had been shot by the police, his wife had disappeared and his one room shack on the Location given over to a drugs gang. At the time, Joshua had not known what to do with this disturbing knowledge and had stored it away as another one of those puzzling features of his teenage world. He simply accepted as fact that on Sundays Buyisiwe would go to the Portuguese shop on Commissioner Street to buy a carton of milk, a loaf of bread and a bottle of cheap gin. Everybody knew it and nobody cared. In the world of Krugerburg, he was just another drunk old kaffir in a woollen cap shuffling about on odd shoes, too big for him; he was a bit of a nuisance, but nothing to get worked up about.

Titch wasn't looking where he was going and Joshua watched the car and Buyisiswe converge on intersecting courses. He was conscious as it happened that for the first time he was applying the knowledge of physics and geometry that he was working at in his textbooks on the table in his bedroom to the real world, calculating the relative speeds, distances and angles of the two moving objects but in the detached state that he found himself increasingly existing in, he saw no danger until too late. Titch wasn't going very fast, but then neither was Buyisiswe and when the car collided with the man, there was no squeal of brakes hastily stamped on, or slide of skidding tyres, just a dull thud; the same sound as when his father's car had hit a honeybadger on the road at night.

Joshua broke into a trot to see what had happened. He knew how to call the police when things like this happened because they happened so often and still being just a bit of a *jong* himself, he liked to flaunt his skill at being able to do it. He was often the first to call the police from the phone in the Portuguese shop or from the Caltex, mainly because the adults preferred to rubberneck, or didn't want the hassle of going to the station to fill in the forms, especially if it was just a kaffir. Telling the police what they had witnessed, at length and in great detail, they would do quite happily, but going to the station and writing things down....Joshua knew that many of the good citizens of Krugerburg weren't really convinced of the necessity of being able to write down anything longer than a shopping list.

Buyisiswe was spread-eagled, faced down in the dirt road and the milk carton was glugging its contents gently into the dust when Joshua got there. A small crowd of onlookers was already gathering and going inside the cinnamon and hessian scented store to the make the call, he heard Titch swear, crank open the door of his beloved car and begin complaining loudly.

'Can you *fokken* believe it, hey? The dirty black bastard! Look what the *fokken poes* has done to my car!'

There was a metallic clang as the front bumper detached itself from the baling wire holding it to the radiator grill and dropped to the ground, like a broken bell. A hiss of steam announced that Titch's repair of the Ford's cooling system had not been as successful as he had supposed, and all that was left of the roaring throttle was an ominous ticking.

'The *bladdy* useless *fokken* kaffir,' he shouted. 'The *poes*!'

By the time that Joshua was replacing the receiver, Titch's swearing was beginning to hit new peaks and as he stepped out into the bright sunshine, it seemed that the volume amplified accordingly. Titch was standing over Buyisiswe now and the old man, stunned but not fatally injured, was beginning to stir.

'You *fokken* useless kaffir!' he shouted. Buyisiswe flopped over like a dying fish and Titch spat straight into his face, a glob of grey green sputum that stuck to his brow and then slid down into his eye. 'Do you know how much time I have spent on making this car work?'

Buyisiswe groaned, as though he had just woken to a hangover. Titch took a pace forward and stamped down as hard as he could on the old man's face. Then again, and again, in a frenzy of hate until with a crack, like the sound of popping corn, the old man's skull broke and a mass of yellow grey brain and blood spurted out of his ear like a ruptured boil. Titch swore again and kicked the head like a football, so hard that the woollen cap flew off and the bone distorted.

'Look at my *fokken* shoes!' shouted Titch. 'Look at the *fokken poes* kaffir mess on them! And here was me up all night polishing them to a shine!'

A young woman, narrow faced, in her thirties wearing a crimpoline blouse and a gingham wraparound skirt called out from the gathered audience.

'Alright Titch. Leave him now. You've made your point.'

'Made my point?' he answered, swinging round. 'Ja? And who is going to pay for the damage to my car? Answer me that? Now I got to pay out to a *bladdy* mechanic because some stupid old kaffir, who should never have been born if there was a true God in heaven, cannot look where he is going and is already drunk on a Sunday morning.' He booted Buyisiswe in the head again, spreading crimson gore into the pooling milk. 'Kaffirs! We should just kill them all and have done with them.'

There was a brief half-hearted wail as a siren announced the arrival of the Krugerburg police paddy wagon. The car pulled up and a heavy set officer, with sweat soup plates at each arm of his blue shirt, climbed out of the vehicle.

'What?' said Titch in disbelief. 'Why was it necessary to call for the police?'

'You killed him,' said the young woman, with no more outrage than if he had broken the shop window with a cricket ball. 'Someone will have to clean up.'

'*Ag man*,' replied Titch dismissively. 'Just get some other kaffirs to take him to the dump and then run a broom around.'

The policeman came around Titch's Ford to stand over the body. There was a look of intense irritation on his face.

'Jeez, Titch! Why do you do these things? On a Sunday morning? Do you know how much paperwork this means for me?'

'Ja, I'm sorry, Piet,' replied Titch. 'But it wasn't my fault, you know. And it's just a kaffir.'

'You got to think before you do these things,' complained the officer. 'The kaffirs get upset and it means we got to go out and *donner* them some more. It's a pain in the *gat*.'

'Ja, Ok, I'm sorry,' said Titch. 'Hey, can you give me a tow back to my place? I can't leave the car here now.'

'Will it not start?' asked the policeman. 'Open the bonnet, let me take a look.'

Titch stepped over Buyisiswe's corpse and felt for the catch. 'Mind you shoes, hey? There is *fokken* kaffir *kak* everywhere.'

Officer Piet grunted, hitched up his belt and peered into the engine compartment.

'You fixed this up yourself?' he asked, shaking his head in disapproval. 'FORD – Fix Or Repair Daily. It is a heap of *kak*, Titch. Everyone knows not to buy Fords. Why did you buy a Ford?'

Titch looked suitably castigated. 'It will be fine, once I repair the damage, again.'

'OK,' said the policeman. 'You know how to take a tow? You got to keep your foot a little on the brake so we don't kangaroo along like a couple of queer coons, ja?'

Titch nodded.

'What about Buyisiswe?' asked the woman. 'You can't just leave him in the street.'

'Who called the police?' answered Officer Piet.

Joshua stepped forward.

'A *laatie* like you called the police? That is very fine work,' congratulated the policeman. 'Now go and call for the kaffir ambulance to take him away, hey?' The rest of you,' he beckoned the small audience to him. 'Give us a shove so that we can hook this car up and take it to a mechanic.'

By the time that Joshua returned from making the second call, Titch was behind the wheel again, being towed away by Officer Piet and the crowd had dispersed, tut tutting, going home or to the pub. Only the young woman was left, standing over Buyisiswe, frowning at the bloody mess. Joshua looked at her and he saw her weighing him up, wondering if he was thinking what she was thinking.

'What have we come to when a *joller* like Titch Janssens can kill a black man for any reason he chooses,' she said, finally. 'Any reason. *Or no reason at all.* He should have some *madala.*'

Joshua heard the word coming but by the time it had arrived, he had pulled the arms that protected him close to his chest, just in time to try to block it out, to stop it before it reached his brain.

Madala: respect.

It felt like a ten ton truck hitting his chest. And it felt just like he was feeling now; his life owed to Sanchez, beaten to a pulp in the next bed.

05

Happy Families

20th May 1980

'*Ag* you'll be right as rain in a day or two,' said the medic. 'Ja, it looks worse and feels worse than it is, really. You can talk to the Intelligence officer. She will be here just now. You want me to throw the kaffirs out now?'

Joshua was groggy from the painkillers, but as he blinked awake he looked over at Corporal Sanchez and his escort.

'The kaffirs stay,' he said. 'And they are not 'kaffirs'. They are Bakongo soldiers fighting for South Africa against the communists.'

'Whatever you say,' chimed the medic, scribbling on the chart and replacing it on the bedstead. 'Captain Mostert is a welcome sight for sore eyes, I will tell you now. She is a tonic for this *troupie*, for sure. *Check die lekker anties,* hey?'

'Thank you for your consideration, Detective,' muttered Sanchez through swollen lips, as the medic left. 'And I glad to see you are feeling better. We make a rather distressed pair, do we not?'

'Attention!' barked CSM Landsberg, coming through the door like a tank. 'Lie as straight as you can. Eyes Front! Officer in the ward. Lie, easy.'

Captain Trudi Mostert was indeed a tonic for the troops and Joshua could only wonder how she kept hold of her knickers this far from civilisation with only several regiments of testosterone for company. She was blonde and young and tanned and pretty with her hair in a pony tail and her beret was tucked into the epaulette of her military browns, but the uniform could do nothing to hide her feminity. Even the combat boots seemed to emphasise the slim length of her legs rather than diminish them to a military uniformity. And although Joshua was used to seeing women in uniform he was surprised to see that this one was nonchalant enough to be carrying a copy of *Cosmopolitan*. Somehow it didn't seem right to him that a woman should be reading *Cosmopolitan* in a border war that was supposed to be off-limits to women. It seemed too *civilian*, as though women had no right to be going into a war zone at all and even if they were so allowed, he reasoned, they should not be reading Cosmo.

'Which one of you is Smith?' she asked.

His eyes travelled up from her perfect swan neck, across cheeks that sang of tennis parties and swimming pools, starry nights in the Graaf-Reinet desert and the soft sigh of the sea on Wilderness beach.

'I am,' he said, with a gulp.

She looked at him and Joshua believed that he had never seen such perfect blue eyes. All he could think of was girls in their gowns at the Police balls in the Coldstream Club off Kerk Straat on a summer evening. Sanchez stirred uneasily.

'And you are the detective?' she asked, ignoring the drooling and laying a briefcase on the bed.

'It is,' Joshua replied. 'What brings you here?'

'The bomb in the Company office,' she rapped.

'I remember it,' answered Joshua, drinking in a faint floral scent.

'Don't be a ...' CSM Landsberg was about to say *poes*, but abruptly decided against it.

'Any information you have, we need it,' rapped Captain Mostert again.

'I wouldn't know,' answered Smith. 'Did the cleaner, Mopboy, plant it?'

'Don't think so,' she replied, pulling out a sheaf of papers from the briefcase and handing them to him. 'Can you identify him from these?'

He took them in his uninjured right hand and looked at the top one. It was a Personnel Form which the black ancillary staff were supposed to fill in when they applied for a job with the military. He had used similar things in the police and knew how unreliable they were. Nobody ever checked the accuracy of the information there because no-one could really be bothered going around the Locations to check. Everybody knew they were 90% made up and as long as they contained a reference from a pastor or a priest, accepted the fiction. The photographs were always poor quality, so that all black people really did look alike; a pair of white eyes behind the smudge of an inky fingerprint. He let the forms drop one by one on the bed and then answered in the negative.

'We think Mopboy's real name is Sixpence Ndwandwe.' she said, consulting a notebook. 'Did you ever get threatening letters while you were here? It's a common MO for the ANC.

They think they are being democratic if they warn you before they murder you. As to the bomb – well, we think that will be SWAPO. It's more in their line.'

Smith kept the knowledge of the note to himself.

'Are you here because of Colonel Dietz and Admiral Steyl?' he asked.

'They have been evacuated to the rear,' she answered. 'I am 23.'

'Merriman?'

'Back in the jailhouse.' She picked the papers off the bed, ignoring his attempt to look down her shirt. 'The idiot was picked up trying to thumb a lift over to our base area.'

'Why would he do that?'

'Because he's an idiot. Strydom is in the cells with him. It was him that let Merriman go free when him and his pals did this to Corporal Sanchez. He says the clerk told him Sanchez was the murderer just before the bomb went off.'

'Actually, the clerk didn't say that,' said Smith. 'He just said that the murderer had been in the jail. Strydom knew it wasn't himself but he's too thick to think that it could be a white man.'

'Yes, we've gathered that,' she said. 'So you still need to catch a murderer – or maybe two.'

'Was Lieutenant Keay murdered? Or was he just shot?'

'He was double tapped,' she said. 'That means it was one of ours that shot him. SWAPO just spray bullets around like they're carrying garden snakes.'

Captain Mostert put the papers into her briefcase and got ready to leave. '23 have got an interest in this case now,' she stated. 'We will be speaking again.'

'You will be welcome anytime, miss.'

'It's *Ma'am* to you, Sergeant. And CSM – I expect Corporal Sanchez to be treated with the same dignity and respect as any white soldier. This is an order.'

CSM Landsberg came to attention, saluted and then followed Captain Mostert out. The room suddenly seemed bereft, very empty, as though all the flowers had been taken away from a wedding breakfast.

Joshua turned to Sanchez, ready to thank him for saving his life.

'You need not say anything,' said Sanchez anticipating. 'I did it because you are the only thing approximating to the law in this 41st Mechanised Regiment and I would like justice for what Strydom did to me. And I might have been next for Mr. Sixpence Mopboy Ndwandwe. The ANC do not have much love for 23 Battalion. And we are not flavour of the month with SWAPO either.'

*

22nd May 1980

Two days later, when Sergeant Smith was discharged from the infirmary it was evident that Colonel Malan and Major van der Merwe had instituted a number of changes to the way things were done in 41 Mech. For a start, there had been a review of the state of discipline brought on by Strydom's attempted lynching of Sanchez and instead of the more relaxed approach to military formalities common on the border, the rule of the garrison had been enforced. This meant parades every morning and evening, which in turn meant inspections, creases ironed into scrupulously clean uniforms, equipment polished, oiled and scrubbed, barrack rooms swept out, beds made in the regulation fashion, with the three lines woven into the blankets running down the exact centre of the perfectly squared off cot. Guards were mounted, wearing boots specially issued for the sole purpose of being bulled up to the point where CSM Landsberg could see his face reflected in them. Chromed bayonets were polished up and soup plate tin helmets issued so that the carefully choreographed drill, the stamping to attention and the cracking off of salutes so sharp that one could almost hear the elbows click, were made all the more impressive. Men now marched around the base in squads regulated by NCOs calling out the time, their previous habits of slouching and mooching on their way like civilians, knocked away by the military metronome. Evenings were spent in the laundry, or over ironing boards, rather than puffing on *skyfs* and slurping beer in the canteen, and meals were wolfed hurriedly as the men were harassed from one task to the next according to a timetable so tight it was hardly possible to meet the ever advancing deadlines. Compulsory physical training had replaced the voluntary rugby and cricket, and before daylight the Ratel crews would emerge, hacking and coughing, from their billets, dreading the ten kilometres of pounding knees and chafing packs that faced them before their first coffee of the day. Having become accustomed to driving rather than running, these sessions were pure torture to begin with and they eyed the ropes, walls and climbing frames of the new assault course rising a little further out of the dust each day with a growing dread. Life for the soldiers of 41 Mech had now become an endless sweat of grit, sand, dust, polish and soap powder washed down with tepid tea, cold mealiepap eaten with grimy fingers and an overwhelming desire for five more minutes of sleep.

Nor did it end there. The fact that the black ancillaries had been infiltrated by ANC or SWAPO operatives meant that a full security sweep had to be carried out. This meant that all the cooks, cleaners, bottle washers, shit shovellers and general labourers were withdrawn from service and penned up in a wired in compound some distance from the base while Captain Mostert attempted to comb out the wolves from this flock of black sheep. While she did this, the soldiers of 41 Mech had to take over their duties, adding to the burdens that Malan and van der Merwe had already laid across their shoulders; they underlined the reason for this unwelcome new regime by putting Strydom to work in the latrines whenever he was allowed out of the jail.

For the labourers, this was just another humiliating and bewildering episode in their ground down lives. Most of them had been recruited in the Bantustans, the native reserves that the black people had been shovelled into by Apartheid, and as the qualifications most valued by the Labour Agents for this kind of work were docility and lack of education, they accepted imprisonment as somehow being part of the natural order. They were people to whom things happened, not free agents who expected to shape the world that surrounded them. Shuffling along in their blue denim overalls or clumping into the pen in wellington boots, they looked like the coffle of slaves they were; debased, doped with dagga and cheap booze, quarrelsome, as uncooperative as cattle, their humanity beaten out of them by sjamboks, truncheons, tear gas and bullets. They had come to resemble what the Broederbond said they were; barely more than animals dependent on their keepers; they were paraded as the justification for Apartheid; they had become its self-fulfilling prophecy; the black man was a lower form of life, to be treated as such, and here was the proof. And yet among them were those who kept the dream of freedom alive, feeding it, polishing it, burnishing it and sharpening it whenever the authorities were not looking.

Joshua learned at first hand of the trials and tribulations endured by Captain Mostert at her work because he was detailed to help her. Merriman was saying nothing and until the mystery of why he had been trying to reach 23's base could be solved, there could be no more progress on the case, so van der Merwe had attached him to her in the hope of making it. Most of the black men and women employed on the base had so little education that they were barely able to write their own names; none could read and it quickly became apparent to both of them that the Personnel Forms had been filled in by hands other than their own. Perhaps a student or teacher eking out a miserable income as a professional writer had filled them in? The handwriting was often similar and the details too coincidental to be true; all the people whose names began with 'A' had the same birth date. When she tried to match the names and photographs to the faces of the poor souls marched, one by one, in front of her, she realised the impossibility of using the Personnel Forms for any kind of intelligence work. Apart from the dreadful quality of the photographs and the smudged, illegible pink and mauve Banda copies, there were also forms duplicated on over used carbon with broken, semi-functioning typewriters to decipher. When she asked the people for their names, she was met by a wall of incomprehension, silence, sometimes dumb insolence, but mainly a defensive suspicion, as though offering up any information at all would result in deleterious consequences for themselves or someone they knew.

'Name,' she would demand.

'Huh?'

'Wat is jou naam?' she would repeat.

'What?'

'Name. Tell me your name.'

'Yes. Goed, Dankie.'

'Your name is 'Dankie'?'

'Huh?'

'Jou naam is 'Dankie'?'

'Geen problem, Missy. Suid-Afrika is an wunderlike land. Goed Dankie.'

And so it went on, hour after mind numbing hour, until only her dogged persistence had produced a list of two hundred names which corresponded to the annotated cover sheets now attached to the original Personnel Forms. She had also generated new documents to cover the workers who had no records and who seemed to be subsisting on charity or sharing the jobs of the other workers. Once this was done, she felt able to release some of them to their duties, although this did not immediately unburden 41 Mech because she insisted the labourers carry out their duties under guard. Kassie Strydom gained some company, though he wasn't 100% glad of this.

Looking for the wolves came next. This was a doubly frustrating task because not only were the two hundred suspects uncommunicative as a matter of habit, she was sure that anyone who was ANC or SWAPO would have scarpered by now. Either that, or they would be so cool headed and well trained that they would be impossible to identify. All she had to hand was the working hypothesis that anyone involved with SWAPO would probably speak some Portuguese because that was the language of their Angolan hosts. The chances of a native of a South African Bantustan knowing Portuguese would be minimal. She could also work with racial features, on the basis that a South African Xhosa or Zulu black did actually look different from a Namib black, although this was complicated by the fact that there were as many Ovambos in SWAPO as there were in 23 or indeed, the SAPS; the Kavangos were difficult to tell apart from a Xhosa or Zulu too. Himbas were easier because they had a sort of red colour to their skin and the Bushmen were easy, because they were quite small. None of this, it occurred to both her and Joshua, was very much to go on.

'Ola. Bom dia,' she would say, looking closely at the skin colour, general features and mien of the suspect in front of her.

'Huh?'

'Nome?' she would ask, watching for a flicker of understanding.

'Huh?'

'Onde e a sua casa?'

'Yes. Goud, Dankie.'

'Voce entende?'

'Dankie. Suid-Afrika is an wunderlike land....'

It was hopeless and all she could recommend was that the labourers be allowed to continue with their duties but under close supervision and that they be returned to their wired in billet as soon as those duties were completed. Colonel Malan had little choice but to agree, even though he understood how cumbersome this arrangement would be. Brushing aside van der Merwe's reservations about imprisoning people who were essential to the running of the base and were probably innocent to boot, a system of guards, sentries and escorts was introduced alongside a paper system of registers, chits, dockets which was supposed to regulate the activities of the labour force. Captain Mostert knew that this system would not work; reams of paper never did; she already had the proof of that to hand in the pile of useless, but neatly stacked Personnel Forms and she confessed as much to Joshua.

'Can you imagine Kassie Strydom doing book keeping?' she said despairingly, as they walked past the wired in compound where blue figures squatted dejectedly against the peeling walls of the long, low, wooden billets. 'But what else can we do?'

'This is not a good way to treat the labour,' said Joshua. 'If that was me, I would be thinking that maybe the ANC was not such a bad idea.'

Captain Mostert blew out a sigh. 'You know, none of this will work. Everyone with any sense knows this. But what can we do? It's either Apartheid or Communism and Communism is not much of an alternative. Look at the disaster of Africa to the north! Look at the mess Idi Amin is making of Uganda, kicking out all those Indians like that. Look at Bokassa – he thinks he's the Emperor Napoleon. Look at Nyerere ruining the farmers of his country.'

Joshua went back to the infirmary twice a day to check on Sanchez as a break from this mind-numbing chore. Not only did he feel a debt of gratitude to him, but he also felt that their shared ordeals gave them a connection; he had the uncertain notion in his mind that being beaten to a pulp by a lynch mob and being blown up by a bomb were in some way related and that they constituted a sort of shared experience. Johua was still in a fragile state, still bandaged and stitched, his hands sometimes shaking involuntarily and though he fought them down, there were moments when unexplained tears welled up in his eyes. Sanchez too was still heavily bandaged, his face badly bruised and his arm still strapped up, but he seemed to be in better spirits now that Captain Mostert and the escort from his own regiment was present. He was also glad to be out of the jail and no longer being treated as a suspect and showed this in a willingness to speak openly to Joshua in a kindly and almost avuncular way. Joshua in turn saw in Sanchez someone whose university education and experience of war might be of help, but he knew he could not confide anything near the truth of his situation. He could not tell of his orders to kill Merriman, nor of the threatening demand to leave him him be, but the fact that the black man appeared to be on his side was strangely comforting. In a strange sort of way, a way he could not explain, he felt an affinity with Sanchez; he felt safe with him.

'How goes the investigation?' asked Sanchez on the second day. 'This is a very serious matter for me, you will understand.'

'We're getting nowhere combing through the black staff,' Joshua replied, lighting a cigarette and passing it over. 'I really need to find out why Merriman was heading for your base. It has to be connected to the death of Lieutenant Keay. It's possible he has an accomplice over there. Missy Mostert says she will help me through the personnel files.' He lit a second one for the escort, who took it and with a nod from Sanchez, then went outside.

'Have you asked Merriman himself?'

'Major van der Merwe interviewed him personally,'replied Joshua lighting up a third cigarette. 'He is saying nothing.' He blew out a column of smoke at the flies circling below the thatch. 'CSM Landsberg offered to beat an answer out of him, but van der Merwe would not allow it. He wants it all done by the book.'

'By the book?' said Sanchez, blowing another column of smoke out. 'Which book?'

'*The* book,' said Joshua, catching the note of surprise. 'Ja, I know. But he has got some military law manual from somewhere and is reading it quickly.'

'Well, that is better than nothing, I suppose.' Sanchez paused for a moment. 'Actually, I think it is a lot better than nothing. Even bad laws imperfectly applied are better than no laws.'

Joshua nodded. He didn't really understand everything that Sanchez said but he appreciated that he sounded wise and was willing to trust his judgement. For a moment a surging desire for catharsis made him want to blurt out his dissatisfaction with life as he presently understood it, but he had carried secrets for long enough to know not to drop them, and caught himself in time. Nothing good ever came of blurting out secrets; the most important truths were best kept locked away. Even so, he could not resist eliding his situation to Sanchez as he lay there, swaddled and smoking like a wounded sage.

'Listen, Sanchez,' he said. 'Supposing – I mean, *just supposing*…'

Joshua paused, sucked on his cigarette and then dropped it on the floor, grinding it out with his heel.

'Just *supposing*,' replied Sanchez.

'Ja. Just *supposing* that a bloke had like a *dilemma* where he couldn't really do right for doing wrong…'

'You mean *hypothetically*?' said Sanchez.

'Ja, probably,' Joshua replied. 'Caught like between the Devil and the deep blue sea.'

'OK,' said Sanchez. 'What's the dilemma?'

'Well, like if a soldier was given two orders to do things but could only carry out one of them…'

'Then the soldier would naturally seek clarification from his superior officer,' said Sanchez.

'Yes – no,' said Joshua, scratching the back of his head. 'What if he got two orders from two different officers who didn't really get on with each other?'

'Then he should go to his superior officer….'

'No – yes,' said Joshua. 'It's not like that. What if he had to make up his mind without being able to talk to either superior officer?'

'Then the soldier must make a decision himself,' said Sanchez. 'But it seems to be an unusual situation. Personally, I would follow the last order that I had received.'

Joshua thought about this for a moment.

'What if he knew that the other superior officer would punish him if he carried out the order of the first superior officer?'

'Then I would say that the soldier would be in a very peculiar army,' said Sanchez, shifting on the bed and handing Joshua the end of the cigarette for disposal. 'And that he would be best advised to become the pilot of his own storm and do whatever seemed best.'

'Like in that poem?' said Joshua, stubbing the cigarette out on the floor. 'The one about being the master of your own fate?'

'*It matters not how strait the gate or how charged with punishments the scroll, I am the master of my fate, the captain of my soul.* It is called 'Invictus' and I would say that the man who is the master of his own fate is a lucky man indeed,' said Sanchez, shifting again. 'Most of us are more like Hamlet - subject to outrageous fortune throughout our lives. What I mean is that you must try to steer a course between the two of these superior officers until they have resolved whatever differences led them to issuing two contradictory orders to the soldier in question.'

'That could take some time,' said Joshua.

'Do you have something that you wish to get off your chest, Sergeant Smith?' said Sanchez.

'More than you could possibly imagine,' he replied. 'Sometimes I think I'd like to get my whole life off my chest.'

'I am ready to listen if you think it will help you.'

It was on the tip of his tongue but he swallowed it back quickly as the door opened and the escort soldier returned.

'Sanchez,' he said, getting up to leave. 'I would not know where to begin'

*

It was back in 1974, the day after he had survived the initiation ceremony at the Graaf-Reinet Police station that Konstabel Williams had taken him up the steep drive to the Valley of Desolation. He was hung over, his mouth as dry as the Karoo desert surrounding him, and he was still wiping away traces of the black make-up he had been smeared with, before being tied to a post outside the black Location, adorned with a placard that proclaimed him to be a queer *kaffirboete*.

'Come on, I'll show you your beat,' said Konstabel Williams. 'And show you the landscape, too.'

Williams was retiring at the end of the week and newly qualified Joshua Smith was his eager replacement, so it seemed natural that the old guy should show the new guy the ropes. Almost as soon as they were out of the station and into the car, however, the heavy silence that seeped out of the desert and into the car gave Smith the feeling that Williams had something he wanted to get off his chest, some bit of wisdom to impart perhaps, or some long nurtured, pithy distillation of his experience. As they took the road out past the Prussian blue waters of the dam, he could see the flesh on his gaunt face working, gathering itself as if to cough up a fur ball from under the yard brush moustache. Williams stared straight ahead, dark circles under his eyes, his once blonde hair patchy, limp, sparse and torn across his pate in a poor comb-over. As the tarmac whirred under the tyres on a road that ran straight towards the horizon through scrub that ran flat to the mountains of the Sneeuberg, Smith stared at the indigo sky and waited for whatever was coming.

About fifteen minutes north, the older man swung off to the left and pushed the engine, labouring, up a steep, winding valley. The gradient was so fierce that several times Williams dropped down to first as the engine seemed almost to run out of breath; as they reached the top of each false crest, he revved and gunned it to gain momentum for the next, as though he was never sure that he would make it. It took twenty minutes to reach the top and when Constable Williams got there he announced the fact by wrenching on the handbrake so hard that Smith thought he might have torn it off.

'We call this the Valley of Desolation,' he said, waving a hand around the rust coloured rocks. 'It's a good name.'

Out of the vehicle, Smith followed Williams' baggy shorts and scarecrow thin legs as he led the way up a short rocky path to a viewpoint high above the town.

'Graaf-Reinet,' said Williams, sweeping out an arm.

Fifteen hundred metres down below, the town was laid out like a carpet, its white, wide streets shaded by the feathery purple jacarandas and red flame trees and its neat red and green corrugated iron roofs gleamed in the sun as though they had been enamel glazed. There were bright green lawns, iridescent against the desert scrub and the horseshoe line of the Sundays River that ran around three sides of the town was traced by the paper bark and waving fingers of the bluegum trees. All around the mountains ran like tawny lions racing towards the horizon, while the kites cried and circled and rose on the thermals below them.

'Beautiful, huh?' said Williams, screwing up his eyes.

'Ja,' answered Joshua. 'A real peach.'

Williams ran his eyes around the horizon and then put a finger to his chewing lips.

'Not a peach – a rotten apple,' he replied. 'Look over there.'

Smith had not expected this and he felt a lurch in his stomach that was nothing to do with the residue of last night's alcohol. He followed William's gaze to the black township, east, away from the pretty whitewash and the comforting shade.

'Kroonvale,' he named it. 'The people who live there now used to live in the centre of the town, right by the church and the Drostdy. They lived there for generations; some of them were freed slaves and were given sanctuary down there, right on Kerk Straat. Not now.'

'So what is important about that?' said Joshua. 'It's the same everywhere.'

'Look at this hill here,' continued Williams, ignoring the question, and pointing out a huge shouldered koppie, topped with red sandstone cliffs and capped with mounds of earth, like thatched round huts. 'This is called Spandau Kop. You know where it gets its name? I'll tell you; it comes from a German guy who came here a hundred years ago and thought it looked like a fortress in his home town of Berlin. Spandau is a prison now. Spandau has also got a machine gun named for it. Spandau Kop: a prison and a machine gun, here overlooking our town. What do you think of that?'

'It's very impressive,' answered Joshua, stupidly. 'I mean....'

'It's where the bodies of troublemakers – black troublemakers – get buried when the Inspector loses his patience with them,' said Williams calmly. 'Just like the Nazis used to do with people they didn't like. Just like the Communists in Russia do now. Was your father in the army, at all? Did he serve in the war?'

Joshua shook his head.

Williams grunted acceptance of this.

'I served in Europe. You know what I discovered there?'

Joshua shrugged.

'I was in Normandy in 1944 with the artillery. I saw Brits, Canadians, Yanks, Poles, Jews, Germans, Africans, Cossacks, Russians, every race known to man fighting there; I even saw a Turkish Cypriot in a kilt. He was playing the bagpipes for a Scottish regiment, can you believe?'

Williams turned to look directly at him, his eyes hawkish under lowered brows.

'The best soldiers were the German SS. Tough, trained, experienced, motivated, intelligent, determined and you know what?' He jabbed at Joshua's chest. 'It didn't do them a scrap of good, because we had more shells, more aircraft, more steel, more of everything than them. They blew our tanks apart – ever heard of *Operation Goodwood*? No? Well they did. But it didn't matter, because we kept shipping them ashore, driving them up to the line and shooting back no stopping. It didn't matter that they had all the experience and we had none. A few weeks after the landings, the SS made a big counter-attack and they gave us real hell, but it didn't matter because we put such a storm on them that they could not resist. Shall I tell you what I learned there?'

'Go on,' said Joshua, fidgeting.

'I learned that no matter how good you are in a fight, you will always go down to numbers in the end. And I will tell you too, that there is no difference between men of one race or another. Does that shock you?'

'Is this some kind of a test?' replied Joshua. 'Does the Inspector want to know if I'm a communist or something?'

Williams looked at him with a patient frown. 'No,' he said. 'These things I tell you are what you need to know if you are to survive. I have not much longer to live. It's cancer and I will not survive six months more. But you have your whole life ahead of you and unless you make Graaf-Reinet something more than a prison and a machine gun, you will not survive long either.'

A kite glided up on a thermal, screeching and then banked away into the cornflower blue sky. The wind was hot and dry up here and Joshua could see the curve of the horizon away to the south.

'Why did you join the police, Smith?' asked Konstabel Williams.

'So I didn't get conscripted for the army,' replied Joshua.

Konstabel Williams looked at him sideways. 'I suppose that's something. Why don't you want to go to the war?'

'Catching criminals seems a better thing to do than shooting at people who just want to live their lives like we do,' replied Joshua.

Williams snorted and smiled. 'You sound like me when I joined up after the war – before all this Apartheid rubbish started.'

'Why did you stay a policeman if you don't like it?'

He stretched out his arms and then shook his hands in front of him. 'My bones ache,' he said by way of explanation. 'And in answer to your question, the truth is that at first I did not believe the National Party were serious about racial segregation and then I thought it was just a passing fad and then, when I realised they were indeed serious and it was not a passing fad, it was too late to do anything about it.'

'Too late?'

'Mortgage, family, life insurance, car, pension, bullshit,' he said, raising his eyebrows. He turned away and began to head back towards the car. 'So you get out of that uniform as soon as you can. Become a detective. Uphold the law. Catch criminals. The people who wear that uniform are not policemen, they are thugs so don't you become one too.'

*

It was a day or so later that Joshua had his formal welcome to the Graaf-Reinet police and it came in the form of a braii around Inspector Du Toit's swimming pool. As well as the rest of department, all the wives were there, sashaying back and forth from the tennis court to the kitchen to the sunshades and the deck chairs in empire-waisted mini dresses that showed off their tanned legs and bare arms. Joshua noticed the daring trouser suits with flared legs under flowing pilot shirts but was more drawn to the peasant blouses that billowed in the soft summer breeze like flowers in the meadow. As he came through the gate, he caught sight of the servants' house, a square shack with two windows and a door to the front and corrugated iron on top and could not help thinking of Ayize. He wondered where she was and what she was doing but it was more than two years since he had last seen her and though he felt a pang, the wound had long healed; two years was a long time in the life of an 18 year old. There was a hiss and a flare from the braii as oil got onto the charcoal and the rich smell of toasting meat filled his nostrils.

'Hey there, young Joshua,' called the Inspector, waving tongs. 'Come on over and have a beer man. Ag, it's hot today, hey?'

Inspector Du Toit was a fleshy man in his forties and though still fit, bore more than a passing resemblance to Oliver Hardy. He had the same button nose and small mouth, the creased brow and above it the small, black shock of hair so black it was almost blue. He was dressed in his habitual empire-builder shorts and military style shirt whose only concession to civilian fashion lay in its differently shaded pockets. Most of the other policemen were similarly attired, but there were a couple of *jongs* like himself who affected spoon collars and would have worn tank tops if it had not been such a bright, sunny day.

'Ja, can I have a cold one?' said Joshua, threading through the crowd of guests and trying to sound grown up. Over by the pool, two blonde girls in swimsuits were dipping their feet in the cool water and pretending not to notice the appreciative glances they were attracting from the male company. There were several more shrieking with laughter over at the tennis court while the boys from the rugby club tossed a ball around.

'How are you settling in then?' asked the Inspector, adjusting the meat. 'Your rooms are fine?'

'Ja, I'm staying in a self-contained unit down by Caledon Street,' he replied, trying not to stare at the girls by the pool. 'It's a bit of a fixer-upper but it is just fine.'

'A bachelor pad, hey?' said the Inspector, with an indulgent leer. 'And you a good looking young man with money in your pocket. How times have changed, hey? *Ag*, what with the pill and all this free love, I wish I was young again myself.' He looked up and waved the tongs again. 'Not that I would swap my wife for all the tea in China. This is the *lekker* life here.'

Joshua looked around and agreed. The Inspector's house was a large house built in the colonial style with Dutch gables, solid beams, intricate iron work along the back stoep and large square white framed windows under a grey tiled roof. There were lawns to the front, sides and rear all perfectly manicured, lush beds of agapanthus, oxalis and proteas, all hedged in by plumbago and kept watered by the two garden boys. Inside the house, 17th Century furniture stood on yellow wood floors, polished to a glazed and shining perfection by two maids in the spare hours between cleaning the seven bedrooms, three reception rooms, separate dining room, kitchen, pantry and hallway.

'And this would be the new addition to the force, would it?'

A middle-aged woman with an enormous bust appeared from behind him and Joshua almost spilled the beer he had been handed. He stuttered for a moment and blushed a little as he became quickly conscious of looking down at her deep cleavage before addressing her face.

'Meet Mrs. Meyer,' said Inspector Du Toit. 'She is the wife of Jannie and she is very big in the church.'

'To which congregation do you belong, young man?' she asked.

Joshua looked into her florid face, partly shaded by a hat that was a little too fashionably floppy for her and saw two piercing blue eyes looking straight back at him. They were searching eyes, which though appearing kindly on the surface seemed to betray a harshness beneath.

'Oh, er, I'm not really religious, Mrs. Meyer,' he stuttered. 'Ja, er, Christmas and Easter of course but…'

'Never mind,' she said, cutting him off. 'I'm sure that you will lend your support to our fund raising activities anyway. We bake a little and we have a monthly whist drive in aid of the blacks on the Location. The black Pastor is very nice considering.'

'Oh, er, sure, Mrs. Meyer,' answered Joshua. 'I must just get my duties under my belt first though, hey?'

'Duties?' she scoffed. 'There are no *duties* here in Graaf-Reinet. The blacks are perfectly content and we are so far from anywhere that there is nowhere for a criminal to escape to. Really, it is a very easy life here for a policeman.'

'She's right,' said Inspector Du Toit, as Mrs Meyer coasted away. 'Apart from when they drink too much on a Friday, the blacks are quiet here. Ja, sure, we get the occasional trouble but nothing a few sjamboks can't sort out. It's a good place for a young policeman to learn the ropes.'

'Is there any work for a detective here?' asked Joshua, remembering Konstable Williams' advice.

'Not much,'said the Inspector. He took a handful of sweet herbs, dipped them in water and laid them on the braii. 'Well, not here in the town at any rate. There are sometimes some problems on the farms with the kaffirs stealing anything that isn't nailed down but we haven't had a murder – a white murder – since I can remember. The blacks murder each other, though, especially if they have been drinking too much but it does not take a genius to solve these mysteries. We usually just round up whoever and cart them off down to Port Elizabeth jail. Like I say, this life is *lekker*. Family, church, the Coldstream Club, braii, tennis and pool parties; who needs excitement, hey?'

Joshua looked at the two girls by the pool. 'This is *lekker*, you're right.'

'Where do your people come from?' asked the Inspector.

Joshua thought of his father back in Krugerburg and inwardly winced. The fat, old drunk had hardly spoken to him since Joshua had left home. He thought of his mother in Cape Town and winced once more. She had shown some interest when he joined the Police but it didn't last for long, but it was long enough and Joshua knew from the look on her face when she went back to Cape Town that she was ashamed of him. When he first told her he was going into the Police, she had swallowed hard and asked him if he had ever thought of emigrating.

'Never mind,' said the Inspector, reading his face. 'This is a small town,' he said, handing Joshua a plate and then placing half a kilo of rump steak on it. 'Keep your nose clean, stick together with us and you will prosper. We your family now.'

Joshua took the plate and nodded. Looking around once more he saw the beaming smiles, the happy camaraderie and all the easy comfort of a village. This was not Krugerburg. On a first impression, the people seemed more relaxed, less *coarse*, and it seemed that here was a welcome and a sense of belonging that he had never experienced before. It was not District 6 either, but that place was becoming fainter and fainter in his memory and anyay, it seemed more important to focus on the present and his new future. This place was different; it was away from his parents; it could become his own place, his independence, his *escape*. He wanted to belong somewhere and this pretty town way out in the Karoo desert seemed far enough away from his past. Feeling the warmth of the sun, smelling the spice and woodsmoke of the braii and hearing the tinkling laughter of beautiful girls, he decided then and there that he would put aside the negative parts of Konstabel Williams' advice and begin a new life, here, fully as a policeman rather than as someone who had just joined up to avoid the army.

'Thank you, Inspector, Sir,' he said, reaching for the monkey gland. 'I'll do my best. You can count on it. Yes, Sir, I am part of the team.'

*

24th May 1980

The medics had declared Sanchez fit to travel and as Captain Mostert had come to the conclusion that there was little chance of any further progress at this end of the case, both she and Joshua had decided to accompany him back to 23's base at Echo Tango. Sanchez was still heavily bandaged and splinted, but his eyes were opening and the infections around the cuts and stitches were a little less angry now and he was understandably keen to be back with his own unit.

'You don't mind if I keep you company?' said Joshua, helping him into his trousers as Luis the 23 escort soldier fitted the boots onto his feet. 'Captain Mostert has got a Buffel waiting for you and I would not like to think of her taking advantage of you in your present, weakened condition.' Joshua winked. 'Not while I'm in with a chance, hey?'

Sanchez snorted. Outside the heavy sound of a powerful engine drawing up announced the arrival of their transport and while the Luis fastened Sanchez's laces and his belt, Joshua did up his shirt buttons. 'You are far too ugly and I think your stitches are in a worse state than mine,' said Sanchez, smiling. 'And also, it is said that once a woman goes with a black man, there can be no going back for her. Missy Mostert looks to me like a woman who knows what is good for her.'

'You have got more chance of being struck by lightning, *bru,*' returned Joshua, picking up both his and Sanchez's webbing belts. 'That is a refined lady who needs someone of wit, charm, sophistication and craggy good looks - like me. Strydom has more hope of a jump than you.'

Outside, as they helped Sanchez climb over the side of the Buffel, banging their unwieldy FN rifles on the sides like greenhorns, they heard the distinctive crack and thud of rifle fire from the direction of the butts, while the cadenced crunch of boots came clearly, rhythmically, from the parade ground. The now completed assault course was also in use, and the cry of orders told them that A Company was being put through infantry fire and movement drills at a breakneck speed. This was more like recruit training than war, thought Joshua, and he was glad that his injuries excluded him from taking part.

'Looks like Colonel Malan is working them hard this morning,' Captain Mostert said. 'He is going to make SWAPO pay a lot for that bomb.'

'Are we expecting more deployments?' asked Joshua. 'I thought Operations were over.'

'Not until the fat lady sings,' answered Mostert, swinging the door shut. 'We think SWAPO and FAPLA are going to try to take back something of what they have lost in these last weeks.'

'What date is it?' said Sanchez.

'It's the 24th May,' she said, standing up to take hold of the bar that ran the length of the compartment. 'I reckon that we must have another week or so before it winds down. We have hurt them a lot, but I think we must hurt them a lot more.'

As the ugly vehicle started to move, Luis lay down, stretching himself out along the length of one seat, bored, ready for sleep. Joshua and Sanchez stood up, balancing awkwardly, and took hold of the bar alongside Captain Mostert. It was the best way to avoid travel sickness, even though it meant the risk of sun burn, wind burn and guaranteed a thick coating of dust. The military road that ran out North-West towards the 23 base at Echo Tango was black top all the way but it was still a journey of some hours and Joshua reminded himself of the effort and determination that must have driven Merriman to attempt the journey on foot. This would be no easy trek on foot; even tougher without preparation, a weapon and plenty of water and Merriman was no greenhorn when it came to the perils of the desert. Something urgent must have prompted him to make the attempt though and Joshua sensed that whatever it was lay at the root of the mystery.

Whatever that was, it could wait. There were some hours between Oshadangwa and Echo Tango and he had learned long ago that travel between bases and operations was a time to be enjoyed, savoured even. Luis, who was now fast asleep, obviously knew this secret, as all experienced soldiers did. It was a kind of stasis, when all decisions and power over those decisions had evaporated with the cough of the starter motor. He was in the hands of the driver, who knew his way, and there would be no need for him to intervene, direct or question. He was not in charge, not responsible for once, but was doing what he was told, going where he was sent and not expected to do anything more than do it. Sometimes it was a neutral space too where the differences in rank or race dissolved because everyone was under the command of the driver and he wondered for a moment if all strife could not be solved by sending the disputing parties on a long journey together in which they would have no choice in the direction of travel or the destination chosen. It might just happen that once they had all got bored of avoiding each other or staring at the horizon or anywhere but at their fellow passengers, they would just try to get along for the sake of it and then everyone would be a lot happier. He looked at Luis, who was now snoring, and then back at Sanchez, who was looking out over the yellow back of the vehicle. He looked forward at the nape of Captain Mostert's neck too and then gave up on his philosophy; if she was the only woman on board any voyage would end up in a row. It was the way of the world; rubies, riches, power and women always put men at each other's throats; look at Fletcher Christian and his mutiny in paradise.

As the warm wind came off the cab like the scent off an animal and ruffled his hair, Joshua took in the strong colours of the landscape, narrowing his eyes against the whip of the dust, and followed the flowing lines of the dunes and the scribbled lines of the thorn tree thickets as they passed by. He was used to the Karoo desert, in the centre of which sat Graaf-Reinet, but up here in the Namib the layers of cinnamon, burnt umber, siena, terracotta and straw yellow seemed more powerful and starker and went on for longer. They lay in sharp edged lines as though painted by numbers, and the golden light of the morning sun heightened their definition, making them crisper still against the deep cornflower blue sky.

He could see that Captain Mostert was enjoying the landscape too. Her skin was tan and had the same expensive sheen that Scholtz's had and he couldn't stop himself from noticing the clear complexion and the same, fine atheletic suppleness that came with good food, sun, swimming pools and compulsory competitive sport at exclusive boarding schools. She was concentrating on a line of white gemsbok trekking across a distant dune, their long curved scimitar horns blending into a single lance at this distance, making them look like unicorns on a quest and standing directly behind her, he could not help notice her perfume, a distinctly un-military fragrance of citrus and orange, strawberries and summer freshness. The contrast came as a shock and he immediately noticed his own, slightly stale tang. The cumin smell of men's body odour was so common that he had stopped noticing it and was only dimly aware of variations in its intensity when the smell of diesel, hot rubber on tarmac and mouldy canvas was momentarily camouflaged by the smell of beeswax and polish in the Officer's Mess. This fresh scent of femininity, he almost gasped for now as a release from the tough world of men and war and sand and bullets and the reek of those Lieutenants in their bodybags back at Oshadangwa. There was a whiff not of grapeshot, but of freedom about it and it seemed to hint of a future when he might be released from the uniform that imprisoned him. For a moment, he trembled at the possibility, but then she moved and an eddy in the flowing air dismissed the perfume and replaced it with cigarette smoke from the cab. He closed down all thought and gave himself up to the hypnosis of movement.

It was some hours later when the driver changed down and the the deeper tone of the engine broke the spell that it had cast over the vehicle. Luis started momentarily, then turned over. Sanchez gave a little grunt and swallowed a painkiller, then offered one to Joshua, who took it. Captain Mostert was brought out of her trance by a jerk of the gearbox that set her a step back before she recovered her balance. Joshua put a hand up to steady her and then pulled it back before it was needed and then regretted that he had not taken the opportunity for even a fleeting physical contact.

'Where do you call home, Captain?' asked Joshua, striking up a conversation instead.

'I live in Franschoek,' she replied, turning to take the hair out of her eyes. 'They say it's the prettiest valley in South Africa but looking out here, I'd say they were only half right. Look.'

She pointed towards a family of giraffe, eleven of them, tall, stately, as graceful as an odd God could make them and positively glowing in the daylight.

'Your family are in the winemaking business?' asked Joshua, taking in her delicate elbow and the soft sheen of diffused sunlight on the hairs of her arm. 'Is that what you do when you are not an Intelligence Officer?'

'We have a wine farm,' she confirmed. 'But I really want to branch out on my own, you know? Be my own boss. Maybe open a gallery for artists, you know? This war is a pain in the neck. What about you?'

'I have a house in Graaf-Reinet,' answered Joshua. 'Before that, Krugerburg and the Cape. I was born just by the old District 6. My mother knows Merriman's mother, in case you ask.'

'Ja. Black Sash and all that. One of my aunts was in it. She lost her husband at El Alamein and took the view that as he had died to stop Nazis taking over in Europe, the least she could do was to do her bit to stop them taking over here.'

Joshua looked out across the flat arid landscape. There were no dunes here, just dry grass and thorn trees, without even the hint of a waterhole.

'How long till we get to Echo Tango,' he asked, shading his eyes.

'About an hour,' she replied, reading his thoughts. 'Merriman must have really wanted to get there, hey?'

There was a movement in the straw grass and a stocky bush pig trotted towards them frowning, its tusks up and its tail high in the air like a periscope.

'Warthog – down there,' pointed out Sanchez. 'The best meat there is. Like smoked roast pork done on a spitbraai.'

Joshua remembered the taste of roast pork and gemsquash. He could almost feel the crackling squirt and crunch under the carving knife and made a vow that as soon as this service was finished he would take a trip down to the Cape and get his mother to make some. He wondered what it would be like to take Captain Mostert with him; he wondered what it would be like to have that normal pleasure but got no further in his speculation because a beetle pinged off the cab and hit him hard on the mouth.

'What about you, Sanchez,' he asked, spitting out the insect. 'Where do you come from?'

'Luanda,' he replied. 'But I have not been there since I left for Lisbon many years ago. My home has been in the bush for most of my life since then. Now, I am an exile and my family is with 23.'

'Family?' said Joshua, puzzled.

'Family,' replied Sanchez.

When they finally made the farm gate at the entrance to the base at Echo Tango, Joshua was immediately aware that this was an outfit run on different lines than 41 Mech. For a start, everyone seemed to be that little bit older than the boys and young men of 41 and as the vehicle pulled up by the thatched rondavel guardroom to be swept and searched for booby traps, he guessed that the average age of the *troupies* here was somewhere in the mid-thirties rather than the mid-twenties. Some of them were grizzled veterans, all bone, muscle, sinew and seriousness and he realised with a start that thoughtful, determined men like Corporal Sanchez were the rule here rather than the exception. 23 Battalion was not composed of *jollers* and conscripts, but professional soldiers, battle hardened beyond even the most experienced of 41.

Waved on by the guard, Captain Mostert directed the Buffel past a squad of purposeful men concentrating on a lecture and Joshua took in the fact that white soldiers were mixed in with black soldiers as though race had never been thought of. Looking around at a squad jogging across a dusty parade ground he saw a black sergeant giving orders to white soldiers, a thing that he had never considered possible.

'No Apartheid here in 23,' said Captain Mostert, catching his surprise. 'Apart from the bathrooms.'

'Who are the white guys?' asked Joshua. 'I guess they aren't in the Broederbond.'

'Some mercenaries, some Americans, Brits, Australians, French, Belgians and a lot from Rhodesia, but mostly from South Africa,' she replied. 'There are some Portuguese and Puerto Ricans too. It's like the *bladdy* United Nations here.'

Further on, Joshua spotted a set of goalposts beyond the airstrip and a collection of black kids hoofing a football around amid the shrill happiness of school yard games. Beyond the posts, he could see a two story building, divided into classrooms with blue painted balconies and white washed walls and to the left a village of rondavels around a central boma enclosed within a stockade. There were women in printed cottons and fatigues hanging out washing on lines and pumping at a standpipe for water while infants splashed in the concrete basin below. There were goats there too and a whiff of black smoke from a stovepipe.

'23 have their wives and children here with them,' explained Mostert. 'It's part of the deal we made when we recruited them. Where the troops go – the families follow.'

'This is fucked up,' cried Joshua. 'Kids in a war zone?'

'It is family,' said Sanchez. 'Where else must they go?'

'But…what if you lose, Sanchez? What will happen then?'

'When the French left Algeria back in 1962, they took their Algerian soldiers back to France with them,' replied Sanchez, his tone that of the professor in a lecture theatre. 'Those who did not leave were massacred by the newly independent government.'

'Ja, well, you should not count on escaping if South Africa is defeated,' replied Joshua, his eyes still on the village as the Buffel pulled up by a rusted, grey nissen hut sweltering in the sun. 'The only place we can go to is Antarctica and I will promise you that the National Party will not be handing out free life-rafts to blacks.'

'Communism is in front of me in Angola,' replied Sanchez, gravely. 'And Apartheid is behind me in South Africa. Yet the prospect is not all so bleak.' He touched his chin, as though remembering his orator's tricks but then winced as the movement tugged at a cracked rib. 'For it is my objective analysis that Apartheid will not survive long for it is also my objective analysis that South Africa will need *all* of its peoples if it is to triumph over the communists. This is something that even the National Party know. And for these reasons, I do not fear the future, for a united South Africa will be truly invincible and might even go forward into Africa and liberate my Angola. Antarctica will not be necessary. Now help me down from the truck, please.'

'You have big hopes, Sanchez,' replied Joshua, swinging open the rear doors and prodding Luis awake with his boot. 'I still think this is fucked up though.'

'You think that's fucked up?' declared Captain Mostert, collecting Sanchez's kit. 'Did you know the CO of this unit has his brother in jail for anti-Apartheid activities?'

Sanchez climbed down from the Buffel stiffly and then, his feet on his own *terra firma* gave a sigh of relief.

'It is good to be home,' he said. 'Luis, let us leave the Captain and Sergeant to their business and get back to ours.'

'Sanchez,' said Joshua, raising his voice above the grumble of the departing truck. 'Thanks for what you did.'

'We need each other,' he said, wafting away the fumes and then holding out a hand to shake Joshua's. 'Comradeship and a healthy respect for the law are all that is really necessary for life.'

'You think so?'

'I hope so,' said Sanchez, taking hold of Luis' arm and beginning to hobble away. 'Catch the killer fairly and according to the law.'

Joshua watched them go, unsure for a moment of whether to follow, whether to offer to carry some kit for them or whether to just let them go. Somehow he felt that this was a parting and that he would never see the man who he owed his life to again and he felt diminished by it. It seemed to him that Sanchez might be the sort of guide a man in search of redemption would need and he wished he could call up the transport right now, load him aboard and drive straight back to Police Post 156 where, with Sissingi and a bottle of Redheart, he could start trying to find it.

'Get on with your work,' called Sanchez, without looking back. 'We are not parting forever. This is another village in the middle of nowhere and we cannot escape running into each other. When people here say the world is a small place – they mean it.'

'He's right,' said Captain Mostert. 'You'll see him in the mess later. Come into my kingdom.'

She opened the door into the grey, rusting nissen hut. Joshua shook his head, tugged at his nose and followed. 'I'll get the beers in,' he called. Sanchez raised his hand in acknowledgment.

*

'This is the Intelligence Section,' she said, waving an arm airily at a room full of desks and typewriters, behind which sat two or three silent, concentrating people. Above them a single ceiling fan ineffectually rotated, while the machines clacked and the paper ruffled in the weak breeze. Along the wall were arrayed a series of maps replete with coloured pins and aerial photographs, while notice boards and blackboards displayed organisational charts, unit strengths and scribbled unresolved hypotheses. Below them on pieces of fraying string dangled books and banda sheets, logs, pencils and set squares. 'The brains of the operation. Top Secret. This is where we fight the MPLA, FAPLA, the ANC, MK, PAC, SWAPO, PLAN, the Cubans, the DDR and the Soviets.'

'Jeez,' said Joshua. 'There's a whole alphabet of enemies.'

'No 'U',' replied Mostert, with a smile.

'UNITA?'

'No, they're on our side now. They used to be Maoists but the communists *donnered* them so now they're something else. Mind you, once Rhodesia becomes *Zimbabwe*, it'll be a fair A-Z. Especially if you throw in the Swedish Council of Churches; never mind our own, home-grown opposition.'

'And they all know about this war? I thought it was Top Secret.'

'It is.'

'What's to stop me blabbing it to our own newspapers then?' Smith asked.

'Don't worry. Believe me, if you tried to defect to SWAPO with all this neatly packed up in a suitcase, our Ovambo trackers would run you down before you got ten kilometres.'

'Is that what Merriman was doing when you picked him up, do you think?'

'*Ag*, if you want to find out what Merriman was doing heading our way,' she replied, raising an eyebrow like a patient teacher. 'Then you must look in the Personnel Forms. He must know someone here.'

'He might just have been deserting.'

'Then why head north-west, rather than east towards Botswana or south to Windhoek?'

She had a point, conceded Joshua later, as he began to plough through the files. Merriman had not bolted east, south or even directly north towards the Angolan border and enemy lines. He had headed for 23, which was an unlikely source of refuge, and unless he was hoping to be picked up by a random SWAPO patrol, he must have known that he would be recaptured within a very short time. If Colonel Dietz was right about Merriman having an accomplice -

and if his own growing conviction that Merriman was the murderer was correct – then it was possible the accomplice was in 23. CSM Landsberg had said Lieutenant Keay had been double tapped from a distance, which indicated a 23 soldier had done it, and the look of surprise on Merriman's face when he found out about that last murder, meant that he had drawn his own conclusions about the identity of the killer. The evidence pointed northwest towards the filing cabinets of 23 and here he was among them.

'Good luck,' said Captain Mostert, rapping her knuckles on the nearest grey cabinet and pulling the top drawer open. 'Let me know if you find anything.'

'Thanks,' replied Joshua. 'Is there coffee here?'

She smiled and pointed at an urn at the end of the hut.

'Help yourself,' she said, heading for the door. 'I'll be in the Officer's Mess.'

'I'll let you know when I find something then,' he said, under his breath. 'And make mine a Klippie and coke. It's alright for some.'

One of the silent, concentrating people looked up as the door closed. He gave Joshua a vulpine grin made more alarming by the eye patch above it.

'It's alright for Lieutenant Visser,' said the Eye-patch. 'Lucky bastard.'

Joshua opened up the filing cabinet and pulled out a handful of folders.

'Story of my life,' he replied. 'Only shit things ever happen to me.'

'Boo hoo,' replied the Eye-patch, grinning again. 'Boo hoo.'

Joshua started with the white mercenaries, seeking by process of elimination to exclude them from the investigation on the grounds that a *poes kaffirboetie* surfer like Merriman would be unlikely to choose them as his bosom pals. They were a slippery bunch, with gaps in their records that sometimes looked suspiciously like time spent at Her Rooinek Majesty's Pleasure or breaking rocks in a Texas penitentiary. Some had names that were ludicrously false – he was tolerably sure that D.O. Wellington, H. Nelson and G.A Custer could only be construed as *noms de guerre*. Others still had gaps that stank of time spent doing things best forgotten in places best forgotten; Smith had heard all the stories of what mercenaries had got up to in the Congo, Angola and just about anywhere else that the British, French, Portuguese or Belgians had abandoned to post-colonial chaos. There was nothing to connect them to Merriman though. Even the Rhodesian files, where there might conceivably be a family connection, turned a blank.

Ditto the South Africans. Of course there were officers and NCOs from the Cape and Cape Town, but there was nothing obvious to connect them to Merriman. Ditto the South African blacks, which he was surprised to find in the ranks of 23 as soldiers rather than cooks, cleaners and labourers. What the Broederbond or the ANC would make of this was beyond him. As to the bulk of the 23 blacks, the old *Frente Nacional de Libertação de Angola*, he could find no link at all.

There were six hundred files to get through and after five blank hours, he decided to call it a day and join Sanchez for a drink. He needed to clear his head and come up with better ideas than the ones he was having or Colonel Dietz's rankling accusation would turn out to be justified. *Do you have any idea about how to conduct an investigation?* Although Joshua had not graduated from the Police Academy at the very top of the class, he had not failed the course either and he was beginning to feel that matters of professional pride were at stake, especially as he was a copper surrounded by soldiers. But then, catching his reflection in the window the question that he had been avoiding, the real question, the question that had been lurking in the background ever since he had seen old Buyisiwe murdered by Titch Janssens intruded on him again; *do I really want to jail those who killed these broederbond bastards?*

Above him, he could hear the steady needle drill whine of mosquitoes circling in the darkness and from outside he could hear the chirping of the cicadas filling the night. Eye-patch and the others had long since knocked off and there was no other sound but his own breathing and the sound of his own pulse slowly pushing the blood around his unredeemed self. He was here, he told himself, because of an Apartheid system that had always seemed alien to him, right from the beginning. It was why his parents were divorced and he had been taken from District 6 in Cape Town to Krugerburg. It was why there was a war. It was why he had joined the police. It was why he had been sent to Police Post 156. It was why he had been sent up to Oshadangwa and it was why he had been bombed, threatened, almost murdered. It was why he could make no plans beyond reaching his next birthday and adding another notch to the twenty five already there. And he was only here, now, because a black man had saved him.

His mind went back to what Konstabel Williams had told him to up on Spandau Kop; *don't be a thug – solve crimes and catch criminals.* This was pretty much what Sanchez had said - or something like it; the law was the essential thing about civilisation and only by adhering to a lawful order could South Africa be saved from the coming wrath. He also remembered a lecture on something along these lines in Police College and wished he had paid more attention; it had only been a short one, he excused himself, and the day had been hot. The problem was that all this legal theory implied that he would have to find the killers of the three officers whether he wanted to or not, because whoever had killed them had killed them unlawfully. They might be horrible; they might be pro-Apartheid; their families might be *Broederbond;* but none of that meant they were not outside the protection of the law.

He threw his pencil down, closed up the files, winced at the tug of one of his stitches and went in search of the canteen, trying not to think at all.

Corporal Sanchez was eating *galina africana* and rice left handed with a spoon when Smith found him. Joshua nodded a greeting, went over to the counter and procured two tins of beer and a plate of chicken and rice before clumsily pulling up a chair to join him. It was dinner time and the long bare room echoed with the rumbling conversation of soldiers while a fug of blue smoke hung under the whitewashed wooden joists of the metal roof. Joshua reached for the salt cellar but his splinted fingers fumbled it and a good pinch poured out onto the table. He took a little and threw it over his left shoulder.

'You are a superstitious man, Sergeant Smith,' said Sanchez with a hinted smile.

'Not really,' replied Joshua, sweeping the rest of the salt up and sprinkling it on his chicken stew. 'It's just bad luck not to do it.'

Sanchez gave a little laugh. 'So what is the difference between luck and superstition then?'

'Search me,' replied Joshua. 'It's probably something to do with religion.'

'Did you study the concept of probability at school, Sergeant Smith?'

'What? No. What is it?'

'It is the reasonable assumption that *ceteris paribus*...'

'What's that?'

'It is the reasonable assumption,' continued Sanchez with exaggerated patience. 'That, all other things remaining equal, a coin tossed in the air one hundred times, will fall on Heads or Tails an equal number of times. So, armed with this idea, we can say that good luck is when you call 'Heads' and it lands fifty five times out of a hundred in your favour; and bad luck is when it lands only forty five times in your favour.'

'I once called 'side' in a toss up before a match,' said Joshua.

'What happened?'

'I got sent off before the game even began.'

'That is bad luck indeed,' laughed Sanchez.

'Not really,' replied Joshua, taking a mouthful of stew. 'It was my own stupidity and cheek - but I always thought that it was an original way to beat the odds, you know; by thinking a little differently.'

'By thinking *laterally*,' corrected Sanchez. 'Are you familiar with the idea that if everyone in the world was reduced to half size then the world would be four times bigger?'

'That is fucked up however lateral it is,' answered Joshua.

Sanchez smiled again. 'Are you any nearer to bringing your suspects to justice?' he said, slowly chewing the stew on the left side of his mouth. There was a a spot of dried blood on the right hand side where one of the stitches had worked loose.

Joshua cracked open the two cans of *Castle* before shaking his head. 'There's nothing here about Strydom and nothing to suggest Merriman would find sanctuary here. Nothing that leaps to mind, at any rate.'

'Private Memfeliz report to the Company Office,' squawked the tannoy, a battered megaphone on a pole in the corner of the room.

'Jeez. Don't you hate those fucking things?' Joshua chugged on the beer. 'You'd think the *bladdy* officers could just leave you alone for a little while, hey? Just while you got your scoff down you?'

'Private Memfeliz report to the Company Office,' repeated the tannoy, with added annoyance. One or two heads looked up.

'That would be Corporal Alvarez on the tannoy,' said Sanchez, carefully scooping up more rice. 'He can sometimes be a little impatient when he has not had his food.'

'Private *Mem...*' the tannoy was cut off and Joshua turned to see a weary troopie holding the plug and flex in his hands. He held it up, took the nods of assent as permission to proceed, and pulled the plug off the flex and put it in the pocket of his fatigues. There was a weary cheer.

'Heironimo,' said the irritated troopie, to Corporal Memfeliz. 'Finish your meal and go see what Alvarez is getting his knickers in a twist for.'

'*Memfeliz*,' commented Sanchez, picking up a chicken leg as Hieronimo scraped his chair away. 'It is an odd name for a South African. But I understand there are many Portuguese in Cape Town so perhaps they have different names there. I am not an expert.'

'What does it mean?'

Sanchez shrugged. 'Nothing. *Feliz* means happy. That is all.'

'I knew a girl called 'Felicity',' said Joshua. 'I thought it meant 'lucky'.'

'You would be correct if you were referring to its Latin usage,' said Sanchez, taking the salt and sprinkling it on his food.

'*Heironimo Memfeliz*,' said Joshua, rolling it around his mouth. 'You know I love foriegn sounding names. They always seem to sound better than just plain old *Joshua Smith;* and Afrikaaner names like *Gertrude Bezoudenhout* sound like I'm about to spit. *Heironimo Memfeliz* – that has a certain ring to it, like it should belong to a flamingo dancer or something.'

'*Flamenco*,' corrected Sanchez, sucking on a bone. 'It is pronounced *flamenco* not *flamingo.*'

Joshua took another pull on the beer. 'And he should have a really grand middle name, like maybe *Rodrigo* or *Fabio*. Nothing common like *Pedro* or *Carlo*.'

'My name is Pedro Carlo Sanchez,' smiled Sanchez. 'Corporal P.C. Sanchez, *Douter em Filosofia*. And his middle name is Ortez.'

'Sorry,' laughed Joshua. 'I didn't know. But look, it is still the same, what I say. *Heironimo Ortez Memfeliz. H.O. Memfeliz* – now that is a name to put in lights over a playhouse, eh?'

He reached for the second *Castle*, presuming that as Sanchez hadn't touched it, he didn't want it.

'*H.O. Memfeliz,*' repeated Sanchez, carefully.

'That's the one,' confirmed Joshua. 'What?'

Sanchez looked straight at him.

'*H.O. Memfeliz* – put the words together and you have 'Homem Feliz'; Happy Man.'

'A lucky name,' said Joshua, taking another swig.

'Or perhaps a *Merry man,*' said Sanchez.

'Fuck me,' said Joshua, the can poised in front of his face as the hairs on his arms stood up. 'Merriman.'

*

Captain Mostert was still in her uniform when Joshua called her out from the Officers Mess and although Joshua could smell brandy and coke on her, she wasn't drunk and had not had enough to displace the freshness of her perfume.

'You think you got a lead?' she said, thoughtfully.

Joshua noticed that her military blouse was open just one button lower than the regulations advised and that she was a little flushed. He waited for her to put her hair back up into the pony-tail before telling her of Sanchez's potential breakthrough.

'Let's take another look at the Personnel Files,' she said, fastening up the button on her blouse and smoothing her trousers down.. 'It might be a false name but I cannot put Memfeliz under arrest straight away. I think he's due out on Ops in a couple of days anyway, so he isn't going anywhere.'

'Will he be going with Lieutenant Visser?' asked Joshua, slyly.

'He's in his platoon,' asked Captain Mostert with a sniff. 'Why do you ask?'

'Just wondered,' answered Joshua.

She took up her beret and briefcase from a polished table just inside the door and led the way back to the Intelligence Section, her hips swaying gracefully in the gloaming. Joshua dandled along like a still hopeful dog, intoxicated by the blend of perfume and alcohol, thinking of all the brandy and cokes and all the hoolyjuice that he had drunk with girls just like her on glorious beaches, at braais and on green lawns, striped for tennis. She was willowy, just as he liked women to be, and he was certain she had had the trousers tailored to fit tightly across her perfect, heart shaped bottom.

'Keep this knowledge to yourself, Sergeant. No-one but us knows we're here,' she ordered, unlocking the door, pushing it open, ignoring the main light and switching on a lamp on the nearest desk. For a moment Joshua had a memory of being led into a bowls club pavilion not disimilar to this hut, but for a very different reason. He shook his head to clear it. 'Pull his file out,' she said.

Joshua fumbled through the manilla until he found the one marked *H.O. Memfeliz* and handed the folder to her. She took it gently, laid it on the desk and invited him to come closer, so that they could read side by side. He felt the blood begin to pound in his heart and ran a finger around his itchy collar.

'It's OK, Sergeant Smith. I'm not going to pounce on you,' she said.

'Feel free,' he answered and came closer to peer at the document. There was the usual poor quality, much reproduced passport photo showing the dark complexion and wiry hair common to those classified as Cape Coloured. There was a wide mouth there too and stark eyes that though colourless in monochrome, stood out as unusually determined. Joshua scanned on through to the personal details.

'Fuck me. No, sorry,' he said, looking at Captain Mostert and flustering. He jabbed his finger at the top of the document. 'There; June 6th 1955– same date of birth as Merriman. Do you think they are twins?'

'Memfeliz is Cape Coloured,' replied Captain Mostert, giving him a sideways glance. 'But if I was to give a false date of birth, it would have to be one that I remembered easily, so a brother is possible.'

'Place of Birth is given as Girassol, Benguela,' said Joshua, moving his finger down the page. 'There is a place called Benguela in Angola, but I never heard of Girassol.'

'*Benguela* is also the name of the ocean current off Cape Town,' she said. 'Father's occupation?'

'Doctor,' replied Joshua, looking up thoughtfully.

'As in the wind that blows through Cape Town in Spring – 'the Cape Doctor',' answered Mostert.

'Mother's occupation is given as 'Nurse'.' Joshua paused, and pushed his finger back up the page. 'What's *Girassol* mean? I mean *sol* is, like, *sun* in a lot of languages.'

Mostert put her hand to her forehead remembering her Portuguese.

'It's portuguse for *Sunflower*,' she answered. 'Yes, definitely. *Sunflower*.'

'*Zonnenbloem*,' said Joshua, pulling out the chair and sitting heavily on it. 'District 6. The cocky bastard. They are definitely related. There is no question that this is a coincidence.'

'So Memfeliz is maybe a half-brother, do you think? Or a touch of the tar brush in an otherwise shiny white family tree?'

'It's possible,' conceded Joshua. 'David Merriman's mother was Black Sash so perhaps she liked black...other black things too.' He coughed.

'Ja,' she replied. 'Those religious housewives screw black buck like rabbits. They get all holy and righteous and worked up so much that they need a good rogering to calm them down. How do you think we have *coloureds* in the first place?'

'But it's not allowed,' said Joshua. 'I mean...'

'When did 'not allowed' deter anyone from screwing?' she said, removing her beret.

The phone rang. Joshua looked at it for a moment, willing it to stop.

'Kak,' said Mostert.

She went over to the next desk and picked up the reciever.

Yes, Sir. I understand,' she said, calmly, after a while. 'No arrest until you say so. Yes, Sir, it's crystal clear.'

She put the phone down and did that wriggle that women do when their bras aren't fitting correctly.

'Have you got a cigarette?'

'That the Colonel?'

She nodded, took the pack and matches and then slipped one out and lit up.

'News travels fast here, hey? The CO's got wind of something already. We can't question or arrest anyone in 23 – that means Memfeliz. Not after what 41 Mech did to Sanchez and not after....' she stopped herself, inhaled deeply, then blew out a long cloud of blue smoke. 'Your reputation as a detective preceeds you, apparently. The Colonel wants hard evidence before he allows an arrest.'

'We're never going to get one then,' replied Joshua petulently.

'And you have to be off the base first thing tomorrow,' she added, blowing a smoke ring and flicking her hair back.

06

The Uncertainties of Confessions illicited by Torture

25th May 1980

'So Memfeliz was sent on Ops last night,' said Joshua, climbing into the Buffel carefully and knocking on the cab roof for the driver to start up. The Colonel had meant what he said and two soldiers had been sent over to ensure that he was up, washed, shaved, newly bandaged, breakfasted and then posted back to 41 Mech and Oshadangwa before the sun was over the fence line. 'I heard the helicopters going at first light. Was that a coincidence or was the operation brought forward by accident?'

'No coincidence at all,' she replied, climbing in as the engine started up. 'I tell you, 23 looks after its own. They don't care if you've got a questionable past as long as you loyal to the battalion. Actually, a questionable past might be an entrance qualification. He's been sent into the bush to hide from us.'

'Us?' said Joshua. The vehicle grumbled and began to roll forward. Joshua slammed the rear door closed.

'You, mainly I guess,' said Captain Mostert, taking hold of the bar above them once more. 'But the Colonel wants me to stay on the case because of Lieutenant Keay's death. I'm to report directly to him.'

'You are spying on me,' said Joshua.

'Are you surprised?' she said. The vehicle gathered speed and grunted up through the lines toward the gate, the open veldt and the morning sun. 'Whatever it is, Memfeliz has to wait until we talk to Merriman again.'

As they slowed up at the guardroom, much to his surprise, Joshua saw Sanchez, as smartly half dressed as bandages and splints would allow, holding a clipboard and waving them through. Joshua gave him a polite wave and a big grin as they drove past onto the track to which Sanchez responded by holding up the clipboard up in acknowledgement and calling out 'light duties' as though it was an excuse.

'Will he be OK?' Joshua asked.

'Like I say,' Captain Mostert replied. '23 looks after its own.'

Out on the salt road heading back to Oshadangwa, the stasis of military travel descended quickly and within an hour the distance of rank had fallen away. Joshua lit cigarettes for them and Hopkirk the driver, while Captain Mostert poured hot tea from a flask into a shared cup. It was a fine blue day against the white of the road and as the engine settled down into a steady whine and rumble, so Captain Mostert began to hum quietly to herself. She took off her beret and tucked it into her epaulette, the better to enjoy the golden light, the warm morning wind and the clear air of Africa run through her hair.

'What's the tune?' asked Joshua, eyeing her hips and noticing for the first time the pistol that sat on the right one.

'It's called *Ride to Agadir*. The guys sing it when they get together after they've had a tough fight. Do you know it? It's by a guy called Mike Batt.'

Joshua shook his head. 'I've heard of the Wombles though.'

'Will I sing it for you?'

'Please do,' he said.

Letting the hair out of her pony-tail, she looked out to the north and tilting her head back, sang the words in a sweet wavering soprano, a small brave voice against the run of the motor. She sang as though she had heard the song being sung by men who had killed and suffered loss and although the words were warlike, they carried with them a longing sadness, a regretfulness that war was the lot of the singers, and a wish for peace and farms and families. It was an odd song for the Christian soldiers of Apartheid to be singing but there was something in the way the tune rose and fell that spoke to the sea vistas of the Cape, the deserts of the North West, the wide veldt of the Free State, the spears of the Drakensburg mountains and the forests of Angola, so that each soldier felt a connection with it and with the other soldiers singing it. It was a song that was much bigger than its words and music, a song that had left its composer far behind and taken on life and meaning of its own. It was a song that contained silence and dreams and the stillness that comes from forgiveness and forgetting when the times of trial were over and Joshua was mesmerised as much by the promise of such things as by the impossibility of him ever achieving them.

On the Atlas mountain foothills leading down to Marrakesh,

For Mohammed and Morroco,

We have taken up our guns

For the ashes of our fathers and the children of our sons.

Though they were waiting,

And they were fifty to our ten,

They were easily outnumbered by a smaller force of men.

She finished the song and Joshua saw that the sounds and the words and the silences and the portents had transported her back to her wine farm and forward to a future of galleries and paintings. He waited for her to return, which she did, with a shy smile, a little embarassed to have let her guard down so much.

'Do you think that's how long this war is going to last?' asked Joshua.

'How am I supposed to know?'she said, too quickly, too snappily, closing up the chink in her armour. 'I'm doing service the same as you. They don't consult me on a regular basis,' she drew the hair aside from her face. 'I just want to get it over with.'

Joshua nodded in sympathy.

'Why did you join? I thought it wasn't compulsory for girls.'

'It isn't. But it's a good career move. I have no intention of just sitting around like a good *boerefrau*, waiting out my life in a sewing circle and a baby shower. If I want to have my own business, I have to convince people with money that I can really manage people and achieve things, so this is what I am doing.'

'Is this a Women's Lib thing?' asked Smith, watching a flight of egrets scatter out of baobab tree.

'Ja,' she said. 'Something like that.'

'Does this mean you have burnt your bra?' He winked as she gave him a Captain's stare.

'No it does not.' She rolled her shoulders. 'But I wish I had bought a better one. Do you know there isn't a decent bra between here and Pretoria? Not since SWAPO put that bomb in Woolworths in Windhoek. Why did you join up?'

'It just seemed like a good idea at the time,' replied Joshua, turning away. 'I didn't have the money for further ed after Matric, so I thought I'd join the SAPS,' he said, trying to sound nonchalant. 'That way, I would have better pay than the army and get a career too.'

'That it?' she said.

'That's it,' replied Joshua.

She gave him the briefest of looks. 'Light some skyfs up,' she said, and turned away.

The Buffels was running straight now, with the high pitched hum of heavy tyres on tarmac instead of the hiss and rattle of the salt road, and Joshua was happy when an ostrich started out of the bush and began to pace alongside them the road, as though it was a dog chasing a car. Hopkirk, the driver, began to indulge it, sometimes slowing down so that it could overtake and sometimes veering off the road to try to get closer to it.

'They are such ugly things,' cried out Captain Mostert, smiling again. 'Always looking startled like they have been goosed by a cheeky boy.'

They had not spoken for an hour or more and Joshua regretted that he had been so abrupt. He seized on the opportunity for more conversation and answered quickly.

'Yeah, but you got to be careful of them,' he agreed. 'We have wild ones all around the roads in the Karoo and if they give you a kick then you are in trouble, hey? Some of the farmers are using them as guard dogs these days. Look at that fellow go!'

The large male bird was jogging in its ungainly way, building up its speed gradually, stepping high like a marathon runner upping the pace to break the following pack.

'That one looks like that ballet dancer in the Disney movie,' said Captain Mostert, laughing at its ugly, plucked thighs. 'How come you got posted to South West Africa?'

'Ja,' laughed Joshua, catching the question. 'Or a burlesque dancer chasing the gin. It just worked out that way; South West Africa, I mean.'

Hopkirk slowed as he drew alongside it and then braked heavily as the great feather duster jinked right in front of the vehicle and sped ahead onto the patch of salt road where the tarmac gave out again.

'They don't like the tarmac for some reason,' called out Joshua. 'Maybe it sticks to their toes when it gets hot. Boy he's really moving.'

There was a hiss and crackle from the radio, and Mostert leaned it to hear it. A moment later she was banging on the cab roof and telling Hopkirk to follow in the direction of the ostrich.

'The Colonel likes ostrich fillet,' she explained, drawing out the pistol from the holster on her thigh. 'Take me in as close as you can get before it goes deep into the bush.'

The ground here was rocky and the sun, rising up into a wide cornflower blue sky, had already parched the green out of the grass, but there were still large patches of thorn, still lush from the rainy season and gathering around the wet *vleis*. Some of the trees seemed to exist in two parts, with a thick lower skirt and a luxuriant upper level, joined together by a trunk stripped naked by the mid-level grazers.

'You'll find lion in the shade of those bottoms,' said Joshua, as the vehicle rattled across a patch of white gravel. He ducked as it whipped through a band of stunted trees, then winced as it bounced through the ruts of a drying out stream, rattling his ribs. 'And sometimes leopard up above. What did they want on the radio?'

The ostrich jinked again, as though it suspected that the nature of the game had changed and Mostert rapped her knuckles on the cab roof again.

'Step on it, will you? You drive like my granny.'

Joshua gave a wry smile.

'Are you going to try out for the rugby team too?'

'What?' She was concentrating on the pistol in her hand, trying to draw a bead on the ostrich as it banked left, almost making a u-turn. 'Are you some kind of game ranger in real life?'

The Buffels braked hard and slewed around to the right catching Joshua off balance and sending him hard against the side of the truck.

'Shit,' he winced. 'That was my rib.'

'What?' she shouted as she let off a shot at the ostrich, which banked right now and began to stretch out for a line of denser bush two hundred meters ahead. 'What? I thought these birds were supposed to bury their head in the sand at the first sign of danger?' She cracked off another bullet, missing a second time.

Joshua pressed his right hand to his ribs and held his breath as the vehicle charged forward.

'This guy can really run.' She braced her legs wide apart, trying for a better stance, and put both hands on the gun.

'Just try not to hit any giraffe, hey? They like this kind of bush.'

'Giraffe? What does it taste like?'

'Please. Do not shoot a giraffe.'

She let off another shot and pursed her lips. 'My eye must be out this morning.'

'Do you hunt back home?' asked Joshua, as the driver swung left again, trying to anticipate the ostrich's next move.

'Only the baboons when they come down for the grapes at harvest time,' she replied. 'Other than that it's easier to get meat from the shop.'

*

26th May 1980

'Ja, the ice machine has packed up again,' said the medic as he checked over Joshua's bandages, shaking his head in quick dismissal. 'The kaffir who is supposed to mend it is locked up in the wire compound refusing to work on. He says there is a part needed but he cannot get it because of the sanctions, which is bullshit, I say. He's just pissed off about being locked up but what can we do, hey? I'm not a frigo repair man, am I?'

'Has no-one sent the bodies back to Pretoria?' asked Joshua, wrinkling his nose and gagging slightly.

'We waiting for paperwork. Dietz and Steyl, their pappies are in the hospital, I think, still. Keay, we still waiting to hear from the family.'

'Are they rich?'

The medic scribbled on his clipboard. 'Which of them are not?'

As if on cue, the door opened and a black orderly with a scarf tied around his face entered. He went over to the door connecting the ward to the makeshift morgue, pushed it open a fraction and poured in half a bucket a disinfectant before quickly closing it again. A cloud of fat flies spurted out from under the door jamb and then fizzed there, tormenting themselves to find a way back in.

'Jeez,' said Captain Mostert, helping Smith up. 'I think a little fresh air would do you good. You still looking a little pale.'

'I'm fine, really,' replied Smith. 'I laced my own boots up this morning. It only took me three goes.'

'Well you have a nice day, now,' said the medic. 'You might feel a little like a *krimpie* still for a while, but that is because of the bruises, and this will pass.'

Outside in the bright sunlight and warm air, the smell of Dietz, Steyl and Keay was still strong and although the temperature was only in the low twenties, both Joshua and Captain Mostert knew that there were probably another ten degrees in the day before late afternoon.

'Van der Merwe wants to see us,' she said, heading in the direction of the Company office. 'Look, I think it's better not to mention Merriman's possible brother, just now. It can only complicate things.'

'If your CO has any sense he will have sent H.O. Memfeliz very deep into the bush by now,' replied Joshua, still fuzzy. 'Do you know if Lieutenant Keay was connected to the *Broederbond* at all?'

There was a falter in her step.

'The *Broederbond* are involved?'

'Dietz and Steyl were both connected.'

'This is not good news. Look, Sergeant Smith,' she said, coming to a halt. 'I have nearly *kaked* myself out there in contacts with SWAPO, but I am a lot, and I mean, *a lot*, more afraid of the *Broederbond*. And I will tell you that if the Colonel hears they are involved then he will send Memfeliz a million miles away with a million bucks and a new passport to keep him out of their hands. I told you, the CO's brother is in the *tronk* for being anti-Apartheid? Ja? Well he is loyal to his family and to his regiment and to his country but he is *not* National Party. He is fighting *against* communism, not *for* Apartheid, hey?'

'You afraid of being caught between the devil and the deep blue sea then?'

'Isn't this how we all live in South Africa now? If we choose to go with the blacks we get communism and if we stick with our own kind we get the National Party.'

'Is this why you do not want to tell van der Merwe about Memfeliz?' said Joshua.

Their attention was distracted by the sound of urgent hammering coming from the rebuilding of the Company office up ahead. As they turned a corner, Joshua saw a third plywood wall being fitted into place behind Major van der Merwe as he sat at a trestle table animatedly talking on the phone. Up above were two black men in blue overalls re-thatching the roof with grey reeds, as though it was the silverback of a large gorilla.

'The last thing we need is someone like Strydom in 41 Mech starting up a private bush war with 23, hey?' said Mostert. 'And do you want to be in the middle if my CO and Colonel Malan take it into their heads to get tribal? So too, if we are going to question Merriman about this half-brother, then we should not let it leak out to other people.'

Joshua sucked his teeth for a moment and considered his Police issue shirt. It was still not brown enough for the army.

'You are right. And loose lips sink ships,' he agreed. 'There's CSM Landsberg now.'

He was standing like a caryatid at the front right corner of the building, his lanyard perfectly laid through his epaulette and his shirt pressed, starched and clean, toe-caps shined and stick in hand, as though he were about to take a parade.

'Major van der Merwe wants to see us,'said Mostert.

'Indeed he does, Ma'am,' replied Landsberg, saluting. 'If you and Sherlock Holmes would like to go straight in, Ma'am – and pardon me but the door has not been replaced yet – Sergeant Smith, you will be billed for it as you broke it – just joking. In you go, Ma'am.'

Joshua followed her and went through the door to stand side by side, in front of the trestle table. Major van der Merwe was frowning into the telephone.

'And there is no way we can bury them and disinter them later?'

He acknowledged them with a half salute.

'Well, when *can* I get an answer?'

Van der Merwe's brow darkened. The cloying, sickly odour was sticking to the back of his throat, causing him to be on the permanent edge of a retch.

'Well tell the *bladdy* airforce to buy some disinfectant. You think I should drive them all the way back to Pretoria in a backie?'

Joshua shot a veiled glance at Landsberg, who responded with an almost imperceptible shake of his head. Van der Merwe slammed the phone back in its cradle and took a deep breath.

'You know you could wash them over with petrol,' offered Joshua. 'It will keep the flies down for a little while.'

'Thank you,' replied the Major, tightly. His face was shaded by the rising plywood, but Joshua could still make out a thin white line of frustration on his lips. 'Did you find out what Merriman was up to on the road? Did 23 tell you anything about that?'

'We have some leads, sure...' began Smith.

'... but they are tentative, just provisional, Sir,' broke in Mostert. 'And we must just talk to Merriman once more, if we may, Sir.'

Van der Merwe sniffed.

'And what is your interest in this now that you have reclaimed Corporal Sanchez, may I ask?'

'There may be an intelligence angle to this, Sir,' she replied, looking down. 'Three officers dead, Sir. It looks suspicious.'

Van der Merwe looked unimpressed.

'*Suspicious*?' said van der Merwe, tersely. 'And you think we have spies here in our ranks?'

'That isn't our priority,' she replied. 'The enemy get everything they need from the blacks here,' she replied.

Van der Merwe looked up at the two men thatching the roof.

'Not them,' said Landsberg. 'They are POWs.'

'I'm sorry, I didn't hear you right,' said Joshua. 'Did you say POWs?'

'Prisoners of War,' confirmed Landsberg. 'Tough men, good bushcraft but badly trained and led by terrible officers. When we picked these two *laities* up by the Cut Line they were barefoot, riddled with the clap, sweating with malaria and looking at a 300 klick walk back to Xangongo. They hadn't eaten in a week, so we made them an offer they couldn't refuse.'

'Which was?'

'A job with regular pay and as much mealiepap as they could eat.'

'And that was enough?' said Joshua, looking up at the diligent, impassive faces peering down at him.

'What more do these chaps want?' answered Landsberg.

'Do you think you can get this case wrapped up soon, Captain?' said van der Merwe, impatiently.

Joshua noted the irritation in van der Merwe's voice and wondered if there was more to it than the sweet smell of bodies. He also noted that the Major had not once looked directly at CSM Landsberg but he could make no further observations because outside, two more POWs were lifting up the last plywood wall ready to fit it into place passing nails from mouth to hands and drawing hammers from loops in their overalls. They hefted up the wall as though the white men were invisible, entombing them as the dark filled the room. The only light left came from the blue sky seen through the partial thatch and the rectangle of haze coming through the hole where the door used to be. It was like being in a coffin, thought Joshua as the workers began to hammer in the nails.

'Ja, things are progressing,' said Captain Mostert. 'Is it OK to go talk with Merriman just now?'

Van der Merwe stroked the mole on his cheek and waited for the hammering to stop.

'Petrol, you say?'

Ja, or vinegar,' confirmed Joshua. 'It has the same pickling effect as when you prepare biltong. Just tell the *joller* that he must not smoke while he is working.'

Van der Merwe picked up the telephone once more. 'Alright, do what you must,' he said, dialling.

*

'Petrol,' said Landsberg as they walked across the square to the jail.

'Biltong?' echoed Mostert.

'Begging your pardon, Ma'am,' continued the CSM. 'But this copper is a *p...* a *mompie.*'

The sickly smell from the infirmary was still detectable over the smell of oil, hot rubber and grease coming from the Ratels. Smith smiled out of the corner of his mouth.

'Ja, maybe not my finest hour. But it works. And you watch – there'll be no vinegar for the chips for a week. How is Merriman?'

'A little more subdued than before.'

'Do you think he has thought better of his ways?' asked Joshua, facetiously.

'I doubt it,' replied Landsberg, striding out and running his eyes across the *troupies* at work. 'He's quieter because I kicked the shit out of him for deserting. Pardon my language, Ma'am. Hofmeyer! Fix that mounting before you try to attach the wheel. Did I not send you to school to learn such useful things?'

'Sorry CSM. I am a *poes*,' replied Hofmeyer, wiping down the axle. 'Sorry Ma'am. I didn't see you there.'

'Indeed you are,' said Landsberg.

'Carry on,' echoed Mostert.

'Good man,' added Joshua.

'*Mompie*,' said Landsberg, eyeing Joshua.

'You beat the shit out of Merriman?' said Joshua. 'How did van der Merwe feel about that, he being all for things done in a legal fashion?'

'He is not happy,' replied Landsberg, unconcernedly. 'But there are some things that NCOs are required to do to preserve the honour of the regiment even if it means putting up with a bollocking from time to time.'

The guard was changing as they approached the jailhouse and Joshua watched as the two Corporals there made a show of saluting, handing over the watchbook and generally acting in a manner calculated to produce an impression of stiff military bearing for the approaching party. As he came closer, he noticed a ground out cigarette butt just behind the newly erected and carefully painted sentry box, which had also gained an array of white washed stones in front, like rounded milk teeth.

'Morning Sergeant Major, Sir!' said one of the Corporals, stamping to attention.

'Morning, Corporal Mason,' replied Landsberg, touching his stick to the peak of his cap. 'How are the chimps this morning?'

'Strydom is still under restraint and Merriman is still under the weather, CSM,' barked Mason stiffly, the clean nostrils of his sharp nose clearly delineated by the backward tilt of his alert head.

'Strydom: under restraint?' asked Joshua.

'We have kept him chained up these past days,' explained Landsberg. 'We are not sure if he is a hero or a momping great villain yet and he, himself, has even less idea.' He turned back to Corporal Mason. 'Has he not gone to his shithouse duties yet?'

'He is going just as soon as I have handed over to Corporal James, here, Sir.'

'Good man. Carry on Corporal James, then. Take our very own Missing Link to the honeybuckets, there's a good man. That just leaves Merriman,' he continued, as the Corporals went about their duties. 'Do you want me to sit in with you?'

'I'm sure you have more important things to do CSM,' replied Mostert, rather coldly. 'I think we can handle this from here.'

'Very well, Ma'am. As you wish,' he touched his stick to his hat once more. 'But do not hesitate to call on me if you decide young Merriman needs another kicking.'

'I am sure he has learned a suitable humility at your capable feet,' said Mostert. 'And Sergeant Smith here can fill in any gaps in his education, if necessary.'

They focussed for a moment on the sight of CSM Landsberg's square, creased departing back and then on the tinkling sound of keys from inside the jail and the answering bass protests of Kassie Strydom being led to his daily bread. The big, mulish figure emerged blinking into the light, his handcuffed hands holding a mop and a bucket, awkwardly, as though he was in danger of tripping over them. As he caught sight of them, he pulled away from the escorting Corporal and Joshua smiled as his beetling brows came down first and then shot up as the idea of appealing to the two non-41 Mech personnel woke him up like pink grapefruit for breakfast.

'Hey! Hey! Mister SAPS, Sergeant! Miss!' he called out, a wheedling look of hurt replacing his *eureka* moment. 'Please! Is this any way to treat a human being? I mean, they treating me like a kaffir *sommer* and making me clean the bogs.'

'I thought you were used to shovelling shit,' scoffed Corporal James. 'You're a farmer.'

'Ja, but that is animal shit and so it is good fertilizer,' protested Strydom. 'It's the kaffirs' job to clean up human shit.'

'Really? Well why don't you make a complaint to the Colonel, eh?' sniggered the Corporal, giving Strydom a shove in the small of his back. 'Sorry about this, Ma'am.'

'Ja, it's not fair,' whined Strydom, clattering the mop against the galvanised tin bucket as he moved on, head down. 'It is *fokken swak.*'

'Have you done any interrogations?' Joshua asked as Strydom clanked off.

She shook her head.

'The guys do them. I just collate the info and write up the reports.'

Joshua looked at her and wondered if she knew what happened to prisoners interrogated by the military and police authorities in South West Africa. He decided not to ask.

'OK, well let me handle it, hey? There is an art to it, you know. You have to learn it.'

'Is it a 'good cop – bad cop' thing? One hands out a beer while the other beats him up?'

'No, I'm not big on torture actually. It's more about getting the suspect's co-operation so he incriminates himself,' said Joshua. 'It's very manipulative and can look a bit unfair to the untrained eye.'

'How so?'

'Well, we make things up sometimes and see how they react. Or we watch their reactions when we ask them basic questions,' explained Joshua. 'It's like, well, sometimes if we ask a suspect a question and their eyes go up to the right, it means they are remembering something; if they look down to the left, it usually means they are thinking up a lie.'

'Is it?' she said.

'Ja. I know there is doubt in your voice but this is something that is true.'

'Any other trade secrets?'

'Lots. Just let me do the talking, hey?'

She took off her beret and put it under her epaulette.

'My CO needs cast iron answers. This, he will insist on.'

Joshua tilted his head to one side. 'Then we must have a confession.'

'No torture,' she said. 'No torture, understand?'

Joshua doubted his ability to conduct an interrogation without some form of violence. It was true he disliked the really heavy types of torture that he had witnessed, like electrocution or cigarette burnings, but even Konstabel Williams had been known to slap a suspect or two. Sure, it was supposed to be a case of 'innocent until proved guilty' but there wasn't a copper in the SAPS who believed this for one moment. Most of the time the 'innocent' were as guilty as hell and the easiest way to get them to admit it was to hit them with a sjambok a couple of times. Even if the guy was actually innocent, the technique still worked because you could tell from the way the suspect stuck to his story or not whether he was telling the truth.

'Does "no torture" mean I can't give him a little tap or two?' he asked.

'No torture,' repeated Captain Mostert. 'I mean it. I'm sick of the way you guys just seem to think it is the answer to everything.'

'OK,' said Joshua, as they went inside.

The smell of fresh paint mingled with the damp smell of stale sweat and as they looked down the row of cages for Merriman they both caught the cumin smell of biryani left over from his ratpack breakfast. He was sitting miserably on his bunk, an empty mess tin at his feet, still clutching the spoon in one handcuffed hand. His lip was split and swollen and his black eye was only one of a number of contusions, cuts and abrasions that several bouts of CSM Landsberg's punishment beatings had marked him with. His blonde hair was matted and parts of it were bloodied where it had been torn out by the roots and he sat, hunched, beaten, transformed, with none of the spark that he had challenged Joshua with last time they had met.

'They *donnered* you good, huh?' said Joshua.

Merriman looked up, recognised him and then looked away, subsiding.

'I want a lawyer,' he mumbled, as though the act of speaking involved aggravating splintered teeth.

'And I want a Jensen Interceptor,' replied Joshua.

'And I need to see the doctor. I'm pissing blood again.'

'Well look,' said Joshua, glancing at Mostert. 'You co-operate and we will see what can be done.'

'I'm not telling you anything until I've seen the doctor.'

Joshua wasn't fooled. He recognised the catch in Merriman's voice that betrayed him. He had heard it several times before in the cells back in Graaf-Reinet. It told him that the suspect was close to breaking and would soon confess.

'Look man, just tell us what you know and it will all be over.' He came closer to the bars. 'You know you want to get it off your chest.'

'I want a lawyer. You have to get me a lawyer. And a doctor.'

'If I get you to the doctor, will you give me a confession?'

'I want a lawyer.'

Joshua looked round to Captain Mostert. 'You studied law didn't you?'

She looked straight back at him and frowned.

'No torture,' mouthed Joshua

'Ja,' she said, cottoning on reluctantly. 'Ja, I will qualify when I finish my service here.'

'I want a proper lawyer,' insisted Merriman, mumbling down at the floor. His mouth was dripping a thin mixture of saliva and blood. 'Not some army *stukkie*.'

Captain Mostert's hackles came up at being referred to this way but Joshua motioned to her to cool it.

'She's all you are going to get,' he said. 'If you don't want her, then I can let her go. But she came all the way down from 23 to help you. And I will tell you that she is very pissed off at the way 41 Mech treated Corporal Sanchez, so she is as much on your side as anyone you are going to get.'

Merriman considered this for a moment before spitting out a globule of red saliva.

'I need a doctor,' he repeated.

'Ja, look,' said Joshua. 'I got you a lawyer so now you must give me something, hey? I can hardly take you to the infirmary just now while there are three Lieutenants in there rotting away and stinking the whole place down. Just tell me why you killed them, hey, and then we can talk about the doctor.'

'I don't have to say anything. I didn't do anything. And you can't prove anything,' Merriman hissed, as though the air was ice cold against a missing filling. 'You are not fooling me, really.'

'It will be easier this way in the long run,' coaxed Joshua.

'You going to beat me up more?' Merriman's voice cracked again.

'Look, I'm giving you a lawyer and a deal for the doctor.' He indicated for Captain Mostert to start moving down the corridor towards the door while Merriman's eyes were still downcast. She took the hint and, folding her arms in front of her, began to move. 'So take some time to think about this, hey?'

Merriman issued what might have been taken as either a snort or a sob.

'And you should know this,' said Joshua, dropping his voice to a conspiratorial whisper. 'The *Broederbond* are interested in this case, Merriman. Ja, I thought that might get your attention. They are interested in *you*. So the *23* Captain, the *stukkie*, who is also a lawyer, is your only very slim chance of getting any justice, hey? I'm helping you as a fellow pommie, ja? But I can only go so far. So think on it good while we go for some tea.'

*

'Good start,' declared Joshua, once they were outside. 'Now he will not be so confident. Did you see him wince when I mentioned the *Broederbond*?'

'Sergeant Smith, I am not a lawyer,' replied Captain Mostert. 'What is this bullshit?'

'*Ag*, it's just technique, like I told you and as torture is not allowed I must have some other way to soften him up. All you have to do is sit by him and nod like you know what you are doing from time to time. For now we must have a proper room for the questioning and you will be seated by his side on the other side of the table from me, like you are his friend.'

'A proper room? What's wrong with the cell?' They began to walk across the dusty road towards the canteen.

'He is like an animal in his own cage in there,' explained Joshua. 'We have to put him somewhere unfamiliar, somewhere which is our territory, not his.'

'You have an office or another place?'

'I thought you might pull rank with CSM Landsberg,' Joshua smiled. 'I think he has a soft spot for you.'

*

Two hours later, Merriman was delivered to a bleak room at the back of one of the administration blocks, scrubbed militarily bare but for three chairs, a trestle table and a bucket. There were no windows and no chinks to allow the light in and the low plywood roof made everyone who entered it stoop involuntarily as though they feared to bang their heads on the ceiling. It was almost airtight too, but the smell of the canteen mingled with the smell of the corpses found its way in, seeping through the woodwork like a ghost. Joshua was already in the room sitting on a chair behind the table directly under the weak bulb dangling from the cable overhead. Captain Mostert slipping into her role as prisoner's friend took Merriman from the guard, brought him in by the elbow and seated him carefully on the uncomfortable wooden chair. He was shuffling painfully, his hands still cuffed and his wrists chafing where the metal had rubbed the skin away. She sat down beside him and placed a sheet of paper in front of him.

'I'll get you a pencil, if you like,' she said, with a grim smile of understanding.

'Not writing anything,' Merriman muttered, showing his cuffs. 'Fucking can't.'

'No need to – yet,' declared Joshua, matter of factly. 'Let me tell you your fortune first.'

It was hot, stuffy and claustrophobic in the dim light and Joshua felt the first bead of sweat run down the inside of his shirt. He picked up the water bottle that he had brought with him, took a small sip, then screwed the cap firmly back on.

'You killed Lieutenant Dietz with a bayonet, right?'

Merriman kept his eyes on his cuffs.

'You then killed Lieutenant Steyl with two shots to the head, right?'

Merriman's eyes shifted to the paper and then back to his cuffs. He snuffled, but did not otherwise respond.

'Your accomplice...'

Merriman's eyes clicked up to meet Joshua's.

'Your accomplice then killed Company clerk Bornmann with a bomb that was probably intended for Admiral Steyl and Colonel Dietz, right?'

Merriman's eyes went up to the right and then his head turned as his eyes travelled down to the left.

'You feeling happy about Bornmann?'

Merriman looked up again. 'That was a mistake,' he mumbled.

'So you admit you have an accomplice here?'

Merriman's eyes went down to the left, then he leaned back and let out a sigh. He nodded.

'Name?'

'What does it matter?' he muttered. 'He's dead now.'

'You should tell everything now,' said Captain Mostert, gently.

'His name was Sixpence Ndwandwe?' demanded Joshua.

'I only knew his cover name.'

'Would that be 'Mopboy'?'

'It would,' said Merriman, snorting back mucus from his nose.

'So, was your accomplice involved with the murders of Lieutenant's Dietz and Steyl?'

Merriman was about to say something but then checked himself, spotting the trap before he answered.

'Well was he? Did Sixpence put you up to it?'

'I don't know anything about Dietz and Steyl,' he muttered.

'Do you need some water?' asked Joshua, holding up the bottle, and then replacing it at his feet before Merriman had time to answer. 'No? OK. Let's go on. How did you and Mopboy communicate?'

'Communicate?'

'Yes, communicate. How did you get your orders? I'm presuming he was the one in charge.'

'Oh,' said Merriman, his eyes going down to the left again. 'Ja, we passed notes to each other.'

'Where?'

'Where?'

'Where did you pass the notes? In the canteen, the shithouse? Where?'

'Just anywhere, really.'

'Just anywhere? No, you must have had a system.'

'I just passed them to him whenever I saw him,' said Merriman.

Joshua's eyebrows went up.

'So you wandered about the base and went on Ops with these notes in your pocket, just on the off-chance you might bump into him?'

'Ja,' said Merriman, snuffling.

'Bullshit,' said Joshua. 'Let's go back to when you murdered Dietz up at Chetequera, hey?'

'I told you, I didn't kill him.'

'Ja, I heard you,' replied Joshua. 'Tell me how you lost your bayonet again.'

'I can't remember. It was a hot contact.'

'And someone found it and stabbed Lieutenant Piet Dietz with it.'

Merriman shrugged. 'Wasn't me.'

'Hmm,' said Joshua. 'And I'm sure the judge will believe that. You were in his Ratel with Hofmeyer.'

'Ja.'

'Who was driving?'

'Gerrit. He always drives.'

'And you went with Dietz when you dismounted?'

'No,' said Merriman looking Joshua straight in the eyes. 'I went the opposite way to him. Ask Hofmeyer.'

'I will. Any theories on who stabbed Dietz through the heart with *your* bayonet?'

Merriman demurred. 'Like I said, it was a hot contact. There were Cubans.'

Joshua sniffed at this and scratched his armpit. 'Not broken any laws yet have I, Captain?' he asked, looking across.

'Everything is just fine,' she replied. 'Now that we know he has an accomplice we can charge him if you like.'

'Ja-Nee. I think we must ask a few more questions yet. Is this OK with you Merriman? Not feeling oppressed or anything?'

Merriman did not respond, but kept his eyes on his cuffs. There was blood there, fresh, and oozing up from within the black encrusted scabs around his wrists.

'OK. So let's talk about Lieutenant Steyl. Did Sixpence give you a note to kill him or was it your own idea?' said Joshua, opening what felt like a new chapter.

'I didn't kill him,' answered Merriman. 'I told you that already.'

'Ja and I don't believe you, so I thought I'd ask it again. Tell me, when did you hear the order to unload magazines that day at Dombondola?'

'I don't remember any order to unload. What would I want to unload for in a contact? We were shooting.'

'So that we wouldn't be able to count your rounds,' observed Joshua. 'So we couldn't narrow Steyl's murder down to you.'

'You are crazy, Sergeant.'

'I'm crazy? And you are the one trying to tell me that you are happy to shoot *terrs* in a contact but then help them put bombs in the camp.'

*

Joshua and Captain Mostert locked Merriman in the room behind them and went outside for a break. The heat of the day was building and they could hear the sound of Strydom's galvanised tin bucket clanking from the back of the canteen. There were gunshots too, but these were the measured cracks of target practice and Joshua noticed that Captain Mostert hardly heard them. He scratched his nose with his splinted finger and then, unable to resist the urge to scratch, drew blood from a mosquito bite on his ear.

'So we have established that he is not a traitor at least – not with a made up bullshit story like that,' said Joshua, irritated at himself for scratching and pinching the bite to stop it bleeding. 'He was not connected to Sixpence Ndwandwe. He killed Dietz and Steyl for other reasons.'

'Memfeliz?' asked Mostert, putting her head back to enjoy the daylight.

'Something like that. Did you see the way he jumped on my offer of Mopboy as an accomplice?'

'Ja. Why did he do that?'

'Because he is very stupid,' replied Joshua, scratching at the back of his head where he had discovered two more bites. 'Most criminals are very stupid, you know. Even quite clever people become very stupid in jail as well. They think that they have worked everything out and that no-one will ever have thought that what they have done has been done before.'

'You know I heard a rumour that you are under investigation yourself,' said Mostert. 'Is it true?'

Joshua wrinkled his nose. 'It is true,' he replied. 'It is bullshit, but it is true.'

'What did you do?'

'It's nothing. Just some bullshit from a couple of scraps I got into on my last leave down at the beach. How did you find out?'

'I'm an intelligence officer, remember? And Graaf-Reinet is not at the beach.'

'Let's go back in,' said Joshua, evasively. 'He should have sweated a bit more by now.'

*

'So where were you going when you left the base?'

Merriman kept his head down. Joshua waited for a long minute.

'It's an easy question.'

'I just needed to get away,' said Merriman quickly. 'Everything here was just, like, fucked up. I needed to get my head together.'

'Don't waste that surfer-dude bullshit on me. You were deserting to your SWAPO friends weren't you?'

Merriman seemed to consider this idea for a moment, turning it over to see if it was viable, before rejecting it. 'I was just fucked up,' he said, miserably. 'I think I'm a little shell-shocked, you know.'

'Ja. Oh dear,' replied Joshua. 'My heart is pumping purple piss for you. Now tell me what you were really doing.'

Merriman put his head down on the table. He was breathing heavily, rasping as though his lungs were full of fluid. Joshua left him there, signalling to Mostert not to intervene.

'You ever know District 6 in Cape Town?' said Joshua, lightly.

Merriman stopped breathing for a moment.

'I was brought up there as a kid,' continued Joshua, tempting. 'Exciting place. It's gone now though. Progress, and all that. It all got knocked down for rebuilding. To tell you the truth, I really miss the place.'

Merriman brought his head up and leaned slowly back in his chair.

'I know it,' he said, warily. 'So what?'

'Just wondered, as you are from the Cape, originally, I mean.'

Merriman did not blink.

'You know they gave it another name, but I don't recall what it is. Do you know it?'

'No.'

'No?'

'No.'

'And you a Cape Town boy? I am surprised by this. Hey, I got an idea,' Joshua's eyes opened wide. 'Why don't I get my mother to give your mother a call and then she can tell her what it is now called, and then she can tell me what it is now called, and I can then tell you what it is now called?'

Merriman said nothing, but he licked his dry lips nervously.

'Only joking,' said Joshua. 'It's called *Zonnenbloem*. As you well know.'

A fly buzzed in on the fetid breeze and settled on the table, rubbing its front legs busily, as though it were about to eat a meal. Joshua wafted it away.

'You need a drink of water? You look a bit done in,' said Joshua, reaching for the water bottle. Once again, he did not wait for an answer before putting it back down. 'No? OK no problem. Why were you heading for 23 at Echo Tango?'

'I wasn't heading anywhere.'

'*Onde voce estava indo?*' said Captain Mostert, an unexpected voice in his ear.

'Nowhere, I told you.'

Joshua smiled at Mostert while Merriman frowned, uncomprehending of the significance of the exchange.

'What?' he said, looking from one to the other. 'What?'

'*Voce entende portugues,*' said Captain Mostert. 'You understand Portuguese. That would be useful if you were meeting someone at 23.'

*

When the purple sky began to turn as livid as a bruise, Joshua decided to call it a day. From the moment that he had revealed his knowledge of Portuguese, Merriman had stonewalled, refusing to say any more, refusing to give any answers, refusing to walk into any more traps. It was as though he had acknowledged that he was in a more dangerous minefield than he had first thought and that his only safe course was to stay absolutely still. Even when Joshua had got Captain Mostert out of the room for a moment and then reached over the table to jab him with a straight, strong finger directed into a tender, hot, bruised gum, which was meant to hint at a lot more violence to come, he had refused all contact.

'We'll leave him with a bucket and a bottle of water over night,' said Joshua. 'He'll soften up. You want a klippie and coke?'

'I'd kill for one,' she replied. 'Where can we get a drink round here?'

'You could invite me into the Officers and Sergeants mess,' he replied. 'The CSM won't let me. He is of the view that it is the world's most exclusive club and not to be sullied by mere Police Sergeants.'

'Ja, it's such bullshit. I'll stand you a drink. I don't think anyone will kick up too much of a fuss if I say we are still conducting business.'

'Thanks,' said Joshua, walking alongside her. 'Tomorrow, we should break him. We are clear that he killed Dietz and Steyl and it seems equally clear that brother Memfeliz, or whatever he is, killed Lieutenant Keay. That was a pretty neat trick of yours – the Portuguese bit, I mean.'

'Thanks,' she said, returning a smile. 'My CO won't let us prosecute Memfeliz though, not without a confession, and we'll never touch him without we first get a confession from Merriman.'

The strong smell of beeswax and polish over damp wood greeted them as they went into the Officer's mess, Captain Mostert leading and scouting out the bar as if she was reconnoitring an ambush. The place was empty, so she went behind the wooden counter as if she owned it and poured them both brandy and handed up cokes.

'What sort of an outfit doesn't have ice,' she complained, rooting through the refrigerator below the counter.

'The sort of place that has a three troublesome corpses in the morgue,' replied Joshua, his eyes travelling over her behind.

Mostert turned and caught him looking. She smiled and shook her pony tail. Joshua swore there was a hint of blush there.

'What did they do with the Company clerk?' she asked.

'He isn't *connected*,' replied Joshua, taking the bottles of coke and knocking the tops off them. 'So he goes into the ground over in the cemetery.'

'Isn't that the way of things,' she said, pouring Klipdrift. 'I dread to think what they do with the blacks that die out here.'

'That's a point,' agreed Joshua. 'What did they do with Mopboy?'

'Shovelled him into a shallow grave somewhere, I guess.' She put the stopper back in the bottle. 'Minus his ears, which are probably being tanned for a souvenir right now.'

*

26th May 1980

'So we are still working on the idea that Memfeliz is connected to Merriman and that he is responsible for the death of Lieutenant Keay?' said Captain Mostert.

Joshua nodded as they walked towards the temporary interrogation centre at the back of the warehouse. It was still early and the light was soft. Above, a helicopter clattered off in the distance drowning out the last cry of a hyaena.

'What do you think the motive is?' asked Captain Mostert.

'Ja, that's a puzzle,' conceded Joshua. 'It may be something family or something to do with the *Broederbond* – I cannot ignore this connection – but well, you know, I do not think there is much premeditation in this and I am not buying that Merriman is ANC or SWAPO or whatever connected. But I hope to find out this morning.'

Merriman's appearance had not improved over night. His scabs had attracted a plague of flies that had chosen the moisture of fresh blood and tears over the fetid stench of the faeces and urine in the rancid bucket, while the overnight heat had dehydrated him to the point that his cracked lips were now marked by a thin white line of caked and dried spittle. Sometime in the night, his scalp had bled again and the dried blood had sculpted his fair hair into a series of punk points while the chafing of the cuffs had smeared rusted blood from his finger nails to his elbows. Yet even through the gag of his body odour, the odours of the dead officers' bodies was still detectable in the morning air and as Joshua and Captain Mostert stood back to let at least some of the stink out, it was the thought of what another thirty degree day would do to those three week old corpses that made them summon up the courage to go in to the hot room.

'I think a direct approach is probably best this morning,' said Joshua grimacing. 'Unless you want to stay all day in there.'

Captain Mostert put her hand up to cover her mouth and nose, swallowed hard and then signalled her agreement with a short wave. 'How long will it take?'

'How long is a piece of string? But we can make the effort to get it over with quickly,' he answered. 'Have you got your paper and pen to write down what he says? Normally we would just get him to sign the paper and we would fill in the confession for him afterwards but as this a special case, it will need to be done the other way round.'

She wafted the air with her pad.

'OK. Let's start.'

Merriman hauled himself up onto the chair from his sleeping position on the floor.

'Give him some water, hey?' said Joshua. 'And I will just get rid of this bucket. Where is Kassie Strydom when you need him?'

Merriman grunted and put his head back as Captain Mostert trickled water from a water bottle across his lips and into his mouth. He gulped at it, ignoring the pain as the fissures in his lips opened and swelled with the reviving moisture.

'More,' he croaked. 'More.'

'Don't take too much,' she coaxed, pausing. 'Just a little at a time.'

'Can he talk yet?' said Joshua, reappearing.

Mostert nodded. 'A little, I think.'

'Can you talk, Merriman?' demanded Joshua. 'Are you ready to tell us everything we want to know now?'

Merriman held his cuffed hands up in supplication for more water. Mostert raised her eyebrows at Joshua and he gave her permission. She poured more into him, faster, until she had emptied the whole bottle.

'Shall I get more?'

Joshua nodded. He wanted her out of the room for this next bit. It would only take her five minutes to get more from the bowser parked up by the storehouse wall, but five minutes would be enough. He pulled out a coke and popped the top off it with an opener from his pocket and waved her off. She looked at the bottle and smiled, remembering just how many brandies he had necked last night.

'OK Merriman, let me just give you this coke and then you can tell the nice lady lawyer and Captain everything so she can write it down and we can all go home and you can go back to the nice *tronk* for the rest of your born days.' He came around the table and stood behind the prisoner. 'You like coke?'

Merriman gave the weakest of nods.

'It's the real thing,' said Joshua and seized Merriman's hair. He dragged his head back, almost cracking the neck and ignoring his own pain, pulled him backwards, so that the chair was on two legs and Merriman's mouth and nose were open to the sky. Merriman tried to struggle, but he was too weak, too broken and he could do nothing as Joshua poured the fizzy drink into his nose, into his nasal passages and into his exploding brain.

It was as though he had had smelling salts punched deep into his nostrils. For what seemed like an infinity, Merriman experienced a galaxy of pain as the soda crackled like electricity in his sinuses, swelling and bulging in an effervescent mockery of epileptic pain, his eyeballs bursting with colours, squeezing out a panic that blotted out all other consideration but that the agony should stop. Yet it went on and on, a Niagra of violence spinning like a Catherine wheel through his head, overwhelming every pleasure or pain he had ever remembered and substituting it with a permanence of crackling, white phosphorus burning that found every hole in his broken teeth, loosened his bladder and turned his bowels to a shuddering looseness before he collapsed. He came to on the floor, soaked in his own sweat, filth, urine and humiliation.

'OK, Merriman,' said Joshua, hauling him back on to the chair. 'The Captain is coming, so now we can begin, OK?'

Merriman's head went up and down and his sightless eyes rolled in the wonder of such all pervading agony.

'Everything is fine?' she said, coming back in. 'Do you want more water, Merriman?'

He shook his head in refusal and she sat down beside him, pen and paper at the ready.

'He is a mess,' she said, touching her temple significantly. *What have you done to him?*

Joshua ignored her.

'You have a brother or a cousin or something, called Heironimo Ortez Memfeliz,' began Joshua. 'Born June 6th 1955 in Zonnenbloem, District 6, Cape Town. I don't know if he is your twin, your half-brother, whether he is legitimate, illegitimate, adopted or something else. But I do know that he killed Lieutenant Keay with a shot to the head, possibly two, and I am going to charge him with murder. What I don't know is *why;* perhaps it is to do with all the people being moved out of District 6 to make way for Zonnenbloem? Although technically I don't really need to know this, it will make life less complicated for the judge when he sentences him to hang. He is in the 23 *tronk* and Captain Mostert here is keen to know the details so that she can help with his defence. For me, I don't give a shit and am happy to shoot him like a dog and bury him in a ditch. Want another coke?'

Merriman pulled in his hands and if they had not been cuffed he would have wrapped them around himself. Instead he hunched up and began to rock back and forth like an animal driven mad by confinement. He muttered a little, inaudibly, but then came suddenly to a decision, which he indicated by nodding his head vigorously and bouncing up down on his chair.

'You want more coke?' said Joshua.

Merriman shook his head and then his whole body followed up with a fit of shivering.

'I killed Dietz and Steyl,' he said, through his broken, spluttering mouth. 'And Keay. I killed them.'

'Write this down,' ordered Joshua to Captain Mostert. 'No, wait. Not the Keay bit.' He directed his stare back to the trembling Merriman. 'How did you kill Keay when you were in jail?'

'Doesn't matter,' stammered Merriman. 'I did it. Make no difference to you who did it. I confess it; it was me.'

'You want to cover up for your cousin? Wow, that is very noble. Why?'

'Doesn't matter,' repeated Merriman, dribbling blood. 'Just do me for it. You get yours. Everything's over.'

'Tell us why you did it,' insisted Captain Mostert, sympathetically. 'There must be a reason.'

Merriman looked down at his left hand.

'Like you said,' he stuttered. 'They're *Broederbond* and they knocked down my house in District 6.'

Joshua looked at Mostert and shrugged. He didn't believe it but it was a motive. He didn't believe it but if the coke trick couldn't get the truth out of him, nothing short of real torture would and he decided to settle. The case could hardly be said to have been cracked but he was already convinced of Merriman's guilt and if Merriman confessed then that was that.

'As you wish. You confess to the murder of Lieutenants Dietz, Steyl and Keay, right?'

'Ja,' said Merriman.

Captain Mostert wrote his words down verbatim.

'You want to sign?'

Merriman nodded enthusiastically, shaking dried blood out of his hair. Captain Mostert put a pencil into his cramped hands and pushed the paper sideways towards him for him to sign. Joshua gave a little shrug of incomprehension in response to her unspoken question. Merriman drew his signature on the paper.

'It's the real thing,' said Mostert, when she handed him the confession written in her own neat ball and chain hand and signed in Merriman's smudged and broken scrawl. 'That's that then.'

'I killed Lieutenant Visser too,' said Merriman.

'Lieutenant Visser isn't dead,' said Captain Mostert.

Then her eyes widened in horror.

06

Mother Knows Best

The 23 Battalion Alouettes were in the air before Major van der Merwe had put the phone down in the Company office and CSM Landsberg had two Ratels racing for the Cut Line only moments later.

'Visser and Memfeliz are setting up an OP just over the border,' said van der Merwe, tersely. 'There are two sticks of four out there and they are under radio silence until tomorrow. They will not switch on until then.'

'Shall we not send the rest of the Company out?' asked Captain Mostert.

'We shall not. It would serve no point. If CSM Landsberg and the 23 Alouettes can't find them, then they are lost indeed. I see no reason to alert the enemy further than is strictly necessary and the last thing I want is notices in the foreign press that the South African Defence Force is involved in a large scale cross-border operation that contravenes every international law you can think of. Especially as Pretoria has not given its authorisation.'

'So we just wait to see if Visser gets double-tapped?' said Captain Mostert, anxiously.

'Let us hope it will not come to that,' replied van der Merwe, clenching his buttocks once more and stroking the mole on his cheek. 'And we only have Merriman's word that the Lieutenant is in danger. You say he has admitted to the other murders?'

Joshua handed over Merriman's confession.

'Yet, it is not possible that he killed Lieutenant Keay?'

'That's right, Major,' said Joshua.

'And you think he is covering for someone who is probably his a cousin or a half-brother; this Corporal Memfeliz?'

Joshua nodded.

'Because sometime in the past, they were relocated against their will from District 6, possibly by business interests controlled by the Dietz, Steyl and Keay families? And they are taking their revenge.'

Joshua nodded. He was reluctant to mention the *Broederbond* by name in front of the Major in case he turned out to be in it too.

'It seems a coincidence that two – whatever relation they are, exactly - in two separate units should find four separate sons of their blood enemies under their guns and at their mercy in a remote location all at the same time. It seems *very* coincidental. *Too* coincidental.'

'It's all we have to go on right now,' answered Joshua.

'Do you give credence to this coincidence too, Captain Mostert?'

Mostert thought for a moment.

'It is true that it seems unlikely,' she said, slowly. 'Merriman's story is threadbare certainly, but we have no other thing to go on. Not until we can question Memfeliz.'

'And if Memfeliz turns out to be an officer killer, what then? From what I can make out, you have no evidence at all against him. And little chance of gathering it if Merriman sticks to his story.'

Mostert conceded that this was true. 'We must just question him and see, Sir.'

Van der Merwe rubbed his mole again. 'I suppose that we have to be thankful that Memfeliz and Visser are in 23 and that we are not the only unit riddled with madness.' He stood up, scraping back his chair and paced a little, his hands behind his back fiddling with his belt. 'Get over to 23. I'll call ahead and tell them you are coming.'

'Is Visser in the *Broederbond*?' asked Joshua as they left the office on their way to collect their kit.

'I don't know,' replied Captain Mostert. 'It's not like they wear badges.'

'I know this. But you are from 23, maybe you know if he is connected?'

'All I know is that he is from Cape Town.' She strode ahead a little, then stopped and turned. The blue light of the sky framed her soft figure so that she seemed to glow under the hot sun.

'Look, he's OK. He's a decent guy, right?' she said. 'I don't know what his parents are into and I don't care. All this District 6 crap happened when I was a kid and as far as I know no-one ever made any money out of it because no-one wants to invest in such a toxic area. Last time I looked, most of it was just a bulldozed wasteland. It isn't worth killing for. What is?'

'Are you sweet on him?'

'None of your business!'

'So you are then.'

'Just get your kit and I'll meet you by the transport,' she said striding off.

Joshua watched her bottom move under the stretched tailored fabric of her trousers and drew in a deep breath of longing. 'Bastard,' he said to himself. 'That is a classy *choty goty*.'

*

Joshua and Captain Mostert were in the second of the five vehicles, each of which was packed with troops, stores, tools, spares, guns and ammunition and a terse, tense expectation of trouble.

'No chances being taken this time,' said Joshua, impressed by the show of force and suddenly feeling very safe. Whoever had written that note would have to have a very long reach indeed if they intended to pluck him out of an armoured convoy manned by 41 Mech. Sure, Mopboy was dead, but he was under no illusions that the ANC wouldn't have other, equally handy operatives around these bases.

'It's a good time for us to move and strike,' replied Captain Mostert. 'It would be nice if this was all for us, but really, they will take us to 23 at Echo Tango, pick us some of the guys there and then will be off to strike at SWAPO bases over the border. The further back we can push the weapons caches and supply dumps, the tougher it is for them to make their incursions.'

The light was strong and the scents of the bush rose up as the vehicles picked up pace and then spread out along the road. High above, a single vapour trail screeched across the sky startling a family of giraffe into a graceful, slow motion gallop across a sward of thin grass. Joshua looked about him at the soldiers, many of whom had sported beards before Strydom's vigilantism had brought the wrath of Basic Training bullshit down on them. Now they were cleaner, sharper, yet still exuding an air of easy confidence, as though this were just another day baling, fencing or harvesting down on the farm. In the next vehicle forward, he saw two of the *troupies* trading playful punches, cuffing each other about the shoulders before their leader told them to cut it out and get serious.

'You think we might expect trouble?' asked Joshua, above the run of the tyres.

The landscape always seemed so empty that it could hardly be possible for an enemy to move un-noticed in it.

'I think that SWAPO might,' she replied. 'This time of year is our time because the bush is thinning and we can move through it more easily. Most of the time we don't bother even with the roads.'

'Bundu bashing,' he called out.

She nodded, but without enthusiasm. The vehicle was picking up speed now and the sound of the engine combined with the rush of the wind to make conversation more difficult and he could see that she wanted to enjoy the sensation of freedom that came with driving high atop, as though she were remembering being on the back seat of an open top roadster hurtling down along the sea road on the Chapman's Peak highway. She brushed the hair away from her face and, in a motion that Joshua was beginning to see as her defining characteristic, removed her beret and folded it once more into the epaulette on her left shoulder. He envied Lieutenant Visser his good luck but then withdrew the thought when he remembered why there were troops on the road and in the bush and helicopters in the air. For all he knew, Visser was stuck with a bayonet or dying alone in the bush with a double tap to his head. For all *she* knew, too.

He shifted his stance and looked out at the thin bush. He could do nothing about the note, he told himself; he would not think about it; he could not think about it. Instead he focussed on thinking about the curious relationship of David Merriman and H.O. Memfeliz until the hum of the motors and the warmth of the sun sent him into a doze which lasted until the lead Buffel slowed to allow the farm gate at Echo Tango to swing open. Up above, the sound of rotors on the skyline could be heard coming from the direction of Angola.

'Do you think they found them?' asked Joshua, surfacing.

Captain Mostert shaded her eyes and peered into the distance.

'They are all coming back together so the answer is probably *yes*.'

'We have to question Memfeliz straight away,' he replied. 'Get him while he's off balance.'

'That's if anything has happened,' she replied, biting her bottom lip.

'Ja, true. I'm sure we raised the alarm in time,' he said. 'But I am not sure what we will be able to charge him with if he has done nothing.'

'He killed Lieutenant Keay,' said Captain Mostert, her eyes still fixed on the helicopters.

'Officially, Merriman killed him. It says so on the piece of paper he signed.'

She murmured something in reply, but Joshua didn't catch it and all further conversation was drowned out by the noise of an outgoing hunting convoy of armoured vehicles and then the percussion of helicopter rotor blades sweeping above their heads. He looked up, right into the teeth of a grinning CSM Landsberg and an equally grinning black soldier, who gave him a cheery thumbs up and then pointed at another stork-like helicopter taking off from the base. It had two chest freezers slung beneath it and was heading in the direction of Oshadangwa. And it was in that unlikely image that the beginnings of a solution to the case of David Merriman and Heironimo Ortez Memfeliz came to him.

*

'Corporal *Memfeliz*,' said Joshua, holding the file in front of him. 'Corporal *Heironimo Ortez* Memfeliz.'

There was no mistaking the family resemblance now that he was sitting in front of him on the opposite side of a desk in Captain Mostert's nissen hut. Memfeliz had the same wide mouth and strong brow as David Merriman, though his nose was finer, his cheekbones sharper and his chin a little more pointed. They had the same blue eyes, too, but what marked Memfeliz as different was his light milk-coffee complexion and his wiry, black hair.

'Corporal Heironimo Ortez Memfeliz, of Zonnenbloem, Cape Town,' he said. 'What is your date of birth?'

Memfeliz's hands were in cuffs and he stared at them as he sat stiffly before the desk. He did not reply.

'June 6th 1955,' said Joshua, supplying the answer. 'Do you know your – what is he? Cousin? Half-brother? - is being held for the murder of three officers?'

Memfeliz kept his eyes down and continued in silence.

'He's a good whatever he is to you. Not only is he coughing up to the murder of two officers that he did kill, he's put his hand up for one that *you* killed too. What do you think of that then?'

There was no reply. Joshua expected as much; 23 soldiers did a basic course in anti-interrogation techniques.

'Pretty witty, giving your place of birth as *Girasol, Benguela* and your father's occupation as a Cape Doctor. Were you born in the Peninsular Maternity? Which street did you live on?'

The silence remained. Mostert raised an eyebrow in question.

'Well, OK then,' continued Smith. 'Let's assume that you and David Merriman are related on some level whatever that may be. Why did you change your name?'

There was the slightest flicker of movement in one eye. Joshua waited for a long while but nothing more came.

'So you did change your name?'

Nothing. The metal hut creaked with the heat and a fragment of rusted paint dropped off the ceiling to land with a ping beside them.

'I wonder, did you change it *from* Merriman *to* Memfeliz, or were you originally called something entirely different?'

Memfeliz's eyelid flicked once more.

'Of course, silly me,' said Joshua. 'You would have to change it to *Heironimo Ortez Memfeliz* or you wouldn't be able to use your initials to spell *HOMemfeliz*. Question is, therefore, just what is your real name?'

Memfeliz's eyes flicked up and held his for a fleeting moment.

'You know what?' said Joshua, after another strategic pause. 'I don't think that your name is *Merriman* either.'

Mostert raised an eyebrow again. He had not consulted her about the line of questioning before they had entered the nissen hut and the hypotheses he was laying out were a mystery to her.

'It stands to reason, see?' he continued. 'Your mother's name was *Merriman* and when she took David home from the Peninsular Maternity Home, or wherever it was you were both born on that same day in 1955, I think she left *you* behind. So although you carry your mother's name today – or something approximating to it – this is an assumed name. It isn't your real one.'

Mostert was frowning, puzzled. Memfeliz made no sign that he had either heard or understood.

'It's 1955,' continued Joshua, folding his hands and looking up at the ceiling. 'The Immorality Acts forbid inter-racial sex and the Church forbids any kind of sex outside marriage. Now, follow me closely, hey? Mrs Merriman, a Churchy white liberal Englishwoman has a bit of a fling around the back of the marquee at a Black Sash tea party with a handsome black or Cape Coloured. Man, she flushes hot when she remembers this, hey? And then flushes a hell of a lot hotter when she finds she has been knocked up good and proper. But then she starts counting her rosary beads and thinking of how many times she did the wild thing with her rightful partner and husband in that month and, boy oh boy, does she start to cross her fingers. And then the Doc tells her it is twins! Everyone is happy! Everyone is looking forward to the birth and the christening and the baby shower and all the presents and candles and churchy stuff and happy families all round. Except Mrs Merriman has now got more than her fingers crossed, hey? She's wishing she kept her legs crossed behind the marquee now, hey? Just in case the proud father turns out to be the wrong colour and she's got a couple of cuckoos in the nest.'

Joshua leaned back in his chair and shifted his gaze to the far wall.

'And then the time comes and we are all rushing off to the Peninsular and dad is told to walk up and down outside and smoke cigarettes anxiously while the woman do all that messy shouting and pushing and – pow! Out pops junior number one and he is whiter than white and fit to be advertising soap powder and everyone is very happy, Mrs Merriman most of all. Jeez that must have been a relief! Can you imagine it? No more worries about what happened behind the marquee or in the back of the bioscope or in the British Hotel in Simonstown. Lady Luck has smiled down on her and all her prayers have been answered. Only they haven't, have they?'

Memfeliz drew his head up.

'Because then out pops junior number two and although he isn't as black as the Devil's arse, he's got enough of the tar brush in him to raise more than a few eyebrows up at the Church of the Immaculate and Disapproving Conception. What to do?'

'Is that possible?' blurted Captain Mostert.

'Stranger things have happened,' replied Joshua, cutting her off. 'But, I repeat: what to do? Any theories, Memfeliz?'

Memfeliz said nothing, but dropped his head again.

'Well, how about this one?' Joshua continued. 'Now District 6 being District 6, this isn't the first time a white woman has ended up with a baby that is the wrong sort of colour. So up pops Sister Consuela or the Mother Superior or whoever and whips away the offending child to an orphanage somewhere discreet, where the child of sin can be properly looked after before being palmed off on a grateful family who happen to be the right colour for the job. What do you think, Memfeliz? Or do I have to get hold of Mrs Merriman herself and put her through the third degree? Tea break, I think.'

'Jesus, Sergeant Smith, when did you come up with that one?' said Captain Mostert, once they were outside the room.

'*Ag*, man, it's the oldest story in the *bladdy* township,' he smiled, trying not to sound too pleased with himself. 'Why do you think there are laws against it? It came to me on the way over here. It's clear as day when you think about it.'

'Clear as day? That you can have two babies at the same time that are different colours from two different men?' She put her hands on her hips and shook her head. 'You must have taken a different biology class to me.'

'No, I learned it from a book about Ancient Greeks and Romans,' he replied, with a smirk. 'Castor and Pollux were twins but had different fathers. Ja, I thought it was not possible either but I asked a Doctor I knew once and he said it was indeed true. He told me the name for it, but it was long and I wasn't so interested, you know?'

She looked at him with admiration.

'You are smarter than you look, Sergeant Smith.'

'Ja, that would not be very hard, hey?' he replied, pointing at his stitches.

'Don't put yourself down,' she replied. 'And though I am glad Visser is not dead, he is not my boyfriend, OK?'

'As you wish, Ma'am,' said Joshua, saluting.

'Ja you want to turn me into a *bakvissie* now? A little giggly girl who must just be thrown back into the pond, ja? I'm already feeling stupid. What do we do next?'

'Let him sweat. He will not want us asking his mother, so he will go along with the story and will try to prise out more of what we know.'

'We don't know anything else.'

'Ja, but he does not know that. We must know why he has a false name and why he has joined 23 and why he has killed Lieutenant Keay.'

'Is that all?'

'I think it might be enough to be going on with.'

Once back inside, Joshua began his magisterial interrogation again. He was feeling happier on several counts now, not least of which was the news that Lieutenant Visser was not as lucky in love as he was popularly believed to be. Captain Mostert sat down on a chair slightly behind Memfeliz's eye line on Joshua's advice, in the hope that it would make him look up and around more often.

'So, now, Corporal Memfeliz. Will it be necessary to contact your mother now?'

Memfeliz held still, as he had been trained to.

'Hmm,' said Joshua, trying to look smarter than he looked. 'This tells me that I am right about Mrs Merriman being your mother, otherwise you would have advised me to go right ahead and contact her.'

'Why?' he said, unexpectedly.

'Because if we do contact her, she will confirm the story – or one close enough to it, at any rate.'

'So you say.'

'Ja, I do. Now when exactly did you make contact with her again?'

'Good trick, *Konstabel*.'

'Ja well, it was always worth a try. Now, your name, please. Your *real* name.'

*

'So Lieutenant Visser is still with us and we can consider him safe from his own soldiers for the time being,' said Commandant Kobus Korff, sipping at a cup of rooibos tea. 'Nor can we charge Memfeliz with murder, or even attempted murder, because there is no evidence, apart from the word of a possible brother, who has not only confessed to a murder that he did not commit, but also to a murder – that of Lieutenant Visser - that has not taken place. Can you imagine what a lawyer would make of that in court?'

No-one who met the Commanding Officer of 23 Leopard battalion would ever have mistaken him for a soldier on first acquaintance. Being short, paunchy, overfed, pale and staring anxiously out from behind oversized spectacles he resembled an accountant about to break bad news to the Board of Directors rather than the best thinking soldier since General Smuts. That those spectacles concealed a troubled, divided intellect was general knowledge in 23, and considered to be largely as a result of his brother being incarcerated in an unpleasant jail near Rooigrond for voicing vociferously anti-Apartheid views and refusing to shut up when told to. The paunch too was deceptive, for Commandant Kobus Korff, was a veteran of many gruelling cross border operations in Mozambique, Zambia and Botswana as well as Angola and even at forty could still cut it.

'And yet you are convinced that Memfeliz is an imposter and responsible for death of Lieutenant Keay,' he took another sip of rooibos and held the cup before him, like a grail. His office was as spartan as van der Merwe's, except for his one permitted luxury, a small spirit stove on which he brewed his own tea. 'Tell me, what will you do with this knowledge if it is indeed correct?'

'Put him on trial, obviously,' said Captain Mostert.

'And have you considered what will happen if he does confess to the murder?'

'He will be sent to jail or to the hangman,' she replied.

'Have you had much dealing with the law, Sergeant?' He fixed a piercing eye on Joshua. 'I mean, the proper law, with judges and witnesses and lawyers who have not been bribed and evidence that has not been made up.'

'A fair amount,' said Joshua. 'But mainly just giving evidence in the Graaf–Reinet courthouse.'

'Where no-one ever doubts your word. I see,' Korff took another lingering sip of tea. 'And if at the trial of – let's just stick with *Memfeliz* - the defence produce Merriman who has already confessed to the murder, do you not think this will produce *reasonable doubt*? Yes, I can see by the cloud gathering on your brow that you agree with me. So Memfeliz walks. And then you bring Merriman to trial and his attorneys produce Memfeliz once more, who has already been cleared of the murder, and say that he is really responsible, because the police have his confession in their possession.'

'I never thought of that,' admitted Joshua.

'I thought not. Now who will benefit from bringing such a trial into the public eye?'

Mostert pursed her lips.

'Ja, the enemies of the Republic who would like nothing more than to see her armed forces discredited. They would have a galloping field day with this. We are at war, people, and in this kind of war the weapons are newspapers and trials and diplomatic sanctions just as much as Ratels and rifles. So to win, we must take this into account, for to lose is unthinkable. We must come up with a creative solution to the problem.'

'*Creative*?' ventured Joshua cautiously.

'I do not mean a shallow grave, Sergeant. We are not barbarians or *terrs* here.'

'Glad to hear it, Sir.'

'I thought you might be.' He drank some more tea, sat back in his chair and pronounced judgement. 'Find out everything there is to know about Memfeliz and then come back to me.'

'And how will we do this, Sir?' asked Captain Mostert.

'You are an Intelligence Officer and he is a Police Detective and we have files and files and files of information at our disposal,' smiled Korff. 'But Sergeant Smith here has a much better source than any of these.'

Mostert looked blank.

'Ask Sergeant Smith's mother,' said Korrf. 'Mothers know everything, don't you know?'

*

'Mom is that you?'

'Joshua! How nice to hear from you. Two phone calls inside one month. This must be a record.'

'Ja, I was meaning to phone more but...'

'Are you in trouble, Joshua?'

'No, Mom, it is the case that I am working on.'

'A case? Like the other one? What sort of a case?'

'A case, Mom. A *police* case.'

'My, I forget what a grown up boy you have become.'

'Mom, look. I need to ask you for some information.'

'What? Speak up. I say, this is a very bad line. When the sanctions are lifted we might get a proper telephone network. Do you know, Mr Cox has just received a letter telling him he must appear in a court case in Pietermaritzburg for speeding faster than the permitted limit and now he...'

'Mom, look, I must...'

'...must drive all the way back there to answer charges because the police say he was wasting fuel by driving so fast. Cape Town all the way to Pietermaritzburg!'

'Mom...'

'...and how is that supposed to save fuel, I ask? And which way will he go? The Transkei is not very safe, so he must drive perhaps, all the way around Basutoland...'

'Mom, listen...'

'...and through the Orange Free State and then to Newcastle...'

'Ja, Mom, it is a long way...'

'He will be gone a week at least and what will we do without his car to take the old folk to the Church to play Bingo?'

'Mom, I must ask you about Mrs Merriman once more...'

'She does not have a car. How can she drive the old folk?'

'No, Mom. It is related to her son, David.'

'David? Oh, he was a nice boy. How is he? I hear he is in the army now, poor boy.'

'Ja, Mom, he is just fine.' Joshua crossed his fingers behind his back and looked up at the fan circling below the rafters in the Intelligence Section. Captain Mostert was leafing through Memfeliz's personnel file with a wry smile gathering at one corner of her mouth. The telephone was set to such a volume that she could hear each word screech through the tinny speaker that came off a spur and sat on her side of the desk, like a little frog. 'But I want you to tell me something about his Mom.'

'Mrs Merriman?'

'That is her.'

'Are you being sarcastic with me Joshua?'

Captain Mostert raised her eyebrows and tipped her head to one side in warning.

'No, Mom.'

'Is it to do with the Police?'

'Yes, Mom...'

'You are not in any sort of trouble are you, Joshua?'

'No, Mom, I *am* the Police...'

'Oh, dear, I'm sorry. Of course you are. Now what do you want to know?'

Captain Mostert let out a small giggle. Joshua glared.

'It is a little difficult, Mother. Sensitive, you know?'

There was a crackle of static.

'Are you still there Mother?'

'I'm listening Joshua. Is it about a girl?'

'No, Mother, it is about Mrs Merriman.'

'Has David got a girl into trouble? Is this why you are calling?'

'No, really, Mother. It is not David that I am calling about.'

'You called about him last week – was it last week? Maybe it was longer now I come to think of it. Why would you be calling about David twice?'

'I'm not calling about David. I want to talk about Mrs Merriman.'

'Whatever for?'

'*God give me strength,*' he mouthed to Captain Mostert. 'It is to do with a case, Mother. A *police* case.'

'Joshua, I am not stupid. Please do not speak to me like that. This line is bad and I am not responsible for the General Post Office.'

'Yes, sorry, Mother.'

'Now, what is it that you want to know?'

'I want to know about Mrs Merriman.'

'What about her?'

Joshua fidgeted a little.

'Do you know that your accent is getting more English?' said Captain Mostert.

Joshua ignored her and wished that he had prepared better for this encounter. Now that it came to ask the questions he needed to ask, he was really not sure about how to go about asking them.

'Mom, look, *ag*, it is a little tricky, Ja?'

'You know you sound more like an Afrikaaner every day, Joshua? I should never have agreed to you going to an uneducated backwater like Krugerburg with your father. If I had kept you here with me you would have got your Matric...'

'I *did* get my Matric!'

'Yes, but what did you do with it? You should have gone to the university here and become a lawyer.'

Joshua caught himself. Captain Mostert's smile broadened and she sat back in her chair, as though it were a ringside seat.

'*Mother*, I need to ask you some questions about Mrs Merriman. Police questions. Delicate Police questions. Please.'

'Police questions?'

'Police questions, Mother.'

'About Mrs Merriman? Not David?'

'Yes. No.'

'So David has not got a girl into trouble. This is good news. I would not like Mrs Merriman to be embarrassed by any unsuitable behaviour like that. She does good work for the Church and although we are all *human* and can expect God's forgiveness in due course, it is always better to be spared trouble like that. People can lose their reputations so very easily on just a bit of tittle-tattle and once they are gone, they are hard to get back.'

'Mother...'

'I'm sorry, Joshua. I interrupted.'

'That's OK, Mother. Now...'

'Mrs Merriman...'

'Ja, yes. It is about David's father.'

'Not Mrs Merriman?'

'Yes, Mother. Do I need to explain to you the facts of life?'

Captain Mostert screwed up her eyes in delight.

'Joshua?'

'Yes, Mother, listen, sorry, hey?'

The line crackled.

'*Mr* Merriman is not very well at the moment. He still has tear gas in his eyes from being at the demonstration last week.'

'Oh, I'm sorry to hear that; *Demonstration?*' he mouthed at Captain Mostert. 'But I need to know if he and Mrs Merriman had a *completely* happy marriage.'

'Joshua?'

'I know it is delicate, Mother, but I need to have this information.'

'And how am I supposed to know?'

'Well, I thought that as you have known her for a long time...'

'...that I would be party to confidences. *Personal* confidences.'

'Well...yes.'

'And you think I am the sort of person to pass on such confidences? Like a common tail-bearer and *stoep* gossip?'

'No, Mother. I didn't mean it like that...'

'Well how did you mean it?'

'It is *police...*'

'Intelligence gathering' murmured Captain Mostert.

'...intelligence gathering, Mother...'

'Collation of evidence,' murmured Mostert once more.

'...collation of *evidence...*'

'Mary Poppins was a Lesbian.'

'...Mary Popp..... no, listen Mother,' he glared at Captain Mostert, who smiled wider than before. 'It is important.'

'You are not spying on our protest activities are you Joshua? You wouldn't betray your own Mother surely? Tell me, Joshua. I insist.'

'No, Mother,' he narrowed his eyes furiously at Mostert. 'I am not spying on you or Mrs Merriman. I just need to find some things out about her background.'

'I call that *spying*, Joshua. What do *you* call it? Is this the influence of your father?'

Joshua held the phone away from his head for a moment and took a deep breath.

'Mother: you and Dad did not get on, am I right?'

'Well I would have thought that was rather obvious.'

'And did Mr and Mrs Merriman sometimes not get on?'

'Marriage isn't a bed of roses, Joshua.'

'Please, Mother...Did they sometimes not get on a long time ago. In 1954 or 1955?'

'In 1954? How could they not be getting on? They had only been married a year or two. My how they worked hard for the Black Sash then! They set up their own Advice Centre in the old District Six.'

'And did they have a bust up for a while, perhaps?'

The line crackled uncertainly.

'Joshua, why do you want to know this information?'

'You need it to clear David Merriman,' suggested Mostert.

Joshua put his hand over the mouthpiece. 'You want me to lie to my own Mother?'

'Not if it is your first time, obviously,' she replied.

Joshua considered hard for a moment.

'It is to help David Merriman out of some trouble,' said Joshua, blushing.

'You are filling up like a glass of red wine,' laughed Mostert. 'It's quite cute really.'

'I thought you said he was not in any trouble. Has he got a girl in trouble, Joshua? I deserve to know this after the last time...'

The line crackled.

'The *last time*, Mother?'

There was another crackle and a hiss.

'Joshua?'

'Mother?'

Joshua counted the fan above make six and a half slow revolutions.

'If I tell you this, it will help David, yes?'

'It will,' said Joshua.

'And it will go no further?'

'Mother...' Captain Mostert waved her arms violently from side to side, warning him not to give such a promise. 'Mother, you know that will depend. This is *evidence*.'

There was another crackle and the sound of laboured breathing could be heard clearly, as though it were no distant than next door.

'Joshua.'

'Mother.'

'This *will* help David?'

'Tell me about the other baby, Mother.'

The fan made another six and a half torpid revolutions.

'Then you know.'

'The Peninsular Maternity Home.'

'Joshua, things were very hard then...the Pass Laws and...the Coloured people were being deregistered as voters...we thought this was the beginning of...what the Germans did...what the Germans did to the Jews.'

'What happened to the baby, Mother?'

'We couldn't believe it! Sheila – Mrs Merriman – she only fell once, Joshua. She swore! It was just once when Clive and I had been arrested and she was frightened and needed some comfort. They had fallen out...it was a mess...a mistake.'

'Clive? Who is Clive and when were you arrested?'

Captain Mostert was listening intently now. 'Don't ask questions,' she murmured. 'Let her talk.'

'Let her talk?' mouthed Joshua. 'You bet I'll let her talk! She was *arrested?*'

'Clive! Sheila's husband. He and I were arrested at a protest in Hermanus. That's when I started courting with your father. Your father knew the Police well and so got us out without us being charged or mistreated. She thought that we...'

'I thought you met father at a Church social? You told me you met him at a Church social! Since when did Church social events take place in Hermanus Police Station? Was Elvis Presley playing *Jailhouse Rock* in the band, hey?'

'Joshua...'

'Sergeant Smith!' hissed Captain Mostert. 'The baby!'

Joshua took a deep breath.

'OK, Mother. Tell me about the baby. What happened to the baby?'

The ceiling fan turned slowly.

'Well we knew at once that she could not keep it so...do you remember when you were little, Joshua? Do you remember we had a big pram? Big enough for two?'

'What?' Joshua had a dim and vague memory of a blue, four wheeled carriage and a rush of memory brought back the feel of satin and the smell of milk, spit and teddy...and the presence of someone else in the pram. 'I had a black foster-brother?'

'Joshua...'

'And you wait until now to tell me?'

'Joshua, it was only for a little while.'

'I have a black foster-brother?' Joshua was beginning to hyper-ventilate.

'No! Don't be silly. Don't over-react, Joshua. He stayed with us only for a short while. Of course, your father hated it...'

'Now why would that be?'

'Because he had *views* about black people that I'm sure you are fully aware of. He thought that if there was a black child sharing your cot, you would be tainted and grow up as something less than a man.'

'Sergeant Smith!' hissed Mostert again. 'Where did the baby go?'

'We *fokken* know that don't we?' he spat.

'Joshua, please don't swear in that fashion. We did the best that we could do at the time and you cannot possibly understand how fraught with difficulty those years were.'

Joshua looked at the surrounding walls, festooned with arrow marked maps and diagrams of Soviet military equipment as supplied to the enemies ranged against him and felt a twinge from his cracked ribs.

'I'm sorry, Mother,' he said, breathing hard and trying to control himself. 'It was a slip of the tongue. What happened to the baby, Mother?'

'We only kept it for a little while...and Angola was not such a bad place then. There were plenty of Portuguese families – good families; Christian families – who were only too willing to take in an orphan. You know the mortality rates for children up there were terrible twenty years ago...'

'Ja, and I'm sure the Communists improved them...'

'Joshua!'

'Sorry, Mother. Please go on.'

'Well the father thought it would be a good idea to go to Angola too. He said he knew people there.'

'Do you have a name for the baby, Mother?'

'Well...actually...I named him.'

Mostert thrummed.

'We knew that Mozambique or Angola was probably the best place for him...and the father agreed to take him there.'

'So, the baby was a *boy*?'

'Yes, certainly he was a boy. A beautiful bouncing baby boy of six pounds...'

'*Name*,' urged Mostert, through gritted teeth. 'Get a name.'

'And his name, Mother. We don't need to know his weight.'

'Well...I liked to do crosswords then and we, well, thought it might be necessary in the future to have, well, like code names...'

'Mother?'

'I named him *Heironimo Ortez Memfeliz*.'

'Of Girasol, Benguela. Father: the Cape Doctor. Mother: Nurse. What was your job back then, Mother? Yes, I know: a nurse. Don't tell me.'

'You know all this, already? Then why are you asking?'

'Mother, like I said, it's a police case,' sighed Joshua.

'Are *you* in trouble, Joshua?'

'No, Mother. I'm not in trouble.'

He looked across apologetically to Captain Mostert, who was lighting up an amazed cigarette.

'So I need not worry about this package that was delivered for you here this morning?'

'Package, Mother?'

'Joshua, you know I have some experience in these matters. It looks like a Writ.'

*

'So Memfeliz is who he says he is and who we think he is,' surmised Mostert, through the end of her cigarette. The phone was back in its cradle now and Smith had his hands around the back of his neck, massaging the nape. 'Question now is: when did the two brothers become aware of each other?'

'It can only be through military service,' said Joshua. 'It *must* be. We should look at where they served.'

'We should find out when Memfeliz returned to South Africa, certainly,' agreed Mostert, crushing out the stub into the old tuna can she was using as an ash tray. There was a fizz and a slight odour of fish oil lifted up. 'Do you think it worth questioning him again yet?'

'Let's leave him in the *tronk* overnight, hey?' answered Joshua.

'Your accent is Afrikaans again now, you know?'

Joshua continued to knead his collar.

'Do you think your Mother has anything else to tell us?' she asked.

'Not unless she puts her Church pals under the cosh,' he replied. 'I think that's all we'll get out of her for the time being. She's probably praying for forgiveness now, in case she has unwittingly become a police informer without knowing it.'

'The best kind.' Mostert flipped Memfeliz's manila folder closed. 'What was that about a Writ?'

'Like I say,' answered Joshua, stretching. 'Some crap from my last leave. Can we call it a day now? I need a drink.'

The 23 Battalion mess was much more informal than that of 41 Mech and Joshua met with no difficulties when he entered in Captain Mostert's wake. The room was airy and as light as thatch and bare light bulbs would allow, with bare joists and roof trusses painted against the ants that devoured everything in the torpid heat of the savannah. Behind the bar, the steward was polishing the tankards one by one and hanging them up in their allotted places among the unit shields, flags and photographs and mementoes of events known only to those who had participated, like a collection of private jokes displayed in an equally private code. Two or three young officers and junior NCOs nursed cans of *Castle* around a record player listening to *Blondie* and *The Boomtown Rats*; Commandant Korrf himself was leaning against the wooden counter in an attitude of such casualness that Joshua almost mistook him for some rustic barfly in at early doors.

'Have a drink?' said Korrf, motioning them over. 'Fill me in on the details.'

Captain Mostert gave the Commandant a précis while the steward drew brandy and cokes. He listened intently, peering down into his tankard, swilling the contents around from time to time and giving a short, sharp nod each time he counted a salient point.

'So you have confirmed your knowledge rather than expanded it,' he pronounced. 'And your Mother has revealed to you a family secret, Sergeant Smith. Are you comfortable with the knowledge that you shared a pram with a black brother.'

'He isn't my brother,' answered Joshua.

'It seems that in other circumstances, he might have been a foster-brother.'

'In other circumstances, maybe,' conceded Joshua.

'Does it alter your view of the situation now that it has sprouted family connections?'

Joshua shook his head. He had not really had time to digest the information, but on the quickest of considerations he dismissed it as superficial; Memfeliz had shared a pram with him for a little while; so what?

'Does it alter the way you *feel* about Corporal Memfeliz, on any level?'

'Why should it?'

'Because family is a very odd thing, Sergeant Smith. No doubt you have been around this battalion long enough for someone to have enlightened you as to my own situation...' Mostert quickly looked down.

'...it is, I believe, common knowledge. I read that there are those of a radical persuasion who believe that the days of the family as an institution of society are coming to an end, consigned to history by easy divorce, the pill, the permissive society, a general, growing and pervasive decadence. I have read that in the future there will be things called 'families of choice' which will be associations of friends, more or less fluid, consciously chosen. What do you think of that?'

'I think its bullshit, Sir,' replied Joshua.

'I am inclined to agree with you, but I would be interested to know your reasons for believing this.' He beckoned to the steward for a refill.

'Well, I'm no philosopher, Sir, but there have always been families and even when everyone in any particular one seems to hate each other, they all seem to be drawn back together at Christmas time.'

Korrf chuckled. 'And when was the last time anyone over the age of twelve and under sixty can put their hands on their hearts and say they completely enjoyed a full, no holds barred family Christmas? Have you ever seen that movie *The Lion in Winter?* No? You should. It is about an old English King visiting his family in a castle which he keeps his wife imprisoned in. That would add a new twist to Christmas, hey?' He took the replenished tankard and continued. 'But there is a serious point here and what you say is correct; the bonds of family are very powerful and they draw people back together from long distances and long distances in time too. Brothers and sisters who have not seen each other for decades appear at the bedsides of parents they have not seen in years – ja, even when there is not a will to draw them out of the woodwork! Are you familiar with polygamy at all? I mean the traditional type - not like in Hollywood.'

'I'm not married even once,' said Joshua.

'I know the Africans often have more than one wife and that some of the Muslims down in Durban have four,' Mostert chipped in. 'But I don't know how they square it with the law.'

'And I bet Donny Osmond is a busy chap...' added Joshua, stupidly.

'For myself, as a married man, I will settle for just one wife,' interrupted Korrf. 'When you *have* been married for a little while you will appreciate this wisdom. But no, my point is this: when an African man decides he would like to take a second wife, he does not divorce the first one, but begins to visit the second one in her hut and gradually cohabits with her over a period of time, all the while keeping the first wife in the dark about his little secret.'

'Bastard,' said Mostert.

'Ja,' said Korrf. 'It is the question of bastards that forces the arrangement. For when wife number two produces a baby, his friends will insist that he tells wife number one because this will make for less trouble in the long run. They will say that a few tears – smoothed by putting *dagga* in her mealiepap – are better than a whole new family turning up at his funeral and demanding a share in the inheritance.'

'That would be a difficult interview,' smirked Joshua, ordering another brandy and coke.

'It would indeed,' agreed Korrf. 'So the institution of Right-hand wife and Left-hand wife was invented to deal with it. The first – the Right-hand – wife gets top dog status in the village, while number two – Left-hand wife - gets to build her hut on the other side and both get security for their children. In between, the husband builds his hut where he can have a bit of peace and quiet. Are you burning your bra yet, Captain Mostert?'

Mostert blushed and took a large slug from her glass. 'Everything is fine for *him*!'

'Ja, but this is not where it ends, you know.' Korrf helped her to more coke. 'Because each of these betrayed ladies will very often take a lover or two and so pay him out in his own coin.'

'Serves him right too,' said Mostert.

'Ja, true,' agreed Korrf. 'And the man must take those children as his own and care for them too.'

'This is very complicated,' said Joshua.

'It is,' agreed Korrf again. 'But the point is that each of the men and women, the husbands, wives and lovers could make life much simpler for themselves by moving away and setting up on their own. But they don't. Because the bonds of family are seen as so important that they outweigh all the heartbreak, lies and deceit that each of them experiences and engages with in their varying measures.'

'Sir,' said Joshua. 'Are you saying that we will never get a conviction of Merriman and Memfeliz because they will not rat on each other? Because, with respect Sir, we have already worked that one out.'

'What I am saying is that you should look into the *family* connections more. Mrs Merriman was perhaps, for a little while, acting like a *Left-hand* wife. So *who* was her husband?'

*

27th May 1980

'You know your Commandant has a way of making me feel like a *doos*?' said Joshua, replacing the phone in the cradle. He had tried three times without success already to call his mother in Cape Town.

'Don't worry about it, Sergeant,' replied Mostert, sitting down with a pile of box files full of newspaper clippings. 'He does that to everyone. He's got a Ph.D in Lit from Wits, you know. It didn't occur to me to ask the name of the father either.'

She pushed the top box towards him.

'According to the regimental records, Memfeliz arrived here in 1975 with the rest of the Portuguese refugees after the Marxist take-over in Angola. He joined 23 a year later, in '76, and has been based here at Echo Tango ever since. No mention of parents in his file, but I'd guess they probably came to South Africa at the same time.'

'Any periods of leave in Cape Town when he might have run into the Merrimans?' Joshua asked. 'Although I guess it's not exactly the place where a black would go for a vacation, is it?'

'*Ag*, man, in the Cape he could pass for white with a push,' she replied. 'As long as he had his papers...' she leafed back through Memfeliz's file. '....but no; nothing in here. These 23 guys are supposed to be hush-hush so a blow out in Swakopmund is about all they can expect unless they're very white or in the Officer's Mess.'

Joshua took the box-file. 'I hate paper work,' he remarked. 'What am I looking for?'

'Photographs; his name in any of the reports; family; anything.'

Opening the box, he viewed the pile of inky clippings cut from the pages of half a dozen newspapers. He recognised the letter heads of the *Johannesburg Star*, the *Cape Argus* and the *Natal Witness*, as well as a number of smaller, more local papers, his own *Graaf-Reinet*

Advertiser among them, and then, grasping the first handful, saw that there were some purple roneo evaluation reports in among them.

Scanning the first couple, he read how the Portuguese colonists, some of whom had been there for centuries and who knew no other place to call home, had been summarily booted out of Angola and Mozambique in 1975 and sped on their way with threats of massacre. There were grainy black and white photographs in the pile too, enlarged prints of the pictures embedded in the text showing columns of civilian vehicles heading south through to Ruacana, all full of sad, exhausted people. One, taken at Johannesburg railway station showed a group of teenagers in flares and feather cuts clutching suitcases, as though this was a school trip; only the empty eyes showed that it was not. Another one showed thirty or so people of all ages posing before a truck at the border. The truck looked like it was on its last legs, overloaded with the collection of bedding, cases and packages that had been swept up in panicked hurry and overflowing with sadness. All the people, every single one, even the babies, had the same expression of desperate worry stamped on their frowning faces.

'It's funny when you look at refugee photos,' he said, almost to himself. 'You expect them to be black people or Jews going to America or something. These people look like us.'

'It *will* be us if we don't win this war,' replied Mostert.

Joshua went back to the pile.

'You know I heard a story from a refugee family back then,' said Mostert, after a long pause broken only by the slow swish of the fan. 'They lived up in Luanda in a big house and ran a business employing – shit, I don't know – thirty or forty people. They paid for schooling and medical care for them and the kids and, you know, really looked after them. Then one day, the servants walked into their house and said that it was all theirs now and that if they did not leave straight away, they would murder them and their children.'

'Savages,' said Joshua.

'Well, they saw a photo of their house and business recently.'

'You don't need to tell me the rest,' he said, leafing through another report. 'The Africans had wrecked it.'

'Joshua, do you worry about what will become of us? I mean, like, all of South Africa, blacks included, if ever the ANC was to take over?'

'I see nothing but roses in my future,' he replied.

'It's just that...well, I just know that there are none of the workers on our farm who are capable of managing it. If we whites had to leave...what would happen to them?'

'They would fuck it up.' He turned over a few more sheets of newpaper. 'Or someone like my mom and Mrs Merriman would take it over and try to run it like a Church social. So it would take a little longer for it to be fucked up.'

They worked on, in silence.

A fruitless hour later, Joshua piped up.

'You know we could just ask Memfeliz who his old man was.'

'He was adopted. He won't know.'

'Didn't the father go up to Angola with him? Maybe he stayed up there with him? Maybe the old man told him who his old lady was and that he had a brother? Unless the two boys just happened to bump into each other by accident.'

'He's not talking, remember?' sighed Mostert, turning over more photographs. 'We need to find something to get him to talk. See if his name is on a list somewhere: a photo with a caption that reads *The Memfeliz family arrive in South Africa and are very grateful* would be ideal.'

'I'm going to call my mom again.'

'Why don't you go to the horse's mouth and ask Mrs Merriman?'

'She doesn't have a phone. I checked the Directory.'

'Jesus, some people are living in the dark ages.'

Joshua dialled.

'Hey Mom! Howzit?'

'Joshua? *Again*?'

'Mom, what you told me yesterday, hey? I just need one more thing.'

'I will *not* tell you the name of the father, Joshua.'

Captain Mostert rolled her eyes.

'How did you know that is what I was going to ask?'

'Mothers know everything,' muttered Mostert.

'Joshua, I have known you since before you knew yourself. This is not information I wish to divulge.'

'Mother, please,' said Smith, making an apologetic face for Captain Mostert.

'Mrs Merriman deserves some privacy and I do not see how this can possibly help David Merriman – or his...brother.'

'No, Mother. This is really very serious.'

'Is this line being tapped by State Security, Joshua?'

'What?'

'Are you working for the Bureau of State Security, Joshua? You know how I disapprove of State Security.'

'Mother? Is this for real?'

'I have been having coffee and cake with Mrs Merriman this morning, Joshua and she is not happy at all with your enquiries, Joshua.'

'Not happy, Mother?'

'She is not keen to remember those days. It was a terrible wrench for her and she has kept this secret in her heart for all these many years. Joshua, she is a married woman and you should remember this.'

'It sounds like she should have remembered too.'

'Calm down, Joshua,' said Mostert. 'There's a good boy.'

'*Fok jou, Ma'am*' he mouthed in reply. 'Mother...'

'Joshua, that is a very un-Christian thing to say and you were not raised to say such things out loud to your mother.'

'Sorry, Mother, but this is really important...'

'What would happen if Clive found out? Have you considered this? Why, can you imagine what Freda Stein would make of this if it got out? Sheila would lose her place on the Church committee in an instant.'

'Mother,' pleaded Joshua. 'Mother, I just need the name so I can eliminate him from our enquiries.'

'Liar,' said Mostert, smiling.

'What *enquiries* are you making, Joshua? This is not a State Security investigation, is it?'

'Why would State Security be interested in Mrs Merriman's twenty five year old affair?' answered Joshua, pressing his splinted fingers to his temple.

'You must tell me that. How should I know?'

Joshua waved the telephone in the air as if he was about to beat God to death.

'Mother, please,' he began again. 'It is not a big deal...'

'It is to Mrs Merriman...'

'...so just save me a lot of time and trouble and tell me...'

'Wait a moment, Joshua. There is someone at the door.'

The sound of the handset being placed down on the side table cut off the conversation.

'Is your Mother like this? Honestly?' said Joshua.

'You have got that English accent again,' she replied, without looking up from the file. 'It's quite a bit sexy, you know?'

'Ja, I feel very sexy right now.'

'It's gone again.' She turned over another photo. Looked again carefully and then held it up to the light. 'Hello, we might just have something here. Let me just check with the card index. Back shortly.'

'Take your time. And bring a Klippie and coke back, hey?'

'It's ten o'clock in the morning, Sergeant Smith,' she chided.

'Ja and it's six o'clock somewhere and I still have to have this conversation with this crazy old woman.'

The phone crackled.

'Joshua, I do hope that you are not referring to me?'

'No, course not, Mother. There is someone else here...'

'I hope you were not referring to me,' teased Mostert, gathering up a few papers. 'That would be *insubordination*, hey, *Sergeant*?'

'Mom, Mother, look...'

'Are they from State Security?'

'Who?'

'The people you are with...'

'No, Mother – who was at the door?'

'It is Mr du Plessis. He is taking your package to the Post Office so that it may be redirected to you. Where should I tell him to address it to? He is waiting.'

'My usual address will be fine.'

'But you are not in Graaf-Reinet, Joshua, and you have not been there for months now.'

Yes, but the Police Station there will know where to send it to.'

'Are you on a secret mission for State Security?'

'No, Mother, I am working on a sensitive case, that is all. So please send it to the usual address.'

'Do you think you will be home for Christmas?'

'Mother, it is May.'

'Yes, but it is important to make arrangements early so that no one is left out and arrangements are well worked out in advance. Yes, Mr du Plessis, the address is in the book – under 'J' for Joshua...yes, that is it. No...the other one...wait a moment...'

The telephone relayed the muffled sound of a distant polite conversation and then rumbled as it was picked up again.

'Yes, thank you for your kindness. Yes...'

'Are you talking to me now, Mother?'

'...yes, I know Mr du Plessis. Children can be so impatient and demanding. But thank you again...yes, please...a receipt would be very nice...'

'Mother!'

'Joshua, please do not be so impatient....yes, thank you. You can see your own way out Mr du Plessis? Thank you again...yes, Goodbye and please give my regards...'

'I think we may have something,' said Captain Mostert, returning with a new file clearly marked *Bureau Of State Security*.

'*Where did you get that*?' mouthed Joshua, eyes wide as he pointed to the file.

'Has your Mother confessed yet or will we need the electric chair?'

'Please, get it charged up to maximum,' replied Joshua, clenching his fist and banging it against his forehead.

'Now Joshua, where were we?'

'You were going to tell me the name of Mrs Merriman's lover and the father of her extra baby.'

'I was not. And *extra* is not really respectful of a human being.'

Captain Mostert leafed through the BOSS file and pulled out a photograph, which she compared to the one she had lifted from the pile of press cuttings.

'Mother, you can be assured that I will spare Mrs Merriman's blushes and not tell Clive about her bit on the side.'

'Where did you ever hear such an uncouth expression? I am shocked. Well maybe not so shocked. Have you seen your father recently, Joshua? Are you still sending him money?'

'Oh, yes, Mother, I am still keeping the bar of the Krugerburg Hotel in business.'

'He is still your father, Joshua.'

'Mother, can we leave dad out of this for a moment? I need to find out who the father of Heironimo Ortez Memfeliz is at the moment. So please, Mother, spill the beans, hey?'

'Ask her if it is *Onele Nonyana*,' said Captain Mostert, holding up two photographs side by side.

'Joshua? Who is speaking that name? Did you know all along? Joshua....Joshua....Are you still there....'

But Joshua did not answer because he had dropped the phone and was outside the Intelligence office puking into the dry flower bed and shaking like a man in the last throes of a fatal fever.

07

No Greater Love.

'Ja, I'm fine thanks. No, no. It's just something I ate – the medication. Is my mother still on the line?'

Joshua was wiping sticky, bitter liquid from his chin and brushing away the half-digested and identifiable remains of the bacon and porridge breakfast that had spattered his boots.

'I hung up for you,' replied Mostert, a sympathetic hand on his back. 'Are you sure that you do not need to lie down or something?'

Ja, ja, really. I'm OK.'

'Do you want to see the medic?'

'No, no, honestly...'

'I can help you over there if you like...'

'*Fok's* sake, no! I'm fine.'

'Touchy, hey? You must be feeling a little better.'

'Tell me about...' the name stuck in his throat. 'Tell me what you found out about Memfeliz's old man.'

They went back into the office, the cool darkness a relief from the heat and the glare of the strong daylight. Mostert picked up the newspaper photograph and handed it across to Smith, who was wiping his hands on a bit of rag.

'Do you want to clean up first?' she asked.

Joshua saw that he was rubbing his hands too hard and nodded. 'I'll just use the bathroom quickly and then we can get down to work.'

The washroom at the end of the room was lit only by a single bare bulb and by what light could squeeze through the horizontal bars of the ventilation grill. The smell was damp and close and concrete and the water coughed out brown and spluttering for a few moments before the air lock shifted and it flowed free. Joshua put his hands under the tap and began to wash them, then scooped up the water to dash away the cold sweat on his pallid face, all the while being careful not to catch his reflection in the deteriorating silver of the cracked mirror above the basin. He looked at the backs of his hands, inspected the nails there and then flexed those fingers that were not splinted together. He wished that he had brought clean sticking plaster to replace the sweat and dust grimed, frayed dressing that held one broken finger to another and then considered using the meagre worn cake of soap to scrub at it. He dismissed the thought; the bandages were like his soul and would never scrub clean. Turning around, he pulled at the lavatory paper that hung from the fitting in the cubicle there and screwed it up into a temporary plug for the basin, aware that his hands needed something to do if they were not to begin shaking uncontrollably. When the basin was full, he took a breath and then plunged his head under the water, keeping it there for as long as he could before flipping up again and spraying water around the small room. The water was brackish but cool enough and he repeated the baptism two or three times more before he felt ready for what Captain Mostert was going to tell him. Putting his hands against the wall, eyes closed and pushing hard, he steadied himself, then took out the plug, and tossed it into the lavatory without looking in the mirror.

'You better now?' she said, as he emerged.

He nodded and gave a weak shrug of his shoulders. 'The painkillers on an empty stomach.'

She waited a moment for him to sit down.

'You want to see what I found out?'

He nodded again, trying to look as though his stomach was not tremulous with a leaden anxiety.

'You sure? You look like shit.'

'Never felt better,' he replied, coughing back acid.

She took a long, querulous look at him.

'What?' he said. 'It's puke OK? You never had too much Hooly Juice?'

'Ja,' she said. 'But normally it comes with a hangover.'

'I'm OK,' he insisted. 'Stop looking at me like I'm a *bergie* come to get drunk on your nice Cape Town wine farm.'

'As you wish.' She shrugged and pushed the first photograph towards him. *Portuguese Flee Communist Murders* announced the caption; *Cape Families Respond to Calls for Hospitality.* 'They are on the left of the group.'

Joshua ran his finger along the queue of displaced people at a reception centre somewhere. It was hard to distinguish Memfeliz from the other people there because his complexion was no darker than many of the other refugees and the tartan suitcase and brown paper package he was holding were interchangeable too. It was not difficult to spot the only black man in the picture however and though he was not facing the camera directly, Joshua could tell from the easy pose that the two men were father and son. He felt his stomach lurch.

'So?'

'So, the man with Memfeliz has an uncanny resemblance to...' she pushed a second photograph towards him, this time from the BOSS file. '...this man. I wonder if they are related?'

Joshua took the photograph and felt his heart begin to beat faster. It was a standard numbered front and profile of a detainee, but from out of the frame came the dark, unflinching, sulphurous hot eyes of a furious man bent on revenge. He recognised them; he could not mistake them; they were seared into his brain.

'Are you sure?' he said.

'Looks pretty similar to me – and don't give me that crap about them all looking alike.' She took the photograph back. 'Let's see what the file has to tell us about Mr *Onele Nonyana*, shall we? Here we go; born 1935, Transkei – what was he doing in the Cape then, the naughty boy? Or was that before the Pass Laws came in? No matter...Hey! He's a rich boy, is our Onyele, educated at Fort Hare and ...oh shit....'

Joshua felt his mouth fill with a sahara.

'Jesus, Sergeant Smith,' she said, the blood draining from her face. 'His old man went to school with Nelson Mandela...the Commandant is going to have a fit, man. Memfeliz's old man is ANC! Now *that* is a motive for killing Lieutenant Keay if ever I saw one.'

Joshua said nothing. A weight was crushing down upon him now, a weight strong enough to crush all the future out of him.

'There's more here...' continued Mostert, now excited. 'Active in the youth movements...Sharpeville...Soweto...busted twice....thought to have been in Angola in the late fifties! Yes, that's him then. And...last seen four years ago in...Graaf-Reinet disturbances...Wait,' she said, looking up. 'Isn't that your neck of the woods?'

Joshua did not respond.

'He's probably in Russia or Bulgaria or Cuba now,' she said, reading on.

'Probably,' agreed Joshua, through strained lips.

'Let's talk to Memfeliz, hey? Then we can have a full story to tell the Commandant. Looks like I'd better do the talking this time.'

Joshua nodded his agreement. His face was cold, as if all the blood had run from it.

*

Memfeliz was still silently defiant when he was brought in. He kept his cuffed hands between his knees and did his best to focus his eyes only on them, but as Mostert laid out the photographs in front of him, then added some more mined from the box files, he could not help but flicker over them. Joshua watched the corner of his eyes creasing, his lips working, watched the nostrils flair and the frowns that grew or diminished in intensity as each of the pictures was displayed.

'So, you are who you say you are,' began Mostert gently. 'But at the same time, you are a different person than the one we thought you were. Do you want to tell us why you joined 23 Battalion, Heironimo?'

There was no reply beyond a working of Memfeliz's mouth, as though he were chewing. Mostert opened his personnel file.

'No complaints of your military behaviour in here,' she continued, in the same soft tone. 'Promotion, recommendations from Officers and NCOs alike, plenty of experience.'

She paused as though reading. Memfeliz's eyes were casting uncertain glances at the pictures before him. She went back to the BOSS file.

'Not a sniff of disloyal activity here from you...until you shot Lieutenant Keay.'

She flipped some loose leaves back and forward, making a show of cross-checking information.

'You really are on our side aren't you? Unless you are some kind of...what do you call them, Sergeant Smith?'

'Sleepers,' replied Joshua. 'Agents sent to burrow deep into an organisation so they can rise up through the ranks and betray it all the more.'

'I know what a sleeper is,' said Memfeliz, quietly. 'And I am not one.'

'Well, what *are* you then?' asked Joshua.

Memfeliz ignored the question and focussed on Captain Mostert.

'Let's ask about your family background, then,' she said. 'White mother, black father, illegitimate birth – not really usual that, but not *that* unusual either – all involved in anti-Apartheid activities. You are spirited away by your father to live in freedom in the Portuguese colony of Angola where you are cared for by...someone, the file doesn't say...but we can infer that you had regular visits from your father who continued with his political activities. Would you like to tell us something about *them*?'

'My father's politics are his own affair. Ask him.'

Mostert gave a little high pitched hum of agreement.

'Well tell us about growing up in Angola then.'

'I grew up, went to school and then got kicked out.'

'That it?' she said. 'No, I'm curious. We had some family friends up there before the revolution back in...when was it?'

'1974.'

'That's right. Where did you go to school?'

'What?'

'Which school did you go to?'

'It was run by nuns.'

'Ja, nice,' she produced a packet of cigarettes and put them on the table. 'Smoke?'

Memfeliz held up his cuffed hands.

'Are these really, absolutely necessary?' she asked Joshua, pointing to the cuffs.

'Yes,' said Joshua. 'They are.'

'Can you smoke with them still around your wrists, Heironimo?'

'*Corporal Memfeliz*,' said Joshua. 'Call him by his proper name.'

Mostert looked from one to the other and then repeated her question: 'Can you smoke with the cuffs on, *Heironimo*?'

He shot an irritated dart at Joshua and nodded. 'Score me a *lus.*'

She took out a cigarette from the packet and handed it to Memfeliz, waited for him to manipulate it towards his mouth and then lit it for him. He inhaled deeply and blew out a volcano of blue smoke.

'Which high school did you go to?'

'Just high school.'

'English or Portuguese?'

'Portuguese.'

'And the people who looked after you?'

'Portuguese.'

'Churchy?'

Memfeliz drew on his cigarette again and nodded as he exhaled.

'So, you grew up thinking of yourself more as a Portuguese person than as a South African?'

'Luso-African,' he replied. 'More *Luso*, than African. My first language is Portuguese, with English second and my Xhosa is just enough to buy a beer and say hello to my father.'

'How did your father feel about that?' She kept her eyes on the file.

'He said we were living in exile, that such things were to be expected and that one day we would go back to South Africa. He was right about all those things, especially the last bit.'

'So you and him fell out over the revolution?' she said, thinking out loud. 'Let me make a wild guess and say that he was in favour of beating up the colonial oppressors, while what you saw was all your friends being mistreated and dispossessed. Must have been tough getting kicked out by the forces of black liberation.'

'You will have to ask him about his politics.'

'Am I on the right track?'

Memfeliz drew on the cigarette again and nodded.

'Did you know who your mother was?'

Memfeliz tensed up suddenly, as though he had been kicked.

'So the answer is *no*,' said Joshua, too loud, too urgent.

'I knew *of* her. I was adopted by a Portuguese family,' replied Memfeliz, letting go of the tension.

'White?' asked Joshua.

'White enough.'

'Were you angry about this?' said Mostert, slowly, dropping her voice, yet keeping a lilting quality to it.

'I was a baby. I didn't know anything until '74.'

'1974?' coaxed Mostert. 'Go on.'

'I didn't have a *Portuguese passport...*'

Memfeliz dropped the cigarette end and crushed it out under his heel.

'They were to send for me,' he said bitterly. 'I was to go to Lisbon and then to the university and become a doctor or a lawyer, whatever....'

'But your father intervened,' said Joshua, surmising. 'Liberation first, *then* education, hey?'

'Have you seen them since? Did they get in touch from Lisbon?' asked Mostert.

'I have not heard from them in more than five years. I have no address for them and they have no address for me. I have no way of finding them short of a miracle and I cannot go to Portugal to look for them *because I have no passport.*'

'So your real father, Onele Nonyana, brought you back to South Africa as part of the refugee crisis,' said Mostert. 'Jeez.'

She sat back in her chair and pushed a hand over her forehead.

'And in Cape Town at the Reception Centre, your real mother, Mrs Sheila Merriman found you.' Mostert offered the cigarettes once more. 'And *you* found David. That must have been hectic, hey? One hell of a shock.'

'One hell of a shock? Yes. Several one hell of a shocks. The biggest one was receiving my racial classification.'

Captain Mostert had tucked her beret into her epaulette again and had stopped taking notes.

'I had to go to an office in Cape Town and queue up with some of the other refugees to get papers or a *passport*,' said Memefeliz. 'Then, some guy comes down the line and started sticking his pencil into peoples' hair and making some of them go to a separate window at the counter. He came to me, stuck his pencil into my afro, left it there a moment and then directed me to the window; that's how I became Coloured.'

'Apartheid is a very scientific system,' said Mostert.

'And so now I couldn't live with Sheila– I could not call her 'mother' – and David and Clive -,'

'How did *he* take your arrival?' asked Joshua. 'Not very well if he's anything like my old man, I bet.'

'Clive,' sighed Memfeliz. 'Clive knew just exactly what I was, but he just couldn't work it out. To his credit, he didn't ask either and so we all played a game called 'Don't tell Clive' for the best part of a year.'

'Some investigative journalist, huh? You didn't tell him?'

'What would have been the point? Besides, I had come to realise that frankly, I was looking at a future that wasn't black or white in any sense of the word and in which this new, old family would not play any part. I had to make my own way; this is the refugee's truth. I had to eat; I heard of 23; it sounded like a good idea at the time; it *was* a good idea and still is, even though it is like a state of suspended animation.'

He looked up at the ceiling.

'You know, if you have never really had a real family, the army is a great thing,' he said. 'It is also a good *university*, even though it will not give you the qualifications necessary to go to university to become a lawyer or a doctor, it teaches you a lot about yourself and about life.'

'So who are you fighting for?' asked Joshua.

'For me, of course,' replied Memfeliz, as though the question was impertinent. 'And my regiment.'

'No, I mean, *politically*,' said Joshua.

'Oh *politically*, you mean,' he mocked. 'The answer is the same. Who do you think I should fight for?'

'The ANC, like your old man.' Joshua's voice was hard, too hard.

'The ANC?' replied Memfeliz, dripping sarcasm. 'Those people who are friends with the MPLA Communists? The people who took my family home and business and my university prospects and my chance to choose my own life in Angola or Portugal? Yes – they are first on my list of people to fight for.'

'Where is your father now?' asked Mostert.

'We lost touch,' replied Memfeliz. 'I haven't seen him since I joined up. You can check that.'

Joshua felt the tightness in his stomach dissipate like mist on a mere and reached for the cigarettes.

'What about David?' asked Mostert.

'David,' said Memfeliz, carefully. 'Was not a good character. His parents considered themselves to be very *modern* and had some new ideas about parental authority that would not be given much attention in Angola. You have heard of Dr Spock, no doubt...'

'Ja, he's that pointy eared guy...'said Joshua. Mostert silenced him with a lift of her chin.

'So he was not *disciplined.* He would not take any responsibility for himself. I learned this very quickly. I am not surprised that he took two attempts to pass his Matric.' Memfeliz grimaced. 'To give up an opportunity that someone else would give anything for...he only went to university so he could defer his military service. He talked all the time of trying to get an Irish *passport*. And so I left him behind too.'

'Pissed off because he could go to university or that he could get a passport? When did you last see him?' said Joshua.

'I became aware that he was with 41 Mech when he was called up in November last. At a braii. He does not like the army.'

'Is that why he killed those officers?' coaxed Mostert.

'I have no idea why he killed those officers,' replied Memfeliz.

'Why did you kill Lieutenant Keay?'

Memfeliz sat back in his chair, dropped his head onto his chest, put his cuffed hands into his lap and said no more.

*

'He's offering us a deal,' said Joshua as they walked over to the Mess. 'He'll tell us about Lieutenant Keay if we get him a passport so he can bugger off to Lisbon and get on with his life.'

'How can he think we can do that?' replied Mostert.

'You showed him the BOSS file. If they can't get a passport, who can?'

'Why does he think we will trade?'

'Perhaps what the Commandant says about family bonds is not correct in all its particulars? Perhaps he has been so fucked about that he doesn't care anymore. Man, that braii smells good.'

'Makes a change from the aroma of 41 Mech, for sure,' agreed Mostert. 'Who would think families could be so complex, hey? What happened to 2.4 kids and four *krimpies*? Can you imagine what he feels like? I mean, he gets to be black, gets his whole world turned over by the communists, can't achieve his ambition to be a lawyer or whatever and ends up fighting for a system that will never let him rise up.'

'Especially when he discovers brother David is a *mompie* who can go to university but doesn't want to and ends up here fighting for a system that *he* doesn't agree with either. All it needs is the communists to come and fuck his life up as well and they will be *real* twins,' said Joshua. 'Ja, this is one fucked up case.'

They pushed in through the Mess doors and took in the rich smell of charcoal grilled meat wafted over them by the ceiling fans.

'Grade A Grass-fed Limpopo beef is the best,' declared Joshua. 'Though the local stuff is pretty good too.'

'You got your appetite back then?'

Joshua nodded.

'Can I ask you something, Sergeant Smith?'

'Go ahead.'

'Have you ever *not wanted* to catch a murderer?'

'Is that the Commandant waving to us?' answered Joshua.

Commandant Korff was sitting dumpily at a table with a mound of yellow mealiepap and boerwors before him.

'Get your food and then come join me,' he called. 'Man, this is *real* food.'

Joshua and Captain Mostert filled plates from the buffet and went over to sit at the plain trestle table set a little apart from the other tables. Korff talked as he shovelled in the corn porridge.

'They call these *grits* in America,' he said, between mouthfuls. 'But they use a different variety of maize, I think, and then mix in butter and white pepper. It's isn't as good to my mind, but then I suppose it is what you are used to that is most familiar. It is the same with sausages; the English people in England only have pork in their bangers and in Israel, it is always lamb with spices. Do you think a person's character is formed by the food they make and can this be applied to a whole nation, hey?'

'You are what you eat?' offered Mostert, joking uncertainly. 'The French call the English *rosbifs* and the English call the French and Germans *frogs* and *krauts*.'

'What I mean is that Italian food is created from very basic ingredients that would be available to the poorest farmer – flour, eggs, tomatoes, herbs. Would the fact that the farmer's wife has created a great cuisine from so little limit the farmer's ambitions to eat more expensive meat, to expand his business to pay for it and so guarantee that he remains poor? And is our present predicament here a result of our desire to eat a lot of meat? For you know that to raise cattle and sheep commercially in South Africa requires a lot of land and that desire for land resulted in the Dutch and the other Europeans pushing the African off *his* lands.'

'If the Europeans had not come to this land, it would never have been so productive,' replied Joshua. 'You are what you don't get to eat in Biafra.'

'You may be right, Sergeant Smith. Many of our historians would agree with you, though many would not. The problem with our country is that every race thinks that they are the original oak and that every other race is just a vein of strangling ivy, when in reality everyone planted their own oak here and then, like the ivy they claim to despise, clambered on each others' oaks.' Korrf took up another forkful and chewed. 'Does that make sense? Perhaps I have mixed up my metaphors. No matter.' He cut at a piece of sausage. 'Have you seen famine at first hand, Sergeant Smith? I have; in the place that you name, and now the Israelis are warning that there is a Red Terror going on in Ethiopia that will end in a famine to make Biafra look like the gap between lunch and dinner.' Korff added another mouthful and swallowed. 'You would think that the world had bigger things to worry about than South Africa, but apparently, it has not. Tell me about your investigation.'

Joshua and Captain Mostert exchanged glances and then she filled in the salient details of Memfeliz's background.

'Another odd tree in the orchard of South Africa,' said Korrf, when she had finished. 'Eat while I think,' he said, getting up to fetch his own tea.

'He's a bit philosophical, isn't he?' remarked Joshua, quietly. 'I mean, for a soldier.'

Mostert did not reply but followed the form of Lieutenant Visser as he came through the Mess doors and headed for the buffet. He was tall, blonde, built for rugby and the farms.

'He's a lucky man,' said Joshua, following her eyes.

'He is indeed,' she replied, looking down. 'Do you think Memfeliz was going to kill him?'

'No,' replied Joshua. 'I don't. But I think Merriman might have, given the chance.'

'So you don't think Memfeliz killed Keay either?'

'Tell me about Keay,' said Joshua. He poked his food a little. 'How long have you known him?'

'Not long,' she replied, laying down her fork. 'Although he is officially 41 Mech, he wants to join the Special Forces so he was seconded to 23 only a couple of months ago. To be honest, I've hardly spoken to him. He's been out on Ops quite a lot. The Commandant thinks he needs the experience.'

'So not long enough to piss Memfeliz off for any reason?'

'Not long enough to piss anyone off.'

'And you say he lacked experience?'

'So?'

'It's just the whole collusion aspect of this that has me confused,' he said. 'The Liquorice Allsorts brothers meet at a braii and cook up a scheme to kill a bakkie load of officers over their families' involvement in some Apartheid *kak* in District 6; Merriman does his bit with Dietz and Steyl; Memfeliz is supposed to bump off Keay and Visser. Except that when Keay is bumped off, Merriman is *Jo! Jislaaik!* with surprise and comes running over here; is caught and then coughs to the murder of Visser, who isn't dead, but *is* out in the bush, safe and sound and happy as a sandboy, with Audie Murphy Memfeliz who could double tap him in no time, no witnesses, no questions asked, but hasn't. And now, the Prodigal Brother is offering us the answer to the mystery in return for a passport out, while the *dagga* Brother is volunteering for crucifixion.'

Commandant Korrf returned with his enamel tea mug and shuffled back into his seat.

'And he wants a passport to go to Lisbon, you say? Well, it could be arranged, I suppose. There are enough men in this unit with the know-how to provide him with a false one, but his loyalty and service have earned him something better I think.' Korrf slurped at his tea and then blew on the rim of the mug. 'And with three dead officers, Corporal Sanchez beaten up and relations with 41 Mech rather strained, we must have answers. The families must have answers. And if the answer he provides is unsatisfactory, his brother Merriman is willing to carry the can for all three murders. It would seem a neat solution, were Memefeliz to find himself in Lisbon. The problem would at least have gone away.'

'Could he be trusted not to tell the world about 23? We are supposed to be secret, Commandant,' said Mostert. 'What happens if he casts doubt on Merriman's guilt once he is away from here in Europe?'

'Oh, the arm of BOSS is long, Captain Mostert,' replied Korrf casually. 'It would be made clear that a quiet life going up the Santa Justa lift to the cafes in the Largo di Carmo in Lisbon's fine climate would come with certain guarantees of discretion, I dare say. Make him the offer.' Korrf paused as though reconsidering. 'No. He has done his time here and served well. The regiment must be seen to do right by its own. Memfeliz is one of *us* and we are his family, if what you tell me is true. That must count for something, even if he has killed an officer. Tell him, he has my word, but only on the rendering of a full account.' He looked out of the window to the distant horizon over the landscape that lay olive, tan and bleached like sea salted wood. 'Tell him, if he holds anything back, or we suspect him of doing so, then he also has my word that he will be cast away on his own resources. And it is a long way to *anywhere* from here.'

*

29th May 1980

'You shot him by *fokken* mistake? Do you expect us to believe such *kak*?'

'Do you wish to explain the circumstances of this tale, Corporal?' said Mostert, pushing her beret back and throwing her pencil down.

'Or should we get Pinnochio in to tell it for you?' Joshua smacked his hand down on the table and winced as the pain reverberated through his splinted fingers.

'And then you can explain why you did not bring this information forward earlier,' added Mostert.

'What do you expect?' replied Memfeliz, rocking backwards and forwards in his desperation. 'Who would believe me? Two officers down...my brother held responsible...and have you noticed the colour of my skin? Ok, I should have owned up earlier but...'

'We didn't know it was your brother...' protested Joshua.

'Was it so difficult to work out? I'm amazed it took you so long! Or are you as stupid as the rest of the SAPS?'

'You need a kicking, Memfeliz?' shouted Joshua.

'I'd love one,' taunted Memfeliz, standing up and brandishing his cuffs. 'Go get your friends, *poes,* because you will need them.'

'For *foks* sake! Sit down! Both of you! That's an order, *Sergeant* Smith and *Corporal* Memfeliz. Do I need to open a window to let out some of this *fokken* testosterone?'

Memfeliz held Joshua's eye without flinching and Joshua saw the family resemblance – only the burning eyes were not those of David Merriman but those of Onele Nanyana.

'You need I put you back in the same pram and so you can both hit each other with your teddy bears and rattles, hey?' said Captain Mostert.

'Same pram?' said Memfeliz. 'What are you talking about woman?'

'*Ma'am* to you. Meet your *fokken* foster brother! And don't call him a *poes* in front of a lady, hey?'

'He's not my foster-brother!' said Joshua, clenching his one functional fist at the end of a pumped up forearm.

'Close enough,' answered Mostert. 'Now *fokken* shut your mouths. Both of you!'

'Foster-brother?' said Memfeliz, subsiding into the chair and putting his forehead down onto the table. 'Tell me, missy, do I have any other relations that I do not know of?'

'How the hell should I know?' she replied, dismissively. 'Look, OK, you shared a cot with him for a little bit before you went to Angola. That's all.' She looked around at Joshua. 'You have gone pale again. You want me to get a palm frond and fan you? No? Good. Sit!'

Joshua sat once more and dug his nails into his palms. His hands were shaking again and he did not want anyone to see.

'You ready now, Sergeant Smith?' she asked.

He jammed his hands into his pockets.

'Good,' she said, picking up the pencil. 'Corporal Memfeliz, on with your story. You shot Keay by mistake?'

He sat back in the chair again, his legs wide apart, his cuffed hands between them and a look of sour frustration spread across his supplicant features.

'We were out with 41. They were running around the bush in their Noddy cars, getting in the way and generally raising up the dust and every kind of trouble they could think of. We, *us*, Lieutenant Keay, me and three others were supposed to be clearing a bunker when we started taking fire. It was not very serious but Keay got all John Wayne on us and ran forward firing from the hip in the way that no sensible soldier ever does. SWAPO had a concealed 23mm and let rip and so the rest of us lay down, watching for the flash and the smoke and then returned fire. That's when Keay popped up, right in our line of fire – he was charging it, for Christ's sake – and that's when I hit him. Double tap. He just popped up like a jack-in-a-box in my line of fire just as I fired. It was an accident. What else can I say?'

'Anybody see you or can vouch for you?' asked Joshua.

'The bush was pretty close there.'

Mostert wrote a note and then laid down the pencil.

'What did you and David Merriman discuss when you met at the braii?' she asked. 'Because he seems to have a different view on these events than you do.'

Memfeliz put his hands to his mouth and blew into them.

'He smokes too much *dagga*,' he said. 'Those months we spent together in the Cape? He was never without it.'

'You didn't use it too?'

Memfeliz shook his head. 'It turns you into a zombie or an idiot.'

'So... the braii?' prompted Mostert.

'The braii...' Memfeliz ran his bottom lip over his top.

'You tell all, or there is no passport,' Joshua reminded him.

'He is still my brother,' answered Memfeliz.

'Ja, like I am,' said Joshua. 'So tell me and we will keep it all in the family, hey?'

Memfeliz considered for a moment.

'He was shot away, just like I remembered,' said Memfeliz. 'A stupid grin and red eyes. He said he had been on to his – our – mother and that she was involved in some court case or other. He said that she and Clive and some others were trying to bring civil proceedings against some of the officers up here, as part of some big case for compensation.'

'Would that be related to District 6?' asked Mostert.

Memfeliz assented. 'Apparently, the deeds to the properties there had been spread about various rich families and family members to make it more difficult for cases to be brought. Each separate deed meant a separate court case and separate costs and so on. He told me that Lieutenants Dietz, Steyl, Keay and Visser were all holders of deeds to property in District 6. The plan was to serve them with writs actually on the bases and so expose both the District 6 issue and the extent of the war here in South West Africa and Angola.'

'Was my mother involved in this too?' blurted Joshua.

'I do not know your mother,' said Memfeliz. 'But if she is a friend of Sheila Merriman's it is possible.'

'Carry on, please,' said Mostert, writing. 'As fully as you can, please.'

Memfeliz swallowed. 'He said he had a better idea.'

'To kill them...' said Mostert.

Memfeliz nodded.

'And you went along with him?'

'I thought he was full of bullshit,' he protested. 'Do you know how many times soldiers talk about double tapping an officer? Every time they get put on stag! Every time their boots aren't shined! Come on! You know this!'

'So...what did you say?'

'I told him to have another *Castle* or a big bottle of Klippie or Redheart or whatever it was he was fucking himself up with! What do you think I said?'

'Did you not put two and two together when Sanchez was arrested for the murder of Dietz?' Mostert looked up from her notes. 'Or Steyl?'

Memfeliz shook his head quickly. 'Not after the first one. And I just thought Steyl was a coincidence.'

'Did he mention Keay as part of this list of people to be served up?'

'Yup. Keay came to us a little time after the braii.'

Joshua took the pencil from Captain Mostert and wrote: *That would account for Merriman's surprise. He must have thought that brother Memfeliz was on board at last.* She looked at the note and nodded.

'Did you know he came looking for you after Keay was killed?' she asked.

'I heard,' said Memfeliz. 'Grapevine.'

'Why do you think he did that?'

'I have no idea. Speak to him.'

*

'Well,' said Korrf, wrinkling his nose in distaste. 'He is certainly clever enough to go to university and he will probably find himself head of a faculty very quickly, if he goes on like this. A mistake, you say?'

Mostert looked down at her boots.

'So I will lose a good soldier, for no good reason.' He poured hot water from the small black kettle on the spirit stove into the enamel mug that sat upon his desk jotter. 'I suppose it is of no matter. I am getting more Rhodesian volunteers than I know what to do with these days.'

'We had no idea,' offered Joshua. 'But it happens sometimes that there is a coincidence.'

'This is true,' agreed Korrf. 'But we have still been played by Corporal Memfeliz. Are you sure he gave up everything.'

Joshua shrugged in a passive sort of assent. 'As far as we can be without roughing him up a bit.'

'I don't like torture,' said Korrf, sipping at the tea. 'Unless it is done properly and over a long period, or in the immediate moment when the guy is terrified out of his wits, you can never rely on the answers given. And I would face many problems from the mercenaries and volunteers here, if I resorted to torturing my own *troupies*. So Memfeliz will get his passport and Mr and Mrs Keay will get a tragic hero who died in combat, the details of which I will make up shortly. No doubt I will be able to replace him with a Rhodesian.'

He gave a sigh of finality.

'So your work here at least is over, Sergeant Smith,' he continued. 'Sanchez will recover, Visser is still hale and hearty and Lieutenant Keay's death is accounted for. 23's interest in this matter is at an end and Captain Mostert here can return to more regular duties – tracking down proper *terrs*.'

'I'd like to continue on the case, if I may Sir,' said Mostert, eagerly. 'There is still the issue of why David Merriman owned up to killing Keay and Visser.'

'Neither of which problems are ours, Captain Mostert,' answered Korrf. 'As I understand it, David Merriman has confessed to the killing of Dietz and Steyl; that will convict him alone. We don't need any more answers.'

'But, Sir...' protested Mostert.

'And I, for one, do not propose to look for any more.' Korrf cut her further protest off. 'Merriman deserted, took the wrong road and headed in this direction rather than due south, north or anywhere else. I choose to believe this. You should too. If 41 Mech wish to believe something else, that is their affair. Sergeant Smith...'

'Sir?'

'Major van der Merwe has requested your presence back at Oshadangwa and I suggest that you join him at your earliest convenience.' There was no discussion in Korrf's voice. 'Transport will leave at first light tomorrow. Thank you for your help. Have a nice trip. Good bye.'

'Sir,' replied Joshua and turned to go.

'One more thing, Sergeant Smith.'

'Sir?'

'Please ask 41 to return my chest freezers.'

08

Spandau Kop

'Well, that's that then,' said Captain Mostert, holding her third brandy and coke. 'Everyone's happy, although we still have no idea why Merriman killed Dietz and Steyl.'

'So you aren't going with the District 6 motive then?' replied Joshua, holding a couple of ice cubes.

'It's feasible enough for 41 Mech and that's all that matters apparently.'

Joshua dropped the ice cubes into her glass.

'But you still don't believe it?'

'Who cares what I believe?'

'What *do* you believe?'

'I don't know what I believe,' she said, swilling the ice cubes around. 'But I just can't bring myself to believe it's because someone knocked a few buildings down in Cape Town and upset Merriman's mummy.'

'You think it's not because of family reasons then?'

'Perhaps he had a guilt trip about having a black brother...'

'*Coloured*, technically speaking...'

'...or he smoked too much *dagga*...or he once had a black, sorry *coloured*, girlfriend – you know Chinese people are classed as *Coloured*? I wonder what an Eskimo married to an Italian would be? Smith...'

'Mostert?'

'Joshua?

'Trudi?'

'*Sergeant*?'

'Ma'am?'

'Does anyone really believe this Apartheid crap? I mean, *seriously*?'

'Plenty,' said Joshua. 'But most sensible people have learned the trick of not thinking about it all. Look around you. Look at 41 Mech. All good, fit, happy, handsome young men in their prime having the time of their lives with guns, helicopters, Ratels, rugby and braiis. The only thing they are missing is women and girls. If you ask them what they think about Apartheid they will probably mutter something about the bible or how the blacks are happy with their lot or that they personally don't agree with it, but hey, what can I do?'

'I mean – pour me another...'

'You sure?'

'I'm sure. I mean, did you believe all that religious crap in school? That stuff about Noah and Ham?'

'No, I didn't,' replied Joshua with a smirk. 'You know President Kruger thought a giraffe was really a camel because otherwise it couldn't exist because it isn't mentioned in the bible?'

'You lie! You made that up.'

'No, it's true. Corporal Sanchez told me. He's an educated man, you know. He'll probably end up teaching Memfeliz in Lisbon one day.'

'We could have reunion there after we have won the war and sanctions are over and we can go on holiday somewhere other than Israel and Cyprus,' she giggled, glassy eyed. 'Discuss the case, hey? Find out what the fuck was really happening here?'

'*Ag*, stop thinking about it.' He topped her up with coke. 'There is nothing more we can do about it at all. Talk about something else, can't you? Like giving me your address and phone number back in Cape Town, hey?'

'Are you tuning me, Sergeant Smith? You asking for a date, is it?'

'Ja, well, it was just a thought.'

'OK. I'll do it. I'll give you my phone number in Cape Town, but you got to do one *little* thing for me?'

'You name it, darlin'.'

She looked him straight in the eyes and gave him a broad, teasing, drunken grin.

'You got to tell me why you are lying about that Writ and why you *kakked* yourself when the name *Onele Namyana* came up.'

The glass slipped from Joshua's hands and shattered.

'Get a full bottle of klippie,' he replied.

*

It was back in '76. There had been trouble in the Location. Word had arrived that there had been a big demonstration in Soweto about which language was to be used to instruct the school kids there and the school in Kroonvale had gone up in protest too. Inspector Du Toit was furious. He did not like politics or politicians in the first place, but if they failed to belong to the National Party then they did not count even as politics or politicians.

'*Ag*, man,' he swore, when the first reports started to come in from the informers. 'More *bladdy* black agitators. What do they want now? They are burning down their schoolroom now, you tell me? And this is what they call Liberation, is it? How are they ever going to get a decent job without first being able to speak in Afrikaans? Don't they know that what we are doing for them is for their own good? When did the Kaffirs ever get such a good education before? *Ag*, I blame the missionaries for teaching them to read in the first place. They were happy when they were savages and now they are just dissatisfied because they think they can compete with the white man. And how is that supposed to work, you tell me? Don't they understand about evolution?'

All this was delivered in an irritated bustle as he got up from behind his metal desk, tied on his Sam Browne belt, checked the pistol in the holster and pulled out a shotgun from the cabinet behind him. His flesh wobbled as he struggled out from behind the desk and plucked at his button nose.

'Konstabel Smith,' he ordered. 'Go and get Hennie from out of the Coldstream and tell him to get the rest of the boys out, then go around to Jannie's place and get him out of bed. We must just nip this in the bud.'

It was one of those blue autumn days when the flame trees still had buds on them and the white painted houses looked as though they were made from adobe. In the centre of town stood the gothic church in grey and chalk white like a space rocket ready on the launch pad, while the brown louvred shutters on the windows of the bank gave a Mexican feel to the desert silence of the sleepy dorp. The Coldstream stood just across from the church and was busy as usual because it was a Friday lunchtime and police wisdom had it that it was better to get a few beers in early because the kaffirs would be on the bottle later and if there was going to be trouble at the Location, it would be on a Friday night. Hennie was already three beers in when Joshua brought him the unwelcome news.

'This early?' he remarked, scratching the blonde hair on his head. 'And they have set fire to the school, you say? Because they must learn Afrikaans?'

Hennie was phlegmatic about these things. He was not interested in politics much either, but he understood why the people on the Location should not be happy about their lot. He had had difficulty mastering English when he was at school and sympathised with those who were not good at learning languages.

'Ja, Afrikaans is quite hard to learn,' he agreed, blowing out his red cheeks. 'Especially if all the pop music is in English and all the movies are American too. The only time a black man must use Afrikaans is when he is in police custody or talking to the Boer. Otherwise, he is always talking English or his own black language. It must be hard having to learn all those different words for trigonometry and the bible.'

'What must we do, then?' asked Joshua, following him out through the shaded garden and into the car.

'We must just go and *donner* them as usual until they get some sense back.'

Jannie was of much the same opinion, though he was more irritated at having to pull a double shift on a Friday night. He had been looking forward to a few beers in front of the rugby and then a braai and some more beers later in the Coldstream while his wife attended the church social.

'Come on, Jannie,' chafed Hennie. 'Do you need a boomerang to get that belt round your waist, hey?'

Jannie was a big man who squeezed everyone if he had to share a seat in the back of the car. Sometimes, it seemed that he filled the car on his own and his sweat soup plates were always bigger and more prominent than everyone else's. Behind his back, the other officers called him 'Shaka' in the belief that the legendary Zulu king had grown so fat he needed eight men to lift him on their shoulders when he went about on a palanquin.

'*Fok you*,' came the irritated cry from within the house, followed almost instantly by the shrill sound of his wife scolding him for using bad language. Once in the car, he became voluble about how it was time to teach the kaffirs a proper lesson and stop pussyfooting around, but Joshua took this to be more related to his disturbed afternoon sleep rather than any seriously held political positions.

They met up with the Inspector in the place they always met up, on the road out to Kroonvale, just by a piece of waste ground near Lewack Street where Spandau Kop loomed over them, like a titan or a tidal wave. Ahead on the left was the cricket field, while on the right, forming the other side of the glacis for the Location was the athletics field, not much more than a track in the dirt, and just by it the one storey school, from which a thin wand of smoke was rising. There were three or four other vehicles gathered together when Joshua, Hennie and Jannie pulled up, all of them looking as tired and bored as the policemen they carried.

'All right, you know the drill,' said the Inspector. 'Everyone take a *sjambok* and when we get there look for the troublemakers. They will be people we don't know from Joburg or Durban – they always are – so hit them hard and get them in the back and off to the station.'

One of the policemen handed out the *sjamboks* and Joshua took the hard, supple, hide whip in his hand and flexed it, testing it against his leg. It would hurt a lot when he hit someone with it.

'What do we do about the fire?' asked Hennie.

'*Fok* the fire,' replied the Inspector. 'If they want to burn down their future that is up to them. We just need to break a few heads and round up the troublemakers, hey? Then we can get back to our beer.'

There was a general acceptance of the plan. It was no different from the other plans that they had used on the Location, except that this time they were to look out for the ringleaders. Usually they did not bother, but as there was trouble in Soweto, it was agreed that this time they must just make the effort.

'You know, maybe we should get a rugby match up with the kaffirs one day,' said Joshua, as he climbed back into the car. 'Maybe it would use up their energy a bit and get them to be a bit more peaceful and co-operative?'

'Ja, good idea,' replied Hennie. 'Except that they don't play rugby, do they. They play that *poes* game, soccer.'

'Just a thought. Do we know who the troublemakers are?'

'*Ag*, it will be some uppity *poes* from Joburg like Du Toit says,' said Jannie. 'He will be wearing glasses from reading too many books and will be waving a copy of the Communist Manifesto in one hand and the Bible in another. And he will be at the back of the crowd when the fighting starts.'

They drove up towards the school where the demonstration was taking place and parked in a line on the track. There were twenty policemen and two or three hundred demonstrators, but Joshua did not feel outnumbered or overawed while he had a sidearm, a *sjambok* and so many experienced colleagues ranged alongside him. The waving placards that had been distributed to the demonstrators had clearly been made elsewhere as there were no printing facilities outside the rear office of the *Graaf-Reinet Advertiser* and so it seemed to him obvious that they had been prepared by outsiders. To him, the whole affair looked rather half-hearted.

He began to scan the crowd for people he didn't recognise, but there was Solomon Khetshe with his younger brother Ananthi, holding up an expensive looking banner declaring that *Afrikaans is the Language of the Oppressor*, while their cousins Babalo and Feza waved rather cheaper ones, declaring that *Afrikaans Can Go To Hell*. This he dismissed as blether; he knew that all four of them spoke Afrikaans fluently. More disturbing was the placard that threatened *One Settler One Bullet*, while he didn't know what *Azania Now* meant.

Just then, the Inspector took out a megaphone from the boot of the car and began issuing a metallic, bureaucratic call for the crowd to disperse, but he was instantly shouted down by a more powerful bullhorn squealing out a shrill defiance. When he tried again, the crowd responded by chanting slogans in Xhosa which Joshua could not really understand but which made him a little more nervous all the same. He could see that this was not a normal township disturbance. Somehow, though most people seemed half-hearted, there seemed to be a more organised core of people and he began to worry if a trap was not being set; there *were* people with glasses and books at the back of the crowd who seemed to be in earnest discussion and he didn't recognise any of the people sitting on the roof of the school under a banner which proclaimed once more that *Afrikaans is the Language of the Oppressor*. He also noted that the smoke was not coming from the school at all, but from behind it, as though it was being held out as a temptation for the police to take.

At that moment, Jannie called out to a young boy who was in the front row of the demonstrators.

'Hey, Jikela! What are you doing here? Why are you not at work in my garden? Why are you here making a noise with these people? And where is that nice new jersey my wife knitted for you?'

Jikela looked down, sucking his teeth and jamming his hands in his pocket.

'Come here,' demanded Jannie, frowning, wobbling and sweating in equal measure. 'Come here, I say.'

Jikela took a step forward but then many other hands came around him and held him back.

'It is my *job*,' he hissed to his fellows. 'How else can I get money for school?'

The hands drew back as they acknowledged his dilemma, but then one of the men with spectacles appeared and pulled him back roughly.

'Liberation *then* Education,' he stated. 'Do not be a slave to the Boer. Free yourself!'

'You put that boy down, Kaffir,' shouted Jannie, waddling forward. 'Why do you come here stirring up trouble? Go back to Johannesburg, hey?'

The man with spectacles took a pace forward. He was a stocky man in his early forties with a short beard and round face upon which a strong brow had been built. He jutted out his chin, hooked his thumbs into the front of his denim dungarees and confronted Jannie at five yards distance.

'This is *my* land, Boer, and you are not welcome in it. Go back to Holland where you came from. You are like a pig with your snout in my garden.'

'A *pig*, is it now?' said Jannie, putting a mocking hand to his ear, as though he hadn't heard properly. 'And have you been drinking, Kaffir, to make yourself so brave?'

'Do not call me Kaffir, you fat pig of a Dutchman.'

'Or you'll do what? *Kaffir*.' He looked down at Jikela. 'Go home boy, and take your friends with you. You are a good boy and you should not be mixed up with these agitators. Come to work as usual tomorrow and we can forget about all this racket.'

'Did you not hear me, you fat *pig*. Go back to Holland.'

Joshua looked at the man with the spectacles and saw that there was something different about him. He was not like the other residents of Kroonvale and not like any of the black people he had come across in Krugerburg. He had an air, a confidence about him that was unusual and he struggled to put his finger on what it was that made him stand out. It wasn't his dress, although the dungarees were not so faded as a farm labourer's should be and he was pretty sure that they were worn as a political statement rather than as actual work wear. Nor was it the heavy, black frames of the spectacles that gave him the look of a college intellectual, or even the hair, which was fuller than the close crop that the Africans habitually wore.

'Go back to Holland, you fat pig,' repeated the man, enunciating every word, chopping them out of the air as though they were made of rock.

And then Joshua understood what made this man different.

He was not afraid.

He was not afraid of the police.

Everyone was afraid of the police, weren't they?

It was an attitude that he had never seen before in an African and suddenly *he* was afraid. The warning he had been given by Konstabel Williams up on the mountain overlooking Graaf-Reinet came rushing back to him as he looked at the crowd and then at his colleagues; *you will always go down to numbers in the end.* It was with a start that he realised that if the crowd wanted to, they could take them, and all it would need to galvanise them would be a leader who wasn't afraid to lead. A man like the one standing up, chin to chin with Jannie. He felt his mouth go dry.

Three shots rang out and a howl went up from the crowd as it turned as one to run. A half dozen more shotguns sprayed birdshot at the heels of the fleeing demonstrators in a sudden, deafening volley and before Joshua could draw his own sidearm, the man with the spectacles was bowled over by four konstabels. They threw him to the ground, lashing at him with their *sjamboks*, tugging at his arms and legs and kicking where they could not strike with the whips. He struggled, putting up a good fight, lashing out and catching Jannie with a scraping boot that took the skin off all the way down his shin and drawing blood but he stood no chance against the experienced policemen.

'Get him back to the *tronk*,' ordered the Inspector, disdainfully as they ground his face, grunting and tight into the dust. 'We'll clean up here.'

Joshua looked round and was amazed to see that the demonstration had disappeared on the instant, leaving only a single placard face down in the dirt and a slight red haze where the retreating feet had scrambled up the dust.

'Konstabel Smith. Come with me,' said the Inspector, leading the way briskly toward the school. 'We must just kick out this fire and find the Pastor wherever he is. Then *he* can put the embers out.'

They rounded the corner to see a bonfire of rubbish and school furniture burning half-heartedly in the kindergarten section. Joshua congratulated himself on spotting what might have been a trap but said nothing as the Inspector went over to it and kicked it apart, sighing.

'What is the matter with these people?' he complained. 'Why do they not just stay quiet so we don't have to keep doing this?'

Joshua looked around the deserted schoolyard, checking the broken windows for any sign of demonstrators laying in ambush but there was no sign that only a minute or so ago, there had been several hundred discontented people gathered here and on the roof.

'But this is a lesson for you, hey?' he continued, scattering burning sticks and smouldering wood. 'Don't waste time negotiating, hey? You must hit them hard, then they know you mean business – *a whiff of grapeshot* is what the Emperor Napoleon called it. No half measures.' He turned over some old newspapers that had been packed so tight that the flames could not devour them and then stood up straight. 'It's amazing really. Here we are in Graaf-Reinet, from where the Great Trek started, the great epic that confirmed us as the rightful rulers of this land and yet every day we have to relearn the kaffirs the truth that we hold this land by right of conquest. Never mind that the *bladdy* British stole it from us, hey? *We* took it back because they could not beat us, so it is obvious that God meant it to be ours just as the Voortrekkers at Blood River said so. Why don't the kaffirs understand this obvious thing, hey? It would be easier for everyone all round if they just accepted reality, hey? Now, where is that *fokken* Pastor?'

They went straight on through the dusty boards, peeling blue paint and litter that lay strewn down the narrow township lanes. The huts were in need of repair, split by the blistering heat of summer and cracked by the biting frost of winter and waiting for money sent down from the mines in Joburg by those menfolk lucky enough to get work there. The corrugated iron roofs seemed to crackle as Joshua and the Inspector walked through the narrow lanes of packed red earth, impatiently looking for the Pastor. At times, they would push open the rusty iron door to a yard full of chickens or stunted vegetables, disturbing old ladies staring at their hands or old men staring straight up at the sun. Everywhere there was a hot smell of iron and rubbish and dogs and the silence of hopelessness and strangled ambition, and pressure cooker anger bore down on the roofs of the shacks and shanties like a flat, heavy hand.

The Pastor was found in his rough wooden church hall helping the women to pick bird shot out of hands, legs and buttocks while a queue of smarting people holding rag wrapped injuries waited patiently for their turn for treatment. The Inspector went in alone, leaving Joshua outside to make sure no agitators turned up.

'Don't bother arresting them,' he said. 'Just *donner* them, hey?'

Joshua saluted and pulled his hat down. The Inspector sighed and raised his eyebrows.

'You have to be confident' he said. 'You have to give the impression that you can take any number of them on and win. *Aggression* is the key, man. *Aggression*.'

Standing outside in the hot sun, Joshua contemplated on the character of the man with the spectacles. What on earth did he think he was doing challenging Jannie in such an open and insolent fashion? He must have known that he would take a beating for it, yet he still acted defiantly. Joshua was impressed, but he could not decide whether the man was really brave or stupid; he did not see any point in getting into a fight that it was impossible to win or to come out with at least some honour. And that man would never win in a fight with the whole police detachment and he would not come out with much honour either; he would be lucky to come out without serious hospitalisation. Still, there was something disturbing about the man. It was not so much the defiance, nor even the way he had insulted Jannie by calling him a fat pig. It was the fact that he was not afraid that unsettled him. The man was not afraid even though he knew he was going to lose. He acted like he was confident of victory.

'We are in trouble now,' said the Inspector, appearing from the church door, fitting his hat on his head and striding back hurriedly through the prefabs and corrugated iron shanties towards the car. 'That agitator we arrested; his name is Onele Nonyana and we are *opgefockt*. His father was one of the legal team during the Rivonia trial.'

Joshua looked blank.

'The one where all the ANC terrorists were sent down.'

Joshua shook his head again.

'The one that all the foreigners are up in arms about,' explained the Inspector impatiently. 'Don't you read a newspaper?'

'Just the sports pages.'

'Listen to the radio?'

'No. So what?' asked Joshua, mystified.

'It means that there will be lawyers and if they see what Jannie will have done to that *poes* agitator by now, there will be questions to be answered. Irritating ones.'

The Inspector drove back to the station at a speed which suggested impatience but which was not so fast as to indicate that he hoped to get back in time to prevent Jannie from doing what he was going to do to him. Indeed, the sound of Jannie grunting with exertion as he beat the arrested man could be heard quite clearly as they entered the building and neither he nor the Inspector paused before going straight through to the cells.

'Jannie, it would be better if you stopped now,' called the Inspector urgently. 'Oh fuck.'

The man with the spectacles, Onele Nonyana, was handcuffed and slumped against the far wall of the square space, his dungarees sliced open along the legs where the hide whip had cut through the cloth. One shoe was missing revealing a long, bloody sock, ribbed and fat, like a grub. There were blood stains on the wall behind him, on the floor in front of him and as Joshua came through the door he felt a tooth crunch under his boot.

'Oh Jannie,' sighed the Inspector. 'Could you not have waited at least until I got back?'

Jannie was sweating and breathing heavily. His face was contorted into a twist of pure hatred, his eyes glinting out of them like lost points of obsidian, furious, vengeful and merciless.

'He called me a pig,' spat Jannie, grasping the fading man by the hair. 'A Kaffir called *me* a *pig*.'

Onele Nonyana's tongue lolled out of a broken jaw and both his eyes were already closed from convex bruises that were swollen full with blood. The Inspector ground his teeth in frustration and stepped forward to yank up Onele's leg and tear off the sock, dropping it wetly to the floor. He took out a pen from his pocket and drew it down the bare sole of the exposed foot.

The toes curled upwards and outwards.

'Shit,' said the Inspector.

'What?' said Jannie.

'You have damaged his brain, man.'

'So?'

'So this is Onele Nonyana and his father is a prominent kaffir lawyer.'

He dropped the leg.

Jannie shook his head in disgust. 'A kaffir lawyer. What is the world coming to?'

'Who knows about this?' asked the Inspector. 'I mean, who has taken part in his arrest and beating?'

'Piet, Joup and Willie knocked him down and brought him back here like you said,' answered Jannie. 'I mean they roughed him up a bit, but...'

'But you *donnered* him up good?'

'Ja-Nee,' shrugged Jannie. 'We all *klapped* him a bit. It isn't all my fault.'

'Where are they now?'

'They've gone over to the Coldstream for a beer with the others, now the trouble is over.'

'OK,' said the Inspector. 'So you did this and there is only you and me and Konstabel Smith here who *really* knows what happened.'

Jannie gave another shrug.

'So now we must get rid of this body before people who can ask awkward questions come to ask these awkward questions, ja? So put him in a blanket and take him out of here. Take him to the desert and bury him, ja? Deep, so the jackals and leopards don't dig him up, ja?'

Jannie shrugged once more. 'Is it that serious?'

'Ja, it is *fokken* serious,' replied the Inspector, emphatically. 'So you and Konstabel Smith here must do this thing and not breathe a word about it. It will be dark in an hour, so get him ready.'

'He isn't dead yet,' Joshua pointed out. 'Maybe he should go to hospital.'

241

'He will be by the time you are well out in the Karoo,' said the Inspector. 'And you could take him to Christian Barnard in the *groot schur* and he would not be able to put humpty back together again. Now I will be in the Coldstream when you get back and I will have some cold ones waiting for you. Jannie,' he added, with a twitch of his head and a look back at Joshua. 'A word in private, hey?'

They waited for the deep blue of the Karoo sky to darken through its golden sunset to the profound sapphire curtain provided to hang its ticky coin moon on and then wrapped up Onele Nonyana in his blood soaked blanket. He was still breathing, a stertorious, irregular rattle full of mucus and the blood his lungs were filling up with, while his tongue lolled and rolled around loose in his shattered mouth. At the last minute, Joshua tossed the shoes into the parcel and, grunting with exertion, the two of them carried him out to the vehicle and rolled him without mercy or ceremony into the boot.

'He's still alive,' hissed Joshua again.

'Look, man,' replied Jannie urgently, while he gave his hands a quick wipe with a rag to get the blood off. 'To all intents and purposes he has already passed. He is just a cabbage now and we are doing him a service by putting him out of his misery.'

They drove out on the north road, the Voortrekkers road, past the dam and Joshua wound the window down to let out the copper smell of Onele's blood and the more acrid tang of his urine. The warm wind drove it back in though and so he wound the handle all the way down and stuck his head out in the hope that it would blow away the trembling nausea that was creeping from his stomach into the whole of his being. He looked up at the lustre of the Karoo night's pewter stars and thought of old Buyisiswe, whom Titch Janssen had *donnered*. For one terrible moment he thought he saw him in the rear view mirror, sitting in the back seat and his mind reeled as though it was being driven backwards from his eyes.

'Don't worry,' said Jannie, noticing his discomfort. 'We all feel nervous on our first time. It's natural.'

Joshua did not reply but pulled out a handkerchief and put it to his mouth and nose, wishing that it was table cloth sized so that he could wrap it around his head and ears and blot out his sight.

Half an hour further on, they pulled over, crunching off the road up a narrow track and coming to rest under a stand of acacia thorns. Jannie parked with the headlights still on, pointing into the bush.

'This will be fine,' he said, hefting his bulk off the seat. 'The sand is soft here so digging will be easier.'

They took two shovels from the back seat and walking nine or ten yards along the yellow beam of the head lights found a drift of fine sand.

'I'll start with the hole,' Jannie directed. 'You get some rocks to keep the animals off.'

Joshua nodded. He was trembling now and as he picked at the soft, flat sandstone flakes lying along the track his hands were full of pins and needles.

'Watch out for scorpions,' warned Jannie, his tone low and even as he began to labour at the sand.

Joshua stumbled on a loose rock and blundered out of the light, temporarily losing the clarity of his night vision before straightening up and then, drunkenly, rocking over again. He did not fall though, steadying himself by taking up three or four of the stones in his arms and carrying them back to stockpile along the side of the trench that Jannie was deftly excavating.

'Get quite a few,' he ordered, and Joshua staggered away again, returning a second, third, fourth and fifth time, with an ever growing load to add to the rust and umber coloured pile. 'That should do it. Now your turn with the spade.'

Joshua took the tool and slid it into the earth, noting the gravelly consistency and soft fine sand that slid off the blade almost as quickly as he scooped it up. He drove it in again vertically, prising loose a stone there and added it to the spoil, then drove it in again.

'Keep it shallow and even,' advised Jannie. 'We are not digging a well, ja?

Sooner than he expected, the grave was nearly a metre deep and Jannie decided that enough was enough.

'Let's get the kaffir. He should be dead by now.'

They opened the boot only to be greeted by the gurgling breaths of their captive, holding on to life with all the urgency of evolution and all the tenacity of fingers clutching the cliff edge.

'*Fok*,' said Jannie. 'Well let's get him out anyway.'

Joshua took hold of Onele's twitching legs and with difficulty managed to pull them over the lip of the boot. Jannie reached in over him and yanked the rest forward and out, so that the body toppled in a grunting heap of spattering blood and entangling blanket. In the moonlight Onele's eyes flickered white under the bruising, now ruptured, as though clattering out a morse code message for mercy or vengeance.

'Get the spade,' ordered Jannie.

'Can we not use the gun? It would be quicker and less painful,' Joshua stuttered. 'And if anyone finds the body we can say we killed him in a gun fight.'

Jannie shook his head. 'Too late for that. Too many kaffirs saw him taken into custody. He has to disappear properly. And you never know who we might attract with a gunshot. There are still a few Bushmen around and who knows how many *bergies* are hogging their Redheart under the rocks here? So get the shovel. No, wait. Let's move him into the grave first.'

Joshua felt his gorge rise and could not contain himself. He spewed an acrid spray onto the sand and choked through shaking hands.

'*Ag*, man. It's no big deal,' said Jannie sympathetically. 'You get yourself together now and I'll move the kaffir, hey?'

Joshua walked off three paces while Jannie tugged at the living corpse and raised it onto his shoulder in a fireman's lift. He heard him wheeze as he carried Onele towards the grave, heard him curse as his clothing snagged on a thorn and then grunt again as he tore free. Then there was the sound of sliding as Jannie ditched the body and a soft *whump* as Onele hit the ground. Moments later Jannie reappeared with the shovel.

'Ja, he's nicely dead now. That last fall must have finished him off.' He handed the shovel to Joshua. 'Fill him in now. Put a layer of sand over him, then put the rocks on top and then put more sand and dirt on top. When you have finished I'll show you how to camouflage the grave with rocks and leaves and bits of other shit.'

'Are you sure he's dead?'

Jannie did not meet his eyes. 'Ja, he's dead. But if he is not...use the shovel.'

Joshua shook his head slowly from side to side. 'You do it. I can't.'

'No,' said Jannie, firmly. '*You* will do it.'

'I can't. I just can't.'

'You can and *will*. This is from the Inspector. So that you will not be tempted to share our little secret with anyone else.'

'What do you mean?'

'You heard what I said. Me and the Inspector understand each other. We need you to understand us too.'

'Why would I tell?'

'Ja, look,' explained Jannie. 'Choosing which side you are on and then changing your mind is a luxury that you *soutpiel rooineks* have, but us Afrikaaners do not. So this is our insurance policy that you remember which side you are on.' He picked up the second shovel and put it on his shoulder. 'Don't worry man. He is probably already dead. Come on. I'll show you how to do it.'

Joshua looked at the spade in his hands and realised he was gripping it so hard that his knuckles were white and his forearms were beginning to cramp. He took a deep breath, which almost caused him to start hyperventilating, then carefully unfurled each finger from the shaft, slowly, in turn, from left to right. As his eyes followed the light he saw the beam was full on Jannie's broad back while the shovel blade over his shoulder looked like a fist. He put his own shovel on his own shoulder and followed.

Onele Nonyana was still, but it was obvious from the grunting uneven breath that the life in his body was still clinging to it. Jannie had dumped him into the grave and had gone so far as to tidy up the blanket so that it was straight and neat and covered his face, even though it meant exposing his feet and the shoes that had been tossed in next to them. Joshua threw up again.

'You know, choosing who to hate is a big decision,' he gasped. 'You may find you are stuck with such a choice for life.'

'*Ag*, man,' said Jannie, irritated now. 'OK, look. We'll do it together, hey? Would that be better for you?'

Joshua was retching a dry acid now, bending over and his body was shaking like a wet dog, trying to spew out the thick yellow bile that seemed to be clogging his windpipe.

He felt a big hand grasp the back of his collar and give him a friendly, straightening hand.

'We just going to put the shovel on his neck and then stamp down, very hard, for a quick moment and then it will all be done, ja?'

It seemed to Joshua that he had no will of his own as Jannie guided him towards the head of the grave and the sputtering gurgle of Onele Nonyana's last breaths. He hardly knew his own hands as they drew back the blanket and guided the blade of the shovel into the v at the top of the supine man's neck and he hardly felt his left foot as he put it onto the top of the blade and rested it there for a moment as Jannie came in behind him and put his own right foot on the other side. He was conscious of the fat belly pushing into his kidneys, of the hand on his left shoulder and of the laboured breathing below, but he was no longer conscious of an independent self when he looked up to see the pale disc of the hangman's moon in the black hole of the night.

And then he stamped. He stamped with all his might, driving the blade down, into and through the flesh until it touched the bone and snapped through it. Onele Nonyana was dead.

Jannie sent him to sit in the car while he finished off the job of burial.

When he returned, he was carrying something in a rag which he tucked into the glove compartment before starting up and heading back to the Coldstream for a beer. Joshua knew instinctively what it was because there was another one acting as a gear stick cover right next to him. He had been mistaken in thinking it was made from tanned ostrich leather. As if murdering a brave man wasn't desecration enough, Jannie had cut off Onele Nonyana's scrotum for a souvenir driving accessory.

*

'He used *that* for his gear lever?' said Mostert to the darkness.

Joshua took the last mouthful from the bottle and tossed it by the neck into the silence of the scrub and sand by the compound fence.

'So now I am fucked up completely,' he said. 'Even if I don't agree with Apartheid, even if I joined the *fokken* ANC tomorrow, I would still be fucked. I cannot be forgiven; I dare not go to jail; sanctions mean I cannot get a passport and go hide out in *fokken* America or China or *fokken* Timbuktu. I am fucked and there is no coming back from this level of being fucked up.'

'Is that why you are here in South West Africa? Are you hoping to hide here?' She lit cigarettes for them both. 'A scrotum for a gear lever cover. That is barbaric.'

'There is some court case crap. A civil suit following me,' said Joshua. The brandy had not dulled his pain or his senses but had given him a heightened clarity such that when he looked up at the stars, they seemed brighter and closer, colder and more indifferent than ever against the deep ocean of the night. 'The ANC supporters think they can get me in court for the false arrest of Onele Namyana. It will open a can of worms, obviously, so the Inspector pulled some strings, got me a promotion and sent me out to South West Africa.'

'I guess it's in his interests too,' she said.

'Ja, I guess so.' He drew on his cigarette. 'The lawman on the run, hey? Sounds like a crappy cowboy movie down the bioscope.'

'Did you tell anyone else about this?' she asked, her face glowing as she drew on the cigarette.

'Oh ja, sure,' he replied. 'I told my mother that I had executed the lover of her best friend, the father of my foster-brother and shovelled him into a shallow grave.'

'Your father, maybe?'

Joshua drew on his cigarette, building the tip into the microcosm of an inferno.

'Him? Ja, if I told him he would not remember it in the morning and then, even if he did, he would probably sell the story to the *Herald* in the belief that I was now a national hero.'

'That is probably a good thing that you should keep this to yourself,' she said. 'At least until you work out what you should do.'

'What about you?' Joshua replied. He spoke up to the stars rather than turn his head towards her.

'Me?' she sounded surprised. 'Me? Who should I tell? I work for 23 Leopard Battalion; we don't exist officially and we are fighting a war that is not happening either, in a country that we are not supposed to be in. And we have killed a lot more people than you and your *jollers* in the Graaf-Reinet police, I can tell you.' She flicked the cigarette ahead of her in a small, bright orange arc. 'Believe me, Joshua; your secret is safe with me.'

'You going to give me your phone number now?' His voice was bittersweet, brimming with a deep sadness. 'Maybe I'll call you when you finish your service here.'

She folded her arms across her chest and then unfolded them, placing them wide apart on her hips.

'You guys keep it all bottled up, don't you?'

Joshua didn't answer.

'Ja,' she said, briskly. 'Call me when you get there.'

And then, more softly.

'Ja, give me a call, hey?'

*

30th May

It was a blue and silver day with fresh painted clouds of white and the wind was still cool as Joshua Smith sat on the top of the Buffels trying to blow away his hangover on the way back to 41 Mech at Oshadangwa. His stomach was bilious, leaden and his brain seemed to have shrunk inside the balaclava that clothed his emotions about unburdening himself to Captain Mostert last night. What he had mistaken for intimate clarity, was only the foolishness of *in vino veritas* and he trembled at the prospect of her thinking better of her promise in this same clear light of day and going to Commandant Korrf with his story. She had avoided his eye at breakfast and the note that he had found with her number written on it, slipped under his door as he slept, now folded neatly in his shirt pocket was only a thin insurance. Nor did he look forward to the brown A4 envelope that his mother had identified as a Writ moving inexorably towards him, as it surely must be, making its ponderous, elephantine way from Graaf-Reinet down to Cape Town, back up to Pretoria or Bloemfontein, then on to Windhoek and along the slick black ribbon of tarmac to meet him at Oshadangwa or Echo Tango, or somewhere else along the road. Cannons to the left and cannons to the right, he thought to himself; and then there were the cannons right in front of him, the invisible ones that fired notes pinned to bayonets into places where only he could find them. He felt a twinge in his ribs, as though he had been prodded with Sanchez's missing bayonet, and then gave into his fate, lying down on the floor of the vehicle and trying for the oblivion of sleep.

Sometime later, when they turned into the farm gate at Oshadangwa base, the driver banged on the metal wall of the Buffel to wake him.

'One of your *poes* mates is here, *Konstabel*. You going to arrest the whole fucking regiment now?' He flipped a lit cigarette back from the cab, which Smith was both nipped by and grateful for. 'Ag, that would be a good fucking punch up man. You guys would get *klapped* properly.'

Joshua stood up and saw the dog-faced Police Casspir parked just inside the wire perimeter with the familiar figure of Lieutenant Els sitting atop the cab, fiddling with a speaker roughly fixed there. Els looked up and gave him a friendly wave, screwdriver in hand, teeth bared through his Zapata moustache while a scrappy baseball cap perched on his untidy afro hair.

'You don't mind that I borrowed this heap of kaffir-bashing crap do you?' he called. 'My Buffels is fucked and in the shop.'

'What are you doing here?' replied Joshua above the rev of the engine.

'Ja, I'm here for you, *poes*. I'm your *fokken* lift.'

Joshua was about to ask who had sent for him, but a cough from the Buffels chugged out a cloud of choking blue smoke and Els was gone, obscured by the jailhouse as the driver took the corner on what felt like two wheels and drove onto the vehicle park. There CSM Landsberg was waiting and quickly directed him to the Company office, its silver-back thatch completed, its windows watching.

'The Major is pleased with the freezers, as indeed, we all are,' said the CSM, his grin vulpine. 'The atmosphere has improved considerably.'

Joshua sniffed the air; the smell of rotting meat had disappeared, replaced by the more militarily wholesome smells of serge, diesel, dust, sweat and hot cordite.

'I'm being back-squadded, I see,' replied Joshua.

'Your work, for which we are all exceedingly grateful, is done here,' replied Landsberg, touching him with his stick on his chest. 'Now go home and enjoy the delights of whatever a good little policeman does when he is at home. That would make us all happy – van der Merwe, most of all.'

'The case isn't solved, you know? We still don't know *why* Merriman did what he did.'

'Yes, *it is*,' replied Landsberg, his voice cadenced as though he were stamping to attention. 'This is what Major van der Merwe is about to tell you and you *will* agree with him.'

Joshua shrugged. He was too empty and hungover to mount much resistance. Inside the Company office, now an odd mixture of bright light from the windows and gloom spreading down from the thatch mingled with the smells of fresh paint laid over disinfectant on new sawn wood. There was a new sound too, the wheezing hum of a newly installed air-conditioning unit which rattled the papers under their weights on van der Merwe's desk. The Major, in silhouette, back lit as usual was standing by the far window, his shoulders slightly stooped, a sad, decent fellow, whose stance reinforced Joshua's first impression of him as being too sensitive for the job he had been given.

'Sergeant Smith,' he said, without turning round and opening as though this was an unexpected visit. 'Commandant Korrf sends his compliments and thanks for the way in which you have cracked this case.'

'*Cracked*?' replied Joshua.

'Isn't that the term you sleuths use?'

'*Sleuths*?'

Landsberg tapped his stick against his hand impatiently.

'Ja, well, we did what we could, Sir,' said Joshua.

'And thank you for the chest freezers. They have been a mercy. We have been able to send Lieutenant Keay's body for burial; the air force agreed to take him yesterday. It will be a comfort to his family.'

'Yes, Sir. Very pleased for him – you – the family, Sir. The other bodies are to be buried here, I take it?'

'Ah, no, Sergeant Smith.' Van der Merwe coughed a little into his hand and then stepped forward to sit at his desk. 'They will be transported down to Windhoek by vehicle – by police vehicle...'

Joshua thought of Els and understood.

'...from where the families will take control of them. Sergeant Smith...'

'Sir?'

'You will also escort Private Merriman to his Court Martial in Windhoek.'

'In the same vehicle? Will the bodies still be in the freezers?' Joshua felt sick at the thought of spending a long overnight journey in the company of two rotted bodies and the man who murdered them.

'We are on Operations here and I cannot spare even a single Buffels.' He turned, stroking the mole on his cheek nervously. 'Or any soldiers. That is why Lieutenant Els and his driver will go with you.'

'Sir, there are just a few things about this case that...' Joshua began.

'I'm sure there are,' interrupted van der Merwe. 'But Merriman has confessed and Commandant Korrf has given me an outline of the circumstances surrounding, ah, Corporal Memfeliz and the tragic death of Lieutenant Keay. I have spoken to the Dietz and Steyl families also and they are satisfied with the outcome of the investigation.'

'Sir –' began Joshua, remembering how Dietz and Steyl Senior had advised him to resolve the situation.

'It is an open and shut case, as I understand it,' recited van der Merwe. 'And it need take up no more of our time.'

'Sir, we also have –,' Joshua was about to mention the likely presence of an ANC cell on the base but caught himself as he recalled the implications of doing so.

'So we need detain you no further either...'

'Absolutely right, Sir,' said CSM Landsberg. 'I'll see the prisoner into Sergeant Smith's custody right away and then he can be away straight away.'

Joshua crimped his mouth shut and saluted. There was something too quick about all this, he thought.

*

Kassie Strydom being required for Operations, David Merriman now had the jail to himself and he sat, dejected, crushed, shoulders slumped, his hands clasped between his knees, grey with anxiety. From time to time he rubbed one hand over his head, from back to front as though he could wash away the things he had done, the mistakes he had made, the life he had led, the choices he had made. His bruises had changed colour, had become less livid and urgent as they resolved themselves into scars that would never heal or sank into his body, as though they were sins being absorbed.

'How much does he know?' asked Joshua, quietly.

'He knows that Visser isn't dead. Heard it on the grapevine,' replied Landsberg, holding a clipboard. 'Incredible story though.'

'Did he tell you why he was heading for 23 that night? Why he confessed to killing Keay?'

'No,' Landsberg pursed his lips. 'And now I don't have to care and can concentrate on getting on with the war.'

'What happens next?'

'Whatever you like,' replied Landsberg, handing him the clipboard. 'Sign on the dotted line and he's all yours.'

'What if I sign this *Nelson Mandela*?' said Joshua.

'Sign it bladdy *Adolf Hitler*, for all it matters,' replied Landsberg with a grin. 'Who's going to come all the way out here to check?'

Joshua signed it.

'Right, Merriman,' ordered Landsberg. 'Get your kit together. And God rot you for killing two decent men whose only crime was serving their country.'

Merriman hardly stirred, then rose up like a stiff old man.

'I'm going to hang for this, aren't I?' He forced a resigned, half smile across his face.

'If it was up to me,' replied Landsberg. 'I wouldn't waste the rope on you.' He turned to Joshua. 'But it isn't, so please take him away. Feel free to bury him in the garden, like the dog turd he is, should you feel the urge.'

'OK Merriman,' said Joshua. 'Let's go and get this over with.'

Merriman shuffled around his cage, as though he was not sure what he was doing, as though he had Alzheimer's. He picked up a rag of a towel, then wrapped it around a toothbrush and then stuffed both into a mess tin. Coming towards the bars, he held out the objects in front of him, as though they weren't his own belongings and then turned and went back towards the head of his cot to pluck at a pillow.

'Does he have a kit bag?' asked Joshua.

'No idea,' replied Landsberg, taking the key to the lock. 'Not my concern.'

The door to the cage swung open and Landsberg went through it. He seized Merriman by the scruff of his neck and turned him, propelling him through the opening and into Joshua's waiting arms.

'Have a good trip,' he said. 'Do you need help getting him to the Casspir?'

Joshua shook his head. He could feel Merriman's body and he seemed to be as light as a feather and as easily managed as a sleepy child. He took the pillowcase, shook the pillow away from it and deposited Merriman's meagre possessions into it, tying it off at the neck like a sack before taking him by the elbow and gently guiding him down the corridor. Outside, and into the light, they processed at the best speed of Merriman's aged limping gait, like a calvary, the prisoner keeping his gaze fixed on the ground in front of him, lifting each foot tenderly and placing it forward, half a step at a time, turning the corner of the jailhouse and edging towards Els' waiting Casspir. When they were halfway there, Joshua looked back to see CSM Landsberg watching them go; impassive, he seemed, like some great sentinel guarding the path across the desert or a prophet of the veldt watching a departing, doomed trek. Joshua had a presentiment of foreboding and for a moment he thought it was he himself, rather than Merriman who was being led away by the sleeve; but then Merriman tugged at him and Els started the Casspir up.

'He can go in the back with the body bags, hey?' called Els. 'You ride up here, shotgun, on top with me. Wilson here –' he gave a thumbs down. '- drives like a kaffir's granny, but he's even worse as a *fokken* gunner.'

Wilson's arm came up from the top cover and brandished a finger like the Statue of Liberty.

'Ja, OK,' said Joshua, opening up the rear doors. There were flies gathering around the thawing bags already and the corruption of Dietz and Steyl was already detectable. He helped Merriman up and in.

'It's not for long, hey?' said Els in a stage whisper. 'It's just until we get off the base and then down the road a way. Then we'll strap them on the outside.' He winked. 'Don't want to be schlepping all that way and them stinking like a kaffir's black arse on biryani, hey?'

Merriman climbed in and slid onto the seat without protest or complaint. Joshua took a last look at him and then asked, on the spur of the moment:

'Why were you going to Echo Tango that night? Were you trying to contact your brother?'

Merriman cast about the seat, as though he had forgotten something.

'Did you hear me, Merriman?'

'*Fok's* sake, Smith,' called Els. 'Let's get going, hey? And look down there won't you? No, in the corner. In that carton.'

'Did you hear me, David Merriman?'

'Ja, I got you some Monkey Gland,' said Els, turning back to reach into the cab for a machine gun. 'Your man, that kaffir Sissingi, reminded me to get some. You know he worries about you like a *fokken* mother hen?'

'He's not a kaffir, he's an Ovambo,' said Joshua automatically, then closed the door and climbed up onto the cab.

Els banged on the roof, Wilson let the clutch out and the nine ton armoured pig began to roll forward.

'Is he *bosbefock*?' asked Els, tapping his temple with a finger.

'Ja,' replied Joshua, flicking a salute as the gate opened to let them through. 'Went mad and killed two officers. Completely *bosbefock*.'

'Hmm. Depends on which officers,' said Els, banging a magazine onto the LMG. 'Jeez, I wish this war was over.'

'Why would that be, Els?'

'Then Led Zeppelin would come and play Joburg. *Fokken* sanctions, *boet*. Hey Wilson! Can you not get some *fokken* music up here after I went to all the trouble of installing the *fokken* speaker?'

'You don't want to wait until we are clear of the base?'

'Music! *Fokken* music!'

There was a hiss and a scramble of connections and then all conversation came to an end as *Black Dog* screamed out of the speaker between Els' legs.

'This is living, hey!' he shouted, and let off a burst of machine gun fire into the bush.

Forty minutes clear of the base and Els' tape clicked to a silence as he flipped a cigarette butt off the speeding cab.

'Ag!' he said. 'I forgot about your captive! Wilson, slow down and stop for a minute, hey? We need to check on the lunatic and the corpses, ja?'

Wilson ground through the gears and the rumble of the rubber run-flat tyres deepened as the Casspir came panting to a halt like a floppy eared foxhound on the sand by the road. Els and Joshua climbed back across the body of the truck and lifted one of the hatches there. Els went down on his knees and stuck his head in, sniffing warily.

'Ja, they beginning to thaw,' he said, withdrawing. 'Maybe it's time to strap them on the outside.'

'Not better to leave them where they are?' said Joshua, leaning over. 'I mean, if the bags come undone or a branch whips a hole in one...'

'Ag, they'll be fine,' dismissed Els.

'You lost the head of one the last time I saw you,' countered Joshua. 'They're safer where they are.'

'What about your man?' He tapped his temple again.

'Ja,' Joshua put his head in through the hatch. Merriman was leaning up against the rear door, head back, mouth open and staring as though he was deep in prayer. 'Ja, maybe he can come on top with us.'

Els scratched his moustache doubtfully. 'He's not going to go start gibbering and do a chainsaw job on us, is he, hey?'

'Do you see a chainsaw?'

'Ja, well, chop us up with a panga then.'

'Els,' said Joshua. 'You have a machine gun.'

'OK. Ja, you got a point. He can come up top. Shall we chain him or something?'

Joshua directed his eyes to the horizon in front of him then, facetiously shading his eyes, looked all the way around. The ground was flat, the bush thin, the *shonas* empty for twenty klicks in every direction.

'OK, no chains,' said Els. 'You are a fucking funny *poes*, you know?'

'Merriman,' said Joshua, leaning down again into the interior of the truck. 'David – you want to come up here in the fresh air?'

'Can I?' piped up Wilson, the driver.

'Open the *fokken* windows,' replied Joshua. 'David.' He called to him again. 'David.'

Merriman did not respond, but continued to stare at the thin slit of horizontal glass window above the bulkhead.

'There is something not right with him,' he said, straightening up. 'Have you got a medical kit, Els?'

'Ja, let's have a look at the *mompie* then,' said Els, leaping clear of the vehicle to land, like a gymnast, on the sand ten feet below.

Joshua climbed along the top of the vehicle and then handed himself down via the step at the rear doors. He flipped the handle and caught Merriman before he rolled out sideways from his seat.

'Give him some water, hey?' said Els, drawing some off from the tap on the side of the Casspir into a tin cup chained there.

Merriman was in a dazed state and there was a slight blueness to his lips, as though he was short of breath and starved of oxygen. Smith handed him down gently, made sure he could stand and then led him towards Els's chained cup to drink. He took it, sipped, gave a broad smile and then indicated for more.

'Has he been at the *dagga*?' asked Els, reaching forward to lift Merriman's eyelid. '*Fok* me! He is stoned, man! Ag, he must have some good friends in that outfit of his to sort him out at a time like this.'

Joshua looked into Merriman's eyes and frowned. 'Are you in there Merriman? David? Have you been at the *dagga*?'

Merriman gave a grin of idiotic proportions and hummed the opening bars of a Bob Marley tune.

'*No Woman, No Cry*, hey? He has been at the *dagga*,' confirmed Joshua. 'Well, this is going to be his last trip, I suppose.'

'Is that a pun?' asked Els, drawing off more water and handing it on. 'Hey Merriman, I got an idea, hey? You come up the top with us and you can choose the music and stay as high as you possibly can for as long as you can, hey?'

Merriman grinned and nodded and then, without further invitation, climbed up, hand over hand, with all the ponderous, sure footed purpose of a sloth, to stand upright on top of the Casspir. Els and Joshua grinned too.

'Wilson!' shouted Els. 'Get some hippy shit music on and let's go.'

The engine started on the instant, its big wheels turning onto the black top as Els and Smith slammed the rear doors and climbed back up to sit on the cab roof. Merriman stood two yards behind them, almost in the exact centre of the vehicle, leaning forward a little for balance and then, as the Casspir gathered up its grumbling speed, extending his arms out to the sides like Christ the Redeemer riding a surfboard.

'What sort of hippy shit?' shouted Wilson.

'Any kind!' bawled Els, cocking the machine gun. 'As long as it's LOUD!'

There was a moment's slackening of pace as Wilson's foot came off the accelerator while he rooted through the cassette box. The Casspir lurched a little, sending Merriman off balance which he countered with no more effort than if his surfboard had wobbled before taking the wave, and then as Wilson inserted the chosen cassette, the hiss and clatter of an uncertain connection announced the coming of the urgent drumming and screaming guitars of the rock music.

'Step on it Wilson, you *poes!*' cried Els, sending a chugging burst of bullets into the air. 'Let's *really* cruise, hey?'

Wilson obliged and the Casspir roared forward, with Merriman swaying forward, back, side to side, eyes narrowed, head back, feeling the wind comb out his hair and the music wash over him in an ecstasy of sensation. A soft heat and a strong sunlight shone bright on him, suffusing him with beaten silver light, beatifying him with a diffused pearl glow flecked through with the glitter of gold, and as he moved his chin up and down to fully enjoy the breath of God upon him, it seemed as though the dust and blood and sweat of guilt were sluiced off him, making him anew, baptised, reborn, innocent.

From time to time Els lit cigarettes for them, directed the choice of music so that Merriman might never come down and passed beers. Wilson was driving fast enough to keep the smell of corpses from coming forward and had borrowed Els's pilot shades to screen out the insects that blew in like hornets and bullets, sucked in by the wind and the smell. Els was enjoying every minute of it, even as he concentrated on the road ahead, automatically scanning for the tell tale scrapes of new laid mines. He cocked the machine gun and fired off rounds from time to time adding a counterpoint to the beat of the music and then, as they drove south east to skirt Etosha pan towards Grootfontein Airbase and Otjiwarongo, when the sun crossed the meridian to wester in a purple, silver and red sky, he slipped tracers into the magazine and fired them out, like the hot sparks of shooting stars into the gathering night.

Joshua too sat back to enjoy the ride, the music and Els's antics, glancing back from time to time to see Merriman still caught up in his fragile fantasy, taking pleasure in his last golden taste of freedom and wondering how far down the road it would be before his own crime would catch up with him and send him to the same place that Merriman was bound for. It was no comfort when Els decided that enough was enough for the day and they should pull over and bivouac for the night. If Joshua had had his last wish granted, he would have them drive on and on, forever, never stopping, until he had at last outrun death and fate and found a beach where he could swim, eat and lie with Trudi Mostert to the end of time.

Wilson pulled over by a stand of acacia trees as the eastern sky began to turn from Canaletto blue to mauve, lavender and silver while on their right hand side the setting sun turned the sand around them tawny, tobacco, cinnamon and umber, and the *shonas* became sheets of brass and gold. They handed Merriman down, still high and dazed, and sat him by one of the wheels, then Els got a fire going and Wilson tinkered with the truck.

'It's just tins,' said Els. 'But we got plenty *Castle* and some *Klippie*. We will survive, I think.'

'You think so?' called Wilson, hefting up the bonnet to check the oil. 'These bodies will soon attract every hyena and lion in the *bladdy* bush.'

Wilson's fears were not groundless. As soon as the smell of diesel, oil and rubber from the Casspir had cooled, the miasma of the rotten, thawing corpses began to rise up to greet the millions of flies that were congregating like a black fog inside the vehicle.

'We must just light some wood and hexamine or something and put it inside the vehicle to fumigate it,' said Els grimacing. 'And we must take turns on stag with the machine gun.'

Els quickly got a fire going and Wilson took a brand and some coals on a tray to slide inside the rear doors of the Casspir. The odour of the decomposing bodies and the glare of the firelight had attracted more and more insects until there was a regular crack of winged beetles colliding with the armoured sides, pinging off like bullets, while the hum of flies gave the impression that the engine had been switched on. Nearby, a nest of flying ants had taken wing and were circling above and around them like a swarm of sparks rising up from a bonfire. Joshua brushed the insects off his arm, only to feel himself bitten and stung twice on his neck.

259

'Jeez,' said Els, wrapping a towel around his head like a shamag. 'These cicadas are like to deafen you. We are in for an unpleasant night, I think. And if you don't already have malaria, you are going to get it tonight, for sure.'

Merriman's face was crawling with insects and Joshua tried to brush some of them away. One fly was drinking from the tear duct in his left eye while another danced around his nostrils.

'Do we have DDT?' asked Smith, spitting out a flying ant.

'Do we have airconditioning?' replied Wilson sarcastically.

'Is your prisoner all in one piece?' said Els. 'I wish I could get some quality *dagga* like that. When was the last time we had stuff like that, Wilson?'

'Take no notice,' came the reply. 'He only talks about smoking *dagga* because he thinks it will make him sound more like a hippy when he is showing off his muscles to the girls in Ballito. He is a booze man exclusively.'

'Fuck,' said Joshua, spitting again. 'Maybe if we put some green wood on the fire, the smoke will drive some of these little bastards off?'

'We have some smoke grenades,' said Els. 'They will work for a bit.'

Joshua made sure Merriman was safely sitting with his back against the wheel and then brought out a smoke grenade from one of the panniers. He pulled the pin and tossed it on the ground at his feet where it fizzed and then began to burn, churning and billowing out a thick green cloud, obliterating everything and everyone for a moment, with thick, choking smoke.

'That should do it,' coughed Els, wheezing. 'Hopefully it will keep these off until the sun goes down.'

As the grenade began to burn out, Merriman got up and while Joshua was rummaging in the back of the Casspir for another grenade, wandered lazily into the bush.

'I'll get him,' Joshua volunteered, and went quickly after him into the haze under the trees.

He did not have to go far for Merriman had only gone to pee and the dreamy look of peace and relief that was painted across his features in the green smoke and gloaming light scotched any suspicion that he might be trying to escape.

'Are you still high, David?' he asked.

Merriman shook his head slowly. One eye lid was drooping and the stream of pee was looping around in the dust as he swayed erratically.

'David,' he said, on the spur of the moment. 'Tell me why you did it.'

'Did what?' came the innocent reply.

'Why you went running for 23 when you heard that Keay had been killed.'

'Oh that,' said Merriman, as though it was some unimportant detail of an event long past. 'I didn't want to get him into trouble and I thought I had, you see?'

'No, I don't see.'

'It's when I was posted up here from Bloem,' he began, still peeing. 'My mother told me about some campaign to do with District 6, you know, and how they were going to take people like Dietz and Steyl to court and get compensation or title deeds or something.' He finished and began to shake. 'When she told me who they were – Broederbond types, you know – I thought she had bitten off too much more than she could chew and she would end up in big trouble. So I said to myself that I would sort out this problem for her. I would also pay for what I had done in joining the army; pay for all the people I had shot at and killed; I never wanted to go to the army; but what could I do? I had to shoot back to survive.'

'Go on,' said Joshua.

Merriman began to do up his flies, paused half way through as if he had forgotten how and then continued.

'And then I met my sometime, sort of brother at the braii and I suggested we do it together...'

'...Which he refused.'

'Ja. And so I did Dietz. Man! It was so easy and I thought it would all be written off as combat casualties, or some accident or something, but then you turned up and I thought to myself – this is more serious than I bargained for if the police have come.'

'We had nothing on you, you know?'

'Ja,' he nodded, definitively. 'You were such a *poes*, I thought I could do Steyl as well and get away with it.'

Joshua put his chin on his chest and digested this for a moment.

'Then Keay was killed,' he said, with a sigh.

'Ja. And I guessed it was Ortez and this made me flip a bit and sent me a bit fucked in the head, you know? I thought he had decided to join in the plan but when I knew the police were involved I thought that I had better tell him to stop so when Kassie Strydom got his mob together to *donner* Sanchez, I took the opportunity to go to warn him.'

'You wanted to warn your brother?'

Merriman succeeded in fastening his flies and began to walk back towards the Casspir.

'I thought that as he had had a fucked up life and that he would get more fucked up if he was put in jail and that would make my mother more fucked up too and I am such a fuck up that I thought that if I could save him from being fucked up, I would not be such a fuck up.'

'You did it to help your brother and your mother?'

'Ja,' he said. 'Ja.'

'Not for political shit?'

'Ja-Nee, both.'

'Merriman, David,' said Joshua. 'Is my mother mixed up in this?'

'Ja-Nee,' he replied, his eyes still glassy, glinting with the last rays of the sinking sun. 'Everyone is.'

'Merriman. How much of that *dagga* have you taken?'

'*Dagga*?'

'Ja, *dagga - boom*?'

'Hmm?'

'Come back to the truck and just sit down, hey?'

'It smells there.'

'Ja, but the music is good.'

*

31st May 1980

Joshua rested on the ground by the fire that night but he got little sleep. Wilson had been right about the lions too and from time to time, he heard their throaty, hoarse calls sounding like the breath of titans all around him, echoing through the bush, now sounding close, now far, their voices carrying through the still air. When they laid off, deterred from the smell of the kill by the curious and unfamiliar smells of the fire and the smoke grenade, the diesel, rubber, oil and hexamine, their deep contrast was replaced with the whining and high pitched whirring of the mosquitoes that plagued his ears every time he seemed to be dozing off. Merriman was asleep, propped up against the wheel in a semi-reclining posture that paid tribute to the depth of his intoxication while Els snored contentedly in his sleeping bag, untroubled by the bush, the wild, the war or the world. Joshua let Wilson off his stag early, cradled the machine gun by him and stared into the embers of the fire as though in its hot, white depths lay the answer to his own problem and to Merriman's.

Family, nationality, politics, predicament, upbringing, education, belonging, all seemed more plausible culprits for the murders of Dietz and Steyl than Merriman who, Joshua decided, should never have been required to stray further from a surfboard than a bar. Boys like him were never made to be soldiers, were never made to think their way through political complexities so that they might find their truth, their meaning, their soul; they were life's lotus eaters, whose idle pleasures were our pleasures, and whose childlike irresponsibilities reminded us of the importance of us taking on ours, so that they might shirk theirs. Merriman was decoration, not meat, nor fibre, nor pillar. Left to his own devices, black brother or no, left alone he would have caused no problem beyond a momentary disappointment to his parents, who would reconcile themselves to his lack of career, prospects or drive, in time, and come to value the child in the man. They would come to their own joy when they saw him ride a wave like a dolphin on a straight horizon and they would crack a beer and admit that, perhaps it was not so important that he was not a lawyer or an accountant and that perhaps it was he who had got it right after all.

Nor could he escape his own culpability; if he had been less concerned with getting out of this job and saving his own skin, made a better effort, been a better copper, or at least a more convincing one, then Merriman would never have shot Lieutenant Steyl and the whole thing might have just been brushed under the carpet instead of ballooning into a situation where a butterfly was about to be broken on a wheel. If he had listened to Konstabel Williams up on Spandau Kop and not been seduced by Inspector Du Toit and his cosy dream of team and family and easy community; if he had told his father where to stick his ideas earlier; if...if...if. And who was he to criticise anyone after killing Onele Nonyana? He was, he decided, no better than Merriman; and probably worse.

Merriman snuffled and shuffled in his sleep and in that moment, Joshua decided he was going to let him escape tomorrow. He was going to stop somewhere on the outskirts of Windhoek and leave the Casspir unattended, accidently on purpose, with a wallet of money and a bottle of water and the broadest of hints that Merriman should take them and go. Dietz and Steyl were dead; hanging this fey creature would not bring them back and somewhere, up above, this dereliction of duty might be taken in mitigation for his own murderous despatch of Onele Nonyana. How else could he summon up the courage to face the world, to seek redemption?

When morning came, Joshua's decision to carry out this plan hardened into a determination every bit as stiff as his limbs as he stamped some life into them in the pre-dawn light. Rooting up the embers of the fire and then taking some to put into the back of the Casspir to continue with the fumigation, he thought how it might just be possible for Merriman to hide somewhere on the outskirts of Windhoek, especially if he was able to contact his mother, who would know people who might know people who could put him up until he could be smuggled out of the country to Zambia or somewhere else. Once Merriman was free, he resolved, he would try to come by a passport like Memfeliz and so move on to a better life and escape from his situation as both prisoner and warder of Apartheid.

'You want tea or shall we move on a little first,' he said, as Els appeared from the bush, sporting his machine gun and nut cracker shorts.

'Ja, there must always be time for a brew,' he replied quietly, almost reverently to the retreating night. 'I can find no spoor of lions but they made a racket last night, hey?'

Joshua nodded as Wilson stirred, sat up and rubbed his eyes.

'Give Merriman a nudge.'

Wilson shook the body next to him but all the response he got was a soft groan.

'We should have tea quickly though,' said Wilson. 'The packages will be stinking to high heaven soon and it is OK for you to ride on top while I am in the cab but not for me today.'

Joshua put a black kettle on the fire, lodging it in the embers then busied himself with the makings. Wilson shook Merriman again, but got no response.

'You know, this *mompie* of yours is not right in the head at all,' he said. 'If I am not mistaken he has a concussion like when you have been *klapped* good and proper.'

'What's that?' said Joshua.

'Hush,' said Els, freezing.

Below the sound of the morning breeze, there was another sound, like the beating of spears on shields.

'Chopper,' said Els, relaxing and straightening up.

'Grootfontein is up and about early today,' said Wilson. 'Some kaffirs are going to get *klapped* worse than this *mompie* today.'

Els shook his head. 'This one is coming from the south. Puma, by the sound of it.'

'Let me take a look at Merriman while you make the tea, hey?' said Joshua to Wilson, stepping over the fire and rousing Merriman by the shoulder. 'Wake up, David. Wake up.'

Merriman opened his eyes and they shone like black diamonds as the first horizontal rays of the corn gold sun shot slanting through the bush like tracer. Smith waved his hand in front of them, but got no response.

'I think you may be right about him having a concussion,' agreed Joshua, feeling Merriman's head. 'But surely the medics at Oshadangwa would have spotted it?'

'How can you tell with the amount of *dagga* he did yesterday?' said Wilson.

'That chopper is coming in our direction and flying fast,' said Els, his head cocked. 'I think we should get started now now. If they are dropping stopper groups, there may be a SWAPO Typhoon unit close by. Maybe it was they who scared the lions off, hey?'

Wilson was used to Els and needed no more prompting. He was up and kicking out the fire, collecting gear and stowing it almost before Els had finished his sentence. The rear doors of the Casspir were opened, the coals swept out and the engine started, all before Merriman had been persuaded to stand up straight. As the sun came up, sliding the shadows back towards the light, Joshua herded him into the back, closed the doors and then climbed up on top as the monster shuddered, rolled and shouldered its way back onto the tarmac. Els scanned the bush for signs of ambush and then the sky for signs of the helicopter as Wilson gunned the engine up and headed towards the nervous south.

It was low down when they caught sight of it, its blunt nose tilted slightly earthward, frowning as it raced straight up the road towards them. Els relaxed.

'Whatever it is doing, it is not dropping stopper groups,' he said. 'It looks more like it is either following spoor or the pilot needs the *fokken* road to find his way because the *poes* can't read a map. Watch – any minute now and he will be stopping to read the *fokken* road signs.'

The day came up quickly now and by the time the helicopter was within a kilometre of them, it was clear that this was not an ordinary SAAF helicopter. It was not flying tactically for one thing and seemed to be in far too much of a hurry, its engines racing along much faster than was the usual standard. As it came closer, it swung left off the road, made a wide circle and then came at them from the rear, the wide side door pulled back to reveal several men in civilian suits armed with shotguns. One of them was pointing at them and making signals that they should stop.

'Have we been speeding?' shouted Wilson as the chopper clattered above them. 'Are we to get a ticket? They look like plain clothes coppers to me.'

Els gave a thumbs up sign and told Wilson to pull up. 'Maybe we have won a bingo prize, hey?'

The helicopter hovered massively to the right rear as the Casspir rolled to a halt. Joshua caught sight of a crewman unrolling a cargo net inside.

'They have come for the bodies,' he called out. 'They are going to sling them underneath and take them on from here.'

'Good job,' said Wilson, turning the engine off. 'They will be higher than Gorgonzola in another hour. They already near mush.'

The helicopter backed off and touched down thirty metres away, flinging sand and dust and small stones up around it. Before the haze had cleared four men, burly, in suits that seemed too tight for them, had debussed, donned sunglasses and were striding towards them.

'Which one of you is Smith?' said the leader, a scarred veteran, whose pores seemed like craters on the moon and whose dimpled chin admitted of no facetiousness of purpose. 'You have two bodies with you?'

Joshua jumped down from the Casspir. 'Lieutenants Steyl and Dietz...'

'Ja, we know,' replied the leader.

'They are not in a pretty state,' said Joshua.

'I dare say they will just go straight into the family plot then, without the viewing.' He wrinkled his nose. 'I see what you mean. You have a prisoner too? A David Merriman?'

'He's in the back with the bodies,' replied Joshua. 'Why?'

'Ja, he is to come with us.'

Joshua looked into the eyes of the plain clothes man and saw exactly what those words would mean.

'He's my prisoner,' he protested. 'He stays with me.'

'No, he is my prisoner now.'

A second suit stepped forward and handed him a piece of paper. Joshua saw himself reflected in the sunglasses and quickly dropped his eyes, took the paper and glanced over the order. It was legal.

'I'd still like to take him in,' he argued. 'He's my collar and I want the credit.'

'Don't be a *poes*,' replied the leader, as the second suit handed him another envelope. 'We brought this up for you. It was forwarded by your mother. It's a Writ requiring you to appear in court over the unlawful detention of some kaffir or other.'

The leader nodded to the third and fourth suit, who went to the back of the Casspir and removed the still dazed Merriman.

'Wait,' said Joshua, scanning the document. 'What is this?'

'It's what you've been worrying about all this time,' explained the veteran. 'It's why you got promoted out here. That Inspector of yours back in Graaf-Reinet is as crafty as a *fokken* jackal, he is. You know that you are named in the Writ, but he is not? *Fokken* clever move that, hey? Gets you to bury his dirty work in a shallow grave in the Karoo and then slides out from under, hey?'

'What?' said Joshua, again. 'This can't be right. He said that everyone in the station was being indicted and that this was his way of protecting me as I was still new to the job!'

'You lie,' replied the veteran, unimpressed. 'I would never have believed such a thing possible.'

The two men took Merriman by the arms and began to lead him back up the road.

'What the fuck are you doing?' said Joshua, a panic rising up in him.

'Preventing the escape of a dangerous felon, a traitor and a murderer,' replied the veteran, raising a hand.

'But, he's harmless!'

'Did you check the colour of your skin this morning, Sergeant?'

Joshua turned just in time to see one of Merriman's guards raise his shotgun and blast a hole in his back at kidney level. Merriman's arms went up and out and his head snapped back as the force of the blow threw him down on his face.

'No! No!' cried Joshua, making a move, only to find himself restrained by the touch of a gun barrel under his ear. He froze, the only movements left to him the trembling of his hands and lips and the welling up of tears.

The suits bent down, flipped Merriman over onto his back and shot him once, twice more. Merriman flapped a little like a landed fish, and then lay still.

'Shame about that,' said the veteran, removing the gun from Joshua's ear. 'But the *poes* has had it coming from a long way back and from a long way up. Shot while escaping; that's what the inquest will say. If there is an inquest. Or maybe we'll tell his mother he was a war hero, ja? That will please her, ja?'

Joshua felt a numbness begin to flow through him, a great, all pervading numb shock, a bleak, barren, hopeless emptiness blighting his soul; like ink poured into milk.

'Don't worry about the Writ, hey?' said the veteran. 'Just ignore it. You know how these legal cases often come to nothing. We'll keep a copy though, just in case.'

Joshua dropped to his knees as though poleaxed, put his forehead on the dusty ground and covered his neck with his hands until Merriman's body had been shovelled into a bag and the helicopter rose once more, with the three body bags slung in the net beneath, the four suits receding into the distant future.

'Els?' he said, when there was nothing but tears, heat and silence left. 'Els, what the fuck are we doing here?'

'Ag, sorry man,' said Els. 'Sorry, hey?'

09

Police Post 156

7th June 1980

Sergeant Joshua Smith of the South African Police climbed up the fourteen steps of the ladder to the top of the rusting iron water tank and raised his binoculars northwards to the horizon. There was nothing there but salt sand; flat, white, grey, as though someone had mixed concrete powder into soap powder. Slowly swinging through ninety degrees of unchanging vista, he lowered the glasses and looked southwards along the straight scrape of the road, taking in the grass that straggled across waiting to be shaved off by the blade of the road grader due in two days time and the raised lips on either side of the verge, which went like perspective lines straight to a vanishing point somewhere in the invisible distance. He raised the glasses. The view was the same into the middle distance and the far distance. He lowered them again and looked west. No difference. He looked east. Another identical scrape ran to an equally indefinite horizon. Each day he swung the binos around the horizon at dawn, mid-morning, noon, mid-afternoon and before sunset and saw nothing. He looked up into the blue, the perfect blue, the Canaletto blue of the perfect sky that only changed in the golden hour after sunrise and the lilac and lavender hour before dark.

There was a hiss of static from the radio in the Caspir parked hard up by the wall of the square, white painted concrete police post.

'Get that, hey?' he called.

Konstabel Scholtz appeared from out of the building. He was wearing nothing but veldtschoen and a pair of blue shorts and had not bothered to shave again, hoping that the proof of a beard would make him look older than his eighteen years testified to. He trundled out from the shade of the post, ambled around to the rear of the Casspir and swung up into the back. For a moment there was nothing but silence, the real profound silence of the bare salt desert, the silence that sucks up all sound and turns it into heat, flat light and emptiness and then the sounds of crackled conversation came up from inside the vehicle.

'This is Whisky Golf. Acknowledge, Over.'

Joshua nodded, let the binoculars dangle round his neck and climbed off the water tower. He dropped off the mid-way rung of the ladder, felt the crunch of the sand and rock salt beneath his feet and the give in his knees bend like wishbones. Straightening up, he screwed his eyes into a gritty slit and looked around his vast kingdom once more; one junction, one building, one water tank, one armoured vehicle, one square box of a latrine and one long, stark encircling line of nothingness.

'Sisingi?'

'Smith?' replied Sisingi, from inside the post.

'Tea?'

'That would be a very fine thing.'

Smith touched Sanchez's bayonet fastened on his belt and thought of David Merriman.

'What a waste,' he said to himself. 'What a *fokken* waste this *fokken* limbo life is.'

Printed in Great Britain
by Amazon